A VENGEFUL KING RISES
HOUSE OF CROFT

SOPHIE BARNES

A VENGEFUL KING RISES

House of Croft

Copyright © 2024 by Sophie Barnes

All rights reserved. Except for use in any reviews, the reproduction or utilization of this work in whole or in part in any form by any electronic, mechanical, or other means, now known or hereinafter invented, including xerography, photocopying and recording, or any any information storage or retrieval system, is forbidden without the written permission of the publisher.

This is a work of fiction. Names, characters, places and incidents are either the product of the author's imagination or are used fictitiously, and any resemblance to actual persons, living or dead, business establishments, events or locales is entirely coincidental.

Cover by Carpe Librum Book Design - www.carpelibrumbookdesign.com

ALSO BY SOPHIE BARNES

Novels

House of Croft
A Vengeful King Rises

The Gentlemen Authors
A Duke's Lesson In Charm
A Duke's Introduction To Courtship
A Duke's Guide To Romance

Brazen Beauties
Mr. West and The Widow
Mr. Grier and The Governess
Mr. Dale and The Divorcée

Diamonds in the Rough
The Dishonored Viscount
Her Scottish Scoundrel
The Formidable Earl
The Forgotten Duke
The Infamous Duchess
The Illegitimate Duke
The Duke of Her Desire

A Most Unlikely Duke

The Crawfords
Her Seafaring Scoundrel
More Than a Rogue
No Ordinary Duke

Secrets at Thorncliff Manor
Christmas at Thorncliff Manor
His Scandalous Kiss
The Earl's Complete Surrender
Lady Sarah's Sinful Desires

At The Kingsborough Ball
The Danger in Tempting an Earl
The Scandal in Kissing an Heir
The Trouble with Being a Duke

The Summersbys
The Secret Life of Lady Lucinda
There's Something About Lady Mary
Lady Alexandra's Excellent Adventure

Standalone Titles
The Girl Who Stepped Into The Past
How Miss Rutherford Got Her Groove Back

Novellas

Diamonds in the Rough

The Roguish Baron

The Enterprising Scoundrels

Mr. Clarke's Deepest Desire

Mr. Donahue's Total Surrender

The Townsbridges

An Unexpected Temptation

A Duke for Miss Townsbridge

Falling for Mr. Townsbridge

Lady Abigail's Perfect Match

When Love Leads To Scandal

Once Upon a Townsbridge Story

The Honorable Scoundrels

The Duke Who Came To Town

The Earl Who Loved Her

The Governess Who Captured His Heart

Standalone Titles

Sealed with a Yuletide Kiss (An historical romance advent calendar)

The Secrets of Colchester Hall

Mistletoe Magic (from Five Golden Rings: A Christmas

Collection)

Miss Compton's Christmas Romance

CHAPTER ONE

September, 1817

Alice Irvine hastened along the pleasure garden's illuminated cross-walk. Fireworks popped overhead in vibrant displays of shimmering light while Beethoven's "Moonlight Sonata" drifted between the trees. The air was cool. Soon, the leaves would change color as summer gave way to autumn.

Alice quickened her pace. She could not be gone long before her parents noticed her absence. For now, they were preoccupied with the ballet. But like most of Vauxhall's distractions, it offered only brief entertainment. She had to return to them before the show ended and they realized she no longer stood in the crowd of onlookers.

Up ahead, a small group of revelers rounded a corner. All were flamboyantly dressed in accordance with the masquerade theme. Their joyous mood was evident in their hoots and whistles as they drew nearer.

"Oh no," one of the men in their midst exclaimed, his attention fixing on Alice. "A lonely shepherdess."

Disguised as Harlequin, he pranced toward her and grasped her hand before she gauged his intention. Startled, she nearly tripped over her feet when he pulled her into a waltz.

She did her best to keep up, spinning and twirling across the path. His gaze caught hers and he laughed, enchanting her with his playfulness.

His companions cheered and clapped and one of them, a woman wearing a lavish Marie Antoinette costume, called, "Bring her along. The more the merrier."

Alice's dance partner slowed his movements until they came to a halt. He raised her hand to his lips and pressed a kiss to her knuckles.

"Well?" he asked, his voice slightly muffled behind his mask. "Will you favor us with your company or must we part ways?"

"Thank you for the dance," Alice said, "but I'm afraid it must be the latter."

His eyes pierced hers from behind his black mask. A grin caught the edge of his mouth, concealing the brief disappointment she'd glimpsed a mere second before. "A pity."

He released her with a flourish, executed a deep bow, and spun away, his movements fluid as he darted after his friends.

Alice breathed a sigh of relief and resumed her own progress. Hopefully the mask she wore had made her just as unrecognizable to him as he'd been to her. A soft smile curved her lips as she hastened onward. The anonymity of her encounter added a hint of exhilaration to the pleasure she felt in response to the stranger's attention.

It also made her more eager to reach her destination where heated kisses and ardent caresses awaited.

Her heart pounded faster. She knew the danger that lurked ahead - the undeniable risk of scandal - but she couldn't resist the thrill of meeting the man who promised her passion unlike any other.

Ever since he'd first kissed her in an alcove at the Foxhill ball, she'd welcomed every chance to be alone with him, if only for a few moments. No one had ever affected her so. He made her come alive in ways she'd never before experienced.

Inexplicably, the impropriety and the daring, the prospect of being caught, only fueled her desire for more. As did the rogue himself. The wicked words he'd whispered in her ear when last they'd met still sizzled in her veins.

Reaching a thick copse of trees, she sent a swift glance over her shoulder, then stepped off the path. Darkness closed in around her as she moved forward through the brush, but she wasn't afraid. Instead, she welcomed the increased privacy offered by the secluded location.

Despite the heavy scent of dirt and leaves, she smelled the musky perfume of the man she'd come to meet. She could almost feel the heat of his body encompassing hers, the powerful strength of his presence urging her onward.

A twig snapped and a strong arm encircled her waist, pulling her backward, flush against a masculine chest. Alice's breath caught and her pulse leapt with increased excitement. This was one of the things she loved best about their assignations – his ability to surprise her.

"You're finally here," he murmured, the low vibration of his voice sending hot little shivers straight down her spine as he drew her more firmly against his hard frame.

"Yes," she whispered in anticipation of what would come next. If he wished to claim her in earnest this time, she'd happily let him do so.

His head dipped and his mask grazed her neck as he breathed her in. Alice moaned. Who would have thought such a tiny abrasion could feel so incredibly good? And yet it was nothing compared to the rousing sensations igniting within her when he slid his hands over her body, the intimate exploration making the passion between them burn brighter than any flame.

Heaven have mercy, she wanted more. She wanted

him - needed him - more than anything else in the world. So she leaned back against his sturdy frame, and surrendered to pleasure.

CHAPTER TWO

Chief Constable Peter Kendrick arrived at Vauxhall just after dawn. He stepped from the hackney carriage, paid the driver, and lit a cheroot before proceeding toward the pleasure garden's front entrance where one of his Runners was stationed.

"Lewis," he said, greeting the younger man with a stiff nod. "Give me the details while we walk."

Lewis swallowed, the hesitance in his eyes informing Peter that he had no wish to accompany him. But rather than argue, the younger man straightened his shoulders. "Of course."

Peter set his cheroot to his lips and pulled the smoky flavor into his lungs. He nodded toward the entrance while exhaling through his nose. "That bad?"

"Worst I've ever seen, sir."

Peter considered Lewis. He'd been off duty when

Miss Fairchild had been murdered in June, and again when Lady Camille's body was found last month. Judging from his queasy expression, Lewis was sorry he'd not been off duty this morning as well.

"Right," Peter told him. "Best get on with it then, hadn't we?"

"Aye, sir."

Peter brushed past him and started walking. It wouldn't take long to know if the murder committed last night was connected to the previous ones.

Lewis followed, directing him toward the right and onto a graveled path. A hushed atmosphere enveloped the garden, adding an eeriness made more pronounced by the mist dispersing across the ground.

"A gardener made the discovery," Lewis began. "He was getting ready to trim the tree branches growing too close to the wall when he happened upon the young woman's body."

"Any idea who she is?" Peter asked.

"None. She's still wearing her mask from last night's masquerade. However, a Mr. and Mrs. Irvine did file a missing person's report. Their daughter, Miss Alice Irvine, went missing at Vauxhall yesterday evening."

"How the hell does that even happen?"

"No idea, sir. She must have wandered off."

Peter sent Lewis a sideways glance. "Cause of death?"

Lewis clenched his jaw as he met Peter's gaze. "Her throat was slit and…"

The young Runner drew to a halt and bent over, hands clasped on his shins. His breaths came heavy and fast, as though he were fighting the urge to vomit. When he finally straightened, he looked a touch paler. "No one should die as she did. It's morbid beyond compare."

Peter reckoned Lewis was right. And although he'd suspected he knew what he'd find, he was still shocked by the sight that greeted him when he stepped between the trees moments later and caught his first glimpse of the victim.

Her body, dressed in a light-blue shepherdess costume, was not only still and lifeless, but stained by the blood that had spilled from her throat. It was a ghastly sight, not just a thin slash, but a deep and damaging wound. Her glassy blue eyes stared at the sky from behind her white satin mask, and her faded pink lips were parted as if in a whisper.

Pinned to the front of her bodice, was a square piece of paper containing one word, written in thick black ink. WHORE.

Peter drew a sharp breath as he surveyed the scene. Although this wound was deeper than the ones on Miss Fairchild and Lady Camille, the cause of death was as identical as the note left behind.

Despite having twenty-seven years of experience dealing with the darker side of humanity, Peter still shuddered. The air was thick with the sickly-sweet smell of death, and the sight of the corpse, her skin pale and cold, made his stomach churn. He couldn't help but imagine her final moments. Thankfully, her dress was intact and her positioning gave no indication of any sexual violation.

He closed his eyes briefly and took a deep breath, deliberately cutting off all his emotions so he could be objective. When he was ready, he bent to remove the victim's mask, gently peeling it back to reveal her face.

A quiet rage built inside him as he beheld her youthful beauty. It wasn't fair. What kind of monster had done this?

He glanced at the Runners positioned nearby before fixing his gaze on Lewis. The poor man kept his attention well off the ground. Peter didn't blame him. "Lewis, I'll need to speak with the Irvines – see if this is their missing daughter. You have their address?"

"Yes, sir."

Peter huffed a breath. This was the kind of news every parent dreaded. "Call on them. Take Anderson with you and have the Irvines accompany you to the Bow Street office. I'll meet them there."

Peter watched the two men stride off. Anderson, an older more seasoned member of the force, would lend the support Lewis needed.

Lowering into a crouch, Peter scanned the area for evidence, his gaze fierce and focused. The ground had been disturbed to suggest the frenzied movement of feet. Most likely the victim's as she'd fought to free herself from the killer's grasp. A larger set of footprints were imbedded in the dirt, and Peter quickly ordered measurements to be taken.

There were several broken twigs and branches as well, indicating that whoever had done this had fled the scene quickly. Leaning forward, he examined the body, looking for any additional clues, but none stood out. Hopefully the coroner would have greater success. If they were lucky, they'd find something meaningful under her nails, like a piece of fabric or some hair.

If not…

He sighed and stood, hating the fact that another woman might die before he managed to track down the killer.

It was almost nine by the time Peter entered the Bow Street Magistrate's Court. Interviewing the gardener who'd discovered the victim had taken some time. The elderly man had been so shaken he'd barely been able to speak.

Peter swallowed the last of the bread roll he'd managed to buy from a bakery on his way over and wiped the crumbs from his fingers. He then greeted a couple of Runners and started toward his office, only to halt when Lewis came striding toward him.

"The Irvines are here," he said, his expression grim. "I showed them into your office."

"What did you tell them?"

"That you might have some news about their daughter." Lewis held up a file with some papers inside. "The missing person's report, in case you'd like to go over it first."

"Thank you." Peter took the papers and scanned the description the Irvine's had provided. He then glanced toward his office door. For now, those people had hope. Unfortunately, he was about to crush that. "I'll need some coffee first."

"There's a fresh pot in the back room. I can fetch you a cup if you like?"

"Thanks, but I'll manage." Peter began turning away, then thought of something and said, "See if you can get hold of the rest of Vauxhall's employees and have them come in for an interview. It's possible one of them witnessed something."

Stepping back to let another Runner past, Lewis said, "I can also put an announcement in the paper asking anyone who was there last night to come forward with information."

"Let's wait on that. I'd rather keep the investigation as private as possible for now, though I do appreciate your line of thinking. What you may want to do is locate the files on Miss Fairchild and Lady Camille. Their cases have the same modus operandi."

Lewis nodded and Peter went to pour himself a cup of coffee. He took a sip and savored the heat as it slid down his throat. Right. Time to meet with the Irvines.

He told himself it was part of the job and that someone had to do it. Might as well be him. But delivering bad news never got easier, no matter how many times he did it. Lady Camille's mother, the Countess of

Hightower, had flung herself at him when he'd spoken to her, beating him with her fists while shouting that it wasn't true – that he must have made a mistake. Miss Fairchild's parents had been more stoic, but their pain had been palpable nonetheless.

Despite his feet being heavy, Peter forced himself to walk down the hallway. He had to get past this so he could move on with his investigation and try to find justice for these three women.

On that thought, he opened the door to his office and greeted the Irvines.

They rushed to their feet and stood before him, hope brimming in their watery eyes, like sunshine dancing on dewdrops. The husband stepped forward first and stuck out his hand.

Peter shook it and wished the murdered woman was someone else's daughter – that the awful heartbreak waiting around the corner could be delayed just a little bit longer.

"A couple of Runners came by our house this morning," said Mr. Irvine as soon as the introductions were out of the way. "He told us there was news about Alice."

"Possibly." Peter glanced between the couple. "Would either of you like something to drink?"

Mr. Irvine sent his wife a questioning look, in response to which she shook her head.

"Very well then." Peter gestured toward the chairs they'd been using before his arrival. "Please have a seat. As I understand it, your daughter went missing last night while the three of you were enjoying an evening out together at Vauxhall. Correct?"

"That's right." Mr. Irvine glanced toward the piece of paper Peter had placed on top of his desk. "We gave the clerk a description of her."

Peter kept his expression carefully schooled. "If you don't mind, I'd like you to tell me about your evening, up until the point where Alice disappeared."

He needed to understand what had happened – *how* it had happened. It was vital he got as many details out of the Irvine's before he delivered the damning news. After that, they'd likely be incapable of any coherent thought.

Mr. Irvine leaned forward, propping his forearm on his thigh. He frowned at Peter. "I was led to believe that you'd be the one giving us information. Not the other way around."

"They haven't found her," Mrs. Irvine muttered. "Have you?"

"Please," Peter said, his eyes on the husband. "What time did you arrive at the gardens?"

Mr. Irvine flattened his mouth and leaned back. For a moment, Peter didn't believe he'd answer. But then a distant look entered his eyes and he finally said, "Our carriage dropped us off around eight o' clock. There were six of us, including our sons and youngest daughter. We were all dressed in costume, because of the event."

Peter didn't bother asking him to elaborate on that. The shepherdess costume was already mentioned in the missing person report. "Did you have supper upon your arrival, or did you stroll about?"

"We had supper, after which we went to watch the cascade. There was a ballet performance after that. It was scheduled to last fifteen minutes and I..." Mr. Irvine drew a shaky breath. "It was a very good show. Absorbing. I never noticed Alice's disappearance until it was over and I turned to ask her opinion. Only she wasn't there."

"Did either of her siblings see where she went?"

Mrs. Irvine shook her head. "No."

"Were you familiar with any of the other spectators? Anyone we might be able to call upon and question?"

"I...I don't recall," Mr. Irvine muttered. He reached for his wife's hand and clasped it tight. "The Marquess of Lundquist approached Alice earlier in the evening, at the cascade. They exchanged a few words before he strolled off."

Peter made a note of it. "Are the two of them friends?"

"They've danced together a few times at various social events, but he's never called on her or invited her out for a walk," Mr. Irvine informed him. "I don't believe they're especially close."

"So you would say it's unlikely that the marquess convinced your daughter to meet him for a rendezvous while you were distracted by the ballet." Peter kept his voice soft as he spoke, for he knew what he implied would not be well received.

Mrs. Irvine blanched. "Alice would never resort to

such mischief. She's a decent person, Mr. Kendrick, not the sort to be led astray by a man. Not even by a marquess."

Apparently, Mrs. Irvine didn't know her daughter well. Or maybe she did and the killer had made a mistake? Peter considered that possibility. It had been dark and Alice was wearing a mask when she met her fate between those trees.

"If anything," Mr. Irvine said, his voice stiff, "she received word that one of her friends was in need of help and went to lend her assistance."

An unrealistic theory, Peter decided, considering she had since failed to return. He glanced at his coffee and wished it were brandy, then folded his arms on the table.

"Mr. and Mrs. Irvine," he began while doing his best to keep his voice level, "I regret to inform you that a young woman was found murdered at Vauxhall this morning. She matches your daughter's description, though I cannot say for certain—"

Mrs. Irvine's anguished cry cut him off. Her slender body doubled over in pain as she wept with heaving sobs. Mr. Irvine slid from his chair and crouched before her, his arms embracing her as best he could while tears slid down his cheeks.

He glanced at Peter. "It cannot be true. I want to see her. Just to be sure."

"Of course." Peter stood from behind his desk and crossed to the door. "Take as much time as you need. I'll accompany you to the morgue when you're ready."

He left the office, closing the door on his way out. The Irvines still held on to some small sliver of hope, but Peter already knew this too would soon be gone. There was no doubt in his mind. The woman he'd seen in Vauxhall that morning would soon be identified as Alice Irvine.

CHAPTER THREE

Adrian Croft was still restless when he returned from his morning ride. He'd given the horse its head and savored the rush of cold air on his face while they'd galloped through Hyde Park.

The exercise usually helped clear his mind, but today was different. Uneasiness gripped his bones on account of the news that had reached him before he'd gone out. Another victim had just been named in what had become a horrific series of murders. Miss Alice Irvine was dead.

Knowing the villain remained at large increased his concerns for his sister's security. His stomach clenched with the idea of her encountering any sort of danger when she ventured out of the house.

Setting his jaw, he climbed the stairs and entered his room. His valet, James Murry, was already there, waiting with a bath and a clean change of clothes. He greeted Adrian and proceeded to help him remove his jacket.

"Have my father and sister arisen?" Adrian asked while Murry began untying his cravat. He flexed his fingers, enjoying the strain the action produced in his joints and tendons.

"Your father is already in his study," Murry informed him. "The bell from your sister's room rang just before you arrived. I believe Emma is helping her dress as we speak."

"Thank you, Murry." The cravat was undone and unwound. Murry removed it, leaving Adrian to unbutton his forest green waistcoat. He started to shuck it. "I want a footman with her whenever she leaves the house. At least until the man who's murdering upper-class women has been apprehended."

"Perhaps it would be wise of you to warn her against going out," Murry suggested. He'd been employed by Adrian ten years ago and had not only earned his master's absolute trust in that time but had since become more than his job title claimed him to be. "At least for the foreseeable future."

Adrian glanced at him. "She'll never listen."

Evelyn was stubborn that way, and who could blame her? She was eleven years younger than he and had recently made her debut. Of course she wished to go out and attend social functions. She wanted to dance and consider her marital options.

Adrian tensed on that thought. Did the world possess a man good enough for her?

His thoughts shifted to Edward, his closest friend, and the tension in Adrian's body eased. Yes, he decided. Just the one. Provided Evelyn took the time to notice the admiration with which Edward watched her.

He shook his head and tugged at his shirt's front closure, undoing the tie before pulling the garment free from his breeches.

"I'll see about the footmen then," Murry told him.

"Thank you. That will be all for now." Murry left and Adrian finished undressing before stepping into his bath. As usual, there was much for him to accomplish today. Those who depended upon his father's good graces had to be kept in check.

With this in mind, he bathed quickly and toweled off, his thoughts returning to Miss Irvine and the two other victims who'd come before. The notion of someone preying on innocent women made his blood boil. Whoever this murderous bastard was, he had to be stopped so Evie could be safe.

As was too often the case, Bow Street didn't appear to be making progress in that regard. The first victim, Miss Fairchild, was murdered two months ago, yet the killer had yet to be captured.

Adrian muttered a curse and snatched up the shirt that had been laid on his bed then proceeded to dress. After donning his trousers and waistcoat, he called for Murry to assist him with his cravat.

Once ready, he went to locate his sister, who was now in the dining room enjoying her breakfast.

"I wanted to wish you a pleasant day before heading out," he informed her.

"You're not eating?" She slid her gaze toward him, abandoning the paper she'd been reading. A hint of a smile tugged at her lips.

"I did so before my ride."

"Of course." Disappointment filled her dark gaze. "I suppose I'll see you later then?"

"Tonight," he confirmed. "At supper. Until then, there are matters I need to attend to. In the meantime, I'd like to ask that you don't go out."

"A bit hypocritical of you, wouldn't you say?" She arched her brows before turning her attention to her tea and taking a sip. "I've a scheduled meeting with Rose and Louise. We're to go shopping together."

"Call it off." He doubted the women she spoke of were genuine friends of hers anyway. Most people, he'd learned from his father, hoped to gain an advantage from the connections they made. Experience had taught him that this was true, with only a few rare exceptions.

"Whatever for?"

Adrian gripped the doorframe. "There's a murderer on the loose. It isn't safe."

She raised her chin. "According to the articles I have read on the matter, all three women were killed in the evening while on their own. It's daytime now and I shan't be alone. There's no need for you to worry."

"Easy for you to say," he muttered. Unlike him, she'd been spared from dealing with villains and cutthroats –

men who'd sell their own daughters into a life of whoring if they stood to gain from such a transaction. He'd seen the bleak side of London, the shadowy corners where crime thrived and death prevailed. There was no escaping it in his line of work, but he supposed his sister did make a reasonable point. Nevertheless, he felt inclined to tell her, "I'll not argue further if one of our footmen goes with you."

Her gaze snapped to his and held for a second before she finally answered. "Fine."

Expelling the breath he'd been holding, he eased his grip on the doorframe and wished her a pleasant day before stopping by his father's study on the way out.

"I'm off to speak with Macintyre and Goldie," he told him from the doorway.

Papa glanced up briefly from the ledger in which he was writing. Of stocky build, George Croft still conveyed an intimidating amount of strength and power, despite having reached his seventieth year. His features, however, had slackened a little with age, and the hair that had once been black had faded to grey.

"Let's get some results this time, shall we?" Papa's quill scratched the paper as he made a note. "Your men's last effort was laughable at best."

Adrian gritted his teeth. "I'll handle it myself this time. Rest assured, I know what needs to be done."

Papa's steely blue gaze returned to him once more, and this time it held. "I should bloody well hope so."

Without adding anything further, Adrian took a step back and shut the door. He then went to let Murry know about Evie's plans to go out, before setting off for the gaming hell Macintyre ran.

The place had been transformed from a filthy, dimly lit dump only those who lacked class and pride would frequent, to an elegant place of business where several upper-class gentlemen now chose to risk their fortunes. All at the Croft family's expense.

With several weapons concealed on his person, including a long narrow blade tucked into a specially crafted channel located in the sleeve of his jacket, Adrian alit from the carriage when it pulled up in front of The Devil's Den. Keeping all senses on full alert, he moved toward the front door with swift strides and, finding it locked, proceeded to knock.

A sleepy-eyed woman answered his call. Dressed in a red satin robe, she looked as though she belonged to the brothel where he would be heading next. Her lips drew into a saucy smile as her gaze swept the length of his body.

"You're a welcome morning surprise," she purred, stepping a bit too close for comfort. If only she knew how he loathed the cloying perfume of roses.

He nudged her aside with his shoulder and entered the building, his gaze quickly moving toward the gaming room that stood beyond the foyer. "Where's Macintyre?"

A dainty hand slid over his arm as the woman, having briefly stumbled when Adrian passed her, approached him once more. "Somewhere nearby, I expect. How about we find him together after I show you how a good hostess should greet men like you?"

He scowled at her. "I've no interest in what you're offering."

"But—"

Eager to be done with his task, he stalked toward a pair of glass doors and flung them open so hard he heard their frames crack. "Macintyre?"

Not finding him in the gaming room, Adrian turned on his heel and shouted for him once more. "Macintyre?"

A thud came from somewhere upstairs. Adrian glanced at the woman, who suddenly blocked his path. "Get out of my way."

"Please, don't hurt him."

He didn't have time for this nonsense. Grabbing her upper arm, he yanked her sideways so he could pass then dashed up the stairs while she screamed words of warning to Adrian's quarry. Maybe he should have tied her up and gagged her first. The last thing he felt like right now was a rooftop chase.

Turning left, he started along the hallway, thrusting doors open as he went, searching for the man who'd indebted himself to his father. He found him soon enough, half dressed and with one leg out an open window.

Adrian leapt forward and grabbed him by the shirt collar, yanking him inside with so much momentum they fell back together, onto the floor. Macintyre grunted and started to scramble, still hell-bent on his escape.

Unwilling to let that happen, Adrian jammed his fist into Macintyre's shoulder, knocking the man sideways just enough to let Adrian pin him down.

"Please, please, please," Macintyre cried. "I'll do whatever you—"

Adrian's fist connected with Macintyre's jaw, splitting his lip and sending a thin stream of blood down his chin. "You've said so before."

Another punch to Macintyre's face cracked his nose with an unpleasant crunch. Adrian beat him until he stopped struggling and his head lolled to one side. Only then did he grab him by the front of his shirt and haul him upright so he could deposit him on a chair.

Adrian leaned in, his eyes boring deep into Macintyre's soul. "Everything you own has been paid for by the Crofts. We've built you up and we'll tear you down if you don't meet the terms of our agreement."

"I'm trying," Macintyre wheezed.

"Try harder," Adrian growled. "The club has been thriving these last three months since it was reopened. Your payment to us is long overdue. I want names, details, and fifty percent of the profits."

Just to be sure the man understood how serious he was, Adrian drew the blade he'd concealed in his sleeve and held it against his throat. Macintyre's eyes bulged. He started to tremble, and then the pungent smell of urine filled the air. He'd bloody well gone and pissed himself.

Good.

The greater his fear, the simpler this would be. Adrian pressed the blade closer, until he knew Macintyre felt a sting. "Well?"

"The Earl of Elmhurst cheated last night," Macintyre rasped. "Paid me a hundred pounds to let the incident slide when I drew him aside."

"That's not the kind of information I'm after," Adrian hissed. He already knew the earl to be underhanded. A series of similar incidents filled the file he'd gathered on him.

"All right...all right..." Macintyre's gaze darted toward the door. He leaned back slightly, away from the blade, but Arian only pressed it harder against his throat. "One of the serving girls overheard something about Lord Glendale being pro-French."

Adrian eased the blade a little. This was better. If word got out that the man who'd led a campaign against Napoleon's army and lost might have done so on purpose, he'd be arrested and hanged for treason.

Adrian stepped back, removing his blade from Macintyre's throat in the process. "I'll take the fifty percent now."

"But I—"

"Before you finish that sentence, I urge you to consider what will happen to you if you tell me you don't have the blunt."

"Right. Yes. Of course. I'll fetch it for you right now."

"And don't try to cheat me," Adrian warned. "I know how much you make on average per night."

He left The Devil's Den ten minutes later with nearly three thousand pounds in his pocket, and headed toward his next destination.

"You did well today," Papa told Adrian later when the two men removed themselves to the study for after dinner drinks. "I'm proud of you."

Adrian almost snorted with disdain. He hated what he'd done, hated the person his father had turned him into, and the fact that this hadn't been a one-time occurrence. He'd been his father's enforcer for years now and knew how to make those indebted to him pay their dues.

Thankfully, most of them gave up quickly. Only a few had forced Adrian to resort to real violence. And then there were those who'd betrayed the family – those who'd been taken care of for good.

He set his glass to his lips and downed the contents before saying what had been preying upon his mind for too long.

"I want out."

Stillness filled the room. Adrian forced himself to look at his father, unmoved for once by the anger that burned in his eyes. "There is no out. Not when you're my only son – the heir to everything built by generations of men who came before you. My God, boy. You're supposed to be King of Portman Square after me."

Disgust curdled Adrian's blood. That moniker would not apply to him. "I never asked for any of this."

"And you think I did?" Papa scoffed. "This is a matter of building wealth and power, and the best way to do that is by having the upper hand on everyone else."

Adrian glanced at the cabinet where the files were kept; hundreds of detailed accounts on England's most prominent men, to be used for extortion whenever the need arose. "There's also the assistance we've offered criminals, our blackmailing efforts, the smuggling, and other endeavors the law won't look favorably on."

Hell, if someone were to investigate them and actually manage to prove their criminal undertakings, the House of Croft would crumble.

"Bah." Papa waved a dismissive hand and downed the contents of his glass before pushing himself to his feet. He crossed to the sideboard where he proceeded to refill his tumbler. "You know as well as I that there's nothing more beneficial than putting others in debt. As for the goods we acquire, I'm a firm believer in every man having the God-given right to procure whatever he wants at the lowest cost. But there's a group of puffed-up peacocks who've decided to raise the price of imported corn so none can afford it, ensuring English landowners profit instead. Besides, why should the government take a cut when we're the ones doing all the work?"

"Because it's the law?" Adrian tried.

"A law made by those attempting to gain control

over the masses." Papa huffed a breath while flexing the fingers of his left hand. He frowned before quietly adding, "I'll not be subject to that."

"And I'll not hold another blade to another man's throat on your behalf," Adrian countered. "I want more for myself than that."

"More for yourself?" Papa snapped, his face darkening with splotches of red. He shook his glass of brandy, sloshing the contents over the sides. "How bloody ungrateful of you. After all your ancestors and I have done to secure your life of luxury – your future. And here I was, prepared for you to take on more responsibility. Lord knows it's time. You're almost thirty. But I'll be damned if you make a mockery of your good name by going soft."

"It's got nothing to do with going soft," Adrian said, his voice as hard as the blade he'd threatened Macintyre with that morning. He stood, even as Papa's expression contorted. "This is about me wanting to live a life free from all this. It's about wanting to marry and raise a family without my wrongdoings forever nipping at my heels."

Papa took a sharp breath. He staggered slightly, as though he'd been pushed off balance. Jaw tight, he reached for the bookcase behind him and steadied himself with one hand. Still, his gaze, sharp and unyielding, never strayed from his son.

"In case you're unaware, you'll never be free from all this," Papa spat. "Not as long as my blood runs through your veins."

"I—"

Papa suddenly groaned and his features twisted. He dropped his glass, which exploded upon the floor, sending shards of crystal and brandy across the Aubusson rug. A raspy intake of air followed. He suddenly clutched his chest with one hand.

Adrian rushed to his aid and wound one arm around him, his intention to help him into a chair. "What's wrong?"

Papa's lips parted but no words came. It sounded as though his breath was lodged in his throat. Until it wheezed from his lungs. His eyes went impossibly wide.

Without further warning, he pitched forward, breaking free from Adrian's grasp as he fell to the floor with a thud.

Adrian stood immobile, his posture rigid as the velvet-clad casket was lowered into the family vault beneath St. Paul's. Although the day was temperate, the cool granite with which the tomb had been built made the occasion uncomfortably chilly.

Evie, who suffered the loss of their father more fiercely than he, sniffed as she dabbed away tears. For Adrian, Papa's death had come as a shock. He'd not expected it to happen yet. Despite his age. Papa had not appeared to suffer from declining health. He had, however, been a difficult man for Adrian to love. In fact, he could not say that he missed him.

"Are you ready?" he asked once the pallbearers had left him and Evie to mourn alone, their retreating footsteps echoing the loneliness of this subterranean place. This would be the last time a Croft was confined to eternity here. In future they would be laid to rest outdoors, surrounded by life. He'd make sure of it.

Evie nodded. "Yes."

Taking her arm to lend support, Adrian guided her through the long stone hallway toward the stairs, then up into the north transept of the church and out into the bright afternoon sunlight. There, he escorted her to their waiting carriage and helped her climb in.

She leaned on him the entire way home, quietly weeping while he said nothing. For what could he say? The father she'd known had been so very different from the one who'd ordered Adrian to drown an unwanted litter of kittens when he was but ten years old. He bore no resemblance to the brute who'd whipped him whenever he'd cried or to the unforgiving authoritarian who'd raised him to be ruthless.

Gritting his teeth, he clenched one fist until his nails dug into his palms. He loathed himself for not rebelling sooner, for the real concern and dread he'd experienced on behalf of this man when he'd realized he was unwell. It had waned soon after, but that did not erase the fact that in a brief instant, he'd felt more for his father than what he'd deserved.

"What shall we do now?" Evie asked as they

removed their outerwear a short while later and handed them to Elks, their butler. The older man was not quite fifty years old, yet his neatly combed hair was as white as the snug cravat adorning his neck. Soft features accompanied by a pair of warm brown eyes afforded him with a kind appearance that only a fool would misjudge as weakness.

"I recommend tea in the parlor." There was much for them to discuss, most notably Evie's future. Adrian's fondest wish was to see her happily married, not for convenience as Papa would have wished, but to a man of her choosing. "I'll just have a quick word with Cummings first. Shouldn't take long."

He dropped a kiss on Evie's cheek and strode to the study where he was unsurprised to find his father's secretary waiting. After years of service to the family, Cummings, like most of the senior staff, was more than an average servant. He'd been one of Papa's closest confidants.

As expected, he stood upon Adrian's arrival.

"Sir. May I offer my sincerest condolences once more?"

Adrian bristled. "That's really not necessary."

"The service was lovely," Cummings pressed. He and the rest of the household had been in attendance until it was time for George Croft to be interred.

Choosing not to comment, Adrian hardened his gaze. It was time to defy his father once and for all. "There's work to be done now, Cummings. For starters, I want the Croft files destroyed."

CHAPTER FOUR

April, 1818

Apprehension clung to Peter Kendrick's shoulders as he climbed the steps of Number 21 Albemarle Street. The chief magistrate would not summon him to his private residence without good reason, and Peter very much feared that reason involved him having to stand to account for failing to catch the man who'd murdered Miss Fairchild, Lady Camille, and Miss Irvine.

Inhaling deeply, he drew back his shoulders and used the knocker.

"Yes?" asked the slender middle-aged man who answered his call. His aloof expression left no doubt in Peter's mind that this was the butler, though it did surprise him a little that his superior could afford one. His own salary barely covered his monthly expenses.

"Chief Constable Peter Kendrick to see Sir Nigel Clemens," Peter said, his voice so even and dry there would be no debating that he preferred to be anywhere else.

"Of course. Do came in." The reed-like servant stepped aside, allowing Peter to enter a narrow foyer. "Your hat and gloves, sir?"

Peter handed him the items, then waited while the butler went to announce his arrival. Moments later, he was shown into the chief magistrate's study.

Sir Nigel had always struck Peter as an imposing figure of a man with wide shoulders, thick salt and pepper hair, and sharp eyes.

"Chief Constable," the magistrate said, his voice tight as he rose from behind his desk. "Thank you for coming."

Peter answered the greeting with a firm nod while trying to gauge his superior's mood. "Of course."

Sir Nigel held his gaze. "Would you care for some tea or coffee?"

"Coffee would be welcome."

The order was placed and then Sir Nigel motioned Peter to one of the chairs in front of his desk before returning to his own seat. He leaned forward, interlocking his fingers on top of the mahogany surface as he began to speak.

"Judging from your silence regarding the murderer responsible for the deaths of those three young ladies last year, I'll assume you're no closer to seizing him now than you were seven months ago."

Peter shifted uneasily in his seat. A dressing down it was then. Not that he didn't deserve it. He'd failed those women, failed their families, and failed the city as a whole. Hell, those crime scenes still kept him awake most nights. Despite every effort on Bow Street's part, there had been no progress in finding the killer or identifying a motive for the murders.

All he could do was pray that there was a reason why he'd not managed to track down the villain. Hopefully, the bastard himself had met with a tragic end and no longer posed a threat.

Even as he thought it, an icy shiver slid down his spine. Unfortunately, such luck was rare. Nevertheless, he raised his chin. "Evidence was lacking. The two men I brought in for questioning were quickly let go."

One had provided a compelling alibi. Sir Nigel himself had vouched for Lundquist. Peter hadn't liked that one bit. Given the severity of the case, he'd considered it an abuse of power. Especially since the measurement Peter had taken of the footprint left at the crime scene matched the size of the marquess's.

But what could he do? Not a lot, it would seem. Sir Nigel had simply reminded him that thousands of men shared that size.

"I think we can both agree they were unlikely suspects."

Peter was tempted to argue, but chose to refrain.

Instead he said, "As you are aware, we have deduced that the man who did this is upper class."

"That has been your conclusion, Mr. Kendrick. One based on nothing more than supposition." A maid arrived at that moment. She served the coffee with efficient movements and swiftly departed. Sir Nigel leaned back in his chair, the leather squeaking beneath his bulk. "It is a theory I refuse to subscribe to until you provide me with concrete proof."

A challenge, to be sure. "The fingernails of all three victims were clean."

"I beg your pardon?"

"They showed no sign of struggle."

"Your point?"

Peter stared at the magistrate. How could he not see it? To be sure, rumor did suggest that he'd been unwell of late, but still… He took a deep breath. "The killer was either so stealthy that he was able to sneak up on them and deliver the fatal wounds before they realized what was occurring, or he was someone they had no cause to fear. A man they happily approached with no concern for their well-being."

The deadly wounds had been dealt at extremely close range.

"Again, without witnesses, something left behind at the crime scene, or even a disgruntled suitor lurking somewhere in one of these women's pasts, you're at a dead end."

Peter was well aware of the fact. He hated every second the monster who'd done this went unpunished as much as he'd hated showing the Irvines their daughter's lifeless body.

Some parts of the job were best forgotten. But there had been one thing. Each woman had burned a piece of paper before she'd gone to meet her demise. Remnants had been found in their bedchambers when he'd searched them. He was convinced it had to have been a letter inviting them to their secret rendezvous, but with nothing but ash left behind, he had no proof.

"Powerful people are very unhappy with our incompetence in this matter," Sir Nigel said bluntly, jolting Peter out of his reverie. "Complaints have been made. Most notably by the Earl of Hightower, as I'm sure you can understand."

The earl's daughter, Lady Camille, had been the second victim. Her body had been discovered beneath Westminster Bridge.

"It ought not surprise you," Sir Nigel continued, "that the earl has the whole bloody peerage up in arms over this. The Prince Regent himself has written to me, demanding answers. To put it bluntly, our jobs are at stake, Mr. Kendrick. Yours especially."

The gravity of Sir Nigel's words weighed heavily on Peter. It took a great deal of effort for him not to slump in his chair. Instead, he sat straighter and reached for his coffee. He frowned at the steaming hot liquid before allowing himself a soothing sip.

"I can begin again, review the entire case from start to finish. It's possible I missed something. At the very least, it should appease the public by making it look like we're not giving up."

Sir Nigel sighed heavily. "Unless you expect to do what you've been unable to do until now, within the next couple of days, I propose we come up with something else."

"Sir?"

"I'm not saying we should stop hunting for the killer, but we do need an immediate distraction. A victory if you will. Something that will take attention away from Bow Street's lack of progress in this matter." His gaze fell upon Peter who did his best to refrain from showing emotion. Sir Nigel cleared his throat before speaking again. "I suggest we go after Adrian Croft."

Peter almost dropped his cup. The dainty piece of porcelain dipped, spilling hot coffee on his thigh. He winced and set the cup aside on the desk. "We've tried before without result. Are you sure another attempt won't make us look even more foolish?"

"I'll admit it's a gamble," Sir Nigel murmured. He drummed his fingers lazily on his armrest while seeming to ponder his options. "However, all things considered, it's one I'm prepared to make. If we can remove Adrian Croft, the newly minted King of Portman Square, from the game, everyone of consequence will breathe more easily. The prince included. Instead of demands for answers, we shall be thanked, celebrated even."

The chief magistrate wasn't wrong. Bow Street had

always suspected the Crofts of building their wealth through nefarious means. Acquaintances of theirs had mysteriously vanished on several occasions after speaking against them. According to what Peter himself had managed to piece together, the family traded in damning secrets, playing people against one another, and providing favors in exchange for political gain.

Their influence made them the most sought-after allies and the most hated foes within London Society. And yet...

"We've never been able to prove their involvement in any illegal matters. Everyone connected to them is either incredibly loyal or too afraid of what will happen if they betray them."

"Correct. They've always seen us coming and as such, they've always been prepared. Mr. George Croft was especially careful – sly as a fox, that one. But he's gone now and his son is in charge. Mr. Adrian Croft is younger, less experienced and, most importantly, unmarried."

Peter tried to work out the logic behind those words, only to find himself saying, "I'm not sure how that signifies."

A smug smile stretched Sir Nigels's lips into a tight line. He leaned forward once more, pausing as he folded his arms on the table. "It signifies because it allows us the chance to use The Nightingale Project on him."

CHAPTER FIVE

⌘

Dorian Harlowe stood near the terrace railing, spine straight, hands clasped loosely behind his back. The early morning sunshine spilled from a cloudless sky. It sharpened the colors, brightening the freshly cut grass that stretched toward the forest.

A gentle breeze danced around him, rustling the leaves of the trees. Birdsong infused the air with soothing effect until a disturbance sent the birds soaring, their squawks of alarm announcing the four young women's arrival.

Samantha and Hazel burst from between the trees, racing along the well-trodden path with Tara and Holly close behind. Their lean bodies moved with an elegant ease that could only be reached through vigorous exercise, determination, and discipline.

Their attire, more suited to men than to women, aided their movements. Their shirts and breeches were snuggly fitted, their shoes constructed from a sanded calf-skin that made the leather especially supple.

Shoulder to shoulder, they sprinted toward the ninth obstacle they would encounter as part of the course – a low stone bridge traversing what looked like a natural depression in the landscape. For them it would serve as a tunnel.

Dorian watched the women fling themselves onto their bellies and into a crawl, their arms dragging their bodies forward until they vanished from view. A moment passed before they appeared on the opposite side of the bridge, Samantha now in the lead.

She leapt to her feet, Hazel hard on her heels, and ran for the ramp leading onto a piece of peripheral fencing. Without needing to slow her movements, she made her way along the narrow beam, gaining additional distance to Hazel, if only by a slight margin.

A bothersome fly began buzzing around Dorian's face. He swatted it away, his attention on his protégés briefly interrupted. It nearly caused him to miss Samantha's somersault through the air as she leapt from the fence.

He nodded his approval and checked his pocket watch. She and Hazel were both on track to beating their own personal records while Tara and Holly, the youngest of the four, did their best to keep up.

With the Crown's support, he'd managed to train the women to become the deadliest spies in the country. Only a few select people knew of The Nightingale

Project, an initiative intended to bring England's enemies to their knees, if need be.

Unfortunately, war with the French had ended since the project's inception. Napoleon had been captured and imprisoned. There wasn't the same need for military intelligence as there had been before. His project lacked a reason for implementation, and since he needed to prove the necessity for its continued existence, one of his students had taken on an assignment much too simple for her level of skill.

A satisfied smile tugged at his lips as he watched Samantha circle around and approach the course's greatest challenge - a series of staggered roman pillars gradually rising from the ground in ever increasing height.

To the untrained eye, they would appear like nothing more than a curious folly, arcing from the forest side of the property and toward the roofline of Clearview House. For the women he trained, the pillars tested the contestants' balance, agility, and courage.

The pillars were not for the faint of heart, but they were necessary. If his students were ever chased across the rooftops of a city, this test would make sure they were able to do so as though it were second nature.

Samantha kept an even pace, the toes of her right foot landing on the first pillar. At only ten inches in height, it was more of a tall step. She leapt up onto the next one with her left foot, continuing her upward climb with Hazel second and the other two close behind.

It didn't take long for the women to reach a height equal to Clearview's second floor landing. Still they continued, their nimble pace crafting the illusion that this was a simple feat, easily accomplished by anyone daring enough to attempt it.

Dorian knew this was not the case. One wrong move would lead to disaster, which was why he never let them try it until he was confident they would excel.

"Don't you worry they'll fall?" The question came from Chief Constable Kendrick, who'd just been shown onto the terrace by Branton, Dorian's butler.

Dorian dismissed the servant, then glanced at Kendrick who'd come to stand beside him. "They won't."

He returned his attention to the four women. Samantha had already reached the top-most pillar, so far above the spot where he stood, she was level with the roof-line. Hazel was right behind her with Tara and Holly closing the distance. If Samantha didn't jump soon and the others failed to slow down, they'd collide and lose their balance.

Beside him, he sensed Kendrick holding his breath.

It was expelled in a gush of amazement when Samantha leapt for the roof and vanished from sight. The others followed, disappearing one after the other.

"Look there," Dorian murmured, directing Kendrick's gaze to the right.

Samantha soon reappeared. Gripping a rope attached to one of the many iron rings that had been embedded as structural ties at the top of the walls, she swung herself over the side of the building and started rappelling downward.

With bent knees, she landed in a stance that allowed her to spring back into a run and race to the end of the course. Hazel met her there two seconds later and clasped her raised hand in celebration of their achievement. Tara and Holly soon joined them.

United, yet independently capable.

The camaraderie and support they consistently showed one another pleased Dorian greatly. They would do well if they were ever called into action. He took a slow breath and expelled it, aware that there should be five instead of just four. Melody's talents were wasted in her current position as lady's companion to the dowager Marchioness of Heathbrooke.

He often wished he'd been able to send someone else in her place.

The problem was trust. In this regard there were only five people upon whom Dorian knew he could count without fail. Samantha, Hazel, Tara, Holly, and Melody. He'd saved them from the orphanage where they'd been placed and had raised them with his wife's assistance until her death a few years ago.

His only regret was the shortsightedness with which he'd regarded the project. In retrospect he should have fostered ten more children at least.

Clapping, Dorian shouted his support, then sent the footman who'd been waiting with a tray full of fresh lemonade, glasses, and biscuits to go serve the women their treat.

Turning to Kendrick, he arched a brow. "I wasn't expecting you today."

"I know." Kendrick looked mildly uncomfortable, yet determined. "Please forgive the intrusion, but I've come to acquire an asset."

Dorian stilled so briefly he doubted the constable noticed his apprehension. Forcing a welcoming smile, he gestured toward the cushioned bamboo chairs that surrounded a matching table. "Have a seat."

Kendrick did as he suggested and Dorian took the chair opposite him. Coffee was served. Kendrick had the good sense to wait for the attending maid to be well out of earshot before offering further explanation.

"The order has come from the chief magistrate himself," Kendrick said. "The mission will be—"

"Less laughable than the previous one?" Dorian made no attempt at hiding his bitterness. Installing Melody as Lady Heathbrooke's companion had been careless.

"Miss Roberts is in an excellent position with regard to acquiring intelligence," Kendrick countered. "She sees and hears a great deal from her vantage point in Grosvenor Square."

"Gossip." Dorian spoke the word with distaste. "Nothing substantial."

"Let's not forget that she's also able to spread it," Kendrick pointed out.

This was true. Melody had managed to change two

parliamentary votes by placing suggestive comments in Lady Heathbrooke's ear. Hours later, the information had been reported as fact, the men it referenced losing all credibility with regard to the bills they'd attempted to pass.

Still…

"My downstairs maid is just as capable of achieving such goals. It does not require the skill of a highly trained agent."

Averting his gaze, Kendrick glanced out across the garden.

"I realize you're disappointed," he murmured. His gaze returned to Dorian, sharper this time. "I'd be unhappy too if I'd dedicated over a decade of my life to a cause that's unlikely to live up to what I envisioned. It could be worse though. You and The Nightingale Project could be forgotten completely. Your protégés could be forced to make the same choices as other young women their age, between marriage and spinsterhood. Or something less appealing, given their backgrounds."

Dorian considered Kendrick with care. There was no denying he made a fair point. Sighing, he picked up his cup and sipped his coffee. "What sort of skill do you need this time?"

Kendrick's attention returned to the garden, to the spot where the four women lounged, enjoying their drinks. "Whatever the blonde has to offer."

It took every ounce of training Dorian possessed not to flinch in response to that comment. Keeping his voice cool and level, he said, "Samantha's the best I've got. Unless you're sending her overseas to infiltrate a foreign power, I'm afraid I'll have to refuse. One of the others will serve well enough otherwise."

"Not in this instance."

Dorian studied Kendrick with rising interest. "What the hell are you planning?"

Kendrick reached for his cup and sipped his coffee, using the same stalling tactic Dorian had used a short while ago. "The chief magistrate has his heart set on Adrian Croft."

"Bloody hell."

"He's not the sort of man one arrests for no good reason. Solid proof of every illegal undertaking he's been involved with will be required. No rumors, no maybes, but facts."

"You realize there's a chance Croft might not have taken up the mantle his father left him. According to my own sources, things have been quiet in Portman Square lately."

"As one might expect. It's been seven months since the funeral. Mr. Croft and his sister have been in mourning. I believe things will liven up a little, now that this time has passed."

"If you think Mr. Croft might welcome the comfort offered to him by a beautiful woman with whom he's not acquainted, that he will invite her into his home and give her the chance she needs to find something damning against him, you'd best re-think your strategy,

Kendrick." Dorian scoffed. "Any idiot would recognize that as a trap from a mile away."

Kendrick coughed, then cleared his throat. "We're hoping he'll let something slip."

"Not going to happen." When Kendrick merely stared at him, Dorian sighed. "The Crofts did not evade capture for generations by letting something slip. Devil take it. Who do you think you're dealing with? This man you're after has been raised, much like every other heir in the country, to assume his legacy. He'll know not to trust a stranger with his secrets."

Uncertainty finally showed itself in the tightly knit lines on Kendrick's forehead. "All we have are assumptions, woven together from situations that turned in the Crofts' favor. The problem is those who've been blackmailed, or who might know of men who went missing, refuse to speak out because they're afraid of the repercussions."

"Or that is what you believe," Dorian murmured, "since all of this has yet to be proven."

"Precisely."

Dorian pinched his brow and muttered a curse. "There's no denying that men sat up straighter whenever George Croft entered a room. He conveyed power and an underlying hint of aggression. His fortune was substantial. Have you tried following the money?"

Kendrick nodded. "There's a country estate – Deerhaven Manor – a good three hours' ride from the City. It's on the shore, near Worthing. Apparently most of the Croft earnings come from fishing and the barley Deerhaven grows in its fields."

"Sounds reasonable." Dorian drank some more coffee. "Have you considered the possibility that there may be nothing to find?"

"I don't believe that. They'd need a fleet of boats, not the three I've got on record, and a hell of a lot more land for fishing and grain to support their lavish lifestyles. Besides which there's also the schools they've sponsored and the almshouses they've opened."

"You do truly make them sound perfectly horrid."

"My point is, their fortune comes from somewhere other than where they claim or it wouldn't be large enough to cover these huge expenses."

Dorian knew Kendrick was likely correct, yet he was compelled to make another suggestion. "Secret investments, perhaps?"

"Maybe, but there's something else going on as well. I'd stake my career on it, Harlowe. Grown men don't look like they're ready to piss themselves at the mention of somebody's name, unless they have cause to fear that person." Kendrick's eyebrows dipped. "Last time I mentioned Croft to a smuggler we'd apprehended, he said the smuggling was nothing compared with the killing he'd done. That's how terrified he was – he was willing to hang for a murder I doubt he committed, just so Croft wouldn't come after him for thinking he'd spilled information to Bow Street."

"And did he?" Curiosity hung in the hair. "Hang, that is?"

"No. I released him, hoping he'd lead to more information. Three days later, some dockworkers fished him out of the Thames."

"In other words, it looks like you're on to something."

"Truth is, the chief magistrate needs a win and so do I."

"You probably shouldn't go around mentioning that. Doesn't instill much faith." He chuckled when Kendrick blanched. "If what you suspect about Croft is true, Samantha will find out. But she can't do so in the space of one week. She'll need time – lots of time – so the acquaintance she builds with Croft appears natural."

Kendrick leaned in. "How much time are you thinking, exactly?"

"A month or two at least."

The other man sat so utterly still, it was clear he'd hoped for a much shorter time-frame. He finally nodded. "Very well, but I want regular updates on her progress."

Dorian agreed to the terms and saw Kendrick out before returning to the terrace. Resuming his seat, he allowed himself a peaceful moment to mull over their meeting while finishing off the last of his coffee.

He had every faith in Samantha's ability to see this mission through even though he feared the impact Adrian Croft might have upon her.

CHAPTER SIX

A bothersome ache gnawed at Samantha's left inner thigh. Despite being in excellent shape and preparing herself for today's challenge, she'd still managed to put too much strain on her body.

Lounging in one of the armchairs that stood in Harlowe's study, she stretched out her legs and crossed them at the ankles. Still dressed in the breeches and shirt she'd worn while exercising, she sipped her hot tea while waiting for Harlowe to broach his reason for summoning her.

"Chief Constable Kendrick came to see me today." The words were bluntly spoken, the lack of emotion adding weight to the statement. "The chief magistrate wants your assistance in taking down Mr. Adrian Croft. Are you familiar with the man?"

Samantha tapped her nails against the side of her cup. "If memory serves, I read his father's obituary in the paper last September. Beyond that, I know nothing about him."

Dorian nodded. "Rumor has it the family's been involved in a number of illegal dealings for several generations. Providing aid to criminals and foreign agents, smuggling, counterfeiting, forced prostitution… You get the idea. Unfortunately, no real evidence of this exists, and until it does, we've got nothing to go on but unverified rumors and suppositions, which is hardly enough to convict a man of his station."

Samantha could sense where this was going. "You want me to infiltrate his life and find the proof that will get him arrested?"

"Precisely." Approval turned Harlowe's grey eyes a shimmering shade of silver. "We need you to gain access to Croft's inner circle. Find out exactly where his family's wealth has come from and what sort of dealings Croft himself has been involved in. Documents will be required if we're to build a solid case that can't be refuted in court."

"That's quite the challenge," Samantha murmured, eyeing Harlowe. "Getting close enough and gaining the kind of trust such a task will require is going to take time. Especially since I was never meant for English Society. He'll be bound to question my past, my connection to you, and my reason for suddenly showing up at all the events I'll have to attend for our paths to cross."

"We'll create a reasonable story – one that's close to the truth."

It wouldn't be easy, but she was happy to take on the task. Her pulse already raced with the thrill of testing her abilities in the real world.

Focusing, she narrowed her gaze and told Harlowe, "For starters, I'd like to assemble a dossier on him. If I'm to come up with a workable plan that will lead to success, I'll need every piece of information you have at your disposal."

CHAPTER SEVEN

Having arrived at the Earl of Marsdale's home some twenty minutes ago, Adrian kept to the periphery of the glittering ballroom while chatting with his sister, his host, and the Duke of Eldrige.

It was his first public outing since the death of his father, a return to Society not just for him but for Evie too. An occasion that marked the celebration of Marsdale's thirtieth birthday.

Adrian hadn't wanted to miss it.

Marsdale – Edward Pryce – was a longtime friend of his due to their mothers having grown up together. As such, they always ignored formalities when in private. He was the only man in whose company Adrian was comfortable enough to fully relax. Unfortunately, this didn't include the sharing of secrets. Edward would never approve of the things Adrian had done. He was much too proper.

So Adrian made sure to keep the more personal aspects of his life carefully hidden. Of course, there was no doubt in his mind that Edward, like so many others, suspected him of working outside the law. But admitting it outright was bound to threaten their friendship – a risk Adrian had no desire to take.

He sighed inwardly, relieved that this evening marked a new beginning without fear or shame. This was what he wanted. A chance to start over.

His days spent running around shady alleyways and hunting down those who crossed his father were over. No need to look back when a much brighter future awaited him and Evie.

"According to what I read, the fellow had some sort of mental collapse in the middle of the street." Eldridge's comment caught Adrian's attention, distracting him from his thoughts.

Of slightly shorter build than Adrian, with thick brown hair and a gaze that seemed to reach the depth of one's soul, the duke was among a small handful of men his father had spoken favorably of.

The rest of those entitled cretins will push their dearest friend off a cliff if it serves their purpose. Eldridge, on the other hand, is a man of substance upon whom even a stranger may confidently rely.

Adrian had never discovered what the good duke might have done to earn such respect. Papa had merely said he could trust him if needed. How much, had not been made clear.

"He punched a man who tried to assist him."

Eldridge rocked back on his heels. "Blocked the traffic on Piccadilly for nearly an hour before the constables came to remove him."

"London does have some rather exciting moments," Edward said before taking a sip of champagne.

Eldridge dipped his chin. "I'm not sure the good Samaritan would agree."

Adrian grinned. He'd missed the lively banter one found at social gatherings. Not that he hadn't enjoyed his regular talks with Edward these past few months, but it was different when there were other people present. Especially with Adrian's own wit in scarce supply lately.

Finding humor in anything had been a challenge. He'd had too much to think of – too many worries and concerns for himself, for Evie, and the future of their lineage. Turning his back on his legacy did not come without some degree of uncertainty or risk.

He'd have to find new ways in which to fill his coffers. Those farther down the chain of command – men who'd served his father with unfailing loyalty – had already voiced their displeasure with his intention.

Might one of them choose to break rank and turn on him?

Trust had been at the heart of everything he and his forefathers had undertaken. If rumor had it that he'd gone soft, that no repercussion would follow from his side, would one of his employees try to sell him out?

He was confident enough in the measures he'd always taken to protect his secrets that such a course would pose a challenge for even those closest to him. With nothing damning ever put in writing, it would be a struggle to prove his involvement in any of the illegal activities he'd engaged in while serving his father.

But it wasn't impossible, he reminded himself while chuckling in response to another witty comment spoken by Edward.

He was just about to reply when the next guests were announced.

A hush fell over the room at the mention of the Irvines. They entered with somber expressions, their attire suggesting they still mourned the death of their daughter.

Adrian found their attendance surprising, given the fact that their daughter was murdered just seven months earlier. But then he noted the young lady who accompanied them – another daughter of debutante age.

"It must be terribly hard for them, having to step out in public so soon after..." The duke shook his head with visible sadness.

"An unfortunate necessity," Evie said, her voice filled with sympathy. "If they wish to see Miss Cassandra married, they must ensure that she's seen."

Adrian glanced at his sister. He'd had a similar notion pertaining to her. At eighteen years of age, she should be looking for her life partner. Hopefully this would be easier for her to do now that Papa was gone. He'd always had a knack for scaring off eligible suitors with his mere presence.

All except one…

He considered Edward and wondered for the hundredth time why he'd never asked for permission to court Evie. Although this was one thing they'd never openly discussed, Adrian knew his friend cared deeply for her and that she returned the sentiment, despite their difference in age.

One thing was certain – it wasn't for Adrian to get involved. If Edward wanted Evie for his wife, he'd bloody well have to figure out how to make that happen on his own.

A melodious tune being played by three violins swirled through the air, mingling with the tapping of feet as dancers moved in time with the music. Later this evening, Evie would dance with the duke – an honor Adrian hoped would encourage other men to write their names on her dance card.

Edward had already done so of course. She would dance with him first. But Adrian would like for her to receive more attention, if only to bolster her confidence.

He was starting to wonder if taking a turn of the room with her would improve her chances, when the maître d' announced two additional late arrivals.

"Mr. Dorian Harlowe and Miss Samantha Carmichael."

Adrian's spirits lifted as soon as he saw the older man. He was tall, with a solid bearing that added a great deal of weight to his studious gaze. Whatever hair he'd once had was now gone, but that did not deter from his striking appearance.

This was someone who wouldn't be crossed.

Adrian smiled. Although he'd only met him once when Harlowe'd joined Papa for luncheon at White's, he'd enjoyed the man's straightforward manner. If they'd been of similar age, he might even have been inclined to foster a deeper friendship with him. The stories he'd told of his travels had been engaging. He'd a knack for making his listeners hang on his every word.

Mr. Harlowe turned to greet someone and Adrian's gaze immediately shifted toward the woman who stood at his side. He took a breath, not even aware that he held it until his lungs started to strain with the effort. Releasing it slowly, he did his best to keep his expression impassive – to hide the interest that surged through his body.

Miss Carmichael was beyond lovely with light blonde hair piled into an elegant updo that left a few curls to frame her face. Slender of build, she moved with effortless grace, the ivory silk of her gown hugging her lithe figure.

"How odd," Evie said.

Adrian shifted his gaze to his sister just long enough that when he looked back in Miss Carmichael's direction, the crowd had closed around her, blocking her from his view.

"How so?" he asked, deciding to humor his sister, though he was a little curious himself as to what she might say.

"Miss Carmichael appears to be of a similar age to me, yet I don't recall her debut."

"You wouldn't," said Eldridge. He lowered his voice to a near whisper as he explained, "I believe her parentage to be unknown. Mr. Harlowe and his wife brought her and a few other girls to live with them some seventeen years ago. As you can imagine, their questionable backgrounds would make presentation at court and subsequent debuts impossible when bearing in mind the purpose of this tradition."

"Marrying into the upper class would not be an option for them," Edward said, putting words to Eldridge's unspoken point. "The scandal of having a wife whose mother might one day reveal herself as a washerwoman or worse would be hard for most to survive, I should think."

"To say nothing of the problems that would arise from this knowledge alone," Adrian said, thinking out loud. "Any number of people might come calling, claiming family ties and demanding some sort of compensation."

"Quite right," Eldridge said. "I think we can all agree it wouldn't be worth it."

"A pity," Evie said while staring in Miss Carmichael's general direction. "She might be perfectly pleasant."

Silence followed this comment, most likely because there was little to say. She was right, of course, but that didn't make Miss Carmichael any less risky as a matrimonial partner.

The current piece of music faded and the next set was announced.

"That's our dance," Edward said, smiling warmly at Evie before offering her his arm.

Her gaze held his as she accepted his escort. "I'll see you later, Brother. Your Grace."

Adrian watched as the pair made their way to the dance floor. Feeling the weight of Eldridge's gaze, he turned to face him. They were alone now, trapped in the uncomfortable silence of Edward and Evie's departure.

Although they knew each other reasonably well, Eldridge had always spent more time in Papa's company than in Adrian's. Perhaps on account of him being at least two decades Adrian's senior, or possibly because Papa, as the head of the Croft family, had been on more equal footing with him at the time.

That had since changed. Adrian's world had shifted. He'd gained the power his father had wielded, only to let it flicker and fade like a burnt-out candle.

The duke cleared his throat, breaking the silence between them. "Tell me, for I am damn curious. Why haven't you married yet?"

"My mistress provides what I need." A response that equaled the shocking directness of Eldridge's question. He followed it with a calm jab of his own, "Where is your lovely wife this evening?"

His comment was bold, bordering on impertinent since it was commonly known that the duke and duchess had been estranged for a number of years.

Then again, given the nature of their acquaintance, Eldridge's own remark had been prying. Adrian watched him closely in anticipation of his response.

A flicker of surprise passed over Eldridge's face before it disappeared behind a neutral mask. The duke gave a low chuckle and looked away for a moment before turning back to Adrian and saying, "I'm afraid Her Grace favors the countryside these days."

"A pity."

The duke smirked. Leaning in, he glanced toward the entrance – the very spot where Miss Carmichael stood – and quietly said, "You ought to stop gawking and ask her to dance."

Adrian stilled on the realization that Eldridge had seen straight through his attempt at appearing indifferent.

The duke stepped back, a wry look adding a hint of mischief to his steely gaze. "Enjoy the rest of your evening, Mr. Croft."

With that, Eldridge turned and walked off, leaving Adrian alone as he went to join the Duke of Wrengate. A man who'd always struck Adrian as the callous sort who'd kick a puppy if it were in his way.

Jaw clamped, Adrian headed outside to the terrace for a bit of fresh air. As he stepped through the door, a light breeze ruffled his hair and cooled his skin. He crossed the flagstone paving and leaned against the railing, then closed his eyes in an effort to calm himself.

Shoving one hand in his pocket, he smoothed his

thumb over the miniature he carried with him without fail.

No one was supposed to know his mind, but if Eldridge was able to read his expression, anyone could. He took a breath and acknowledged that he was severely out of practice. Clearly he'd have to do better.

A soft gasp alerted him to the fact that he wasn't alone. Turning, he saw that he'd been joined by the ever-eager Miss Leonora Brighton, a friend of his sister's who often sought him out whenever the chance to do so arose.

Adrian almost groaned. He doubted her parents would be especially thrilled if they knew of her interest in him.

"Are you all right?" she asked, sounding genuinely concerned. "If you'd like someone to talk to, I'm happy to offer companionship."

Adrian stared at her. "Thank you, but I think it would be best for you to return indoors."

He was not the sort of man who could be coerced into marriage because he'd been found alone with someone's foolish daughter. If anyone happened upon them, he'd walk away without second thought while her reputation would be forever ruined.

Ignoring his suggestion, she shrugged one shoulder and moved toward him. "Your father's death was terribly hard on Evelyn. It must have been awful for you as well."

This was not the sort of conversation he wished to have at the moment. Certainly not with her. He pushed away from the railing and prowled through the darkness until they were standing no more than a foot apart. Her eyes widened with some sort of twisted yearning that made no sense. They barely knew one another.

Raising his palm, he set it against her pale cheek and allowed his thumb to lightly caress her. He watched with an almost perverse degree of gratification as her eyelids drooped and a sigh of pleasure drifted across her thin lips. Like a tiny duckling seeking shelter in a lion's den.

"You would do well to stay away from dishonorable men," he murmured. "Set your sights on finding a suitable match instead."

She swallowed hard, her throat working roughly with the effort as she sought his gaze and held it. "How can I when I'm irrevocably drawn to you?"

Not him, he wagered, so much as the thrill of courting danger. It might be time for him to recommend Evie cut ties with this woman.

His hold on Miss Brighton's jaw tightened, squeezing until she whimpered and squirmed. "Three upper-class women were murdered last year, Miss Brighton. The killer has not yet been captured, and until he is, I recommend caution when choosing whom to seek out in dark corners."

Maneuvering her to the side so he could pass, he strode to the ballroom door and returned inside, coming to an immediate halt when he spotted Evie. She no longer danced with Edward. Instead she stood by the refreshment table, chatting with Miss Carmichael.

Unsettled, he studied them for a moment before he made his approach. What were the odds of a woman he knew next to nothing about befriending his sister?

He reminded himself that she was the foster daughter of a man he'd taken an instant liking to. And yet, Adrian could not shake the awareness that if someone were to try and gain access to him, the most expeditious way of doing so would be through Evie.

Or maybe he was simply too jaded.

Evie was more open and trusting. So it wasn't impossible for her to fall into conversation with someone she'd not met before.

As he drew closer, he wondered what their conversation entailed. He was, after all, Evie's brother and while he wanted her to have friends, he also wanted to make sure she was safe in her choices. The last thing he needed was another Miss Brighton.

He cleared his throat as he reached the ladies, drawing both their attention.

"Evie," he said and added a nod of acknowledgement, though his gaze remained on Miss Carmichael.

He watched her intently, taking in her features – the porcelain skin, blonde hair, and almond-shaped eyes of cornflower blue. They seemed to penetrate him as she greeted him with a soft smile.

Something inside him stirred, though he quickly quashed it. He wasn't here to make friends or entertain romantic notions. All he wanted was to discover if she had ulterior motives.

"Adrian," Evie said brightly. "Allow me to present Miss Carmichael. Miss Carmichael, this is my brother, Mr. Adrian Croft."

"A pleasure." Color spread through Miss Carmichael's cheeks. She averted her gaze, conveying a shyness that struck him as uncommonly charming. But was it real?

He clasped his hands behind his back and gave a short bow while making a very deliberate effort to school his features. It would not do for this woman to glimpse his thoughts as Eldridge had done.

"Indeed, the pleasure is mine." He collected a glass of champagne and clinked it against the one Miss Carmichael held before doing the same with Evie's. "It's rare to meet new people in London Society these days. I must confess, I find it refreshing."

"I was just saying the same exact thing," Evie remarked.

"How come we've not met before?" A question intended to get at the truth. Adrian took a casual sip of his drink.

Miss Carmichael cleared her throat then drank some champagne as well. "There's never been cause for me to participate in these kinds of events. I…am not exactly eligible to marry into the upper ranks of Society. But I've always dreamed of attending a ball, so that's what I wished for on my last birthday."

Adrian frowned. "And Mr. Harlowe agreed?"

"He's a wonderful man – extremely kind, thoughtful, and giving." She took another sip of her drink, as though needing to quash her nerves.

"Thank goodness for that," Evie said. She sent Adrian a pointed look. *Do not ruin this for me.* "I'm of the opinion that every young lady should have the chance to put on fine clothes and enjoy an evening of splendor."

A lovely sentiment, though not one likely to offer additional insight. He tilted his head. "As I understand it, Mr. Harlowe took you in when you were a child."

Evie gasped. "For goodness sake, Adrian, that's hardly the sort of thing one mentions immediately after being introduced."

Miss Carmichael produced a timid smile. "It's quite all right. I don't mind talking about it."

Was it just him, or had Miss Carmichael's eyes hardened a little? "How old were you when you arrived at Clearview House?"

"I was seven."

"Where were you before?"

"St. Christopher's home for foundling children."

"Quite a change then." An observation he tucked away with all the others.

"I count myself lucky." She raised her chin. "I went from sharing a room with nine others to having one of my own, from being cold and dirty, to being warm and clean."

"Heavens," Evie murmured. "I can't even imagine."

"I'll wager you also received an improved education," Adrian said, digging deeper. It was impossible to tell from Miss Carmichael that her beginnings had been so humble. Her attire, the way she carried herself, her very mannerisms and speech belonged to a gently bred lady. It was unnerving how impossible it was to discern her true background, even when he knew about it.

"There were governesses," Miss Carmichael explained, "besides which, Mr. Harlowe and his late wife taught us."

"And what—"

"Adrian," Evie chastised once more, grabbing his arm this time and chuckling. "I'm sure Miss Carmichael would like a reprieve from all your questions. You must forgive him, Miss Carmichael, but he's always had an inquisitive nature."

"I only wished to learn what her favorite subjects might have been." A lie. He'd been meaning to ask about the other women in Harlowe's care and what exactly he'd taught them.

Miss Carmichael responded with a weak smile. "Perhaps we can continue this conversation some other time. At present, I'm afraid I must go and find my next dance partner."

Evie turned on Adrian as soon as Miss Carmichael had walked away. "What is wrong with you?"

Crossing his arms, Adrian met her critical gaze. "How do you mean?"

"You cross examined her as though she were a criminal."

"It's my job to protect you."

"From other young women?" Evie narrowed her eyes on him. "I thought you'd be less overbearing than Papa, but it seems you're just as intent on ruining potential friendships for me as he was."

Adrian bristled. His muscles flexed and his jaw tightened as he leaned toward her. "I am nothing like Papa."

Evie's lips parted. She stared at him in dismay, clearly surprised by the level of anger her comment had led to. Of course she'd be stunned. Her impression of their father had been so vastly different. Yes, he'd been overprotective of her, but not for the reasons she thought – not because he worried she might be led astray by a rogue but rather because he'd feared ulterior motives from everyone they associated with.

Adrian had sworn he'd do better. He'd especially meant for Evie to have more freedom. But how could that happen if he didn't let her make her own choices?

"You're right. Please forgive me. It's just that I know you always see the best in people, even when I struggle to find one good thing about them."

A pained look entered her eyes. "I'm not as naïve as you likely believe me to be."

He hoped that was true, though he couldn't quite help but doubt it. "Come on. I'll show you the rest of the house as promised."

"Really?"

Having only visited the Marsdale parlor in the past, she'd asked Edward if he might give her a tour. He'd declined on account of being the host, but had suggested Adrian do the honors.

Starting downstairs, he led Evie through the various rooms, all of them closed off to everyone else for the evening. They visited Edward's study – a space Evie appeared to show great interest in – then headed to the library, the music room, and the dining room before moving upstairs to the gallery.

It was there, while admiring all the faces of Edward's ancestors, that Adrian made a decision. If he was to truly distance himself from Papa's authoritarian rule, then he ought to provide his sister with more flexibility.

Without even glancing toward her he said, "Invite Miss Carmichael over for tea, if you like. It will give you a chance to further your acquaintance and to decide if she's someone you'd like to count as a friend."

"Really? Do you mean it?"

"I wouldn't suggest it otherwise."

Their father had never allowed either one to bring friends into the house. Adrian had known that it was because he'd worried about what they'd hear or see.

Evie, however, had always believed it was due to his hating the disruption such visits posed to his orderly life.

They returned to the ballroom where Edward was still busy being the attentive host. Mr. Harlowe, who stood a bit farther along, was engaged in conversation with Eldridge. Another curious point. Judging from their relaxed interaction, it looked as though they might be longtime friends.

And then there was Miss Carmichael who presently danced a reel with Viscount Stanton's youngest son, Mr. Clive Newton.

Adrian tracked their movements with interest and made a mental note to have Murry investigate further. Despite what he'd just told Evie, he wasn't about to let Miss Carmichael into his home without knowing more about her.

CHAPTER EIGHT

Samantha deliberately avoided Mr. Croft for the rest of the evening. Ever conscious of his assessing gaze, she fought the urge to glance in his direction. A difficult feat, considering the effect he'd had upon her when they'd first met.

She'd not been prepared.

For some inexplicable reason, she'd imagined him to be shorter, lankier of build, and weaselly looking. Instead, he'd been the exact opposite: tall with nearly black hair and piercing brown eyes – extremely imposing. His chiseled features lent him a stern appearance, while his broad shoulders spoke of physical strength and power.

Despite all the training she'd done, learning to feign indifference, to contain every thought behind an inscrutable mask, she knew she'd shown her hand when she'd blushed. His maleness had affected her.

She'd felt the heat creep up her neck and into her cheeks.

But then he'd started to question her and something inside her shifted.

As mortifying as her response toward him had been in the moment, it occurred to her that it complimented the role she would play henceforth. From now on, she was no longer bold and daring, but rather a meek, perhaps even shy and rather unworldly, young woman. Completely nonthreatening.

"How do you feel it went?" Harlowe asked later as they headed back to Clearview House by carriage.

The ball itself had been everything she'd ever dreamed of. She hadn't lied when she'd told Mr. Croft of her wish to experience one such event. As for the man himself…

"I found a subject with which to engage Croft's sister." A quick assessment of the young woman's slouch as she'd shifted from foot to foot had prompted a comment about uncomfortable slippers. "He approached a while later and introductions were made."

"So I saw."

"He's protective of her," Samantha noted, "and suspicious of anyone he doesn't know."

"I assume that's why you decided to keep it brief?"

"Yes. Coming across as eager would not have served our interests."

"Agreed." He eyed her as the carriage bounced along the cobbled streets on its way out of London. "You did well tonight, Samantha. I'm proud of you."

The comment warmed her immensely. Ever since he'd whisked her away to Clearview House for the very first time, she'd felt indebted. As the years had gone by, the fatherly concern and consideration he'd shown toward her had made her increasingly fond of him. She owed him her life and it was time for her to repay his generosity.

The carriage turned, allowing a beam of moonlight to fall through the window and play across Harlowe's features.

"His sister has invited me to join her for tea on Tuesday."

"An excellent start."

Samantha set her elbow against the edge of the window and sought Harlowe's gaze. "I'm thinking of coming up with some sort of excuse not to."

"Why? Getting inside Croft House so you can search for the proof Kendrick needs is your prime objective."

She shook her head. "It's too soon. Croft will be no less wary of me when I show up on Tuesday than when I engaged his sister in conversation tonight. But if I cancel, it will look as though I've no urgent interest in his family, and he might relax a little."

"Which will make it easier for you to do your job," Harlowe mused.

"Precisely." The carriage left the City behind, picking up speed as it travelled the country road. Clearview wasn't far. They'd reach it within another ten minutes. "I'll need a few tools at my disposal – an inconspicuous errand boy who's stealthy enough to double up as a watcher, someone who can help me expand my social network, and a rented room somewhere in the City where I can keep supplies, seek shelter, and catch some rest if need be without the hassle of trekking back here."

"I know a man you can speak to regarding the errand boy. Wycliffe's his name. Runs a gang of thieves out of St. Giles."

"Not exactly the sort of man we'd have 'round for tea then."

"My experience with him in the past has been positive. I'll give you his address once we're home. As for the contact you need, I'm sure Melody can help."

Samantha had already considered speaking with her. "It surprised me that she wasn't there tonight."

"From what I learned, the dowager marchioness was feeling unwell."

"I'll call on her tomorrow then."

"As for the room you wish to rent, I really must ask if you think that's wise. Don't forget the part you're meant to be playing, Samantha. Proper young ladies do not move about unchaperoned. They definitely don't live alone in the City. If anyone were to find out, it could undermine everything."

He wasn't wrong. And yet…

"I need to have a place I can escape to. Especially if I get injured." When Harlowe didn't reply to this, she told him firmly, "I don't know what the future will bring, but I'd like to be prepared for any eventuality instead of trying to muddle my way through a challenge I didn't see coming."

The carriage rolled to a halt in the graveled driveway, and the door was pulled open by one of the footmen. Dorian leaned forward, but before he alit he sent her a backward glance. "Promise me you'll be careful."

She nodded despite her concerns, convincing him as best as she could that he had nothing to fear. "Of course."

CHAPTER NINE

Gray clouds darkened the sky the following morning when Samantha set off. She had two goals to accomplish today: call on Melody and seek out Wycliffe.

The carriage arrived at Number 2 Berkley Square, and Samantha alit. Tilting her head back, she scanned the façade of the tall stone building before her and took a deep breath before stepping forward.

Her call was answered by an aging and slightly hunched butler, who showed her into a parlor where every conceivable surface was covered in crystal and porcelain figurines. Good grief. She was glad she wasn't tasked with having to dust this room.

Her attention bounced around the space, unable to find a suitable spot on which to land. There were so many things, from the heavy green damask curtains, to a series of mismatched rugs on the floor, to vases brimming with bouquets of flowers and...

She sneezed, just as the parlor door opened and Melody entered.

"Bless you." Melody grinned. She stepped toward Samantha and gave her a quick embrace. "What a lovely surprise this is. I've already asked for a tea tray to be brought up."

"Thank you." Samantha swiped at her eyes with the heel of her hand. "I think it might be wise to open a window or two. It's horribly stuffy in here."

"I completely agree," Melody whispered. "But Lady Heathbrooke won't have it. She's worried she'll catch a chill."

"Can't you explain to her that fresh air can be brought in while she's not actually in the room?"

Melody gave her a this-is-a-pointless-topic-for-us-to-discuss sort of look and gestured toward the settee. "Shall we?"

Samantha sighed. It looked like she'd just have to suffer the cloying smell that hung in the air. "Of course."

A maid arrived with the tea as soon as they'd settled into their seats, with Samantha on the settee and Melody in an adjacent armchair. The tea things were distributed and the maid departed, leaving the two women alone.

"You look well," Samantha said, while Melody poured the tea. "I realize keeping an old woman company isn't what you envisioned for yourself, but I do hope you're happy."

"I'm comfortable," Melody told her, "and I suppose some measure of happiness can come from that."

"Harlowe believes you're doing important work." A lie. He hadn't commented on Melody's job at all.

Melody snorted. "I listen to gossip and then I relay it. Or I let information slip in a way that makes Lady Heathbrooke believe she's made a shocking discovery on her own – one that must be related to others at once."

"You find it too easy?"

"I find it too dull." Melody blew out a breath and sipped her tea while Samantha followed suit. "Tell me why you're here. Is it because you need my help with something?"

"Yes. I've received my own mission. As much as I'd like to, I cannot reveal the specifics, though it will require my presence within Society. If you're able to draw me in and include me when possible, I'd be ever so grateful."

"Harlowe's connections surpass my own. Any particular reason why he isn't helping?"

"It's best if it looks like I have my own friends, people I can be seen going for walks with, for example. That way, my presence at various events will appear more natural – less suspicious to my target."

"So there's a target." Melody smirked, but failed to conceal the dispirited look in her eyes. "Lucky you."

Samantha held her gaze. "It's not as exciting as it sounds."

"Liar." Melody actually grinned. Sobering, she paused for a second before saying, "I'll see what I can do. As companion to Lady Heathbrooke, I have limited influence, though I have managed to make a few friends."

"I'm glad to hear it." Samantha's gaze dropped to a side table covered in macramé. A matching pair of candlesticks stood on top, but it was the paper that had been left beside them that caught her attention. Most specifically the gossip column facing upward and the name that stood out.

Samantha scanned the words casting Evelyn Croft in a most unfavorable light, painting her as some kind of desperate wanton. She shook her head and picked up the paper, pulling it into her lap so she could more easily read it.

"This isn't true. I don't believe a word of it. I mean, I was there last night, at the Marsdale ball. Miss Croft and I spoke and she…" Anger on Miss Croft's behalf swept the length of Samantha's spine. "She didn't strike me as someone who'd engage in debauchery while pretending virginal innocence. It's preposterous to suggest it."

"And yet it's been published in print for all of London to read." Melody gave Samantha a sad look. "Her reputation will be ruined over this."

"But why? Who would choose to spread such lies about a perfectly wonderful person?"

Melody pursed her lips. "You're certain there's no truth to it?"

"Of course I can't be certain but instinct tells me this is completely false. I just can't imagine who'd be behind it."

"Perhaps a jealous debutante hoping to marry the same man Miss Croft is after?"

"And what? The paper would buy such a story without triple-checking the facts?"

"I honestly don't know, I… Samantha, please relax. That's Lady Heathbrooke's paper. It won't do for you to rumple it."

Despite wanting nothing more than to tear the paper to shreds, Samantha relaxed her hold and set it aside. Perhaps she should keep her appointment for tea with Miss Croft. The younger woman would need a friend in the wake of this injustice. Hopefully her brother would have the good sense to march into the *The Morning Post*'s offices and demand a public apology.

Unhappy with the awareness of just how cruel Society could be, she downed the remainder of her tea and took her leave of Melody, who promised she'd be in touch soon.

Samantha returned to the carriage, climbed in, and proceeded onward to her next destination. The beautiful Mayfair architecture slid past the window, dimming and transforming as they travelled farther along Piccadilly and closer to where St. Giles began.

Façades began showing signs of cracked paint, the fencing looked increasingly broken with occasional boards missing, and there were significant signs of rot in the wood trim around the windows and doors. It only got worse when they turned onto Dyott Street. The homes here were squatter, more crooked, and jammed together so tightly they looked like they clamored for air.

The light was dimmer here too, as if a large cloud had darkened this part of the city where washing lines hung between the buildings and stray dogs trotted about searching for scraps. This was where the forgotten resided – those the wealthy wished to ignore.

Samantha noted the scrawny woman slumped in a doorway, her tattered clothes covered in filth and her hair in complete disarray. It was impossible to tell if she was dead or alive.

Shuddering, Samantha patted her arms and thighs before checking her hair, just to be sure the weapons she carried were still secure. Her heart raced a bit faster. She wasn't afraid of what she'd find here. Whatever threat might present itself, she'd be prepared, but that didn't change the fact that she'd never actually killed a person.

She knew how, had trained repeatedly to do so, but if it came to it, would she be able to thrust a blade into a man without blinking?

Harlowe believed her capable.

The first time is always the hardest. Not because you can't handle it, but because you will always second guess yourself until you get past that initial death.

Her gaze fell on some boys who wore the expressions of men who'd returned from war. It wasn't fair that their childhoods were stolen. She wished their lives would be easier. Unfortunately, if they lived here, their lives were far more likely to get even harder as they grew older.

The carriage slowed and drew to a halt. This was as far as the coachman would take her. If she was to seek an audience with Wycliffe, it wouldn't do for her to arrive with the arrogant pomp and circumstance attributed to the upper class. Rather, she'd approach him on foot.

Samantha opened the door and stepped down, neatly avoiding a grimy puddle. She sent the coachman a nod, confident he would wait for her to return, and started walking. Keeping her stride quick and precise, she weaved her way through the narrow streets, moving deeper and deeper into the slums.

The smell, a stench of dead carcasses mixed with refuse, made Lady Heathbrooke's parlor seem like a fresh country meadow. A legless man sat on the ground, his torso propped against a wall while he gobbled down some piece of food. Two women dressed in revealing clothes sewn from vibrant fabrics and lace laughed at her as they approached from the opposite direction.

"Fall on hard times, did ya?" One of them, a plump red-head, crooned. She stepped into Samantha's path and dragged a finger along the length of her arm. "You're welcome to join us."

The other woman, a brunette with a sharp nose and

drawn cheeks, chuckled before licking her lips. "A young thing as pretty as you will earn a good wage. We'll happily teach ya, in exchange for splittin' the profits."

"As lovely as that sounds, I've business to attend to." Samantha shook off the first woman's touch and hardened her gaze just enough to make her retreat. Then, smiling broadly, she said, "I'm seeking Mr. Wycliffe."

The women assessed her from head to toe and finally snorted.

"I hope ya know what ya doing," the brunette muttered before shoving past.

"Tell him Regina will give him a month for free in exchange for your gown," said the red-head as she, too, recommenced walking. Their laughter echoed against the slanted walls of the mismatched buildings that lined the alley.

Samantha took a deep breath and continued onward, stepping over a dead rat that floated belly up in a filthy gutter. Rounding a corner, she entered the street on which Wycliffe reputedly lived.

A small group of men had gathered up ahead, busily smoking and chatting. Samantha kept her chin down, her back straight, and her stride deliberate. Slowing her breath to keep her pulse even, she felt for the blades she'd concealed in the carefully sewn channels inside her spencer's long sleeves.

Their hard metal presence calmed her nerves as she drew ever nearer to where the men stood. Without missing a beat, she aimed for the red brick building with the black door, intent on finding Wycliffe without courting trouble.

"Oi." A gruff voice stopped her. "Who the devil are you and where'd you think you're goin'?"

She clenched her jaw and squared her shoulders while raising her gaze, taking a split second to assess her surroundings. There were five men in total. One held a blade while another drank from a bottle that could be turned into a makeshift weapon.

The man who'd initially spoken stepped forward. He was large, stocky of build, and a good head taller than she, but his movements were sluggish. The rest of the men were slimmer. One had a pair of fierce eyes while the one holding the blade was marked by an angry gash on his cheek. The last two were barely more than boys, one with a scruffy mop of black hair, the other, who drank from the bottle, nearly as blonde as she.

"Are any of you Mr. Wycliffe?" she asked.

The stocky man scowled and took a step closer to where she'd halted, his cheroot dangling between his lips. "No."

She offered a venomous smile. "Then I'm none of your business."

He sneered at her while letting his gaze slide over her body. "I beg to differ."

It came as no surprise to Samantha when he tried to reach for her arm. She'd anticipated the move several seconds before, so sidestepping it proved easy. He growled in irritation as she swept past him, her attention already upon his fierce-eyed companion while keeping her senses attuned to the stocky man's movements.

"I've got her," Fierce-eyes said, leaping to block her path.

Samantha stepped forward to meet him, her fist closing around his lapels and pulling him to her in order to bring him off balance. Surprise showed on his face. He'd likely thought she'd attempt to run. Instead, she swept one leg behind him and shifted her weight, then followed him down to the ground.

They hit it hard, with a jarring thud that caused fierce-eyes to yelp and sputter.

"What the hell?" one of the other men shouted.

Aware that they, too, would soon be upon her, she wasted no time in snapping her opponent's wrists. An accompanying howl of pain spliced the air while glass shattered behind her.

One down, four to go.

Abandoning Fierce-eyes, Samantha leapt forward and barely managed to turn before the ugliest one of the bunch brought his blade down over the spot where her head had been seconds before. She grabbed his wrist to control the blade, then jammed her fingers into his throat as hard as she could before bringing her knee up to meet his groin.

His legs buckled, and he fell to the ground with a whimper.

"Pathetic," muttered the stocky man. He gestured toward the blonde boy who held the sharp remains of the bottle. "Take her down, will ya?"

Settling into a combative stance, Blondie eyed her with apprehension while shifting his gaze to his black-haired friend. They shared a nod of agreement, then approached her together – one moving left while the other moved right.

Samantha remained where she was, watching and waiting until they looked ready to pounce. Only then did she choose to remove her blades from her sleeves and slide them into the palms of her hands.

Blondie and Black-hair froze, their eyes filling with apprehension and fear as she swung her weapons. They'd seen what she was capable of without them. Did they really wish to stay and find out how deadly she'd be if she wished it?

As expected, the pair valued their lives and fled, clattering along the narrow street as though Satan himself were giving chase.

Allowing a smug smile of victory, Samantha returned her attention to the stocky man who'd started the altercation. He backed up a step, his brow sweating despite the loathing she saw in his eyes. He hated her, but he was also very afraid.

So she stepped forward, pressed the tip of one blade to his chest. "I want no more trouble. Understood?"

Rather than answer, he tossed the cheroot he'd been smoking and bent to help his companions stand. Both men cursed her fiercely, but Samantha ignored them. She had more pressing matters to consider, like her meeting with Wycliffe.

She returned her blades to her sleeves, then stepped

up to the black door and gave it a few solid knocks. A boy roughly fourteen years old answered her call. He was only slightly shorter than she, his clothes as scruffy as one might expect from a St. Giles resident.

"I'm here to see Wycliffe," she said, her gaze already taking note of the shabby interior behind the boy. Dark and dismal, the walls were cracked and the plank flooring covered in dirt.

The boy raised his chin, pointing his nose in the air. "Got an appointment?"

Samantha almost laughed. As if the man she'd come to see were in need of a make-shift butler. "No. You may tell him Mr. Harlowe suggested I see him."

The boy gave her a dubious look but decided to grant her entry. "Wait here."

He left her in the grimy foyer where water stains marked the ceiling while black splotches tainted the walls. Damp and cold with a humid smell, it felt like the sort of place from which one would only emerge with a number of ailments.

Samantha stiffened her posture and kept her gaze on the door through which the boy had vanished. Voices engaged in hushed chatter filtered down from somewhere overhead while footsteps pitter-pattered about.

"Come on," said the boy when he returned. "Wycliffe will see you."

Samantha expelled a deep breath and followed the boy through a hallway so crooked she feared the ceiling might cave in and bury her alive. It opened up into a larger room where the floors had been covered in mismatched rugs and the grubby windows hung with faded red curtains. Smoke from a fireplace to the right of the doorway clouded the air, and had no doubt lent to the gray shade adorning the walls.

Furniture was sparse, consisting of no more than two red velvet armchairs with a low table between, and a cabinet leaning against one wall.

A man, roughly thirty years of age in Samantha's estimation, stood in the middle of the room, watching her with interest as she arrived. His dark hair was longer than what was deemed fashionable, curling loosely around his shoulders. Equally unfashionable was his beard which, if removed, would likely allow him to change his appearance completely.

"Mr. Wycliffe?" Despite the hard gleam in his eyes, she took a step forward while holding his gaze. Unlike the men she'd met outside in the street – the sort who tried to seem tougher than what they actually were – this man reeked of ruthless danger.

It made her wonder at Harlowe's association with him.

Wycliffe tilted his head, allowing the edge of his mouth to draw upward into a slick smile that caused shivers to dart down her spine. With that expression, he might as well have said, welcome to my lair and your upcoming disembowelment.

Instead, he swept his hand toward one of the armchairs. "Charlie tells me Harlowe sent you and that you came without escort."

"I'm capable of protecting myself," Samantha told him. Though possibly not from lice, she decided while sending the proffered armchair a wary glance. She sat nonetheless.

Annoyingly, Wycliffe chose to remain standing while studying her with a gaze hard as flint. "I trust the tear on your skirt is evidence of that?"

Samantha hadn't realized the lace trim had ripped. She nudged it with her finger and noted that there was a stain on her skirts as well, from kneeling on the ground when she'd snapped Fierce-eyes's wrists. Bother.

"There was a bit of an altercation outside," she murmured, returning her attention to Wycliffe.

He held her gaze for a few more seconds before eventually snorting and, much to Samantha's relief, taking a seat in the other available chair.

"Tell me why you've come."

"I need a reliable messenger. Someone who can also keep a watchful eye on the occupant of a particular address without getting noticed."

Wycliffe glanced at the boy who had shown Samantha in. "Charlie, fetch Isak for me."

Charlie dipped his head and vanished. The tread of feet on the hallway stairs followed. Wycliffe kept his attention firmly upon her but held his tongue. Once again, she wondered how he and Harlowe knew each other and why all she had to do was mention her guardian's name in order to have her request met.

The sound of rapid footsteps approaching made her

straighten her spine. She tore her gaze from Wycliffe and glanced at the door as Charlie returned, followed by a much younger boy who looked no more than ten years of age.

"He's fast on his feet and small enough to disappear into the background," Wycliffe informed Samantha when she sent him a questioning look. Addressing Isak he said, "You're to work for this lady as long as she needs. Do as she says and you'll be rewarded."

An expectant silence followed, all eyes on Samantha. She gave a quick nod. "Five shillings per day. An extra pound at the end of the job, provided I'm happy with your performance."

"Make that two pounds and you have yourself a deal," Wycliffe told her.

"Very well. Two pounds it is, but only if you complete every task to my full satisfaction." She stepped toward Isak, who gazed up at her with much too grave an expression for someone so young. "Fail, and you'll get nothing. Betray me in any way, and I'll see to it that you're sent to a workhouse. Understood?"

If he could manage this task without any Runners standing in his way, he'd have proven his worth.

Isak gave a swift nod. "Yes, miss."

"You'll start right away then by delivering this to Mr. Kendrick at the Bow Street Magistrate's Court." She retrieved a missive from her skirt pocket and handed it to Isak. "Meet me at The Fox's Burrow tavern tomorrow at three o'clock sharp. If Kendrick has a response for me you can hand it over then."

"But what if it's urgent?" Isak asked.

"It won't be that urgent," Samantha assured him. She turned to Wycliffe. "Thank you for your assistance. I'm in your debt."

"I'm counting on it," he murmured with a wry twist to his lips.

Samantha didn't doubt it for a second. Loath as she was to turn her back on the man, she forced herself to do so as she departed. There were more important matters for her to attend to right now than worrying over the sort of person who had no qualms about using children to his advantage.

It was vital she find a room to let – a place from which she could run her operation without leaving a trail directly to Clearview House.

CHAPTER TEN

Evelyn was in high dudgeon. Keen as usual to read the gossip column, she'd snatched up the paper before her brother was able to do so in order to read the latest gossip pertaining to last night's ball. What she had not expected was for her own name to appear as part of an outlandish lie that threatened to ruin her reputation completely.

"This season will be for nothing unless that story goes away," she grumbled, frowning into her teacup. "I still don't understand why someone would write such a falsehood about me."

"Neither do I," Adrian said. Seated adjacent to her at the head of the table, he glared at the paper she'd handed him just a few moments before. "Rest assured, I've every intention of figuring out who's behind this and having them write a retraction."

"Do you think that will help?"

"I expect so."

The tightness in his voice was evidence of his anger. Evelyn knew he attempted to hide it for her sake, but his expression alone was enough to freeze the air in the room.

Hoping to calm him, she thought of changing the subject by saying, "The front page should interest you too. Doesn't look like Mr. Benjamin Lawrence will be recovering from the fall he took last week. The poor man has lost the use of his legs completely."

Adrian tilted his head, his gaze meeting hers so sharply she gasped. "You'll need to be extra careful now," he said.

"Because of Mr. Lawrence?" She couldn't quite follow his logic. "I'm not sure I understand why a horse-riding accident—"

"Never mind Mr. Lawrence," Adrian said. "I'm speaking of your safety with regard to the rot that's been written about you. Let's not forget that whoever murdered Miss Fairchild, Lady Camille, and Miss Irvine seems to have targeted them because they lacked morals. Let's also not forget that he has yet to be apprehended."

"Don't you think he would have been if he were still out there?" Evelyn sipped her tea while considering. "It's been so long since Miss Irvine's death, I'm sure there's no cause for further alarm."

"Perhaps not," Adrian agreed. "Nevertheless, I urge you to stay at home until I get to the bottom of this."

"I have no issue with that. At present, socializing is

the very last thing I'd like to do." She dreaded getting the cut, of being whispered about behind her back, or facing the censure she knew she'd find the moment she left the house.

Unlike Adrian, to her, people's opinions mattered. She wanted to be liked and knew she'd find it hard to ignore the response she was sure to receive because of some writer's words.

"Do you suppose another debutante might have made up the story because they were jealous?"

"I've no idea." He placed his hand over hers and gave it a squeeze. "Don't fret, Evie. The matter will be resolved one way or the other, I assure you."

But what if it wasn't? What if she would forever after be known as the harlot from whom not just one man but two sought their pleasure last night?

"Good lord." It suddenly felt as though there weren't enough air for her to breathe. "Whatever will Marsdale think when he reads this?"

If there was one man in all of England whose opinion mattered to her beyond anyone else's, it was his.

"I'm sure he'll have the good sense to dismiss it as nonsense," Adrian told her.

"You have to make sure." She couldn't bear the idea of Marsdale thinking ill of her for any reason. "Promise me you'll call on him first."

"My intention is to visit *The Morning Post* first. I'll stop by Marsdale House afterward." He huffed a breath and seemed to make some effort to relax as he grabbed a slice of toast and proceeded to butter it. "Perhaps we should get away for a week - visit Deerhaven while the worst of the gossip dissipates."

The suggestion pleased her immensely. The country estate would serve as a lovely distraction. "I'd like that. We could leave tomorrow after Miss Carmichael stops by for tea."

"An excellent idea, Evie. I'll leave you to manage the packing while I try to undo the damage done toward you."

An acceptable plan that kept her mind off the problem for the better part of the day. Until a missive arrived for her in the early afternoon. Her fingers trembled as she tore the seal. The message was brief, yet wonderfully calming. If Adrian didn't return home with answers, she now had the means to find them herself.

So she came to greet him as soon as she heard him arrive a while later. The somber expression he gave her, however, was far from uplifting.

"They've agreed to check the facts," he said as soon as the two were alone in the parlor. "If they find them lacking, a retraction will follow. Until then, I'm afraid we'll have to weather the storm."

"Were you able to speak with the author directly?"

"No." He muttered a curse. "The chief editor was extremely tight-lipped regarding her true identity. I've been assured that if the accusation made against you proves false, a public apology will follow, though it can take several days before this happens. I'm sorry, Evie. Truly."

"What about Marsdale?"

"He's outraged on your behalf. Doesn't believe a word of what was printed."

Evelyn breathed a sigh of relief. Thank goodness. "I've almost finished packing. What time would you like to set off tomorrow?"

"By three, provided Miss Carmichael has departed by then."

Evelyn agreed and went to collect the novel she wanted to read on the journey. The rest of the day passed without incident. Dinner was served at seven o'clock, according to the same routine they'd followed while Papa lived. They enjoyed a glass of port in the music room afterward where she played one of Haydn's sonatas at the pianoforte.

By nine thirty, she expressed her exhaustion and bid her brother good night before removing herself to her bedchamber. There she collected the missive she had received in the afternoon, grabbed her cloak, and descended the service stairs at the back of the house.

Moving swiftly while taking care to keep silent, she crossed to the terrace door, unlocked it, and slipped out into the chilly night air. The path to the fence at the end of the garden seemed more uneven in the darkness. She tripped a couple of times and fought the urge to cry out, lest anyone hear her.

Intended to keep unwanted people out as opposed to the residents in, the garden gate was easy enough to unlatch. She opened it, stepped through, and closed it as much as she could without actually locking it back into place.

The hour was, in her estimation, nearing ten. If she moved swiftly, she ought to be able to reach the appointed meeting place and return home within half an hour at most, provided she took a carriage.

Eager to settle into the comfort of her bed as soon as possible, Evelyn pulled her cloak's hood up over her head, walked to the next street corner, and hailed a hackney, directing the driver to take her to Smithfield Street. From there she'd walk the rest of the way. It shouldn't take more than five minutes at most.

Dressed as she was and without escort, she doubted anyone would think her more than a servant running a late-night errand. The driver certainly didn't pay her much mind. Nor did the two gentlemen she passed later after alighting from the carriage. Neither one acknowledged her presence with so much as the tip of his hat.

Satisfied she would complete her task without Adrian being the wiser, Evelyn crossed the street and entered St. Bartholomew's churchyard. The stones marking the graves appeared like crooked teeth in the darkness. A sweet scent from some nearby plant offered a pleasant escape from the somber surroundings.

Evelyn navigated her way to the back of the church, her eyes seeking the man she'd come here to meet. She heard him before she saw him, the gentle tread of footsteps behind her prompting her to suck in a breath as she turned.

"You came." His voice was whisper quiet.

"Of course I did. If the information you can provide will help put this viscous rumor about me to rest, then there's little I will not do to obtain it."

"Is that so?" He stepped toward her but his face remained cast in shadow. "The missive I sent you. Did you bring it?"

She raised her hand, showing it to him, and allowed him to take it. "You said you know who's behind the attack. Will you give me their name now?"

"A deal is a deal," he murmured, "but before we get to that, I wanted to tell you how much I enjoyed our dance together last night. You're an extraordinary woman. A pity you're not as innocent as you appear."

A chill swept under Evelyn's cloak. She forced herself to remain where she stood, to not back away as concern flooded her veins. "What are you saying?"

"Only that the incidents described by the paper weren't entirely false. Were they?"

Panic descended upon her in full force. "Of course they were. I would never do what that column suggested. Least of all at Marsdale's ball."

"Because you care for him." A humorless chuckle followed that statement. "And yet, you gladly accepted another man's attentions."

"No." She felt sick at the very idea of what he suggested.

"I saw you with my own eyes."

Evelyn stared at him in dismay while fear began squeezing her heart, stifling every consecutive beat. She shook her head. "Whatever you saw, or think you saw, I had no part in it."

"Oh, but you did. There was no mistaking the name your roguish companion used while you sighed in his arms. What astounds me the most is that someone else saw you as well, which can only mean that one illicit encounter was not enough to appease you for one evening."

"No. Something's not right." Her head spun as she tried to grapple with what he was saying. She had no idea how such a thing could be true. It had to be an illusion of sorts. But the lengths someone had gone to in order to wound her were extensive if that was the case.

"Agreed. Young women playing at innocence when they are anything but is rather misleading."

"You mistake my meaning. Good lord, I can't imagine what you must think of me if you believe what you saw to be true." Not that it mattered. He was just one single person, but if he gave her the name of the source who'd passed on the information to the newspaper columnist, maybe she could get to the bottom of what had transpired and change everyone else's opinion. She looked to the man she'd come to meet. "Tell me who the source is and I'll prove you're mistaken."

He was silent for a moment, an unmoving silhouette in the darkness. And then he said, "I'll want a favor in return."

"I wouldn't expect anything less." Aware that time

was of the essence, Evelyn gathered her courage. She could not be gone from home for much longer. "Name your price."

His breathing grew louder. "Your surrender. Right here, right now."

She stiffened. "I don't understand your meaning."

He moved toward her with wraith-like fluidity. The cool palm of his hand settled gently against her cheek before curling around the back of her head and holding her steady. Another step brought him closer still while sending her already trembling pulse into a mad gallop.

"A passionate kiss," he murmured. "That is my price."

Although she had no desire to do as he asked, she reasoned it might be worth it. They were alone in the dark. Nobody else would know what she'd done. But the name he'd provide her with after would allow her to figure out what had transpired last night at the ball, and could potentially save her reputation.

Surely the benefit outweighed the cost.

Still…

"Will that be all?" she asked, just to be certain. "You'll not have expectations of courtship after?"

His answering chuckle had an unpleasant effect on her nerves. "Trust me, Miss Croft. Marrying you is the furthest thing from my mind, but a taste, that's something I can't quite resist."

She ought to slap him for insulting her so. She ought to leave. But she desperately wanted to know who'd betrayed her. So she steeled herself against what came next and gave a swift nod. "Very well."

To her consternation, his mouth did not descend over hers right away. Instead, he reached around her and drew her flush up against him. The action was so unexpected it forced a gasp from her throat.

He responded with a rough sound and pressed himself to her with firmness. Her back hit the side of the church, distracting her from his shift in position and the sudden press of his hips against hers.

"Please stop." She placed her palms against him, prepared to push him away. "This isn't the kiss I agreed to."

"Come now," he murmured, moving against her with added force. "We both know you secretly want this."

"You're wrong."

He slowed his movements, causing a forceful sensation to stir deep inside her. A wicked chuckle echoed next to her ear. "Am I?"

To her everlasting shame, her body responded to what he was doing with pleasure, and the keen desire for more.

It made no sense. She did not long for this man. She yearned for Marsdale, but it was as if some foreign power had taken possession of her free will, igniting a fire she could not control.

"Like that, do you," he asked when a soft moan escaped her. His voice was gruff, almost accusatory. A snort followed. "You almost had me deceived for a moment – made me question whether or not I'd misjudged you. But it's clear to me now that I didn't."

It was hard to untangle his words when it felt like a maelstrom was rising inside her. Before she could sort out his meaning, he captured her mouth in a kiss so aggressive she failed to notice the sharp metal tip pressing into her throat.

CHAPTER ELEVEN

❦

Adrian had barely finished dressing when a knock at his bedchamber door preceded his butler's arrival.

"I apologize for disturbing you," Elks said while Murry ran a brush down the navy-blue superfine jacket Adrian wore, "but there's a Chief Constable Kendrick to see you on what he insists is a matter of utmost urgency."

Adrian frowned and tried to figure out what had brought Kendrick to his home so early in the day. "Thank you, Elks. Please show him to the parlor."

"Do you suppose one of your many associates might have ignored the order to stop using the benefit of the Croft name for business?" Murry asked once Elks was gone.

"Possibly." One thing was for damn sure. If such a

thing were occurring, he'd find the culprit and make him pay for the trouble.

Unhappy with starting the day in a state of annoyance, Adrian downed the last of the coffee Murry had brought him earlier, and went to discover why Kendrick had come. He wanted the visit over and done with quickly so he could address other matters. The late-night call he'd paid his mistress had caused a delayed start to his day.

A clipped stride brought him to the parlor where he found the constable waiting. The man's slim frame was slightly hunched as he studied the porcelain pieces displayed behind the glazed doors of the bureau bookcase.

"Mr. Kendrick."

Adrian's voice caused his visitor to straighten and turn, bringing his oval face into view. His dark blonde hair had been carefully combed to one side and greased with pomade, offering him a neat and professional look.

Blue eyes met Adrian's from beneath a pair of tightly knit eyebrows. The gravity of his gaze was echoed in the straight line of his thin-lipped mouth. A hint of stubble upon his jaw suggested he'd not taken time to shave.

"Mr. Croft. I'm sorry to call on you so early in the day." Kendrick spoke curtly, his posture stiff, as though he was just as unhappy to be here as Adrian was to have his morning disturbed by his presence.

"I trust you wouldn't have done so unless there was

cause." Adrian gestured toward the seating arrangement. "Shall we sit?"

"Thank you, but I…" He cleared his throat and squared his shoulders. "I'm afraid there's no easy way to say this."

"Say what?" Adrian asked when the man said nothing further.

Seconds passed. A muscle worked at the edge of Kendrick's jaw as he seemed to weigh his next words. A sliver of unease spread across Adrian's shoulders. He flexed his fingers and fought the urge to reach for the miniature in his pocket.

A raven landed upon the outdoor windowsill and proceeded to tap the glass with its beak. The constable sent a swift glance toward it and finally spoke, his voice grave as he said, "I regret to inform you that your sister, Miss Evelyn Croft, was discovered in St. Bartholomew's graveyard a couple of hours ago. It seems she's been murdered."

Adrian's first response was a startled laugh as the tension he'd experienced these past few minutes was released. "Forgive me, but I fear you've made yet another mistake. Honestly, as if your inability to catch the man behind those three murders last year isn't enough, you now misidentify your victim."

"There's no mistake," Kendrick said, his voice even. "I've seen your sister enough times in public to recognize her."

A prickly sensation crawled over Adrian's skin as apprehension returned. He held Kendrick's gaze even as his gut tightened. "You're wrong. We dined here together last night and shared a drink afterward before she retired to bed where I am confident she remains."

"It might be prudent to check."

Adrian flattened his mouth and stalked from the room with every intention of doing precisely that. Damn Kendrick for coming here before eight and disrupting what ought to have been a perfectly pleasant morning with a false claim. He'd looked forward to giving his ledgers a quick review before joining Evie for breakfast. His intention was to pack after that so they could depart for Deerhaven Manor after Miss Carmichael came to call.

He took the stairs two steps at a time, marched to Evie's bedroom, and gave the door a soft knock. When no response came, he knocked again. Harder this time.

Silence.

Disquiet rippled through him. Ice curled over his shoulders. "Evie?"

The lack of response made him reach for the handle. He pushed the door open and looked to her bed. It was neatly made, as though it hadn't been slept in.

A tremor raked the length of his spine as incomprehension transformed into fear. She wasn't here, which meant...

He dared not think it.

Kendrick could not be right.

Evie would soon appear.

Perhaps she'd gone to grab a book before bed and

had fallen asleep in the library. The desperate thud of his heart prayed this was the case.

"Elks!" Adrian ran from her bedchamber, nearly tumbling down the stairs in his haste to find her. Maybe her maid knew something he didn't. "Emma!"

"What is it?" Elks asked, appearing behind him in the library doorway while he scanned the room. "What's happened?"

"Where's Evelyn?" Adrian asked, his gaze darting from corner to corner.

"Is she not in her bedchamber?"

Adrian shook his head. "I already looked."

"Perhaps the music room then."

Deep down, Adrian already knew he'd not find her there either. An ache tightened his throat. Breathing became a chore as his body grew heavy. Somehow, he managed to drag his weight forward, toward Emma, who'd just come to join them. "When did you see my sister last?"

"Yesterday evening, when I helped her prepare for dinner."

It felt as though he were sinking beneath the weight of this revelation and what it implied. "You did not help her ready for bed?"

"She never called upon me to do so."

Every inhalation he took stung his lungs. His vision blurred. This could not be. He refused to believe it. But as he pushed his way past his servants, reality started to grip him. Evie had gone out last night. Kendrick had come to inform him that she had been murdered.

When Adrian reached the garden gate moments later, the unlocked latch confirmed it. A sob of pure anguish squeezed at his chest. His sweet sister was dead, her lifeless body discarded somewhere while he'd rutted with a meaningless woman. He ought to be flayed alive for letting that happen. God help him, he should have died in her stead.

"I want to see her," he told Kendrick stiffly, his thoughts in turmoil. He couldn't even recall coming back inside from the garden. Wracked by indescribable pain and anger, he stared at the man who'd brought him the tragic news.

Kendrick inclined his head. "I'm headed to the coroner's office myself. You're welcome to join me."

Adrian almost agreed, only to realize the last thing he wanted right now was to share a carriage with Kendrick. "I'll meet you there."

"As you wish." Kendrick tipped his hat and departed, leaving Adrian with the awful sensation of having the walls closing in around him. He felt as though he'd been trapped in a tiny box from which there would never be any escape.

"Sir," Murry said, his voice sounding as though it came from beyond a vast distance. "Would you care for a brandy?"

Dismayed by the question, Adrian turned to his valet. "What good will that do?"

"I…" Murry shook his head, his expression pained. "I'm so very sorry."

Adrian stared straight through him. "Just call for the carriage."

Murry did as requested then accompanied him on the twenty-minute ride to St. George's Hospital at Hyde Park corner. Rain would have been an appropriate setting for their somber journey. Instead, the sun shone from a clear blue sky with an almost disgusting degree of vibrancy.

Pre-occupied by grief and guilt, Adrian held his tongue. There was so much to say – so many thoughts demanding attention – and yet he could not find the words. So he listened to the dull tread of the horse's hooves and the occasional moan of the axel when they turned a corner.

Yet all he truly heard was Evie's voice, so young and bright and full of joy.

It was unfathomable to him that he'd never hear that sound again. His heart shrank as pain tightened its hold, made worse by the realization of what was to come. In time, the memory of his sister would fade until all he'd be left with was some sort of vague recollection, more akin to her portrait than to the flesh and blood woman she'd actually been.

This was how it had been with his mother, the miniature of her likeness reminding him daily of what she had looked like.

"Do you wish for me to join you or would you prefer to go in alone?" Murry asked when they reached their destination.

Adrian blinked. He'd almost forgotten his valet was

there. Turning to him, he gave his instruction. "Stay with the carriage."

The last thing he wanted to deal with right now was the awkwardness of his valet seeing him fall apart. So he took a deep breath, alit with a heavy tread, and went to join Kendrick, who waited for him by the entrance.

"You should prepare yourself," Kendrick warned once they'd met with Doctor Fellowes. The coroner led them through a long hallway to the echoing sound of their shoes clicking hard against the stone floor. "She was stabbed in the throat."

Adrian clenched his fists. It was hard to believe he'd not wondered about the cause of death until now. Evie had simply been dead. But the truth of it was, she'd been killed. Someone had done this to her, and now he knew how.

The hollowness behind his ribs expanded as he followed Doctor Fellowes into a cool stone chamber where three tables stood side by side. Two of them were occupied by corpses, their bodies outlined beneath the white sheets that covered them from head to toe.

Doctor Fellowes approached the nearest table and reached for the edge of the sheet, then paused. He glanced at Adrian. "Ready?"

Was anyone ever ready to see the remains of someone they loved? Adrian doubted it, but nodded all the same. He had to ensure that the victim was Evie. Moreover, he hoped that seeing her would offer some sort of clue as to who might have done this.

The sheet was pulled back, revealing a mass of dark brown locks that matched his own. Her forehead came into view next, then her beautifully arched eyebrows, a pair of eyelids – closed as if in slumber – with black lashes resting against her pale cheeks.

Adrian had no need to see her nose or mouth for every possible hope a mistake had been made to be destroyed. There was no longer any doubt.

He took a deep breath and almost choked when he inhaled the acrid air. The smell of death was all too familiar. He'd encountered it hundreds of times before, thanks to the family business. What he'd never planned on was of one day associating it with his sister.

Swallowing against the rising discomfort that threatened to make him retch, he gritted his teeth and asked Doctor Fellowes to pull the sheet lower. The doctor sent Kendrick a questioning glance before doing as Adrian asked.

A ghastly wound, stained by dried blood, came into view. The throat had not just been stabbed, it had been cleaved open, leaving behind a gaping display of raw flesh and bone fragments.

Drawing upon every strength he possessed, Adrian detached himself from all his emotions. It was vital he be objective if he was to gain understanding and see justice served on Evie's behalf.

He considered the faint signs of bruising near the side of her neck and the lacerations of the wound itself. "Inflicting this sort of damage would have required proximity."

This was not the sort of wound one received if one were fleeing one's attacker. Whoever had done this had likely held her in place. Pinned down, perhaps?

"I agree," Kendrick said. "It would appear that your sister knew her attacker and had no reason to fear him. Any idea why she might have gone to the churchyard in the first place?"

"No." He'd told her to be careful and not to go anywhere unescorted, so why had she done it? Adrian could think of no reasonable explanation. Unless she'd embarked on a secret liaison with someone she feared he wouldn't approve of.

"Miss Fairchild, Lady Camille, and Miss Irvine were killed the same way, as though they'd walked straight into the arms of their killer."

Adrian turned to Kendrick. "You think my sister was killed by the same individual?"

"I'm certain of it," Kendrick muttered, his sharp gaze holding Adrian's. "Not only because of the method applied, but because of the note that was pinned to Miss Croft's bodice."

Fresh anger spread through Adrian's body. He glanced at the piece of paper Doctor Fellowes produced, doing his best not to snatch it from him and tear it to pieces.

"The bastard murdered her by mistake." Because of a lie some foolish columnist had printed in the paper.

"The wound appears to have been inflicted by a short blade, sharp at the tip and blunter along the edges," Doctor Fellowes reported. "The victim shows no sign of struggle – no damage to her nails, no fibers, hair, or dirt underneath them. It was as though she were caught unawares and didn't see the blade coming."

"You've suggested the previous victims were killed from behind," Kendrick said. "Are you saying that's not the case here?"

"Exactly." Doctor Fellowes used a scalpel to indicate the direction in which Evie's throat had been stabbed. "The angle of this wound shows that this particular murder was carried out while she faced her attacker."

And yet, she hadn't struggled, which could only mean that she had been killed by someone she trusted. Someone who'd taken advantage of that and used it against her.

Adrian stared at the harshness with which the flesh had been torn. "Were the other wounds similar in nature?"

"If you're asking if they looked just as brutal," Kendrick said, "then the answer is yes."

In other words, they were looking for someone who'd hated these women, or at the very least what they each represented to his sick mind. Adrian wasn't yet sure how he'd find him. All he knew was that he would commit himself to doing so from this moment forward.

This awareness brought an odd sense of calm to his otherwise crippled existence. He thanked Kendrick and Doctor Fellowes, then placed a final kiss to Evie's brow before walking away, his stride clipped and precise as he returned to the carriage.

He gave instructions to the driver before climbing in and resuming his seat on the bench opposite Murry. The carriage lurched into motion, setting a homeward course for Number 5 Portman Square.

Speaking with steely resolve, he said, "I'm calling a meeting as soon as we reach the house."

"You're assuming the role your father intended for you after all?"

"The resources offered to me if I head down that path will be beneficial." Adrian met Murry's gaze without blinking. "May God have mercy on whoever did this, for I can assure you, I shall not."

CHAPTER TWELVE

The hackney Samantha had hired blended easily with the other carriages parked on Portman Square. Eager for the extra coin she'd promised, the driver had maneuvered the vehicle into a spot with an excellent view of Mr. Croft's home.

Despite suggesting to Kendrick that she delay all attempts at infiltrating his life out of respect for his most recent loss, the chief constable had denied her request. She re-read the note she'd received from him, delivered by Isak just moments before.

"Is it bad news then?" Isak asked, most likely noting her frown.

After meeting with him that morning as planned, she'd given him his first task. He'd completed it with success, though she didn't agree with the answer he'd brought her.

"A difference of opinion," she answered.

According to Kendrick, Mr. Croft was racked by grief and anger, both of which would surely cloud his judgement. He'd be more vulnerable now, Kendrick reasoned, and perhaps more willing to place his trust in a woman who offered him sympathy.

A movement beyond the window drew her attention. It seemed the Croft carriage had just been brought round. The front door opened in the next instance and Mr. Croft appeared, as tall, handsome, and foreboding as when she'd last seen him.

"Stay here," Samantha told Isak, handing him a warm mutton pie to reward him for a job well done. She watched as he sank his teeth into the flaky crust. "Keep an eye on that building and inform me of any additional activity."

"Aye miss." He departed and Samantha returned her attention to Mr. Croft's carriage, which was presently rolling into motion. She leaned her head out the window and spoke to her driver, "Please follow that vehicle with discretion."

They pulled into traffic and made their way along South Audley Street, turning left and continuing for a good distance before turning right and slowing to a gradual halt. It seemed they'd reached a church, though not one Samantha was familiar with.

Through the window, Samantha watched Mr. Croft alight, her view of him slightly obscured by a steady stream of pedestrians. It only got worse when he entered the churchyard's front entrance and vanished behind a wall.

Frustrated, she climbed from the hackney and went to address the driver. "Circle the church and pick me up from the street behind it."

Grateful for the fashionable wide-brimmed bonnet she wore, she kept her chin down as she walked to the churchyard's entrance.

Mr. Croft wasn't far, his attention it seemed, fixed on a spot immediately to the left of the church's door. Remaining slightly behind him and to one side, Samantha sank to her knees in front of a gravestone and watched him through her peripheral vision.

To anyone who might glance her way, she would appear as nothing more than a bereaved young woman who'd come to visit a dearly departed friend or relation.

Birds tweeted from somewhere nearby. A cloud slid in front of the sun, casting her in a cool shadow. The smell of moss and brambles and weathered old stone drifted around her.

Careful to keep her face shielded from view, she angled her head just enough to be able to peer through the uneven space formed between a series of gravestones. Her line of sight wasn't especially good, and with Mr. Croft's back turned toward her, she couldn't gauge his expression. But the stiffness gripping his body as he dropped into a crouch revealed the anguish and rage that consumed him.

His love for his sister had been evident to Samantha the moment they'd met, and now she was gone. Cruelly taken from him much too soon. Of course he would suffer. The question was who else might do so because of his wrath?

He leaned forward slowly, as one might do when placing an item upon the ground. A hesitation followed and for a brief moment it almost looked like he'd gotten stuck in his forward crouch.

Samantha kept her attention upon him as his shoulders bunched, stretching his jacket taut. A series of movements followed and then he seemed to reach for something. Leaning back, he bowed his head, appearing to study the object he'd found before pushing himself into an upright position. With one final glance directed at the church wall, he headed toward the front entrance, passing Samantha on his way and disappearing from view.

She remained where she was for a long moment after, just to be sure she wouldn't get caught in case Mr. Croft chose to linger. When she eventually stood, he was thankfully gone. Even his carriage, which would have been visible from her position, had disappeared.

Stepping between a series of gravestones, Samantha approached the path that led to the church's front door and made her way to the spot where Mr. Croft had been crouching. There, nestled against the ivy that lined the church wall, was a single red rose, so vibrant and pure in color, it stood out with startling clarity against the dark background.

She took a deep breath and expelled it, forcing herself to maintain her composure, though it took every ounce of her training to do so. The sadness of that lonely bloom compounded the loss of the youthful woman Evelyn Croft had been.

Moving closer, Samantha reached for the church wall and traced her fingertips over the uneven stones. Was this where she'd died? Was that why her brother had come here? To pay his respects and possibly find some answers?

She stared at the ground, recalling all too well how it had looked like he might have picked something up. Evidence perhaps?

If that were the case, she prayed it would help him track down whoever had done this. For whatever her own relationship to Mr. Croft might be, he deserved to get his revenge before she destroyed him.

∽

"Don't let him fool you," Harlowe murmured, so low the words became part of the gentle breeze brushing Samantha's cheek.

Back straight and shoulders squared, she kept her gaze on the ground, and on the deep hole into which Miss Evelyn Croft's velvet-clad coffin had just been lowered. The somber drone of the vicar's voice complimented the dreary drizzle wetting the air and beading on everyone's clothes.

Even so, thirty people or more had come to attend the funeral. Samantha knew only the ones who had been at the Marsdale ball. Lady Heathbrooke was among them. Hunched in a way that showcased the frailty brought on by age, she stood some distance apart from Samantha, her arm linked with Melody's while she supported the rest of her weight on a cane.

"He may have loved his sister dearly," Harlowe added, "but that doesn't make him any less ruthless. It's vital you remember that."

Samantha slid her gaze to Mr. Croft's mournful figure. The information Isak had given her two nights before indicated that he might be up to something. Ten men had visited Croft House the evening after she'd followed him to the church. According to Isak, he'd recognized one as someone he'd once seen Wycliffe meet with.

She continued to study the man whose secrets she had to discover. He stood some ten yards away, flanked by two other men. Servants, she wagered. Pain was etched upon his brow, but rage was visible too in the tightness of his jaw and the hardness of his gaze.

She didn't doubt Harlowe for a second. Mr. Croft had the look of a man who intended to rip the world apart in his search for his sister's killer. And once he found him, he'd likely take his sweet time skinning him alive.

It was, she reflected, what she would do if any harm came to the people she loved.

This thought had barely formed when Mr. Croft snared her with a hard look. Not altering his expression, he dipped his head as though in greeting. She gave a quick nod and blew out a steady breath to keep her pulse even.

She turned to Harlowe as soon as the vicar was done with his sermon. "Shall we offer our condolences?"

"Anything less would be rude." When Harlowe gestured for her to precede him, she traversed the wet ground and approached the man who could potentially have more influence than the Prince Regent himself. Should he embrace his father's legacy.

Seeing that Harlowe, who'd been right behind her, had stopped to greet an acquaintance, Samantha continued toward Mr. Croft on her own. A few other people ahead of her reached him first, so she waited until they'd voiced their regrets and moved on before stepping nearer.

"Mr. Croft," she said, doing her best not to let his powerful presence affect her. It was one thing to watch him from a distance, but close up, he appeared more unyielding than when they'd first been introduced.

His bearing was dangerous, almost threatening, when he pinned her with the intensity of his dark eyes.

"Miss Carmichael, if memory serves." His voice was low but even, as carefully controlled as his inscrutable expression.

"Indeed." It took some strength of will for her to keep holding his gaze – to not let him weaken her in any way. "I enjoyed a wonderful conversation with your sister the other evening, and wanted to tell you how truly sorry I am for your loss. It pains me to know that she's no longer with us."

Just like that night at the Marsdale ball, the penetrating look in his eyes seemed to search for the truth in her words. Samantha willed herself to keep breathing, to not allow doubt or uncertainty to show in something as simple as holding her breath.

"Your consideration is much appreciated," he eventually told her. "Evelyn was happy to make your acquaintance and looked forward to having you visit for tea."

Samantha considered asking if he had any leads that might help find the killer, but decided against it. Now was not the time to address such a distasteful subject.

With that in mind, she simply told him, "Thank you, Mr. Croft. I shall carry that sentiment with me forever."

She started to turn away.

"Miss Carmichael," he said, almost with a hint of warning. "Whoever did this has yet to be caught. I urge you to be careful."

He gave his attention to someone else before she was able to thank him, his manner suggesting he'd already dismissed her from his mind.

CHAPTER THIRTEEN

Although Adrian spoke to several other friends and acquaintances who came to impart their regrets, his attention remained on Miss Carmichael's retreating figure.

Why had she come?

Although she had been invited to join Evie for tea, the two hadn't met more than once, and even then only briefly. It seemed odd that a young lady such as Miss Carmichael would choose to spend a miserable Sunday morning attending the funeral of someone she barely knew.

He could think of only two reasons. She was either goodness personified or in possession of an ulterior motive.

"Anything on her yet?" he asked Murry as soon as the last well-wishers had taken their leave.

"Not much," Murry told him. "According to the

records I've found, Mr. Harlowe raised her and four other girls as though they were his own. One of the others is right over there – Lady Heathbrooke's companion, Miss Melody Roberts. I see nothing suspicious yet, though one might imagine he's trying to find a place for Miss Carmichael next. Either as governess or companion. She is of an age."

"How old is she," Adrian asked. He sent Murry a sideways glance. "Do you know?"

"Four and twenty."

Well beyond debutante age then. What most would think of as firmly on the shelf. "I'm surprised he's waited this long."

Another aspect that made little sense.

"They're a very private family, that much is clear," Murry said. "Finding out precisely why she's starting to make a regular appearance will likely take time."

"Thank you, Murry." Adrian straightened his spine when he saw Mr. Harlowe approach. "Please keep digging."

The order was possibly moot, for the first thing Mr. Harlowe said when Adrian mentioned the lovely words Miss Carmichael had imparted was that he thanked his good fortune for her and her sisters' daily assistance.

"My sight is not what it once was," Mr. Harlowe explained. "And I find myself becoming increasingly forgetful. Were it not for Miss Carmichael's help, I'd be utterly lost."

Adrian studied the older man. He appeared as friendly and pleasant as when they'd last met, but

Adrian knew all too well that this could be a façade. As such, he rarely trusted anyone who smiled too easily. Trouble was Harlowe had the sort of genuine demeanor that invited people to like him. It was difficult not to, Adrian realized.

Still, he did what he could to keep up his guard. "My father spoke highly of you, Mr. Harlowe. I appreciate your coming."

"It would have weighed heavily on my heart if I hadn't," Mr. Harlowe informed him.

The sentiment was welcome – so much so it made Adrian's eyes sting a little. His throat tightened, and for a moment, he found himself struggling to keep his composure under control. By the time he'd collected himself to some degree of satisfaction, the man was gone, along with most of the other mourners.

Adrian gulped down a breath and crossed to where Edward stood, alone in grim contemplation. "Will you return to the house with me for a drink?"

Edward dragged his gaze away from Evie's grave. Unlike Adrian, he failed to hide his emotions. The heartbreak he felt over Evie's death was etched in every aspect of his appearance, from the slightly untidy clothes that looked as though they'd been slept in to the watery brightness of his moss-green eyes.

He swallowed hard before nodding. Moments later, he fell into step at Adrian's side as they left the churchyard behind.

"I realize this is a difficult subject," Adrian said once they were alone in his study. All his life, this room had belonged to his father. It was the place from which he'd conducted his business and as such, Adrian hadn't set foot in it since he'd died.

Until three days prior when he had accepted his lot and, in so doing, realized he needed a place from which to run his own operations. The first meeting with him as head of the Croft business had since taken place in this room. Now that he'd settled upon his purpose, the space from which deadly orders had always been given suited his mood immensely.

"What subject would that be?" Edward asked. He accepted the glass Adrian gave him and took a seat in one of the vacant armchairs that faced the wide oak desk.

Instead of claiming the chair on the opposite side of the desk, Adrian chose the one next to Edward's, then angled himself toward him. "Your fondness for Evie. I now regret not bringing it up before. Perhaps if I'd done so, you would have realized you had my blessing. Maybe then, you'd have asked her to be your wife and she would not have met such a brutal end."

"I loved her beyond compare," Edward said while frowning into the glass he held between both hands.

"And she loved you." When Edward raised his gaze to Adrian with utter defeat in his eyes, Adrian assured him, "It showed every time she looked your way, when the pair of you danced, and even at the sound of your name."

Edward shook his head then took a long sip of his drink. "I don't understand how this happened. The lie in the paper is one thing, but what would have made her leave the safety of her home unescorted? I never would have believed she could be so reckless."

It was a point Adrian had gone over endless times since. He firmly believed Evie's death was his fault, that it could have been prevented if he'd just paid more attention instead of being preoccupied by the need for bedsport.

Disgusted with himself, he'd ended things with Veronica Miles as soon as he'd left the morgue.

"You know as well as I she was trusting. It was the best of her since it made her kind, but it was also the worst of her because of the naïveté it led to." Adrian drank a measure of brandy then set his glass aside on the edge of his desk.

"Clearly, her killer – undoubtedly the same man who saw to Miss Fairchild, Lady Camille, and Miss Irvine's demises – made a mistake in this instance. He thought her a wanton because of the gossip the newspaper chose to spread. But I can say with certainty that they were wrong. Not because my love for my sister has blinded me to the possibility of her having such inclinations but because the results of the examination the coroner gave her proves it."

Edward stared at him. "What are you saying?"

Adrian was fairly sure his next words might result in Edward punching him in the face. Or worse. "I had to be certain, so I asked for a thorough report. Evie's maidenhead was intact."

There was the briefest of pauses before Edward shot

to his feet, hurled his glass at the fireplace, and grabbed Adrian by his lapels. Gripping the garment so firmly it tightened across Adrian's back, Edward lowered his head until their faces met at eye level.

"What the hell is wrong with you," he growled. "You had no right to have her defiled in such a way."

"Of course I did," Adrian countered. "She was my unmarried sister and as such, she was under my protection. Not yours or anyone else's."

Edward held his gaze for a long, insufferable moment before shoving him backward, releasing him in the process. With a loud and very uncivilized curse, he stalked to the sideboard and poured a fresh drink for himself.

"If I am to solve this case and find the man who killed her," Adrian said while straightening his jacket, "I need all my questions answered."

He'd known in his heart that Evie would never play the harlot, but now he had proof. The paper, however, claimed otherwise, and since this was what had gotten her killed, the article they'd written about her suddenly looked like much more than the possible mistake they'd agreed to investigate.

As far as Adrian was concerned, this had been a deliberate attack on her life. Though he still had trouble grasping the notion.

"I don't suppose she ever mentioned a falling out to you," he asked Edward.

"Your sister had few friends due to your father's overbearing manner."

Adrian couldn't dispute it. Evie's life had been horribly sheltered. Even he had likely frightened away more than one potential suitor. Not that Evie would have had eyes for anyone other than Edward, but perhaps the attention would have been nice.

He cast that thought aside. If she hadn't had enemies, then why had that terrible lie been concocted? To hurt *him* perhaps? Whatever the case, he'd stop at nothing until the responsible party paid for this crime. To Edward, he said, "If anything else comes to mind, please let me know."

"So you can pass it on to Bow Street?"

No. He didn't dare rely upon them, and while Edward's question suggested he had some inkling of this, Adrian still nodded. Revealing how far he was willing to go when it came to his sister would be unwise.

At best, it would upset Edward's stomach. At worst, it would cause psychological damage and alter the one remaining relationship Adrian valued.

"I've gone over every conversation I had with her." Edward kept his attention on Adrian. "Nothing pertinent comes to mind, but I'll keep trying."

"Thank you."

In his pocket was the button he'd found at St. Bartholomew's church when he'd gone to leave a rose in her memory. Concealed beneath leaves of ivy, it would have been hard for Kendrick and his Runners to spot in the early hours of the morning. He'd only glimpsed the item because the sun had been in the right position to bounce off the gilded edge. While it wasn't much for him to go on, it was a start.

"I trust you'll let me know if you learn anything?" Edward said. "I'd like to be kept up to date, if possible."

"Of course," Adrian promised, choosing to keep the button a secret.

He got up early the following morning and readied himself for the day with a new sense of purpose.

"Come breakfast with me," he told Murry. He invited the rest of the staff to join him as well – anything to fill the dining room with chatter and to keep him from focusing on the one vacant chair that made his heart hurt.

Somehow, he got through three slices of toast, some bacon and eggs, plus two cups of coffee, all while learning that Sarah – one of the upstairs maids – had a near-blind father.

"Take him to the clinic on Bedford." Adrian told her. "Maybe they're able to help. I'll pay the bill."

Sarah gaped at him then blinked in rapid succession. "I couldn't possibly, Mr. Croft. It's too great an imposition."

"And yet I insist." Adrian turned to Murry. "I'll trust you to offer assistance while I deal with other matters?"

"Of course," Murry promised.

Sarah proceeded to thank Adrian profusely while he finished off the last of his coffee. Ensuring the happiness of his employees was vital to securing their loyalty. So he paid them all exceedingly well, just as his father had done before him, and offered occasional perks, like sending Cook to Ipswich for her niece's wedding and making sure Sarah's father received the best medical treatment available.

He downed the last of his coffee, then collected his hat and gloves and set off by carriage.

Today he'd begin his hunt.

Puddles from last night's heavier rainfall littered the ground, creating an overall sense of wetness despite the sun's effort to force its way through between scattered clouds. Comfortably seated against the plush squabs, Adrian flipped the button he'd found between his fingers.

The markings on the back of it told him where to begin his search. Just to be sure, he'd checked the buttons on one of his own jackets for a similar imprint, and had found that they were exactly the same.

T.G.E.

The Gentlemen's Emporium.

He arrived there soon enough and entered the exclusive shop.

"Mr. Jenkins," he said, addressing the elderly gentleman who worked there. "I find myself in need of a new set of clothes and am hoping you might assist me."

"Of course, Mr. Croft. Your business is always welcome."

They proceeded to look at a series of cuts from various fabrics. Adrian made sure to pick a few especially pricy items, like a waistcoat fashioned from ice blue silk, embroidered in silver thread and adorned with mother of pearl buttons. It cost twice as much as the velvet jacket he also selected.

"On a different note," he told Mr. Jenkins as soon as the purchase had been concluded, "I'd like you to look at this button for me. Couldn't help but notice that it's a different design from the ones you're currently using."

He handed the round gold fastening over and watched while Mr. Jenkins proceeded to study it.

"This was used two years ago. An issue arose with the manufacturer. We found that the quality no longer met with our standards, so we started ordering from a different supplier."

"If it's not too much trouble, I'd like to see your purchase records from that particular year."

Mr. Jenkins's eyebrows rose. He set the button on the counter and gave Adrian a wary look. "That would be a breach of trust between us and our clients. I'm afraid I'll have to deny your request."

Adrian understood him, but that didn't make him less determined. He leaned forward and did his best to try and look pleasant. "I wonder if you follow the news, Mr. Jenkins."

"Yes…I…forgive me. I must confess I was shocked to hear of your sister."

Adrian gritted his teeth. So the old man knew, yet he'd not said a word when Adrian entered the shop. He took a deep breath, tried not to think of the velvet-clad coffin under the ground.

Allowing anger and pain to guide him would only make it harder to think.

"I found that button when I visited the site where she was killed. As you can imagine, I'd like to know whom it belongs to."

"While I sympathize with you, I cannot help you in this. The shop's exclusivity is due in part to the full discretion we offer our clients. This will easily suffer if it becomes known that we're sharing purchase records with anyone who stops by to ask."

Adrian stared at Mr. Jenkins, watching steadily as he adjusted his spectacles. He'd hoped to avoid resorting to his father's methods during this visit, but if he was going to meet with results, he'd clearly have to apply more pressure.

"As I understand it, your son has a well-paid position within the army. He's managed to create a comfortable life for himself and his family. It would be a pity if he were to find himself stripped of his rank because of some crime he'd committed."

A mixture of disgust and fear filled Mr. Jenkins' expression. "You would ensure such a thing if I fail to betray the rest of my clients?"

"There is little I would not resort to in order to find the man who murdered my sister."

"You'll pay for it with your soul," Mr. Jenkins murmured, shaking his head and retrieving a ledger. "If you don't mind, I'd rather you look at it in that storeroom, just to be sure nobody sees."

Adrian thanked him, took the ledger, and stepped into a small space lined with shelves filled with various boxes. He removed a few to create a space for the ledger to sit, then proceeded to browse through the various names.

Given the fact that the killer had managed to lure Evie to him, Adrian had to assume it was someone she knew and trusted. He was therefore especially interested in the men she'd danced with on more than one occasion since her debut last spring.

Unfortunately, The Gentlemen's Emporium was a popular shop. Every single gentleman Adrian thought of was listed. All had made purchases two years prior, which made it impossible for him to rule anyone out. He was no better off than before. If anything, he left the shop feeling worse for having forced Mr. Jenkins's hand.

Unhappy with himself and the lack of progress he'd made, he ordered the carriage to take him home so he could collect a change of clothes and pick up Murry. Together they'd head to Reed's for a much-needed round of physical exertion. All he wanted right now was to punch someone. And to take a rough beating in return.

CHAPTER FOURTEEN

Three short raps at the door followed by a series of faster knocks alerted Samantha to Isak's arrival. She crossed the rough wooden floor of the room she'd rented and threw the bolt so he could enter.

"Your quarry's been spotted on Bond Street. He stopped by The Gentlemen's Emporium." Isak greedily accepted the glass of lemonade Samantha offered.

She crossed her arms and waited while he drank.

"He was there for about an hour," Isak continued, "before he went home, collected a bag, and set off for Reed's with some other man. After that, he returned home again and didn't go out for the next three hours."

"Where is he now?" Samantha asked.

"At White's." Isak drank some more lemonade, then set the glass down. "I managed to sneak inside his carriage while he was there. Without gettin' noticed, mind. Spotted a book, I did."

Samantha waited for Isak to give her the title. When he didn't, she had to ask, "What book?"

"That'll cost you an ext—"

She had him by the throat in an instant. "Listen to me, you little good for nothing thief. I'm paying you daily, besides which I've been kind, and now you're trying to cheat me?"

Isak's eyes bulged as she raised her hand slightly, pulling him onto his tiptoes. He gasped and wheezed while grabbing her wrists to try and dislodge her grip. When she released him a few moments later, he sputtered and coughed and clutched at his throat.

"Well?" she asked.

Glaring at her, he retrieved a crumpled piece of paper from his pocket. She took it and read the clumsy letters he'd copied, the wobbly lines suggesting he'd gripped the pencil with his fist while drawing each shape.

Even so, the word he'd written was clear. *Herakles*.

Interesting choice.

When Isak reached for the lemonade glass, she snatched it away. "Don't ever make the mistake of thinking you can take advantage of me. I'll break one of your fingers next time. Is that clear?"

He gave a defiant nod.

"On the other hand," she told him, "if you keep doing your job as well as you have thus far, I will reward you for it. So what will it be?"

"I'll keep providing the information you want," Isak wheezed.

"In that case, feel free to relax for a moment or two while you finish your drink." She returned the glass to him and considered her options.

For starters, she'd pay a visit to Hatchard's.

The bookshop, located on Piccadilly, provided her with the book she desired when she arrived there later. They were even able to bind it while she took refreshment at the small teashop next door.

When she arrived back at Clearview House around five, she went straight to Harlowe's study to tell him all she had learned.

He leaned back in his chair, elbows on the armrests, his fingers steepled in such a way that his chin rested on their tips. "Boxing is an excellent way for men to expel excess energy or work through feelings of aggression. If he visited Reed's today, there's a chance he'll return there either tomorrow or the day after."

Attuned to his line of thinking, she tilted her head. "My showing up there, in a place intended exclusively for men, will surely raise his suspicion."

"Your paths need to keep crossing somehow, yes?" When Samantha nodded, Harlowe said, "White's is out of the question. So are the streets near his house. The park could be an option if he goes for regular rides."

"My informant has made no mention of him having done so of late."

"Then Reed's might be your best bet at present. At any rate, you can give it a shot, and if he fails to show up, you can try something else."

"There's still the issue of explaining my presence

there," Samantha reminded him. "It's a boxing club, not a sewing circle."

Harlowe chuckled. When he sobered once more he said, "There have now been four murders with the same signature, indicating they've all been committed by the same man. Who, if I may remind you, has yet to be apprehended. With that taken into account, I'm sure you'll think of something."

"Of course." Samantha gave him a wry smile. "I'll take Hazel with me."

The two women set off the following day after breakfast. Hazel was two years younger than Samantha and every bit as fierce as Harlowe's other foster daughters. With fire-red hair and moss-green eyes, her appearance owed nothing to her name.

"Remember, we have no combat skills," Samantha said as the carriage pulled up in front of their destination. "We're not as strong as we actually are, or as quick on our feet."

"We're untrained women whose exercise has been limited to quiet strolls in the park and the occasional morning ride," Hazel said with a grin.

"Precisely."

They alit and entered the white brick building marked by a sign that read: Reed's Boxing Club. Samantha led the way, cutting a path directly across the foyer and through a pair of steel framed glass doors that led to a large rectangular room.

She paused there for a moment to simply observe. Three fights were presently underway, though one appeared to be more of a training session. A few men looked on, perhaps in anticipation of it being their turn, while others practiced landing their blows against leather bags strung from various beams.

Samantha had practiced her punches on similar equipment. No doubt she'd feel comfortably at home in this place, besides actually having to pretend not to.

She took a step forward, only to halt once more when a man began shouting while storming toward her. Instinct compelled her to take a defensive position. She fought it, barely managing to make sure Hazel followed her lead, before he'd reached them.

Large, sweaty, and looking mighty annoyed, he stared them down with no small hint of disdain. "This place is off limits to women."

"Is it?" Samantha asked, feigning innocence. She glanced over her shoulder. "I saw no sign on the door to suggest as much."

"It being a boxing club should be indication enough," he told her gruffly, crossing his arms and leaning forward in challenge.

The air seemed to still and Samantha became aware of the silence now filling the room. Were she to glance beyond the oaf blocking her path, she knew she'd find the rest of the club's members staring.

She raised her chin and tightened her hold on the quilted bag she'd brought with her. It contained her reticule, a shawl, and the book she'd purchased yesterday afternoon. "I've come to speak with the owner."

"Be that as it—"

"Mr. Reed?" she hollered. "A word, if you will?"

"What on earth is…" The words faded as a stocky man strode from a room to one side. He frowned at the oaf and then he frowned at her. "I won't stand for any commotion. This club is for gentlemen only."

"In that case," Samantha muttered, "I'd recommend showing this fellow the door."

The oaf's face reddened. "How dare you?"

Samantha crossed her arms, rolled her eyes for the pure pleasure of vexing him further, and gave her attention to the man she believed to be the club's owner. "Are you Mr. Reed?"

"That I am," he said while assessing her appearance. "And you are?"

She smiled. The man was wise enough to avoid the risk of crossing a peer's daughter. Not that she could claim such status.

"Miss Carmichael," she told him. "My sister and I would like to acquire a membership please."

A second of stunned silence followed and then the oaf let out a howl of laughter that tested her every restraint. She wanted to wallop him just to show him this was no laughing matter.

"Um…" Mr. Reed looked more perplexed than amused. "I'm afraid rules are rules. Women aren't permitted to enter this place. Not even the current members' female relations are granted entry."

"That's quite a shame," Samantha said before taking a quick right step and hurrying straight past the oaf.

She nodded toward the rest of the men, all of whom had halted their practice and either gaped or frowned at her as she headed toward the side room from which Mr. Reed had appeared.

Raised voices behind her indicated some sort of arguing. She ignored it, checking only to see if Hazel had managed to follow her into the room before planting herself on a plain wooden chair that stood beside three others next to a wall. She placed her bag in her lap. Hazel sat down as well once she reached her, and together they waited for Mr. Reed to join them.

It took a moment before he did so, his expression no longer as pleasant as it had been initially. It now showed hints of extreme frustration.

"Miss Carmichael," he began, choosing to stand rather than sit. "I do not appreciate having my hand forced in any way."

"I understand," she told him gently. "Please accept my sincerest apologies. I'm sure it wouldn't have come to this had I not been confronted by that rude individual out there."

"That man is the Duke of Wrengate," Mr. Reed hissed while sending the door a frantic look. "He and the rest of the members come here with every assurance that they may train in peace without female interference. As such, he has every right to be alarmed by your presence."

"I would have imagined they'd like to show off," Hazel muttered.

Samantha tamped down her humor and gave Mr.

Reed a frank look. Having a duke stand against her was problematic, but she was determined to try and work around it. "While I understand such reasoning, I hope you will at least take a moment to consider my proposition."

"Granting you membership is out of the question."

"Why?"

"Because you're a woman," he told her as though there were something wrong with her head.

"And what? Women have no need to defend themselves?" She pressed her lips together and tilted her chin while pinning him with a sharp stare. "Need I remind you that there is a murderer on the loose and that not every woman is fortunate enough to have a brother at their beck and call?"

"Perhaps it would be prudent for you to remain at home until the murderer is caught," Mr. Reed suggested.

"That's a preposterous notion," Samantha told him, "and well you know it. Instead, we are prepared to pay you handsomely for any lessons you may provide."

"I'd risk losing the other members." He shook his head. "Can't quite see the benefit in that. So while I appreciate your interest, I really must ask you to leave. As it is, you've caused quite a stir, not to mention discomfort."

He wasn't making this easy. Then again, she'd not expected him to. The only remaining chance was appealing to his conscience.

"I would urge you to reconsider," she said as she stood. "Imagine if I too get murdered. How will you feel then, knowing I came to you for assistance and that you refused to help? Won't you always wonder if I might have lived had you shown me how to land an effective punch?"

Uncertainty finally flickered in his grey eyes, but anger drew his mouth into a tight line. "That's a terrible burden to place on anyone, Miss Carmichael. For that alone, I want you gone."

Accepting that there was nothing more left to be said or done, Samantha thanked Mr. Reed for his time and departed with Hazel in tow, past Wrengate, who sent her a glare. She answered it with a broad smile, just to annoy him, and yanked the door open.

No sooner had she stepped onto the pavement than she spotted a tall figure striding toward them.

Mr. Croft was returning here and as luck would have it, she was no longer inside. But maybe that didn't matter. Maybe crossing paths here would be more effective. Maybe...

"Miss Carmichael?" His voice was firm, though not without an underlying hint of surprise.

Samantha cleared her throat. "Mr. Croft. A pleasure to see you again. Please allow me to present my sister, Miss Hazel Stevens."

"The pleasure is entirely mine," he murmured, in response to which Hazel's cheeks turned a bright shade of red.

Samantha sent her gaze skyward and sighed. When

she looked at Mr. Croft next, she found him studying her with a puzzled expression.

"I wouldn't have thought to find you here." He jutted his chin toward the building from which she'd just been expelled.

"An unusual venue for any woman, I'll agree," Samantha told him. "I'm ashamed to admit my reason for coming. It seems so ridiculous now, but since you asked, the truth is we're frightened."

His expression hardened. "Frightened? Of what?"

Samantha knit her brow and widened her eyes to affect concern. "Four women have been killed, Mr. Croft, yet the culprit remains on the loose. We just thought… If we could defend ourselves somehow, perhaps we'd be safer."

"While I agree with that theory in principle, I should warn you that my sister knew how to throw an effective punch, yet she still perished." His eyebrows dipped and it was as if a dark shadow fell over his brow. "However, there's no denying the merit of such training."

"My thought exactly," Samantha said. "I tried to explain as much to Mr. Reed, but he insisted on seeing us out on account of our sex."

"Hmm." Mr. Croft glanced at the door. "Allow me to speak with him, will you? If you'll wait here a moment, I'll see if I'm able to change his mind."

"I hate to impose," Samantha told him.

He took a deep breath and straightened his shoulders. "No imposition at all."

"You should have warned me," Hazel said as soon as the door closed behind him.

"About what?" Samantha asked, turning to her while adjusting her hold on her bag.

"About his looks," Hazel hissed. "That man is handsome as sin, Samantha. I'm glad he's not my assignment."

Hazel wasn't wrong, though it was a point upon which Samantha refused to linger. She could not allow Mr. Croft's appearance to muddle her mind. And she wouldn't. Looks were just looks. They had no bearing on who the man was at his core - a high-class criminal whose prosecution hinged upon her.

"You're focusing on the wrong thing," Samantha said. "According to what I've been told, he's a merciless villain. That is what I see when I look at him. Nothing more."

The sorrow shrouding him as he'd delivered that rose to the spot where his sister was murdered and the anguish marring his features during her funeral didn't change that.

Mr. Croft had inherited his father's position as head of the Croft family, an organization reputed to deal in blackmail, to sell information in exchange for favors, and which was also rumored to have arranged the escape of several high value prisoners from Newgate. The rumors surrounding him were extensive.

The problem was there was no proof, and considering the power the family wielded within Society, proof would be required if the court was to gain a conviction. A challenge, to be sure.

The door opened and Mr. Croft appeared, his steely gaze landing upon Samantha at once. "Mr. Reed has extended a rare invitation to you and your sister. Please come with me."

"But what about the other members of the club?" Hazel asked in dismay. "They were very upset by our presence."

"All have agreed to tolerate it just this once," Mr. Croft informed her. He stepped aside and gestured toward the door.

Samantha wasn't sure what sort of deal he'd struck to make this happen, but she reckoned it to be the underhanded sort that ended with an 'or else'. By all that was holy, he'd just trumped a duke.

Unsure whether to be impressed or terrified, Samantha re-entered Reed's Boxing Club with caution. She almost expected one of the men there to launch an attack as some sort of test.

But no. All remained calm and quiet, the members this time continuing their exercise without paying Samantha or Hazel any mind. Including Wrengate. It was the strangest experience. And it got stranger still when Mr. Reed approached.

"I hope you can forgive my lack of hospitality earlier." His cheeks were ruddy, his eyes a touch wary. "I didn't realize you were Mr. Croft's friends."

Samantha managed a smile. "As I understand it, you were merely enforcing the rules."

Mr. Reed expelled a deep breath and nodded. "Yes, but as Mr. Croft has reminded me, there is room for some leeway now and again, under the right circumstances."

Really?

"You told me you came here in order to get a few pointers on how to defend yourselves," Mr. Croft said coolly. "If that remains the case, I'm happy to assist you."

Samantha thanked him while wondering what he was up to. Few people would be so helpful toward a person with whom they weren't well acquainted. There had to be an angle. She just hoped it didn't include him being on to her ruse.

CHAPTER FIFTEEN

With every instinct on high alert, Samantha followed Mr. Croft to a private training room together with Hazel. There, she set her bag on a bench and removed her bonnet, then smoothed a hand over her hair. Glancing sideways, she caught Mr. Croft studying her with interest. He'd removed his hat and was in the process of shucking his jacket.

"How did you make Mr. Reed change his mind?" She was genuinely curious to know, though she doubted he'd give her an honest answer.

He began rolling up his sleeves, revealing a pair of strong forearms banded with muscle. The edge of his mouth twitched as he eyed her. "I just reminded him and all the club members that this place wouldn't exist without my family's investment and that I expect my guests to be welcome."

"I see." Samantha glanced at Hazel who merely

shrugged one shoulder. It surprised her that he'd been so forthcoming though it still didn't explain why he'd chosen to help the two of them.

"Shall we proceed?" Mr. Croft asked. He swept one hand toward a spot on the floor and gave both women an expectant look.

Keeping her tread deliberately cautious, Samantha followed Mr. Croft to a part of the room that allowed for plenty of movement. Quilted mats had been strewn across the floor here, ensuring a cushioned landing for the beginners she and Hazel were meant to be.

Samantha frowned at them. She'd not used this sort of protection since she was a seven-year-old child receiving her initial lessons from Harlowe. Even then, it had only been necessary for the first week, after which the bruises she gained led to faster learning.

"Who wants to go first?" Mr. Croft inquired..

Intent on looking unsure of herself, Samantha hung back long enough for Hazel to take a step forward.

Samantha caught her arm, then met her gaze when she turned back to face her. "Be careful."

The warning was meant to remind her friend to show uncertainty as well as the lack of skill Mr. Croft would expect. He no doubt believed it to reference Samantha's concern for Hazel's safety since he said to her, "You needn't worry. I'll demonstrate the basics with slow and steady movements. No harm will come to Miss Stevens. You have my word."

Had Samantha truly been worried, she would have found immense relief, not so much in his promise, but with the heartfelt assurance with which it was spoken. It struck her in that moment that whatever his faults might be, Adrian Croft was a dependable man.

But that didn't make him less of a criminal. It only proved him capable of conducting himself as a gentleman ought. A true gentleman, however, would not build his fortune through illegal means. It was vital she remember that whenever he used his charm.

Arms crossed, she watched him instruct Hazel on how to position herself correctly.

"You'll want to keep your knees slightly bent to allow for swifter movement. Like this." He gave Hazel a demonstration, then raised his fists and encouraged her to mirror his stance.

Hazel made repeated attempts but consistently failed to bend her knees while keeping her arms in the right position. Samantha almost laughed. If only Mr. Croft knew how severely he was being deceived.

Then again, it was probably best if he never found out since there was no telling how he would respond. Which reminded her to be extra careful when she stepped forward a short while later to take Hazel's place.

"Like this?" she asked when he told her to keep her fist in line with her shoulder when throwing a punch.

"Almost. Now straighten your arm upon impact."

She did as he suggested, but kept her fist slack and leaned backward onto her heels as she struck the raised palm of his hand.

Mr. Croft offered advice on how to correct her

mistakes then encouraged her to have a few additional goes. He blew out a breath by the end of it and scratched the back of his head while eyeing her with a mixture of curiosity and resolve.

"Take the defensive stance I've shown you again," he told her. When she did as requested, he circled around her, vanishing from her view though she sensed his solid frame directly behind her. A brief second of undefined foreboding took root at the base of her spine. It snapped at her instincts, urging her to attack as soon as he touched her.

Slow and steady, she forced her heart to gentle its rhythm and for her breaths to find the calm she required. To remain utterly still, unthreatening, untrained.

Strong hands curled into her flesh on either side of her waist, the pressure of his fingertips sending an unbidden shiver straight down her middle. She tightened her core to negate the effect and allowed him to help her adjust her position.

"Stay like that if you can," he told her, his voice firm as he stepped to her side. His hands caught her wrists next and positioned them just so. "Now hold your footing and your squat while I show you how to move your upper body."

Positioned at her side, yet angled toward her, he extended her arm and brought it back, over and over, until she could no longer fight the instinct to throw her punch smoothly.

"Yes," he cheered, believing he'd finally gotten his point across. "Now punch me in the shoulder."

She lowered her arms and shook them out, pretending she'd found the practice exerting. "I really shouldn't, Mr. Croft. What if I hurt you?"

"I appreciate your concern for my safety, Miss Carmichael, but I think it will be a while before such a thing might occur." An indulgent smile followed. "Keep practicing though and I've no doubt you can achieve the sort of punch that will split a man's lip and send him running."

Hazel snorted with amusement. Allowing a chuckle, Samantha stepped forward and took the stance Mr. Croft had just showed her. Legs bent, back straight, and arms raised to protect her face from potential attack, she waited until Mr. Croft looked ready before attempting a punch that held most of her power at bay.

As expected, it barely made an impact. Mr. Croft didn't budge in the slightest, but that didn't mean the lesson was wasted. What she learned was that solid steel existed beneath his fine clothes. If she were ever to meet him in a fight, she'd have to use skill, perhaps even weapons, in order to win.

"Excellent work, Miss Carmichael." He gave her a nod to reward her efforts before inviting Hazel back onto the mat so she could try punching him too. A few more turns followed before Mr. Croft declared that this was enough for today. "I encourage you both to practice at home in front of a mirror. Doing so will make it easier for you to check your posture and the correct positioning of your arms."

"Thank you, Mr. Croft." Samantha crossed to the bench where she'd left the bag she'd brought with her. "I'm sure you're a busy man, so we appreciate your taking the time to help us with this. It's really not as easy as it looks."

"Learning the right technique is vital, but strength plays a very important role too. If you're not in too great a hurry, I can show you some exercises you'll want to repeat at home."

"That's very generous of you," Hazel said. "Thank you."

For the next ten minutes, Samantha and Hazel watched Mr. Croft perform a series of simple movements intended to build muscle and flexibility in various parts of the body. Samantha was well acquainted with them since most were a part of her daily morning routine.

She had no need for this, truth was, yet there was no denying the satisfaction she found in watching Mr. Croft perform them. His shirt and waistcoat stretched tightly across his back and the rolled-up sleeves straining against the bunching of biceps when he pushed his weight off the floor.

It was hard not to appreciate his physique and overall strength, though the knowing look Hazel gave her was somewhat annoying.

Ignoring her, Samantha thanked Mr. Croft for his demonstration and vowed to make good use of it.

"If you return in a couple of days," he said, "the room next to this one will have been made available for your training alone. Mr. Reed will also have an instructor at your disposal. Bring any friends and acquaintances who'd like to learn."

Samantha fought the urge to gape at him. He couldn't possibly be this nice. It didn't square with the man he was meant to be.

Unable to figure him out, she thanked him again and went to collect her bag from the bench.

Pretending to search the contents, she waited until he came to fetch his jacket before she clumsily drew the bag sideways, prompting several items to spill from within. Producing a huff of irritation, she bent into a crouch and proceeded to clean up the mess, allowing just enough time for Mr. Croft to notice the book she intended him to see.

"Is that *Herakles?*" he asked, a note of astonishment in his voice.

Samantha shoved the book into her bag and stood. "It is."

He looked mildly flummoxed for a second before he managed to school his features. "I wonder what your opinion of it might be."

Despite having finished it, she pretended otherwise. "I find it incredibly moving and thought provoking, though I must confess that I dread the ending which I've been told will be rather tragic."

"Yes." He was staring at her as though she'd materialized from out of thin air. A shake of his head seemed to ground him. And when he spoke next, he did so with perfect control. "I'd like to engage in a boxing match before I depart, but if you're willing to wait, I'd be honored to take you both out to lunch. Perhaps at Mivart's?"

Samantha could have beamed with pleasure. She was finally making headway. But since she did not want to look too eager, or give him cause to believe that she'd engineered any of this, she let her shoulders slump as though with regret.

"Thank you, Mr. Croft, but I'm afraid that would cause too great a delay to our schedule." She didn't elaborate further, choosing instead to collect her bonnet while Hazel did the same.

"Perhaps some other time then," Mr. Croft said.

"Perhaps," she agreed without making any suggestion as to when such an occasion might arise. Instead, she thanked him once more for his assistance, bid him good day, and proceeded to walk away.

If she wasn't mistaken, his gaze lingered upon her, tracking her every move until she'd vanished from his line of vision. But even then, she couldn't escape him completely. His powerful presence stayed with her long after her return to Clearview House.

CHAPTER SIXTEEN

Adrian returned home from Reed's with dozens of thoughts hovering in his mind. He was still somewhat bewildered by his encounter with Miss Carmichael, and he could not help but give her more thought than he intended. He was intrigued by her and the mystery that surrounded her. Loath as he was to admit it, his curiosity was beginning to take hold.

He entered his parlor and was about to pour himself a drink when Murry appeared in the doorway.

"Yes?" Adrian asked. Murry stepped forward, his eyes flicking to the fire that burned in the hearth before returning to Adrian.

"I may have some information about Miss Carmichael," he said. "Turns out she managed to get the woman who ran the orphanage where she spent the first years of her life replaced. Mrs. Thrush, the widow who currently runs it, even claims that Miss Carmichael helps acquire donations. They received nearly a thousand pounds last year thanks to her efforts."

"In other words, she's kind."

"It would appear so." Murry paused. "But there's something else..."

Adrian sipped his drink. "What?"

"One of Goodard's informants, a Mr. Haines, spotted a woman matching Miss Carmichael's description yesterday morning." Goodard, who owned London's largest employment agency, used the individuals he placed in various positions to track down people of interest. He and the Crofts had a long-standing agreement – an exchange of favors that served both sides well. "Haines was on his way to the Bearded Vulture with a delivery of ale when a woman emerged from the woods, riding at a near gallop. She had to rein in her mount to avoid crashing into Haines's wagon."

"A bit reckless perhaps," Adrian murmured, "though nothing especially noteworthy."

"It's not her handling of the horse that's of interest but rather her seat and attire."

"What of it?"

"She was riding astride, sir, while wearing breeches."

This got Adrian's attention. He straightened his spine, his glass of brandy briefly forgotten. Few people had ever surprised him, least of all in a positive way. Yet somehow, Miss Carmichael managed to do so.

He stilled on this thought and met Murry's gaze. "Are we certain it was she?"

"A female rider estimated to be in her early twenties, with light blonde hair, riding in the vicinity of Clearview House. It's hard to imagine it being anyone else."

Adrian nodded. However intriguing he'd found Miss Carmichael before, he found her doubly so now. While she appeared no more than a typical young lady at first glance, it was becoming increasingly clear that she was a great deal more. With her interest in Euripides, boxing, and now this, he couldn't help but wonder what other hidden depths there might be to her.

Recalling the glass he held, he raised it to his lips and took a long swallow of spiced liquid heat.

"She was at Reed's today," he told Murry. He could not allow himself to be blinded by what she allowed him to see, just in case there was something else lurking beneath the surface. He relayed the interaction while going over every detail in his mind. "The book that fell from her bag just happened to be the same one I'm reading. I need to know if that was indeed coincidental or if there might be something more to it."

"You think she might be trying to gain your friendship by crafting common interests?"

He didn't want it to be true, but he'd never been a big believer in fated encounters or chance. "I don't know, but I'd like to find out."

Murry frowned. "Have you taken your book out in public or mentioned it to anyone?"

"No. I keep it in the carriage to read while I travel about, so the only other person who might have seen it is you."

"Then I don't see how Miss Carmichael would be aware of it, sir."

Neither did Adrian, and yet there was something about the entire encounter at Reed's that somehow felt off, like an elusive memory just beyond reach.

Adrian downed some more brandy. "Thank you, Murry. You've been most helpful. Any other information?"

Murry shook his head. "Unfortunately not, sir. Despite his best efforts, Ward failed to encourage his mark to speak of Miss Carmichael. He was foiled every time he attempted to steer the conversation in her direction."

It wasn't unusual, Adrian supposed. Many households employed loyal servants, though he had to admit he was slightly surprised Ward's skill at obtaining information while seducing one of the Clearview Housemaids hadn't met with more success.

Too bad.

"Thank you for the update, Murry. You can tell Ward to call it quits though he ought to do so slowly so he avoids suspicion. In the meantime, tell Mr. Goodard to put all his informants on alert. And let me know if you find anything else."

"Very good, sir."

Murry departed, leaving Adrian alone with his thoughts.

They would have done well to engage Mr. Goodard's help from the very beginning, but as one of London's foremost employment agents, he ran a larger enterprise and wasn't the sort of man Adrian wished to involve in his own private dealings unless the need called for it.

As he believed it did now.

His personal interest in Miss Carmichael urged him to be wary. Too many people from his past had proven to be manipulative and deceptive, some even traitors. He'd learned some difficult lessons from trusting them, and vowed to avoid such people in future.

He worried Miss Carmichael might be such a person while simultaneously hoping she wasn't. Worst of all, he couldn't quite stop the surge of excitement when he wondered when he might see her again, and this was dangerous.

With a curse, he downed the last of his brandy and set his glass aside. He had far more important matters to deal with right now than a beautiful woman who seemed to cling to his every thought.

After enjoying a quick lunch at his desk, he set off again, returning to St. Bartholomew where he encountered the vicar – a middle-aged man with hints of grey in his dark brown hair. The persistent lines marring his brow made him look like he mourned the loss of better days.

Father Elias had been absent the last time Adrian stopped by. According to what the curate had said, he'd been out visiting a dying parishioner.

"Was anyone else on duty that night?" Adrian asked.

Father Elias plodded between the pews, collecting the hymn books left behind from his last sermon. "I was the last to depart. After locking the vestry at seven, I made a quick round just to be sure the church was empty. Finding it so, I left."

"So no one was here at a later hour? Between ten and eleven?"

"Not as far as I know." Father Elias turned to Adrian and told him bluntly, "I already said as much to the constable charged with investigating that poor woman's death."

"I merely hoped you might have recalled something else in the days since." When the vicar gave no indication that this was the case, Adrian thanked him for his time and departed.

He stopped on the pavement in front of his carriage and swept the street with his gaze. There were townhouses here, more modest in nature than what he was used to, but homes nonetheless, whose residents would have been comfortably hidden away indoors while his poor sister succumbed a short distance away.

"Wait here," Adrian called to his driver before crossing the street.

No one answered the door at the first two addresses. At the third, fourth, and fifth, he was met by solemn head-shakes as each person claimed to have seen and heard nothing. They'd been asleep at that hour.

But the young man he met at the sixth house provided him with additional information.

"I was heading home from The Fox's Burrow that night," the man, whose name turned out to be Adams, told him. "Must have been just before eleven because the clock in the hallway struck the hour right as I entered. I came from that direction, see? Had just turned the corner when a man came striding toward me."

"Did you happen to see if he'd come from the graveyard?"

"No." Adams's expression turned thoughtful. "He might have, I suppose. The entrance wasn't far behind him, but I can't say for sure."

Even if the man Adams had seen wasn't the killer, it might be another witness, and as such, Adrian wanted to find him. "Can you recall his appearance?"

"I only caught a brief glimpse in the dark." Adams frowned. "He was roughly my height, but I can't say anything about his features or coloring."

"Of course not," Adrian murmured while disappointment dampened his spirits. He thanked Mr. Adams, gave him his card in case he recalled anything else, and turned to leave.

"There was something of note," Adams said before Adrian took one more step.

"Yes?"

"He produced a crunching sound."

"A crunching sound?"

"As though he were chewing something hard, like a sugar glass treat." Adams offered the barest hint of a smile and shrugged one shoulder. "I'm not sure it helps."

"It very well might," Adrian said and promptly handed the young man a five-pound note before thanking him once again for his help and returning to his carriage.

The sugar glass treat was inconsequential right now, but Adrian knew it had every possibility of becoming a valuable piece of evidence later. So he tucked it away in the mental archive he'd started creating when he'd found the button, and set his next course for *The Morning Post*'s offices.

"Mr. Croft," he informed the clerk when the young man asked for his name. He produced his calling card for good measure. "I wish to speak with Mr. Abernathy at once."

"Do you have an appointment?" the clerk inquired, scrutinizing the sharp black lettering that formed Adrian's full name.

"No."

The clerk raised his gaze to Adrian's. "As I'm sure you can understand, Mr. Abernathy is a busy man. I'll see if he's available."

"He will be," Adrian said, hardening the look in his near-black eyes, "if he wants to keep his position as chief editor of this paper."

"Are you blackmail—"

"Just tell him I'm here."

The clerk backed up a step. His brow started to glisten and yet, he still looked on the verge of arguing further before he thought better of it and hastened away.

Adrian took a calming breath. He didn't like resorting to threats and coercion. He'd much rather people comply without issue. Yet here he was, following in his forefather's footsteps, fulfilling a destiny he had been bent on avoiding.

Until he'd gone to the morgue and seen Evie's body.

The rage coiling inside him, a poison luring him to the darkness, had him in its grasp. There was no turning back. He'd do whatever it took in order to find the answers he sought.

I won't let you down, Evie.

I'll make sure the person who did this gets punished.

"Right this way, Mr. Croft," said the clerk when he returned, not quite meeting Adrian's gaze this time.

They strode through a long hallway with offices on each side. A large room at the end of the hallway housed the press. Several men rushed about in there, operating various parts of the printing process.

The clerk took the stairs next to this room and showed Adrian into an office directly above it. Mr. Abernathy was there, hunched over a simple desk while perusing some papers. Adrian had met him a few times before, most recently six days ago when he'd come to demand a retraction of the column the paper had printed about Evie.

Mr. Abernathy looked up when Adrian entered, and promptly stood in order to greet him. The clerk excused himself, closing the door on his way out and leaving the two men alone.

"I didn't expect to see you again so soon," Mr. Abernathy said. He gestured toward a vacant chair and offered Adrian a choice between tea and coffee.

Adrian declined the refreshment but accepted the seat. "I want to speak with the person who branded my sister a wanton."

Mr. Abernathy lowered his bulky figure to his own chair with excessive slowness. "As I explained, that would violate their assurance of anonymity. We did, however, look into the matter and found the author within her right. Her source has since been interviewed, and according to her, your sister was indeed seen in the sort of indelicate situation that left little to the imagination."

Adrian gripped the armrests, his nails digging into the polished wood. Clamping his teeth together, he breathed past the tightness in his chest and the tension straining his shoulders.

"Impossible." He glared at Mr. Abernathy with every bit of contempt he harbored for him. "Evelyn's innocence has been determined by the coroner. The source is either mistaken or lying, which obviously means..."

Apprehension surfaced in Mr. Abernathy's eyes. His easy expression fell away, leaving something akin to dread in its place. "Are you implying that something one of our columnists wrote resulted in murder?"

"It's what I warned you might happen when I was last here," Adrian said, his voice soft, gentle, calm, in absolute contrast to how he felt. "Forget the columnist. Give me the source's name and address instead and I'll interview her myself."

"Mr. Croft, I urge you to be reasonable. You cannot honestly expect me to give up such information. To do so would undermine everything this paper stands for. It would caution others against coming forward with newsworthy stories in the future."

"I'll pretend you didn't just make the error of suggesting that protecting the lie this paper wrote about my sister, or the part it played in her death, is of less importance than the paper's reputation." Adrian leaned forward, bracing one forearm upon his thigh while staring Mr. Abernathy down. "Instead, I'll ask if concealing a name is of greater importance to you than your life."

Mr. Abernathy's eyes widened and it looked as though a distinct sheen appeared on his brow. "My… my life?"

"I will not be thwarted in this. Understand?"

"You would have me…killed?"

"Whatever gave you that idea?" Adrian collected a piece of paper that sat on top of the desk, tore off a blank corner, and pushed it toward the editor. "The name and address, and I vow no harm shall come to you."

It didn't take more than a second for Mr. Abernathy

to snatch up his quill and jot down the information. Adrian took it and left, allowing an unhappy smile in response to the sigh of relief that followed him from the room.

CHAPTER SEVENTEEN

Adrian knocked on Mrs. Riley's door some fifteen minutes later. After checking to make sure his mistress was home, her butler showed Adrian into a stuffy drawing room where lace curtains, piles of embroidered cushions, and thick carpeting seemed to serve as no other purpose than to collect dust.

The lady, a widow who'd lost her husband five years earlier and had chosen not to remarry, sat in a high-backed velvet armchair, her posture rigid. Dressed in a burgundy morning gown cut from a crisp crepe, she looked like a queen awaiting her execution.

"While I realize your coming here was inevitable, Mr. Croft, you still managed to catch me by surprise. I didn't expect you quite so soon." Her stiff gaze stayed upon him as he stepped toward her. She raised her chin – an attempt no doubt at feigning confidence. "You should know that I did consider asking Henson to turn you away."

He slanted a look in her direction and arched an eyebrow. "Why didn't you?"

A snort – an underlying hint of surrender. "I'm old enough to have known not only your father, Mr. Croft, but your grandfather too. If you take after either, then you're not the sort of man one chooses to cross without consequence."

"And yet, you spoke to a gossip columnist regarding my sister."

"It seemed like the right thing to do, though I'm sure you'll disagree. Which is why you're here, is it not?" She shook her head. "Honestly, I feared what you might do to poor Henson if he tried to send you away."

"No harm would have come to him, Mrs. Riley, I assure you."

"And me?"

He shoved his hands in his pockets, the fingers of his left hand finding the button discarded by Evie's killer. He flicked the item back and forth, felt the uneven texture from the embossed design adorning its surface. "I'm not in the business of hurting women."

She swallowed with visible effort and took a sharp breath. "Then why have you come?"

"For the purpose of understanding exactly what happened." He considered taking a seat but dismissed the idea as quickly as it had formed, preferring the authoritative advantage of towering over her instead.

"What did you see the night of the Marsdale ball? And what the devil possessed you to go to the press with it?"

She flinched in response to the sudden hardness of his tone. "I'd gone to the garden for a breath of fresh air and to simply escape all the noise. At my age, peace and quiet is something I savor, which isn't to say that I don't enjoy social functions, simply that I prefer to attend them on my own terms." A frown creased her brow. She took a shaky breath and gave him a hesitant look before adding, "I was nearing the end of the garden path, where the rhododendrons are planted, when I heard them."

"What did you hear, exactly?" However distasteful, Adrian wanted to know.

"A man's voice at first, though I couldn't discern his words." Mrs. Riley shifted uncomfortably in her seat. She clasped her hands together and gave a small shrug while fiddling with her skirt. "A woman's moan followed. It increased in volume while I stood there. And then the man said…things which really don't bear repeating."

Mrs. Riley clamped her mouth shut and angled herself away from him. The flush in her cheeks spoke volumes.

"Unfortunately, I must insist." Even though he wanted to grab her and shake her until the words spilled from her throat, he forced some measure of calm to his voice. "What did the man say?"

She sat, silent and unmoving for so long she started looking like one of the portraits that hung on the wall. Only the subtle twitch of her fingers suggested she might be gathering whatever courage she needed.

And then, when he'd finally found a strange sort of tranquility in the hush bearing down upon him, she whispered, so low he scarcely heard her, "'Yes, Evie, just like that.' Some panting followed. And then he said, 'I could shag you forever.' Your sister moaned something I couldn't quite hear and then it sounded as though they both reached their crisis."

Adrian stood, frozen, his feet rooted to the carpeted floor while the world spun around him. Until he recalled the coroner's report and everything settled back into place. A precise kind of focus followed. He let himself breathe.

"What time was this?" he asked with a cool detachment that kept his rage at bay and allowed him to keep moving forward, even when he felt as though he were being pushed back by some invisible force determined to see him destroyed.

"Roughly nine o'clock, if I'm not mistaken."

"And did you actually see my sister engaging in the act you've just described?"

"Yes." Mrs. Riley gave him the sort of pitying look that would have led to a punch in the face, had she been a man. "There was a parting between the shrubs which allowed for a glimpse of dark hair and a light-colored gown."

"But you can't say exactly what color it was?"

"It was dark, Mr. Croft, my visibility impaired."

"What about the man's face?" Adrian pressed with rising irritation. "Did you happen to see who he was?"

"As I said, it was dark and—"

"In other words, you made an assumption based upon what an unidentifiable man said." The impulse to grab her and shake her returned. *How much force would it take to crush her bones?*

Alarmed by the thought, he retreated a step. Losing control made men reckless, and that had consequences. Consequences he had no intention of facing. So he steeled himself against the urge to allow his fury full reign, and considered visiting Reed's once this call had been completed.

"I know what I saw and what I heard," Mrs. Riley insisted, her head now set at a stubborn angle.

"And you went to *The Morning Post* with it," Adrian murmured.

"The gossip column's author and I are longtime friends. We met for tea the day after the ball and I mentioned the incident to her."

"And in so doing, you condemned an innocent woman to die."

"I wouldn't say tha—"

"You knew of the murders committed last year, did you not? Of the labels the murderer pinned to each woman? That he remains on the loose?"

"Yes, but—"

"Then it stands to good reason that you bear as much responsibility for my sister's death as whoever related your observations to the public, and the paper who actually printed the lie."

"It wasn't a lie," Mrs. Riley informed him, her voice strong, firm, and filled with so much quiet outrage that Adrian finally understood. Envy made her vindictive. She'd likely suffered an unhappy marriage, had never known the kind of pleasure she'd witnessed between those bushes, and had punished the perpetrators to the best of her ability.

He glared at her. "Consider this then, my dear Mrs. Riley. Marsdale is a close friend of mine. I feel as at home in his house as I do in my own. So on the eve of the ball, when I grew weary of standing about the ballroom, I invited my sister for a tour of his home. A clock chimed while we were in the upstairs gallery. The ninth hour, to be precise, making it physically impossible for my sister to have been in the garden at that exact time. As you've just suggested she was."

Confusion dimmed Mrs. Riley's eyes. She shook her head. "Impossible. Unless I mistook the time."

"What you mistook," Adrian told her darkly, "was the situation as a whole. You heard a name used and fell for a ruse. As a result, a young woman – my beloved sister – is dead."

"No." Mrs. Riley shook her head vehemently.

"Your punishment will be the truth," Adrian continued, not caring what kind of turmoil would sink its talons into this woman as soon as she knew the extent of her blunder. "The coroner made a thorough examination of my sister's body, and do you know what he found, Mrs. Riley? An untouched virgin, innocent of everything you would have her accused of."

Mrs. Riley's stricken expression offered only a marginal piece of satisfaction. "I don't understand."

"Who was the author?" By God, he'd make sure they never wrote anything ever again.

"I...I really can't say."

Anger flashed behind his eyes. "Tell me."

When Mrs. Riley still said nothing, he seethed, "I'll see you cut from Society unless you give me her name, and if that's not enough, then I urge you to think of poor Henson. Wouldn't do for stolen goods to be found in his possession."

Despite visibly trembling, she glared at him as though he were the devil. "Mrs. Thackery."

How easily she'd sacrificed her long-time friend.

Sick of her presence, of the stuffy parlor depriving him of air, and of struggling to rein in his finely controlled temper, Adrian left. Someone had set Evie up by staging the whole bloody thing and using a decoy in her place.

The question preying upon him now, was who and why.

CHAPTER EIGHTEEN

◈

Peter Kendrick returned to his office after his latest meeting with the chief magistrate and poured himself a large glass of brandy. Sir Nigel's displeasure with him had been felt in every punctuated word the man had uttered.

He was most unhappy with Peter's continued failure to catch the killer and with the time it was taking Miss Carmichael to get nice and comfortable with Mr. Croft. Since Sir Nigel had put Peter in charge of that assignment as well, he not only had to explain his own inability to provide answers now but Miss Carmichael's too.

Made him look like a bloody amateur.

He tossed back the drink he'd poured and hissed in response to the welcome burn the liquid produced as it slid down his throat. The smoke from the cheroot he'd lit wafted toward him. He picked it up and took a few drags before reaching for a piece of paper. It was time for him to check in with his agent and, if need be, to press her for some much-needed results.

The tip of his quill scratched the paper with long sloping letters as he penned the note her errand boy would deliver to her. The lad always showed up near the back entrance a couple of times a day, just in case a message such as this needed relaying.

He wrote his initials at the bottom of the note, folded the paper, and sealed it shut with a shiny blob of red wax. Snatching it up between his fingers, he then pushed his chair back and stood.

The boy was exactly where he'd expected to find him, lurking in a doorway, a grey cap pulled down across his brow to conceal his face. Peter approached at a clipped pace, the missive carefully concealed where he held it, flush against his thigh.

As he approached, he whistled the first few notes from "Greensleeves," allowing the song to fade when the boy slowly straightened, stepped out of the doorway, and walked toward Peter. His gait was almost lazy – a scamp on the prowl for the next pocket to pick. When he drew flush with Peter, his hand caught the missive, snatching it away with such skill, Peter failed to notice the action, even when he knew it was happening.

Without looking back, Peter continued to the bakery just around the corner, from which he purchased a steaming hot minced meat pie. If anyone from Mr. Croft's network happened to see, they'd hopefully remain unaware of the secret correspondence taking place beneath their noses.

Two hours later, he read the response Miss Carmichael had written.

Tell your friend to be patient. As it is, instinct compels me to withdraw for a number of days to avoid detection. Unless, of course, you want me to fail, in which case I am more than happy to press ahead without caution.

Brief and blunt.

Peter lit a flint, held the paper to the flame, and watched it burn. Her reasoning was likely correct. An infiltration of this kind was delicate. She had to instill in Mr. Croft a desire to spend more time with her, to get to know her, and to invite her into his lair.

Sir Nigel was being unreasonable to presume such a task could be undertaken in under two weeks. With this in mind, he wrote a one-page report explaining as much to his superior and prayed the man would be willing to show some patience.

Once this was done, Kendrick gave his attention to the four files he'd placed on his desk that morning, before his meeting with Sir Nigel distracted him from his investigations.

The unsolved murder cases plagued him, keeping him from his sleep most nights. It bothered him to no end that he'd not yet captured the scoundrel responsible. Worse was the fact that his leads continued to fall apart. It felt as though he were reaching into a fog, hoping to come up with answers.

Disheartened, he grabbed for Miss Fairchild's file

and flipped it open. Without a substantial trail to follow it seemed foolhardy to keeping pushing ahead. Instead, it might be wiser to start again, at the beginning.

So he read the detailed notes he'd made of the crime scene, only to realize the information invariably led to the same conclusions he'd arrived at before. And until that changed, there was a very good chance additional murders would follow.

∼

The upper-class gentleman stared out of his bedchamber window, his gaze on the recently planted apple tree in the garden below. As distasteful as it was, encouraging a murderer to target a lovely young woman, it had been necessary in determining Mr. Croft's future.

He'd wanted to wash himself clean of his forefathers' sins, turn his back on the influence they'd acquired, in order to what? Live an ordinary life without impact?

That would not do.

Balance had to be maintained.

Without the Crofts around to punish those who stepped out of line, vermin would rise. It had happened before, in 1753 when Mr. Croft's great-grandfather died while his son was abroad. Heinous crimes had occurred until he returned home, took up the reins, and unleashed his wrath.

That could not happen again.

People might not realize it, but the safety of every London citizen depended on the Croft family's existence. They were the top predators in the criminal world and far more capable of keeping other criminals in check than any constable, magistrate, or judge. Only fools failed to recognize Mr. Croft's importance.

But at least now, with Mr. Croft set on catching the man who'd murdered four women, there was finally a glimmer of hope that justice would soon be served. Not in a court of law, but in the manner in which such a vile person deserved.

∽

Dorian stood a few steps behind Samantha and watched as she raised her right arm, took aim, and fired. The small square board she'd hung from a tree fifty yards away danced side to side as the shot made impact.

"Dead center," Dorian said, checking the result through his spyglass. He lowered the instrument and handed it to her.

She nodded with satisfaction, reloaded the pistol, and held it toward him. "I want you to host a ball here at Clearview. An event on our terms where we're in control of every detail."

"You want to manage Mr. Croft's experience with you." A clever notion.

"I'll invite him for a private tour of the house, allow

him to feel like I'm letting him into my private domain – a place reserved for the closest of friends."

"An excellent plan. I'll see to it that invitations are sent out." He made his attempt, not the least bit surprised by his inferior skill. Samantha had started exceeding his capability years ago, and had since taken care to maintain her high standard. He huffed a breath when he saw that he'd struck the target some inches above the center.

A few more rounds followed, his pride increasing with each successful attempt Samantha made. Although he'd seen her do this a thousand times, her constant accuracy never ceased to amaze him.

"I've been meaning to ask a favor of you as well," he said while they packed up ten minutes later.

She straightened, hands on hips, and gave him a serious, no nonsense look. "Name it. Lord knows I could never repay you for all you have done for me even if I were given a lifetime."

"It was never my intention for you to feel indebted." He took her hand and gave it a squeeze – a rare gesture of fondness. "Whatever reason I had for initially taking you in, I want you to know that I always thought of you and the other girls as my daughters."

A faint smile pulled at her lips and for a brief second her eyes seemed to glisten. She quickly buried the emotion behind an inscrutable expression, leaving Dorian to wonder if he might have trained her *too* well.

"Promise me you'll let me know if you're ever out of your depth. This mission you're on is far from simple, so if there are elements you wish to discuss, any doubts you may have or concerns, I want you to come to me for support."

Samantha grabbed the case containing the pistols and held it firmly in her hand. "You needn't worry. While I will admit to Mr. Croft being a far more challenging target than I had expected, I'll gain his confidence eventually. It's just a matter of time."

Turning, she headed toward the house. As usual, her pace was quick and decisive. Dorian fell into step beside her, then lengthened his stride so he could keep up.

"What makes him more challenging?" he asked while they walked, the meadow's tall grass brushing his boots until they reached the footpath.

"He's not easily deceived," she said, then sent him a quick sideways glance. "I can see it in his eyes – a question filled with distrust, like he's expecting a trap. Consequently, I must bide my time. As it is, I already fear I may have overplayed my hand slightly."

Concern tightened Dorian's expression. "How do you mean?"

"I found out what he was reading, purchased a copy of the same book, and allowed it to spill from my bag when last we met. Despite the interest he showed, I think he believed it too much a coincidence given that I also happened to show up at Reed's. My being there before he arrived ought to confirm that he wasn't followed. Still, I deliberately chose to pull back for a bit – allow his suspicions to ease."

"A wise decision," Dorian agreed, though none of what she'd said addressed what he believed to be the most pressing issue of all. Namely Mr. Croft, the man.

He was strikingly handsome, and with his sister now dead, Samantha would have to target him more directly. It didn't take much imagination to figure out where that might lead. The real test, he supposed, would be whether she'd be able to keep her end goal in sight while seducing her way into his heart.

She couldn't afford to develop feelings.

It would undoubtedly be a challenge. She'd have to throw herself head-first into it, or risk all her hard work going to waste. Dorian could only hope she'd have the good sense to keep her heart out of harm's way.

"Don't forget what he stands for," he told her as they returned through a gate that separated the property's wilderness from the more manicured garden.

"Devious manipulation capable of destroying lives," she muttered, the words hard and concise, as though she firmly believed them.

He nodded, confident in the knowledge that she remained true to the cause.

∼

A gentleman impeccably dressed according to the latest style was what everyone saw when they looked at the man who rode along Rotten Row. Murderer would never occur to any of them.

They were his peers. Friends and acquaintances. Some were even relations.

He tipped his hat and smiled at Viscount Ottersburg and his wife as they passed him in their open barouche. A leisurely ride in the park was an excellent way for him to lose himself for the afternoon. Out here, amid the fresh air and picturesque scenery, the visions that crept in when he closed his eyes were easily buried.

"Fancy a race?" asked Gregory St. Croix, the Duke of Eldridge's youngest son. Seated upon his Arabian thoroughbred with his black hair neatly tied in a queue, he glanced at his two companions with mischief in his bright eyes.

"On your mark," said the man.

"Shall we say until the edge of the Serpentine?" asked Nigel Lawrence, the Marquess of Avernail's fifth youngest son. His brother's horse-riding accident and the paralysis this had led to did not deter him from wanting to race.

"As the crow flies, on the count of three." Gregory swung his mount around and waited for his friends to line up beside him. "One, two... Go!"

The horses snorted and angled their necks, creating a straight line from nose to tail as they leapt into motion. The man leaned into his saddle and clicked his tongue, urging his mount into a gallop.

Air rushed across his face. His hands tightened around the reins, squeezing them so tightly his fingers began to burn. The drum of hooves against the ground kept pace with his heart, drowning out his ever increasing need to rid the world of whores.

In this moment, he was at peace, at one with the beast, his only focus on getting to the finish line first. He gauged it to be no more than a hundred yards away now. The water beyond it gleamed in response to the morning sun, creating an orb of light that gave the illusion of liquid fire.

Shoulders tight, he kept his breaths even while jamming his heels against his horse's flanks. "Come on."

No sooner were the words spoken than the air shifted around him, a sort of invisible push and release as Gregory flew past with Nigel in swift pursuit.

With a muttered curse, he made one final attempt at claiming victory over his friends. He slapped his mount's rump and whipped the reins.

It was to no avail. The Duke of Eldridge's son reached the finish line first, narrowly avoiding two ladies who strolled along the edge of the lake.

They glared at him as he gave a victorious cheer. Nigel, ever the rogue, sent the pair a wide smile. "Take pity on him, I beg you. He's not accustomed to winning."

"Don't believe a word he says," Gregory told the two women while circling around and drawing nearer to where they stood. He removed his hat and winked at the pair before dropping his voice and telling them smoothly, "My friend is a terrible liar."

"And you, sir?" One of the women asked boldly, her deep brown eyes falling upon the one man she ought to avoid. "If your friends are liars and losers, then what are you?"

Her friend tittered, a coquettish sound that grated his nerves. Both ladies blushed in response to all the attention they'd gained, the harm that had nearly come to them moments ago completely forgotten.

"A devil in disguise," he murmured.

The lady who'd posed the question, a pretty redhead with a flirtatious smile, fixed her eyes upon him for one second longer than what was deemed proper.

His muscles twitched as he slid his gaze over her supple body, allowing it to come to rest at the base of her throat. The sudden desire to find out whether or not she deserved to live quickened his pulse.

Although he'd embarked on his mission with purpose and took no pleasure in taking Miss Fairchild's life, each subsequent killing had helped him acknowledge the thrill he was able to find in wielding such power. Not to mention the pure excitement that came from hunting his victim and luring them into his trap.

It was intoxicating – a feeling he longed to know again soon.

∼

Sitting at his desk, Adrian returned his seal to its case and blew out the candle he'd used to melt the red wax. There was nothing pleasant about destroying somebody's source of income, but Mrs. Thackery ought to have known better when she decided to write about Evie.

Adrian couldn't allow such dangerous behavior to slide and had, therefore, gone back to *The Morning Post* after meeting with Mrs. Riley, to demand the woman's immediate termination.

He'd since written letters to all other newspaper companies in the City, explaining the situation and warning them against hiring her if she came to them in search of employment. His signature would hopefully add enough weight for them to follow through so he could return to the more important matter of tracking down Evie's killer.

Having the Croft files available would have been useful. He regretted the decision he'd made to order their destruction. The meticulous notes were part of a collection that detailed every piece of information gathered on members of Society, all Croft family associates, and anyone else they needed to know about, including their enemies.

Filled with dirty secrets and illegal endeavors, it was the key to obtaining favors. In his haste to put that life behind him, he'd foolishly had the entire thing burned – centuries worth of intelligence gathered by six generations.

Those files would have been helpful now, considering the answers he might have found between the pages. Unlike Debrett's, which only contained the basic facts about peers, the Croft files might have provided information about Mr. Harlowe, perhaps even on Miss Samantha Carmichael too.

Worst of all was the awful awareness that they would have given him valuable data on the Fairchilds, the Earl of Hightower and his family, as well as the Irvines. Not to mention what he might have learned about everyone else he and his sister had interacted with in the days leading up to her death.

Furious with himself for being so bloody shortsighted and foolishly impulsive, he waited impatiently in his study for Cummings to arrive. The man, who'd been employed by his father, had his own residence and came to the Croft home on Mondays, Wednesdays, and Fridays at nine o'clock in the morning, departing once more at noon.

Adrian stood as soon as he heard the front door open and close. A muted exchange between Elks and Cummings ensued. The soft tread of footsteps upon the hallway runner followed. Cummings appeared in the doorway. In his mid-forties with dark blonde hair and light brown eyes, he was smartly dressed as usual and with that fresh look about him that always suggested he'd gotten a good night's rest.

"Good morning, Mr. Croft." The secretary crossed to one of the armchairs and set the satchel he always brought with him upon the vacant seat. "Is there any urgent correspondence you'd like me to see to before I proceed with the ledgers?"

Adrian glanced at the pile of condolence letters still sitting on the corner of his desk. He'd handle those himself once he had a minute to spare. "No. There is however a matter I'd like to address."

Cummings gave him a curious look. "Yes?"

"The files I asked you to burn…" Adrian scratched the back of his neck, not quite able to meet the other man's eyes. "I don't suppose you might have ignored that order."

The edge of Cummings's mouth twitched, almost with humor, despite every other part of his expression conveying regret. "I wouldn't dare to defy you."

"So then…they're truly gone, not just boxed away somewhere in the attic."

"I'm afraid so."

"Shit." Adrian paced toward the bookcase where several gaping shelves seemed to mock him for his stupidity.

"Of course," Cummings said, "the files kept here were merely duplicates."

Adrian spun on his heels, almost tripping himself in the process. He caught his balance and stared at Cummings. "Duplicates?"

"Something so precious would not exist without safeguards." A slow smile pulled at Cummings's thin lips. "Another copy – the original – is located at Deerhaven Manor."

An incredible sense of relief poured through Adrian at those words. All was not quite lost then. He could still obtain whatever information the files contained. "You kept them up to date?"

Cummings snorted and raised an eyebrow. "Of course."

"In that case, I think you deserve a bonus of say… twenty pounds? Make a note of it in the ledger and have a cheque from Barclay and Tritton prepared for me to sign."

The secretary thanked him and Adrian went to find Murry. Arrangements would have to be made now. The Moorlands' ball would be held in five days – a social function that promised to lure every high-ranking member of Society to it. So Adrian planned on ignoring the state of mourning he ought to be observing, in favor of attending.

After all, the murderer would likely be there, which meant he'd be keeping a keen eye on every guest. If Miss Samantha Carmichael showed up as well, then that would just make for a far more interesting evening.

With no time to spare, he instructed Murry to start packing. They'd have to leave at once if they were to make it back in time for the ball.

CHAPTER NINETEEN

Samantha entered the Moorland ballroom with Harlowe and instantly knew without having to look that Mr. Croft wasn't present. Despite his absence from London these past few days, she'd been certain he would be. The note she'd received from Melody claimed that their hostess had told Lady Heathbrooke of his attendance.

Apparently neither the duke nor the duchess wanted Mr. Croft there. He, Lady Heathbrooke had explained when Melody pressed her, had the unfortunate ability of making most people uncomfortable. It was this very same aspect that had compelled the duke and duchess to invite him.

Confident he would decline, however, due to being in mourning, they'd not expected him to accept.

Samantha smiled politely when Harlowe introduced her to Viscount and Viscountess Stanton, Viscount and

Viscountess Ottersburg, the Earl and Countess of Glendale, Baron and Baroness Midhurst, Mr. and Mrs. Hillford, and countless others.

A Mr. Julian Walker invited her to dance, after which several other gentlemen signed their names to her dance card. But the one man she'd hoped to encounter remained absent as the evening progressed.

"Don't despair," Harlowe told her when he came to give her a glass of champagne after a reel. "Even if he doesn't show, there are other ways for us to use the evening to our advantage."

"I'm already keeping a watchful eye on the men Miss Croft danced with during the Marsdale ball." Except Marsdale himself, who remained as absent as Mr. Croft.

"And?" Harlowe asked, casually taking a sip of champagne.

"None seem capable of enacting such evil." Mr. Walker and Mr. Newton had both been charming partners. As had the Duke of Moorland. She'd spoken with all three men at various intervals, both previously and this evening, and had found their company engaging.

Nigel Lawrence, on the other hand, gave her an uneasy feeling. She didn't like the way he looked at her, like she were a tasty dessert he'd like to devour. But then, he'd not shown the same sort of interest in Miss Croft. A point worth keeping in mind since she could not afford to suspect the wrong person based on her own bias.

A bit of agitation near the front of the ballroom prompted Samantha to glance in that direction.

"Looks like he made it," Harlowe said at the same time as Samantha spotted Mr. Croft.

She averted her gaze before their eyes met. The last thing she wanted was to let him think she'd been waiting for him.

Her interest in him had to be balanced somewhere between curiosity and indifference.

Perhaps she should make herself scarce for a bit, allow him to chat with other guests so it wouldn't look like she was standing about in anticipation of his notice.

"I think I'll take some fresh air on the terrace," she informed Harlowe.

"And I shall head to the gaming room for a round of cards." He clinked his glass against hers, and the two parted ways with Samantha moving smoothly toward the French doors to her left.

Ever conscious of Mr. Croft making his way through the crowded ballroom, she forced herself to look straight ahead, to ignore the temptation of glancing in his direction.

The cool night air was breezy, sweeping through the honeysuckle vines that clung to the stone façade. Leaves rustled, the soft sound mingling with the muted strains of music filling the ballroom.

A few other guests stood scattered about in small groups. Samantha walked past them, choosing the solitude of the far corner. She stepped toward the balustrade, set her glass upon the edge, and took a deep breath.

Dressed in a gown sewn from soft pink silk overlaid with a creamy lace dotted by small crystal beads, she felt so very different from who she truly was. More like a princess than an agent trained to uncover secrets. She smiled at that thought. Nobody here would suspect her of being able to fight a man on equal footing, or to shoot him dead from a distance of one hundred yards.

She picked up her glass and drank, enjoying the sweet, bubbly flavor as it flowed over her tongue. Measured steps gently touching the flagstone caught her attention. She stilled as they drew nearer.

There was no need to turn and look to know who approached. She could sense him in the tightening of her stomach, the soft prick of awareness against the nape of her neck, and the heat creeping into her cheeks as excitement stole through her.

He'd sought her out and had thereby proved his interest.

All was proceeding as planned.

"Tell me something you've never told anyone else," his deep voice suggested.

She grinned, not with pretense but with unexpected amusement. Her laughter froze as that realization cemented itself within her. She shook her head, attempting to banish the curious sensation of possibly finding him charming, only to tamp down the brief emotion and reach for added control. Her job would be so much harder to do if she started to like him.

Again, the memory of him kneeling in order to place a rose at the base of the church wall where his sister was killed flickered in her mind's eye.

She shoved that aside as well and told him, "I've always hated playing the piano."

He produced a low chuckle as he came to stand beside her. "Why?"

"I'm not especially fond of sitting still."

This time he gave a full-bodied laugh – a rich rumbling sound that swept over her like a tidal wave, catching her in its thrall. He angled himself toward her and propped his hip against the balustrade. "Then why do you play?"

"Because it's expected, I suppose." It was the truth. Harlowe believed all young ladies ought to possess certain skills – refinements, he called them. He also loved the sound of music filling the house and she hadn't the heart to tell him she'd rather not play when asked.

"Do you always do what's expected, Miss Carmichael?"

Mr. Croft's voice held a hint of deep curiosity mixed with something she wouldn't have picked up had she not been paying perfect attention. It was a secretive element, as though he'd discovered something she wasn't aware of.

Concern gave her pause as she wondered what he might know. Choosing to err on the side of caution, she tilted her head as though in thought. "For the most part, I suppose."

"You've never done anything…shocking?"

Samantha's mind raced. Why would he ask that unless he'd discovered something about her? But what? She'd done an endless amount of things that would be considered shocking for any young lady to undertake.

So what was it?

Had the men she'd fought in St. Giles reported back to him somehow? Did he know of the room she'd rented near Covent Garden? Was the man she'd almost trampled while riding, one of Mr. Croft's informants?

She'd no idea, but the icy shiver stealing across her shoulders warned her he might be about to turn the tables.

Despite the frantic beat of her heart, she held herself immobile for a couple of breaths before daring to meet his gaze.

The intensity of that stare was so penetrating and seeking, it felt like it drove all the way to the depth of her soul. It made it hard for her to think.

Yet she had to. If she was to answer his question correctly, she had to muddle her way through this with calm, collected control.

"Can I trust you?" she asked, choosing to start by asking a question of her own.

Surprise flickered in his dark eyes. The soft play of light from nearby torches caused them to glow in a way that threatened to reel her in and hold her captive if she weren't careful.

A wry smile only added to his appeal. "Whatever secrets you wish to impart will be safe with me."

It was time for her to take a gamble. If word of her fighting skills and her visit to Wycliffe's had reached him, she doubted they would be having this conversation. Rather, he'd have tied her to a chair in a basement somewhere and demanded she give him an explanation.

Because that was precisely the sort of thing a man with his reputation would do.

If it was the room she rented that he'd discovered...

He'd know she was up to something and would probably choose to steer clear of her henceforth.

Yet here he was, asking questions with what appeared to be genuine interest.

Which had to mean...

"I love to ride, but maintaining balance in a sidesaddle while all those skirts are twisted around my legs is no fun at all. So I usually ride astride instead. Especially if I'm planning to go for a gallop."

The briefest hint of amazement pulled at his features before he managed to mask the response. An element of mischief replaced it. "How very improper."

She grinned, surrendering to the amusement that danced in the air. "That's only the half of it, Mr. Croft."

"Oh?" An arch of his brow challenged her to confess the rest.

Pressing her lips together, she glanced about as if nervous others might hear. She then lowered her voice and leaned a bit closer to him. "I gave up on the riding habit ages ago, choosing instead to wear breeches."

"Why, Miss Carmichael." The warmth in his voice was like melted chocolate – decadent and smooth. "I must confess, I never would have taken you for a hoyden."

An embarrassed chuckle accompanied an averted look. "I'm really not."

"Boxing, and riding while dressed in men's clothes?" He crossed his arms and swept her from head to toe with a gaze so forceful it felt like he'd physically touched her. "I beg to differ. But that's not a bad thing. On the contrary, it sets you apart from all the rest, and that makes you all the more intriguing."

Heat flooded her cheeks and something inside her – a place buried deep behind her breastbone – expanded. She tamped down the feeling with stern resolve even as her lips twitched with humor. "Not nearly as intriguing as you, I'll wager."

His eyes flashed, darkening just enough to warn her that they were no longer chatting like new acquaintances, but flirting.

Aware that she'd ventured too far from shore, she grabbed her glass and took a quick sip, then turned more fully toward him and mimicked his posture.

"It surprised me not to find you at Reed's this past week," she said, her tone light and casual.

"I was away at my country estate for most of it."

"Oh, how lovely. Is it far?" She asked the question even though she already knew the answer.

"It's a good day and a half's ride by carriage."

"Did you grow up there?" Again, a needless question for her to ask.

"Until I was ten. After that, my time was mostly

spent here under my father's tutelage. Unlike Mama, he preferred London to Deerhaven. Always claimed the countryside bored him."

"How do *you* feel about it?"

He gave her a curious look. "I believe you might be the first person ever to ask me that."

"Forgive me. I didn't mean to pry."

"It's fine." He cleared his throat. "Honestly, I favor the peace and quiet the countryside offers. I'd actually hoped to move to a more secluded location, but now, with my sister dead and…"

His gaze shifted toward the garden, staring through the darkness with a vacant look that suggested the only thing he saw right now was a memory.

An unexpected needle-sharp pain pierced Samantha's heart. Mr. Croft appeared emotionally distraught, completely unlike the hardened criminal Kendrick and Harlowe insisted he was.

Could they be wrong?

She reminded herself that it wasn't her place to question either of them. Her task was to carry out orders. And yet, a small, irritating part of her that had sprung to life the moment they'd met couldn't stand to watch Mr. Croft suffer.

Not on account of a cruel injustice enacted against him and his lovely sister. The vigilante inside her demanded the scoundrel be found and punished, regardless of who Mr. Croft might be or what he'd done in the past.

Besides, tracking the murderer down could help forge a bond between them.

"I realize this is a sensitive subject," she whispered, "so please let me know if I'm overstepping, but I'm curious to know if Bow Street have any leads regarding your sister's killer."

"Not as far as I know," he said, speaking to the emptiness beyond the terrace.

"Have you considered looking into it yourself?" When he didn't respond, she told him, "Your sister was the fourth victim. It might make sense to start at the very beginning in order to know the murderer's original motive."

Mr. Croft's gaze slowly met hers. The earlier hints of mischief were lost behind a stern façade. His change in demeanor almost made her regret having given up on the flirting, which was also the most straightforward path to her goal.

But such a course was not one she felt comfortable with on account of her inexperience. Then again, a lack of experience would in all likelihood prove an asset in this instance. Given the role she was meant to play, it would seem more genuine if she appeared a touch shy and uncertain regarding such matters.

Mr. Croft stared at her, almost as though he needed a second to bring her back into focus. Ignoring her question and the point she'd just made, he asked instead, "Would you do me the honor of dancing with me?"

His voice matched the somber mood that had

settled upon them the moment he'd mentioned his sister. It filled the space between them and rather than push her away, it lured her.

Not that she would have turned him down when this was what she'd been working toward. But the pull she experienced as he stood there, grief etched in every aspect of his bearing, was nothing short of terrifying.

And yet, she faced the sympathy and the attraction he'd managed to sow somewhere deep in her conscience, reminding herself, while accepting the arm he offered, to fight it with unrelenting resolve.

They returned inside just as the orchestra struck up a waltz. He led her onto the dance floor and drew her into his arms, the confidence he exuded that of a man who'd partnered with countless women before her. His hand was firm on her waist, his steps sure and strong as he guided her into the dance with effortless movements. She could feel the power in his body, the contained energy humming beneath the surface.

Yet there was an unexpected gentleness to him as well. His touch, while possessive, was not rough. He held her close but did not crush her. And his eyes, as they gazed into hers, gradually softened, allowing her a glimpse of something that looked almost tender.

Impossible.

"There's something about you I can't understand," Mr. Croft murmured, his voice a low rumble between them. "Why haven't you married?"

The question caught her off guard, and for a moment she struggled to form a response. Averting her gaze, she watched the rest of the dancers rush by in a blur. She should have anticipated him asking this and was slightly annoyed with herself that she hadn't.

"My questionable heritage makes me something of a mongrel," she said at last.

"Mongrels have their merits," he said while turning her in a wide arc. "They tend to be smarter than purebreds and have fewer ailments. I personally prefer them."

Her gaze snapped to his and she saw that he meant it. Perhaps dancing with him had been a mistake. At this close range the man was a far more dangerous adversary than she had expected.

She'd foolishly believed herself strong and capable of resisting his charm. Yet he had the most disturbing ability to make her pulse beat faster.

"I also have a responsibility to Harlowe," she said, attempting as best she could to focus on their conversation. "He's done so much for me, I could never leave him."

"Your loyalty is admirable. Harlowe is certainly fortunate to have you." His thumb stroked gently over her waist, sending a shiver down her spine. "But every woman deserves a life of her own. A chance at love, a family to raise, and all the things that make life sweet."

His words echoed the secret longings she'd buried so deep they'd been forgotten until this moment, and for a second she imagined what such a life might be like. A home of her own, a husband who loved her, children with bright smiles and...

No.

She shook her head to clear the images. That life was not meant for her. Duty and sacrifice were the prices she would pay for the privileges she'd been given.

The music faded and she stepped away, breaking the intimacy between them.

"Thank you for the dance." A polite smile was all she dared. "If you don't mind, I think I'd like to rest for a bit. Loath as I am to admit it, the slippers I chose to wear are not very comfortable."

"Of course." Mr. Croft tucked her hand into the crook of his arm. "There are some comfortable sofas in the drawing room where we can sit while we take some refreshment."

The offer was unexpected. It gave her a choice between the reprieve she'd intended to seek and the chance for them to speak at greater length. While she did feel the need for a private moment in which to collect her thoughts, she could not ignore the opportunity he provided.

Added time spent together would help strengthen the bond that was growing between them. If she turned him down, there was a chance he might not extend the offer again.

So she accompanied him from the ballroom to seek out a spot where her imaginary sore feet could find some relief.

Progress was being made this evening. Mr. Croft's interest in her was increasing. What she did not dare to consider was whether or not her interest in him was limited to her assignment.

The problem was that in order to sell her lie, she had to convince herself of it so well she began to believe it. She had to allow herself to like Mr. Croft, maybe even to fall for him, and that was a dangerous game. Though perhaps the most dangerous part of all was how easy she feared it would be.

She buried that thought and reminded herself of her purpose.

Befriend, gain access, destroy.

Affecting a limp, she leaned on him, removing the distance between them and pushing the length of her arm against his. He instantly switched position, bringing one arm around her for added support while continuing to guide her forward.

"There's a vacant sofa in the far corner," he said.

But as they walked, Samantha heard a man say, "To even suspect you of murder is the utmost of ridiculousness. I'm glad you won your case against Bow Street."

CHAPTER TWENTY

Adrian tensed, his grip tightening on Miss Carmichael's back as the comment he'd just overheard registered. Glancing sideways, he saw that it must have been spoken by Mr. Owen Newton, who stood with his brother, Clive, conversing with Viscount Birchwood and the Duke of Eldridge.

Inhaling sharply, Adrian halted his and Miss Carmichael's progress, a smile fixed on his face as he drew her toward the small group. "Birchwood. If recollection serves, you still owe me a bottle of port on account of our most recent wager."

Birchwood's expression cooled. "What an unexpected surprise, Croft. When Eldridge told me of your attendance this evening, I simply refused to believe it."

"It is surprising," Mr. Owen Newton concurred, his manner reserved.

Adrian couldn't argue. Siblings were expected to

observe at least six months of mourning for each other, yet it had been only two and a half weeks since Evie's death. "Had my sister perished from natural causes, I would have stayed home. Seeing as there is a murderer on the loose, however, I'd rather venture back into Society where I am far more likely to catch him."

"Let's pray that you do," Birchwood said, a frown creasing his brow. The pensive look in his eyes faded as he glanced toward Miss Carmichael. A broad smile followed. "Forgive me, but I don't believe we've met."

Aware that introductions were expected, Adrian sent his companion a quick glance before saying, "May I present Viscount Birchwood?"

She dipped her chin, a soft smile gracing her lips.

"Miss Samantha Carmichael," Adrian announced. He released her arm so as not to appear too possessive and immediately regretted it when Birchwood's eyes lit with interest. Schooling his features and squaring his shoulders, Adrian did what he could to squash his annoyance and told the group firmly, "She's under Mr. Harlowe's protection."

"Indeed?" Birchwood's expression turned quizzical.

"Mr. Harlowe took me in when I was a child and has been like a father to me ever since," she explained. "I'd not have entered Society were it not for him."

"Then I must seek him out and express my thanks," Birchwood said. "For I daresay your presence here has brightened my evening. It's an absolute pleasure to make your acquaintance."

The viscount reached for Miss Carmichael's hand

and raised it to his lips while Adrian fought the urge to vomit. Did any woman appreciate such drivel?

He gave Miss Carmichael a sidelong glance and saw to his amusement that her lips were not only pressed together but that they trembled at the corners, as if she were doing her best not to laugh.

Returning his attention to the group as a whole, he caught Clive Newton rolling his eyes, a quirk that suggested the young man found Birchwood's manner equally ridiculous at the moment. So did Eldridge, judging from the look of exasperation he wore. Of course, this might also be a result of Birchwood ignoring the hierarchy of their titles in his determination to greet Miss Carmichael first.

He took his time, too, releasing Miss Carmichael's hand. By the time he'd straightened, Eldridge and the Newtons looked slightly impatient.

Adrian indicated Eldridge. "The Duke of Eldridge."

"A pleasure," said the duke, sketching a short bow.

"And this is Mr. Owen Newton and his brother, Mr. Clive Newton. They're Viscount Stanton's sons."

"We're already well acquainted with the lady," Mr. Owen Newton said, surprising Adrian with the revelation and leaving his spine a bit tenser than it had been before. "We had the pleasure of being introduced at the Marsdale ball."

"The pleasure was all mine," Miss Carmichael said, the softness of her voice a compliment to the flush in her cheeks.

The effect made Adrian gnash his teeth until it

occurred to him that he probably looked as silly as Birchwood, whose glower likened him to an angry dog on a leash. Not the sort of appearance Adrian wished to reflect. So he took a moment to calm his breath and relax his fists, which he'd not even realized were clenched until that very second.

"I hope you'll forgive my curiosity," he said, deciding the time had come for him to broach his reason for interrupting the group's conversation, "but I couldn't help overhear the comment regarding murder and someone being interrogated by Bow Street. Might I ask to whom it refers?"

"That would be me," said Birchwood, his voice grim.

"I must agree with it sounding ridiculous," Adrian said, choosing to lend support in case it led to additional details. "What happened?"

"I was brought in for questioning in connection with Miss Irvine's murder." Birchwood's somber gaze held Adrian's. "Along with Julian Walker and the Marquess of Lundquist. It was...most unpleasant."

Adrian stared at him while trying to come to grips with this information. He'd always been notified of important goings on. Or at least his father had and the information had trickled down to Adrian.

Until he'd decided to slam the door shut on that world.

In the months since Papa's death, he'd remained fairly ignorant of what went on around Town. He'd been disinterested. More than that, he'd made a concerted effort to become the opposite of what Papa had expected him to be.

So he'd relaxed with Evie during the months that followed. They'd visited museums as autumn gave way to winter, enjoyed evenings out at the theatre, and made all kinds of plans for the future.

She'd loved the idea he'd had of buying a cottage near Brighton – a little retreat with a view of the water where they could stroll along the shore and go bathing.

The memory made his chest feel like it was carved from wood – a hollow space within which the beats of his leaden heart echoed. "What grounds did Bow Street have to interview you?"

Birchwood glanced at Miss Carmichael briefly before revealing, "The three of us were…well acquainted with the woman."

"I see no harm in that," Miss Carmichael said.

Adrian had to agree, unless Birchwood meant to imply something else – something he could not say with a lady present. The uncomfortable look on his face suggested this could be the case.

Choosing to hold his tongue for a moment, Adrian raised his eyebrow and hoped Birchwood might elaborate. To his surprise, it was Eldridge who said, "They enjoyed regular visits to Bush Park together."

"But…" Miss Carmichael sounded completely lost. "How does that signify when she was murdered at Vauxhall?"

"I'm sure the constables were just being thorough," Adrian said, his suspicions confirmed.

"It's a terrible tragedy," Owen Newton remarked, the swift interjection steering the conversation in a different direction. "No young lady deserves such a fate."

"Agreed," Clive Newton said. He looked at Miss Carmichael, his gaze increasingly serious. "I hope you'll be extra careful until this blackguard is caught."

"Of course." Miss Carmichael pursed her lips. "I've started taking a pistol with me wherever I go. For extra precaution."

"A wise decision," Eldridge said with approval.

"I doubt this madman would set his sights on you though," Owen Newton told her, his voice gentle as though intending to reassure. "From what I gather, he only targets immoral women."

"I disagree," Adrian said with a bite to his tone.

Silence followed for a brief second before Owen Newton thought to say, "I beg your pardon, Croft. He clearly made a mistake regarding your sister."

"An unforgivable tragedy," Eldridge muttered.

"Unquestionably so," Clive Newton said, though the words that followed were less sympathetic. "Perhaps this scoundrel's motivation is different from what we suspect."

"The note that was found with each of them could not make his reasoning clearer," Birchwood said. He sent Miss Carmichael an apologetic look. "Forgive me. This really isn't the sort of discussion we ought to be having in a lady's presence. Perhaps we should change the subject."

"Quite right," Clive Newton said. He stared at Adrian for a moment as if weighing whether or not to say more. Eventually his desire to do the right thing, however foolish, won out. "I beg your pardon, Mr. Croft, but all things considered, it might be prudent of you to steer clear of your female acquaintances for the present. Until this case is resolved."

"And why would that be?" Adrian asked, deciding to learn what was on the man's mind though he feared it might end with him grabbing the pup by the throat.

"It's only that you're reputed to be a dangerous man whose wealth was built through nefarious means." Much to his credit, Clive Newton kept his chin high even though the slight hitch of his voice revealed a lack of confidence that was further enhanced by the trembling of his hands.

Adrian narrowed his gaze on him. He had an unexpected amount of courage. "I think we can all agree most peers' wealth was acquired in much the same way at some point or other. But if you're suggesting what I think you are – that I might have slit those women's throats, including my sister's – I recommend you remove that notion from your thick skull at once."

"Or what?"

"Brother," Owen Newton warned.

Adrian leaned in. "Or I'll make your life hell."

"That's enough," Eldridge said with the sort of ducal authority most men knew to obey.

Adrian only did so because he could sense Miss Carmichael's increasing discomfort. He leaned back, his gaze locked with Clive Newton's. "Murder is a serious business. You ought to think twice before tossing out accusations."

"I'm sorry," Clive Newton exclaimed. He looked so young and perplexed it would have been easy to pity him had Adrian been a softer man. "This nasty situation makes me see danger wherever I look. I won't rest easy until the killer has been apprehended."

"Don't worry," Adrian said. "He'll make a mistake. And once he does, he will be caught."

"Let's hope so." Eldridge knocked back his drink and excused himself, then strode away, disappearing into the crowd.

Adrian's attention stayed on Clive Newton for one more second before shifting to Birchwood. "How did you prove your innocence?"

"I was sick on the night in question. My butler and the physician he called – Doctor Wentworth is his name – both attested to me being home in bed with a fever."

"What about Walker and Lundquist?"

Birchwood shoved one hand in his pocket. "I've no idea, but I suppose they must have had solid alibis too or else charges would have been pressed against them by now."

Provided neither man had bought his witnesses.

Adrian sent Birchwood a thoughtful look. At least Doctor Wentworth was known to be a man of good standing. He wasn't the sort who'd protect a possible murderer in exchange for a bribe.

"Thank you for the information," Adrian said. "If you'll please excuse us, I promised I'd help Miss Carmichael find a seat and have already kept her from it too long. Enjoy the rest of your evening."

"Please forgive me for stopping to speak with those gentlemen," Adrian said when they'd gone a few paces, "but I had to know more when I overhead the subject of their discussion."

"You need not apologize." Miss Carmichael sent him a warm smile. "I completely understand."

Satisfied with her response, Adrian steered her toward a sofa in the corner of the room and waited for her to take a seat before lowering himself to the spot beside her. "Better?"

"Very much so. Thank you." She toed off her slippers allowing only a brief glimpse of her stocking-clad feet before they disappeared beneath the hem of her skirt. Bashfulness stole across her face when her gaze caught his. "I hope you don't mind."

"Not if it eases your discomfort." A sharp burst of laughter caused him to glance across the room to where Birchwood still stood with the Newtons.

"Are you all right?" Miss Carmichael asked.

He glanced at her. With her cheeks flushed, a few of her locks in slight disarray and her too-tight slippers discarded for the moment, she conveyed a sense of normality that made her all the lovelier.

Adrian hesitated briefly before admitting, "I let Mr. Clive Newton rile me."

"Something tells me you think that a weakness." She tilted her head, studying him with curiosity.

"Only because it is." How many times had his father tested his ability to keep his emotions in check?

"A lesser man would have issued an invitation to Reed's – make sure he got the chance to punch him."

"To do so would serve no purpose other than proving myself to be everything he accused me of." He grimaced. "You're probably wondering if any of it is true."

The prudent decision right now would be for him to sever all ties with Miss Carmichael. Already, he'd caught himself thinking of her much more than what was wise. And tonight when he'd spotted her on the terrace, a lonely beauty gazing into the darkness, he'd gone to her with far too much enthusiasm.

Holding her in his arms while they danced had only worsened the heated effect she had upon him. This woman, with her humble beginnings and zest for life, was like a balm to his tortured soul. The innocence she embodied with her sweet smiles and slightly shy manner made him crave more. But could he trust her?

She was only mentioned briefly in Harlowe's file, which Adrian had read on his way back to London from Deerhaven. Nothing in there warned him to stay away from her, so he decided to let his instinct guide him. Especially since he genuinely liked her company and found her easy to talk to. The only other person he could say the same of was Edward.

Still he hesitated, torn between honesty and shielding her from the ugliness of his world. But as he gazed into her lovely blue eyes, his conscience compelled him to tell her the truth and to let her choose.

"My father was a ruthless man who did terrible things to gain power and fortune. When he died, I did what I could to distance myself from that world, but then my sister was murdered and stepping back became impossible."

Miss Carmichael's eyes widened, but she didn't retreat. "Why?"

"Because someone went to great lengths, convincing the murderer she should be his next victim."

"You're certain of this?"

Adrian nodded, then explained how the column describing Evie's indiscretions had come to be. "Someone is playing a brutal game. I've not yet discerned their motive, but I'm starting to suspect that I am the true target in all of this."

"Are you suggesting that someone engineered the murder of an innocent woman in order to somehow manipulate you?" Miss Carmichael asked, her voice filled with outrage.

"Yes." Anger and guilt twisted inside his chest.

A harsh emotion he'd not thought her capable of until now flickered in the depth of her gaze. "Then I hope you find the responsible party and make them pay."

The quiet fury with which she spoke surprised him. He'd thought her too gentle for rage to grip her, but there could be no denying the pure disgust she experienced in response to his words. All because of a woman she'd spoken to briefly on one occasion.

Her reaction warmed a forgotten place at the core of his very existence. She understood him. More than that, she felt exactly as he did. Hell, if he didn't know any better, he'd think she'd also like a go at whomever the bastard turned out to be.

Yet another thing they had in common, only this time it touched him on a visceral level. He shook his head, cautioned himself against becoming emotionally involved with her.

"I finished *Herakles*, by the way. It was excellent, despite the tragic ending. Don't you think?"

"Hmm?" Adrian blinked, his gaze refocusing on her until he realized they'd sat in silence for quite a long time. "Oh, yes. Tragic indeed."

"Forgive me," she said. "You looked as though you could use a change of topic, so I brought up the book, but I fear it may have made me seem insensitive."

"Not at all. I apologize. I'm just..." He shook his head. "This new information about Walker and Lundquist has me distracted. I need to figure out why the chief constable chose to release them."

"I understand," Miss Carmichael told him, her hand briefly touching his arm with soothing effect.

Adrian sighed. "Sorry. I never should have stopped to talk with Birchwood. It's made me terrible company."

"Considering all you have suffered, it is I who ought

to apologize for making you feel as though you need to be cheerful."

"You did no such thing. I'm simply preoccupied, that's all." He wished he could stay but knew his mind wouldn't find any peace until he dug deeper where Walker and Lundquist were concerned. "Would you mind if I were to take my leave?"

"Of course not."

Unwilling to leave her alone, Adrian extended his hand and helped her rise. He then guided her back to the ballroom and over to Mr. Harlowe, who was chatting with Baron Midhurst.

Adrian exchanged a few pleasantries with both men, then bowed over Miss Carmichael's hand. "Until we meet again."

The answering blush in her cheeks sent a thrill through his veins. Ignoring it, he turned and strode from the ballroom, continuing into the hallway beyond, not slowing his pace until he reached the front entrance.

Only then did he dare a backward glance in the direction of the woman who'd piqued his interest. No, it was more than that. In some confounded way, Miss Carmichael was coming dangerously close to doing what no other woman had managed before.

Her sensitive nature, the element of mystery she embodied, that adventurous streak she'd confided in him, and the fierce gleam of anger he'd spied in her eyes when he'd mentioned his theory pertaining to Evie's death, were a potent combination.

If he didn't take drastic measures, she'd sweep past his every defense and creep under his skin. After that, she'd surely conquer his heart and—

The arrival of his carriage scattered his musings, like crisp autumn leaves carried away on the wind. He climbed in and thumped the roof, then leaned his head against the window and stared at Moorland House as it slid from his view.

Once home, he handed his hat to Elks and tossed his gloves inside, then cut a path straight to his study. The file he sought on the Marquess of Lundquist was quickly located, but only one file was labeled Walker and it concerned Julian Walker's father instead of Julian Walker himself.

Adrian grabbed both files, strode to his desk, and set them down before taking a seat. He flipped the Lundquist file open and riffled through the stack of pages it contained. There were notes concerning bets the marquess had made, dating back to before he'd inherited his title, records of debts he owed, a secret duel he'd once engaged in, even a brief affair with another man's wife, and...

There.

The chief magistrate's name stood out next to Lundquist's. Second cousins, apparently, on Lundquist's mother's side. According to the detailed notes that followed, the marquess's father had taken an interest in the magistrate's son's schooling, paying the boy's tuition at Eton and Cambridge.

So the magistrate was indebted to Lundquist. But

what of Walker? Adrian gave his attention to the next file, only to be disappointed by the lack of information it provided. The only thing of note besides the rudimentary details was the mention of a shipping investment made by Julian Walker's father.

There was nothing beyond the basic information one would find in Debrett's. No link between the family and those with influence over the investigation. Nor a hint of the Walker family secrets.

Which meant they were either exceedingly righteous. Or cunning enough to somehow elude the Crofts.

In all likelihood, it was the former, but that would not be enough to absolve Julian Walker of guilt. After all, even virtuous families had been known to produce black sheep.

Adrian leaned back in his chair, his gaze fixed on the pages that littered his desk. A connection existed between these two men and Miss Irvine. Regardless of Kendrick's decision to let them walk free, Adrian meant to discover if there was more to it than the secret liaisons Birchwood had mentioned.

If one of them killed her, they'd also killed the previous victims, not to mention his sister. And since he didn't trust Bow Street, he'd have to uncover the truth himself.

He steepled his fingers. Miss Carmichael made a good point when she suggested he take a look at the first victim. Whoever the murderer was, their desire to kill had begun with her.

CHAPTER TWENTY-ONE

After consuming a hearty breakfast the following morning, Adrian took his carriage to Fairchild House, arriving there within ten minutes. He rapped sharply on the oak door.

It creaked open to reveal a stern-faced butler. "May I help you, sir?"

Adrian handed him his calling card and waited for him to note the name before saying, "I wish to speak with Mr. and Mrs. Fairchild on a matter of some urgency."

The butler opened the door wider so Adrian could enter. "Wait here while I see if they are at home."

Adrian crossed the threshold, his boots echoing on the cracked marble floor, and gazed at the portraits lining the walls. The Fairchilds looked like a proud family. Private, he'd learned this morning when he'd reviewed their file in preparation for the visit.

This won't be easy.

Dismissing the negative thought, he straightened his spine at the sound of the butler returning.

"Please have a seat in the parlor. Mr. Fairchild will join you shortly."

Adrian thanked him and entered the room immediately to the left of the foyer, coming to an abrupt halt on account of the bleakness he found there. Black crepe still dampened the light attempting to find its way through the windows, casting a shadow over the space. Nearly a year had passed since Miss Fairchild's death, yet the family showed no sign of moving on.

How could they?

His heart ached on account of their loss, which mirrored his own. Unlike them, however, he could not sit and wallow in misery, entombed in dreary despair. He had to move and he had to act. He had to seek justice. That was his process. Killing the bastard who'd cut his beloved sister's life short would help.

"Mr. Croft?"

Adrian turned in response to the gruff use of his name and met Mr. Fairchild's hard gaze. His wife, who'd apparently chosen to accompany him, clutched his arm. A frown puckered her brow.

"Your visit is most unexpected," Mr. Fairchild said stiffly.

"Why have you come?" Mrs. Fairchild asked. "You're not a friend or an acquaintance."

Adrian inclined his head. Had he been his father, he'd not have allowed the insult to slide.

Mr. Fairchild patted his wife's hand. "It's all right, my dear. I'm sure Mr. Croft has his reasons."

"I understand this will be difficult," Adrian said, wishing he were anywhere else and didn't have to do this. "As you may know, my sister was recently murdered."

"Our condolences for your loss," Mr. Fairchild murmured.

"Thank you. You have mine as well." Adrian took a deep breath and expelled it. "Given the nature of Evelyn's wounds, it's likely she was attacked by the same man who killed your daughter."

"I'll not be discussing Gwendolyn with a man of your reputation," Mrs. Fairchild said.

Aware of what these poor people had been through, Adrian chose to ignore the comment. "Any information you can provide will be helpful in bringing the killer to justice."

"We already spoke with the constable," Mr. Fairchild informed him.

"I understand, but—"

"There's nothing more to say," Mrs. Fairchild cried. She turned away, hiding her face and the tears she shed against her husband's shoulder.

"You may not think so," Adrian said, doing his best to infuse his voice with endless amounts of goodwill. "However, there might be a detail you failed to disclose – something you simply forgot in your moment of grief. If you could outline your daughter's final days it could offer valuable insight."

"As I've already said," Mr. Fairchild told him sternly, "we spoke with the constable."

"And where has that led you?" When Mr. Fairchild glared at him while trying to soothe his weeping wife, Adrian said, "The constable has failed in his duty toward you. I aim to succeed where he did not."

"No." Mrs. Fairchild shook her head. "We'll have no dealings with you."

"I'm only try—"

"My apologies, Mr. Croft," said Mr. Fairchild, "but I must agree with my wife."

The couple turned as one, their gazes fixed on the exit they meant him to use.

With nothing else to be gained, Adrian strode past the Fairchilds's sour expressions. He entered the foyer and stopped, surprised to find a young woman lurking near the front door. She looked to be no more than sixteen years old.

Adrian gave her a curt nod then glanced around, seeking the butler. Not finding him, he crossed to the hallway table where his hat and gloves waited.

The young woman rushed forward, beating him to the table. "Allow me."

She handed him his hat while casting a nervous glance toward the parlor where Mr. and Mrs. Fairchild remained.

"Thank you, Miss…?"

"Edwina Fairchild," she whispered. Her throat contracted as she swallowed, and then she was pressing his gloves into his hands along with a piece of paper.

Pleading eyes held his for the briefest of moments before she turned and darted upstairs. Adrian frowned, then lowered his gaze to the note she'd slipped him. He read the brief missive quickly, shoved it in his pocket, and left the house, putting his gloves on as he walked.

Tomorrow would hopefully lead to more answers regarding Miss Fairchild. For the present, however, he meant to learn more about Lundquist and Walker – information Kendrick was sure to possess.

He strode into Bow Street half an hour later, ignoring the curious glances of constables who knew his reputation all too well.

It took a while for the clerk to inform Kendrick of his presence and even longer for Kendrick to step from his office. When he finally did, his displeasure showed in his expression and the sharp clip of his heels against the tiled floor as he crossed to where Adrian stood.

"Mr. Croft." The chief constable's voice was curt, though not entirely impolite. "I never thought you'd come here of your own free will."

"Whyever not?" Adrian asked, refusing to let the likes of Kendrick make any presumptions about him. He smirked – noted how this seemed to increase Kendrick's annoyance – and told him, "I have a question regarding your murder investigation."

Kendrick clenched his jaw. "Any information I have on that matter is classified until the case is closed. If that is all, I a—"

"Why did you release Lundquist and Walker?"

"I have my reasons."

"And what are they, if you don't mind my asking."

"As a matter of fact, I do mind. You have no business knowing."

Adrian shifted his weight, bringing his mouth level with Kendrick's ear. "Your inability to track down the man who murdered my sister makes it my business. So indulge me, or I will see to it that a more agreeable man acquires your position."

Smiling, he leaned back and waited for Kendrick's response.

The constable shifted his gaze to one side, his mouth set in a stubborn line before he eventually shook his head and hissed out a breath. "Damn you, Croft. I had no choice. Walker has an alibi for the time of Miss Irvine's death, verified by multiple witnesses. He left Vauxhall at eight with a number of friends. As for Lundquist, the chief magistrate has personally vouched for his character."

"Lundquist's a lucky man," Adrian drawled, "to have a relation who's able to clear his name."

Only a quick twitch of the lips suggested Kendrick was taken aback by Adrian knowing there was a family tie between the two men. "He would have been let go regardless. There was nothing to justify holding him."

"A mistake on your part. Wouldn't you say?"

Kendrick's eyes flared with anger. "If that is all, I'd like to get back to work."

Adrian snorted and turned for the door. "Don't waste your time. I'll track down the killer myself."

He stalked from the station and headed home.

There, in his study, he found Edward waiting in one of the armchairs. A decanter of brandy and two glasses sat on Adrian's desk.

Edward turned in his seat at the sound of Adrian's entrance, concern etched on his face. "You look as though you could use a drink."

Adrian crossed the floor, filled both glasses, and sank into a chair with a weary sigh before sharing his recent findings with Edward.

"Walker had an alibi and the blasted chief magistrate vouched for Lundquist. Turns out they're related. Second cousins." He downed a measure of brandy and savored the burn as it slid down his throat.

Edward frowned. "Sounds like corruption to me."

"Indeed." Adrian shifted his glass so the light from the fireplace caught the cut crystal. "Miss Fairchild's sister slipped me a note this morning when I went to call on her parents. She wants me to meet her in Green Park tomorrow. Looks like she might be willing to help."

"Are you sure it's wise of you to be getting involved?" Edward tilted his head. "If I were to catch the bastard who did this, I'd have a hard time restraining myself. I'm sure the same goes for you, which makes me worry. You don't want to be the one ending up behind bars, Adrian."

"There's no need for concern. I'm only trying to piece everything together so I can point Kendrick in the right direction." A lie, but a necessary one.

"In that case, I hope Miss Fairchild's sister has

something useful to share." Edward's gaze hardened. "I want the killer to hang."

Adrian had no intention of letting him face a judge. A hanging would be too kind. But he didn't argue. Instead, he took another sip of his drink.

CHAPTER TWENTY-TWO

Heavy clouds heralding rain filled the sky the following morning when Adrian entered Green Park. He strode onto the nearest path and toward a bench where the lady he'd come to meet waited.

Dressed in a lilac pelisse, Miss Fairchild sat with an older woman – a maid, he presumed, whose purpose it was to chaperone her. As if sensing his approach, Miss Fairchild glanced his way and stood in order to greet him.

He tipped his hat. "Miss Fairchild. I wonder if you might be in the mood for a stroll."

"An excellent idea." She gestured for her maid to follow and fell into step beside him. "Thank you for coming to meet me."

He dropped a look in her direction. "I'm hoping you'll tell me something to help me track down your sister's killer. In which case, it is I who should thank you."

Miss Fairchild gave him a pained look, sniffed, and gulped down a breath before saying, "Gwendolyn's death came as a shock. I still expect her to walk through the door any moment."

"My sympathies." A pause allowed the words to bear weight. "Having lost my own sister to the same monster, I know the pain you've been forced to endure."

"My parents have placed their faith in the law, but it has been several months with additional murders and no hint of Bow Street stopping the killer. My hope is that you might do so instead, and if there's the slightest chance you'll meet with success, I'll happily lend my support. Provided of course that I may count upon your discretion regarding what I'm about to say."

"Of course," he promised. "You have my word."

"Very well." She drew a ragged breath. "What no one knows is that Gwendolyn was engaged in a secret romance with the Marquess of Lundquist at the time of her death. According to what she told me, he disapproved of her friends and demanded she end her associations with them. When she refused, he grew angry and jealous. I fear..."

"You fear Lundquist's jealousy led him to kill her?"

"That, and his need for control. He made it clear to her that she wasn't allowed to dance with anyone else – an impossible demand to make of any young lady without it raising suspicion. So she ignored it and accepted the repercussion."

"Which was?"

Miss Fairchild sent her gaze across the park. "He was rough with her the last time they met in private. She came home with bruises."

Adrian gritted his teeth as anger rolled through him. "I'm sorry."

"No more than I, Mr. Croft." She glanced at him through watery eyes. "I knew what had happened, but rather than tell our parents, I kept my sister's secret."

"If it eases your mind, I don't believe speaking up would have changed anything." Adrian set his hand against her arm in the hope of offering some small measure of comfort. "The man we seek selected women he believed to be without morals. Your sister's tryst with Lundquist must have caused him to think of her in such terms, in which case accusing Lundquist of violent behavior would not have served any purpose, besides ruining her reputation. It wouldn't have changed the killer's opinion of her."

"The killer being Lundquist." A remark intended to make him commit to her line of thinking.

He refused to do so. "Possibly."

"Mr. Croft." Her voice was raw with emotion. "Gwendolyn was the first victim. Given the fact that Lundquist was the only man who could have known she wasn't as innocent as she appeared, it stands to good reason that he took her life before setting his sights on additional women."

"You're certain she met with no other men?"

"I know how this sounds, but my sister was good and kind. She wasn't a…a whore."

"Of course not."

They walked a few more paces before Miss Fairchild drew to a halt and faced him. She raised her chin. "I know it's him. I can feel it in my bones."

Hardly enough to condemn the man. Not without knowing more. He released her arm and took a step back. "You've been most helpful, Miss Fairchild."

"I trust you'll make sure he pays?"

"I'll do my best to see justice served," Adrian promised. He bid her farewell and departed, his intention to stop by Lundquist House next. The time had come for him to confront the marquess and, he hoped, acquire additional insight. One way or another, he would find the answers he sought.

A slow drizzle started as he turned onto Piccadilly. It dampened the air and beaded on Adrian's jacket. As he strode, he turned up his collar to protect the back of his neck. Had Lundquist House been farther away he'd have ordered a hackney, but it seemed ridiculous when the walk could be accomplished in less than ten minutes.

Although a wet sheen had already settled on all visible surfaces by the time he turned onto Clarges Street, the area still bustled with activity.

It wasn't unusual. Londoners were accustomed to stepping out in drearier weather than this.

When he'd gone another five yards, a soft prick of

heightened awareness settled against the nape of his neck, stirring the hair at the base of his skull. It was a feeling Adrian was all too familiar with - one he'd experienced numerous times before and knew to heed.

It urged him to send a swift glance over his shoulder. Which was all it took for him to note the two men who stood out. Not because they looked different from any other working-class men milling about, but because of the dogged gleam in their eyes.

These were hounds on the hunt, probably possessing more muscle than brains and carrying blades they'd want to show off.

What he had no idea of was who might have sent them after him or what they might want.

He flattened his mouth and fisted his hands. Lundquist was his priority. He didn't have time for pesky thugs. Then again, he did want to know who they worked for and what they meant to accomplish.

With a curse, he turned at the next intersection and slipped into the first alley he found. It was littered with discarded crates and refuse that must have been dumped there several weeks prior if the stench was any indication. Not even the rain could wash it away.

Grimacing, he pressed his back against the wall, then waited for the men to appear.

They did so soon enough. The tallest of the pair - a stocky fellow with a round face that showcased a bulbous nose – arrived first. His companion's features were slightly more angular, the sharp red line slashing his cheek a souvenir from a previous fight.

Adrian grabbed them both by the scruff of their necks and shoved them against the filthy brick wall. It only worked because he'd taken them by surprise. Once they gathered their wits, he'd lose the advantage. A few seconds was all it would take. If that.

"What do you want?" he snarled, his fingers digging against their grimy cravats. Water droplets settled upon his face, dampening his skin as the drizzle worsened.

Chubbycheeks grinned, revealing an incomplete set of stained teeth. "Ye'll see soon enough."

Adrian wasn't allowed time to ponder his meaning before Scarface slammed his forehead straight into Adrian's.

The impact sent his hat tumbling and made his teeth rattle. Thankfully, instinct born from experience and endless hours of training with Murry enabled a swift and instinctive response.

Fists curling more firmly around the cravats, he dropped to a crouch. The action forced both men off balance and sent them stumbling. Aided by the momentum, Adrian swung himself forward between them while releasing his hold in the process.

He swiveled around as he started to rise, moving fast while doing his best to block out the pain in his head. Once upright, he launched himself at the nearest assailant, thrusting his fist into Chubbycheeks's jaw before he'd regained his footing.

A grunt accompanied the crunch of bone, the force of the blow knocking Chubbycheeks back while blood-stained spittle flew through the dank air. But the time it had taken to complete the strike allowed Scarface to land a punch to Adrian's gut, knocking the air from his lungs.

Despite the force, he remained on his feet, but barely managed to gulp down a breath before both men advanced together. He flexed his fingers in anticipation of their next move. It came soon enough, though not as quickly as he might have feared. The thugs lacked swiftness and finesse, which made it possible for him to dodge their attacks and block their blows as long as he kept his wits about him.

"Damned toff," Chubbycheeks growled when Adrian nimbly avoided a punch to the sternum while countering with a hard blow to the man's shoulder.

"You'd be wise to know who you're after," Adrian told him, his knuckles cracking as they found Scarface's nose. "I've more in common with Wycliffe than with the Prince Regent."

It occurred to him too late that engaging in chatter was foolish. Doing so broke his concentration and slowed his movements just enough to let Chubbycheeks smash his knuckles against the edge of Adrian's eye-socket.

The pain was instant – a sharp sting and a fierce ache that told him the skin had been split. He rounded on his attacker with carefully controlled rage, sending an upward jab into his chin with so much force, it felled him.

"What the hell?" Scarface muttered when Chubbycheeks landed against the wet ground, a groan the only indication he wasn't dead.

Adrian didn't bother explaining how timing, twisting the hips, or coming in at just the right angle could knock someone out. Instead, he took advantage of his remaining opponent's dismay and repeated the strike.

It would take a moment for the men to regain their bearings. Adrian stared at them and wondered once more who they worked for. He needed that answer.

Dropping into a crouch, he searched their pockets, retrieving a few bits and bobs before finding the blades he'd been certain they carried. They hadn't attempted to use them though, which surely meant they'd not meant him any serious harm.

Water dripped from his hair and onto his brow. Swiping the heel of his hand against the edge of his right eye, he wiped away the blood that pooled there before it could trickle over his cheek. It had been a while since he'd taken this kind of beating, the stale taste it left in his mouth prompting him to spit on the ground.

He rubbed his nose and grabbed the blades, positioning them so the tips touched the underside of each man's jaw.

Chubbycheeks came around first, eyes widening with alarm when he realized he might soon get skewered. He sucked in a breath and stared up into Adrian's face with what looked like deep resentment, anger, and fear.

"I'll ask you again. What do you want?" When Chubbycheeks didn't respond, opting instead for a glare, Adrian pressed the tip of the blade more firmly against him. A drop of crimson gathered around it. "Keep in mind, I'll not ask again."

"Your files." Scarface, who'd regained consciousness too, hissed the words. "We was to get them from ye."

"And you thought attacking me would be the best way to do so?"

"Better than breaking in and searching the house in an effort to steal them. Complicated that, what with yer servants and such. Simpler takin' ye hostage and askin' fer them in exchange."

The man did have a point. "Who hired you?"

"Can't say."

Dissatisfied with the answer, Adrian pierced Scarface's skin as well.

"We don't know," Chubbycheeks croaked when Scarface winced in pain. He blinked against the raindrops. "Never saw 'is face. He wore a hooded cloak when 'e approached us two nights ago. Was at the Mad Bull."

Adrian knew of the place—a tavern in the east end. It was known for hosting bare-knuckle boxing matches and dog fights. He tilted his head. "How were you to deliver the files to this man if you don't even know what he looks like or where to find him?"

"Said 'e'd find us."

"If you're lying…" He watched the tips of both

blades disappear beneath flesh. The resulting blood stained the edge of their white cravats.

"We're…not," Chubbycheeks rasped. "Swear it."

There was nothing more to be learned then, besides the fact that someone was after his files.

Rain began falling in earnest while he considered his next course of action. It smeared the dirt in the alley and made him long for a bath. First, he had to decide on what to do with his attackers.

Common sense told him he'd be a fool if he let them go. He ought to slit their throats to make sure they'd never confront him again. His fingers tightened around each blade's wooden handle. It would be quick and easy. Most importantly, it would help prevent future threats.

Body tense, he flexed his muscles while rain danced over his head. A strenuous sigh worked its way up his throat before he eventually pulled the blades back and stood.

He couldn't do it. Not this time.

While Evie's murder might stop him from severing ties with the life he hated, it need not stop him from trying to do better. There was a choice here between killing these men and letting them go, and although he feared he might later regret his decision, he didn't want more blood on his hands.

Not when it could be avoided.

"Get up. Both of you."

The men scrambled to their feet, coughing and sputtering while clutching their throats.

"Be warned," Adrian told them between gritted teeth. "If you ever attempt to cross me again, it will be the last thing you do before you die. Now get out of here. Before I decide to kill you anyway."

Swaying slightly on unsteady feet, they glanced at the knives in Adrian's hands. For one absurd moment it looked like they might be stupid enough to ask if he'd give them back. But then Chubbycheeks gave an unhappy snort, swinging around and presenting his back as he staggered out of the alley.

Scarface followed without further comment.

Adrian shoved both knives into his coat pocket and went to fetch his hat. After returning it to his head he retrieved a handkerchief which he used to wipe his face. As expected, it came away bloody.

Eager to return home so he could tend to his wounds and freshen up, he set his course for Portman Square. Lundquist House would have to wait for another day. Turning up like this, like some sort of madman, would hardly be conducive.

Instead, he needed to clean up and gather his thoughts before he continued his investigation. The soles of his shoes clicked along the wet pavement, splashing water from occasional puddles.

Today's altercation revealed he had yet another foe to contend with.

A coincidence?

He couldn't be sure.

Perhaps he was looking at separate cases. There was no doubt in his mind that nearly every man of consequence in the country would feel threatened by all the information contained in those files. Information that could be used against them for all sorts of gain.

Maybe the real question was how many of them knew the files existed?

He burst through the front door of Croft House ten minutes later. "Murry!"

His valet arrived at a run, eyes widening when he saw Adrian's bruised face. "What's happened?"

"I'll explain later," Adrian said. "First, I need you to help me move the files so they're harder to find. Summon the rest of the staff after that. I want the house on high alert until further notice."

"Of course." Murry's face tightened with concern, but he gave a brisk nod. "Right away."

Adrian's mind raced as he and Murry transferred the files to a secret storage room located behind the book case in the upstairs drawing room. His father had been the last one to use them as leverage and he'd been dead for six months. So why the sudden interest?

When the question continued to plague him, he put it to Murry. The valet closed the book case and regarded Adrian with steady consideration.

"Does anyone know of your effort to hunt down your sister's killer?"

Adrian stared at him. He'd not been discreet. Anyone who bothered paying attention to what went on would know he was trying to do so. "You think the murderer fears the files could aid in his capture? Because of the information they contain?"

"It's just a guess."

"A correct one, perhaps."

"Or perhaps not." Murry shrugged. "Those files have been used against a lot of people over the years. It's possible one of them simply decided now was the time to try and grab them."

"If that's the case, I hope the individual has learned I'm not to be trifled with."

But if the other possibility were true and it was the killer, Adrian prayed he'd make another attempt so he could catch him once and for all.

CHAPTER TWENTY-THREE

Samantha arrived at the Midhurst musicale together with Melody and Lady Heathbrooke, with whom she'd enjoyed a lovely dinner prior to the engagement. Harlowe, who'd had a business meeting to attend to, would meet them there.

She swept the room with her gaze, searching for him until she realized he'd yet to put in an appearance. Instead she spotted the Earl of Marsdale, who stood in conversation with the odious Duke of Wrengate. The Ottersburgs and Glendales were also present, along with several other peers, including the Duke of Eldridge and Viscount Birchwood.

A cluster of younger men, from whom she recognized only the Newton brothers, were having what looked like some sort of debate, judging from their vigorous gestures.

The debutantes were gathered in a separate corner,

whispering and tittering in a manner Samantha found highly annoying. All while sending coy smiles toward the young men.

"Thank goodness we're not like them," Samantha told Melody under her breath.

"What's that?" asked Lady Heathbrooke.

Samantha sent the dowager marchioness a dazzling smile. "It seems we're in excellent company this evening, my lady."

The dowager marchioness snorted and swept past Samantha, cutting a path directly toward a couple of women of similar age with whom she immediately struck up a conversation.

"I must confess, I sometimes wish I were able to be just a little like them," Melody murmured. She nodded toward the debutantes. "Or at the very least able to enjoy the excitement of courtship, with marriage and a family of my own still waiting upon the horizon."

Samantha glanced at her in surprise. "I'm sorry. I never realized you might have such longings."

Wishing for such things had never occurred to Samantha. She'd only ever focused on what she knew her life would be, instead of dreaming of something that couldn't be hers. Seemed rather pointless really, if not a direct path to unhappiness.

"I try to keep these dreams buried," Melody said. "But I do wonder what it might have been like to gain a suitor's attention, to plan for a future with him and… Forget it. I'm being terribly silly."

Samantha placed her hand on Melody's arm. "You

could still have those things if you truly wished it."

An unhappy smile caught Melody's lips. "How? None of the gentlemen of my acquaintance will have a tradesman's by-blow, and I cannot imagine tying myself to the sort of man who would."

"I'm sorry."

"Don't be. I'm better off with Lady Heathbrooke. Everything else is just fanciful nonsense. I beg you not to spare it another thought." Melody turned and her eyes brightened. "How marvelous. Violet Greene and Octavia Burley are also in attendance. Come, I'll introduce you to them."

Samantha prepared to follow her friend but paused when the Earl of Marsdale stepped to one side and a dark, familiar gaze met hers. A slow smile followed as Mr. Croft acknowledged her presence. She took a slow breath, accepted her stomach's fluttery response even as she explained it away as the thrill of the hunt.

He was here. She'd known he would be, but Melody had distracted her with her comment and… She caught Melody's hand. "You go ahead. There's someone I need to greet first."

Melody turned her head, her line of sight aligning with Samantha's. "I'd want to greet him too if he looked at me that way."

"And what way would that be?" Samantha asked, her heart skipping a beat.

"As though he'd like to whisk you away to a private corner somewhere and kiss you senseless," Melody whispered.

"Hush," Samantha chastised, but it was too late. Heat was already consuming her face. She knew she was blushing profusely despite her effort to keep her mind sharp and focused – on everything she disliked about Mr. Croft.

Melody gave her a pointed look before walking away with a chuckle. Samantha took a deep breath and told herself not to worry. Blushing was a good thing. It would help her look less of a threat while also suggesting an interest in Croft – an interest she needed for him to reciprocate since it would aid in her plan.

Cultivating a bit of romance was paramount to the next step.

But she mustn't rush things.

She started forward, moving through the crowd with only one goal in mind. Him. He watched her with bold overtness, his gaze heating with each step she took. Samantha's stomach tightened. The air around her crackled. An almost feverish feeling washed over her skin. She told herself the reaction was normal – an inevitable part of the act.

And then she reached him.

"Miss Carmichael," Mr. Croft murmured, the low hum of his voice making something distinct yet foreign vibrate inside her. Holding her gaze, he took her gloved hand in his and placed a kiss upon her knuckles. "It's lovely to see you again. I believe you must be acquainted with my friend, the Earl of Marsdale, since you were at the ball he hosted."

Samantha withdrew her hand from Croft's, annoyed

with herself for missing the warmth of his touch, and faced the earl. "It's a pleasure to see you again, my lord."

"Indeed, the pleasure is entirely mine," Marsdale said, a boyish smile contrasting the somber look in his eyes. "Croft has spoken of you at great length. It would seem you've made quite the impression on him."

There was no need for Samantha to feign the smile that followed. It was real and full of appreciation, to say nothing of eager excitement. If Croft had mentioned her to his friend, then surely that meant he had more than a passing interest in her.

For the sake of her mission, she prayed this was true.

As far as her own wants and desires went, she dared not consider why Marsdale's comment had filled her with so much pleasure.

"A positive one, I hope," Samantha said, infusing her voice with amusement.

Marsdale laughed while Croft merely offered the sort of slow smile that reminded her of a cat who'd just spotted its prey. He dipped his head. "The best, Miss Carmichael, I can assure you."

Sensing an opportunity to strengthen their bond, Samantha gave her attention to Marsdale. "Your friend and I had a wonderful time together at the Moorland ball recently. We danced and when I complained of my feet aching afterward, he sought out a spot for me to rest. He's very considerate."

"Seems like he made quite the impression on you as well then," Marsdale said with a touch of mischief.

"Without question." She sent Croft a subtle smile and added softly, "I enjoy his company immensely."

"You do me great honor, Miss Carmichael." Croft gestured to someone behind her, and a footman quickly appeared with a tray filled with glasses of bubbly champagne.

Samantha took one and sipped the fizzy drink before leaning closer to Croft so she could discreetly ask, "What happened to the corner of your eye? That's quite the cut you've sustained."

"A minor accident with a low hanging beam," he told her, his eyes twinkling even as his jaw tightened. "It's nothing, though I appreciate your concern."

"Of course." A slow heat curled its way through her like smoke. She didn't believe him for a second. A man of his caliber wouldn't let such a foolish thing happen. The lingering signs of a bruise on his cheek would suggest he'd engaged in a fight.

With whom? she wondered. When they'd last spoken, he'd been preoccupied with his sister's murder. Given the wound and the bruises' appearance, they'd been dealt shortly after. Could it be that he'd gone to confront a suspect?

"It might be prudent of us to start taking our seats," Marsdale said, scattering Samantha's thoughts. "They're already filling. In a few more minutes we'll be stuck with what's left."

"Come," said Croft. He grabbed Samantha's hand and pulled her behind him, straight toward the fourth row where three vacant chairs remained. A young man was just preparing to occupy one when he glanced their way. His eyebrows rose and then his face paled as Croft jerked his head to one side.

The young man retreated and Croft directed Samantha to the farthest chair. He took the next one, positioning himself between her and Marsdale. It wasn't until she was comfortably seated that Croft's high-handedness registered with her. He'd not asked if she wished to sit with him. He'd made it so by grabbing her hand and shooing that young man away.

She frowned at the seat back in front of her. She'd never doubted that Croft was the sort of man who made the rules intended for others to follow – that he enjoyed taking charge and getting his way. This trait was well described in the file she'd gathered on him and made perfect sense when considering all that he was suspected of.

But how did she feel about it?

As someone who'd always balked at being ordered about or of having her thoughts on a matter dismissed, she couldn't deny her simmering anger. Briefly, she thought of addressing the matter, then promptly changed her mind. It wasn't her job to argue with him but rather to entice him.

Butting heads would hardly accomplish that. And besides, she reminded herself, his possessiveness did prove that things were heading in the correct direction. She ought to be pleased, not put out.

A smile surfaced.

Leaning toward him she aimed for a note of sweetness while asking, "What does a man such as yourself enjoy doing when he's not otherwise busy reading Greek plays, engaging in boxing matches, or attending social events?"

"Target shooting is a favorite pastime of mine."

Her annoyance with him from seconds ago vanished. "What's your best distance?"

"Fifty-five yards."

Hers was sixty.

"Impressive."

"And much like you," he added, his voice so low she could barely hear him, "I also enjoy riding astride while wearing breeches."

She actually snorted with genuine humor. "How unfair of you to use the confidence I shared with you against me."

"You mistake me, Miss Carmichael. I have nothing but the greatest admiration for you, I assure you. Most young ladies would shy away from something so daring."

"It's easier, sturdier, and consequently a great deal safer in my opinion."

"You're likely correct. Sidesaddles have always struck me as rather precarious contraptions."

She agreed and told him as much right before Marsdale drew his attention. The two men spoke for a couple of minutes before Croft addressed her again.

"Tell me about the rest of your interests. Perhaps we'll discover more that we have in common."

"I enjoy shopping, especially at some of the markets

where all manner of curious items can be purchased. Archery and swimming are both favorite hobbies of mine when the weather allows. In winter, I eagerly wait for the lake to freeze over so I can go skating."

"It seems you're the active sort," Croft said, his voice thoughtful.

You have no idea.

"Very much so." She flattened her mouth. "I'm horrendous at most of the things young ladies ought to excel at."

He studied her for a moment, his gaze briefly finding her mouth before sliding away. "I suspect that's because you've no interest in them."

It was her turn to study him, this man she was meant to destroy. In some ways, it felt like he saw her better than anyone else ever had.

She cast that thought aside and touched his arm before telling him conspiratorially, "I often wish I'd been born a boy, able to hunt, spit, curse, and get foxed. Such things are surely more fun than needlepoint, watercolors, and learning how to put together a menu."

He flexed beneath her hand, a slight movement that drew her awareness to his muscled physique. Adrian Croft was a powerful man and she was merely an inch away, close enough to lean in and kiss him.

Or slash his throat if she chose.

CHAPTER TWENTY-FOUR

Adrian shifted in his seat. Miss Carmichael's touch threatened to sear him. It felt like a branding of sorts – a potent sensation he wanted both to harness and flee. This past week, since he'd last seen her, he'd wondered if the connection he'd felt with her had been imagined. A fabrication of his overactive mind.

He now knew it wasn't.

The effect she had upon him, the need she instilled for something more crucial between them, had only grown stronger.

Of course, it also helped that Murry had found nothing else to report about her. Had there been a scandal attached to her name, he would have discovered it. As for the file his father had gathered on Harlowe, the information there gave no cause for concern either. According to the notes, he was a private man who'd mostly kept to himself since returning from the travels he'd undertaken during his youth.

He'd married late – or later than what was the norm – being already into his fortieth year when he'd spoken his vows. Now, at almost five and sixty years of age, he maintained his duty toward the women he and his wife had chosen to foster.

Adrian had been correct to take an instant liking to him. He was an honorable sort who'd probably make a good friend and ally.

As for Miss Carmichael…

"I can't say I'm in favor of women behaving like heathens. Besides, getting foxed is extremely unpleasant. I doubt you'd enjoy it."

"It's the idea of it that's enticing, I think. Hypothetically speaking. I mean, how would you feel if you were allowed to engage only in feminine pursuits like painting, embroidery, reading, and playing an instrument? If you were forbidden from going anywhere alone, from attending university, from smoking or arguing a case in Parliament?"

He was honestly dismayed by her suggestion. It went against everything a properly bred Englishwoman stood for. And while he might be prepared to make a few concessions, like supporting that she ride astride, he could not imagine involving himself with a woman who wanted to cast aside all things feminine in favor of living like…well…a man.

"Are these things you wish to do?" It was possible he'd misjudged her.

"No." The honesty he saw in her eyes put him at ease. "But the not being allowed to do them frustrates me to no end."

He saw her point and he understood her. More than that, he found he agreed.

The first few notes of Mozart alerted him to the concert's commencement. All other chatter ceased and he turned to face the musicians. But even as he watched the violinist, cellist, and pianist gracefully embark upon a lyrical journey, his awareness remained on the lady beside him.

The warmth she exuded, her fragrance – a sweet floral scent so subtle he wanted to lean a bit closer in order to better examine the heady perfume – had a wonderfully calming effect. In truth, she as a whole was a soothing distraction from all of his grief, anger, and hellish existence.

He'd looked forward to seeing her, he realized, for this very reason. Like an opium addict longing for his next trip into oblivion.

It helped that she'd known Evie, if only briefly. "It pains me to know that she's no longer with us," she'd said.

The comment provided him with more comfort than the hollow "I'm so sorry" and "My condolences" he'd received from nearly everyone else.

Because of the careful attention he paid her while notes rose and fell all around them, quieting to a near whisper before climbing to an emotive crescendo, he knew when she straightened and when she leaned forward. The distance between them was so very small. An inch perhaps? It would take so little for him to close it.

His stomach tightened as heat enveloped his body. How had it come to this?

He could not say. No other woman had ever held his interest this way, drawing him to her, instilling in him a need for discovery and conquest.

Everything he'd learned of the world compelled him to fight the temptation, to keep a level head, his wits about him. So he took a shallow breath and glanced to his right, past Marsdale, and away from Miss Carmichael.

His ribs instantly curled their way inward, both hands balling into tight fists when he spotted Lundquist, who sat beside his sister, Lady Lavinia. Adrian had gone to their home twice more this past week, intent on confronting the marquess once and for all, only to be told he'd gone out.

He could think of only one reason why he'd not noticed his presence here yet. His attention had been on Miss Carmichael. Not on the man who'd beaten Miss Fairchild.

Muscles straining against too tight skin, he clenched his teeth until his jaw ached. The marquess sat just two seats over, a look of pleasure upon his face as he listened to the music.

Adrian heard nothing besides a relentless pounding in his own ears. This man, so well connected the bloody chief magistrate let him go, was having a wonderful evening while the woman he had abused rotted away in her grave. A grave he might have put her in.

In which case he would have done the same to Evie.

Throat dry and with each new breath coming harder than the last, Adrian stared through the haze of anger that clouded his vision. He knew he was being irrational. Hadn't he thought the same of Miss Edwina Fairchild when she'd insisted on Lundquist being the killer? There was no proof. Not yet, at least.

Going after a marquess without it would be complete madness.

But letting him get away with murder if he were guilty would be unforgiveable.

Someone touched his arm. He registered words but didn't know who'd spoken.

And then Lundquist turned, his gaze going straight to where Adrian sat. A smile followed and the next thing Adrian knew, his hands were at the bastard's throat.

Confusion widened the marquess's eyes. Horror followed as Adrian pushed his thumbs harder against his windpipe. Shouts erupted and chaos descended but Adrian paid it no mind. He had the marquess in his grasp, and he'd make damn sure he paid for what he had done.

Hands grabbed his arms and attempted to pull him away, forcing him to loosen his hold. He swung his arm back, catching the person with a hard jab. A curse echoed in Adrian's ears as he latched onto Lundquist's lapels and hauled him out of his seat.

He was vaguely aware of Lady Lavinia's voice beseeching him to release her brother. For one fleeting second, Adrian thought of revealing he'd seen her enjoying herself a little too much with Mr. Julian Walker a few weeks prior. Not exactly the proper behavior one might expect from a woman being courted by the Earl of Redgrave. But hurting her just to get at her brother wasn't Adrian's style.

Besides, Lundquist's eyes were already wide with shock, forcing a satisfied smirk to Adrian's lips. He wanted the man to suffer for what he'd done to Miss Fairchild. And if he'd had a hand in her murder. If he'd killed Evie, Lady Camille, and Miss Irvine, he'd bloody well put him in the ground.

"What's wrong with you," the marquess sputtered. "Release me this instant."

Adrian's hands refused to loosen their grip. He leaned in closer, disgust scraping his throat as he whispered, "I know what you did to Miss Fairchild."

The marquess paled. He shook his head. "I barely knew her."

"Liar."

"That's enough," a man's harsh voice insisted.

Disagreeing, Adrian pulled his fist back with every intention of rearranging Lundquist's teeth. Even if he weren't guilty of murder, he'd struck a woman so hard she'd had bruises. For that alone, he needed to pay. But strong hands caught him, restricting the movement and pulling him backward.

Adrian struggled to free himself from the unwelcome grasp. "Let go of me, damn you."

"Stop," a familiar voice spoke next to his ear. Edward. "This isn't to your advantage."

"Go to hell," Adrian spat, rounding on his friend in blind fury. All he saw now was betrayal – the person who'd helped deny him his vengeance. Because it wasn't really Lundquist he had been facing, but rather his father.

Even now, as reality rushed in around him, his hands shook as fiercely as they had done two decades prior, when he'd seen the bruises upon Mama's face and realized what had occurred.

Papa had taken him to London after that. The next time he'd seen his mother was right after Evie's birth, at which point she'd been dead.

"Let's separate these men a little." Adrian recognized Eldridge's ducal tone.

"This is outrageous," a woman could be heard saying.

Another agreed. "He's ruined the evening completely."

Adrian tried to shrug off the men who restrained him, but it was to no avail. There were too many now. All, it would seem, intent on preventing the fight he longed to engage in.

"Bloody animal," Lundquist snarled while doing his best to straighten his jacket. He glared at Adrian with contempt. "I want him arrested. Do you hear?"

"I'd rather you issue a challenge," Adrian said, his voice dangerously low, brimming with menace.

"Someone call the chief constable," Lundquist insisted.

Several men leapt into motion, only to halt at the sound of Miss Carmichael's voice. "Gentlemen. Marquess. Let's be rational for a moment. If you please."

"Rational?" Lundquist gaped at Miss Carmichael for a brief moment and suddenly laughed before pointing a rigid finger at Adrian. "He just assaulted me."

"Mr. Croft's sister was recently murdered, my lord." Miss Carmichael's voice was firm. "It's normal for him to look for her killer in every man he meets. Can we not try to sympathize with him a little?"

Uncertain glances flittered around the room as though seeking a place to land. Adrian straightened, his rage fading enough for him to stay still. The hold on his arms and shoulders lessened. He fixed his gaze on Miss Carmichael, anchoring himself to her until the last of the storm had passed.

Only then did he look at the marquess once more. "I am not the one in the wrong here, Lundquist. In fact, I believe there's a good chance you were the last one to see Miss Fairchild alive."

A series of horrified gasps underscored the severity of what Adrian suggested.

Lundquist's brow dipped. When he spoke next, his voice was quiet. "You think I killed her."

Not necessarily, but it was a possibility Adrian had

to examine more closely. "You were romancing Miss Fairchild before she died," he stated, the flicker of apprehension in Lundquist's eyes spurring him on. "But you were jealous. You wanted her all to yourself and forced her to cut ties with anyone you deemed a threat. When she refused, you became so incensed that you—"

"No." The sharp word echoed through the still room, so loud it took several seconds for it to fade. Lundquist stood, anger etched in every strained line of his face as he stepped up to Adrian. He leaned a bit closer, just enough to whisper in his ear. "Have a care, Croft. Her parents are here."

"I imagine they'd want the truth too."

"Not the kind you're about to uncover." A pause followed and then Lundquist stepped back, a meaningful look in his eyes. "Miss Carmichael is correct. You deserve compassion after all you've been through, especially since you've not taken the time to mourn. I suggest you do so now. Take a sojourn from Society until you're more yourself."

"The marquess is more forgiving than I would have been," Eldridge remarked when Adrian hesitated. "You should take his advice, Croft."

He was being put in his place. Boxed in. By the very man he'd begun to believe might be guilty.

Unless he wasn't. The shock and confusion with which the marquess responded did not fit a man who'd done as Adrian alleged.

Maybe in his rage, his need to find a target upon which to pin his grief and vanquish his childhood demons, he'd leapt to conclusions, creating connections that didn't exist for the sole purpose of satisfying his own bloodlust.

Adrian stared at Lundquist and as he did so, he became increasingly conscious of his decelerating heartbeats. His breaths slowed, the tension in his shoulders abated, and he gradually unclasped his fists.

This wasn't the kind of justice Evie deserved. There were still too many questions in need of answers. The irrefutable evidence required to send a man to the gallows on murder charges was lacking.

He gave a curt nod of agreement. Stepping back, taking a moment to gather his thoughts was indeed wise. Behaving like a lunatic would only ensure that the rest of the world viewed him as such. It would hamper his investigation, perhaps even make the killer more careful when this was the last thing Adrian wanted.

Shit.

He'd lost control and in doing so he'd revealed too much.

"Forgive me." Without uttering anything else, he strode for the door, not pausing until he'd reached it. Only then did he dare to glance back, just in time to catch Mr. Owen Newton escorting Miss Carmichael back to her chair.

The chatter started to ease, though several scolding gazes remained upon him. Lundquist spoke to his sister, who sent Adrian an uneasy look before glancing away. Low talking could still be heard despite the bustle of people returning to their respective seats. Someone coughed and all remaining sound dispersed.

The music resumed, dragging attention toward the front of the room, and it was as if Adrian hadn't been there at all.

He turned from the scene and went to find his carriage. Time to get the hell out of here before he did something truly stupid, like whisk Miss Carmichael away with him.

CHAPTER TWENTY-FIVE

"What in blazes were you thinking?" Harlowe demanded as he and Samantha were on their way home from the Midhursts' house. He scowled at her from the opposite side of the carriage. "We could have accomplished our goal this evening and gotten Croft behind bars. Hell, he did the work for you when he attacked Lundquist. It was perfect. Until *you* chose to defend him. Makes me wonder if you might have started believing the role you're playing – convinced yourself you're actually falling for him."

Samantha bristled. "I could never care for a man who encourages women to pay back the debts they owe him by whoring themselves."

But she could care for one who would hunt down his sister's murderer and make sure he paid for his crime, who'd quietly left a single rose of remembrance, and whose loss was felt in every fiber of his being.

She tried not to think too long or hard on that point and where it might lead, while holding Harlowe's gaze. "Had I not interfered, Lundquist might have done as you suggest. Mr. Croft could very well have been arrested on grounds of assault. But it would have been a brief arrest, not the sort that would keep him locked away for good or possibly hanged."

It took some effort to fight the tremor that threatened to jolt her entire being as she envisioned a rope being tied around Croft's neck. He did not matter. He could not matter. This was her job – what she had been trained to do. There could be no room for doubt or personal attachment.

"Kendrick was clear," she added. "He wants Mr. Croft gone for good, one way or the other. That means we'll need more than him grabbing a man by the lapels and throwing insinuations at him."

"You're right," Harlowe said, his voice thoughtful. "With the sort of barrister Mr. Croft has at his service, he'd be home again within hours."

Relief settled firmly between her shoulder blades. Harlowe understood. She would not have to make any further excuses. A soft exhalation soothed her tense muscles and let her relax. "Trust me in this. I know what I'm doing. Gaining Mr. Croft's confidence gradually is the best way forward – the surest way for me to establish a close relationship with him."

"The ball we're hosting was meant to help with that, but after what happened tonight, Mr. Croft is unlikely to attend."

Samantha knew he was right. "I realize this might look like a setback, but maybe we can use it to our advantage."

"What are you suggesting?"

"We invite Mr. Croft to join us for luncheon instead." It was a risk, one that could end up going horribly wrong.

Aware of this, Harlowe said, "Since we've never done so before, he might wonder about the reason, and that could lead to suspicion on his part."

"It could. But in light of all I have learned thus far, I believe Mr. Croft will be far more likely to let down his guard and open up if he knows I'm doing the same. When I confided in him about riding astride dressed in breeches, a bond formed between us. Telling him something I'd not want others to know, sharing my secrets and letting him think I'm being completely open and honest, is the right way to go. By letting him see where I live, I'll be granting him a glimpse behind the curtain, an intimacy that I'm sure will aid in our cause."

"You make a compelling argument." Carriage wheels crunching gravel accompanied Harlowe's statement. "An invitation will also indicate that what happened tonight changes nothing. You and I support him. We are his friends and as such, we're on his side. Nothing to fear."

"Precisely," Samantha agreed even though she disliked Harlowe's phrasing. He made it sound as though they were setting a sinister trap, and in many ways they were, she just… A shake of her head banished the thought and then the carriage drew to a halt.

Harlowe set his hand on the handle, then glanced her way. "Send the invitation, Samantha. The sooner the better."

She exited the carriage behind him and entered the house that had been her home for the past fifteen years. There was no sense in wondering where her current path would lead her, so she did her best not to. What scared her the most was the question of whether or not she'd be able to follow her orders in the end.

Only time would tell.

∼

Adrian berated himself the entire way home. He was furious. How could he have lost control so easily? It was embarrassing to think of. He'd resorted to baser instinct in front of half of London. In front of Miss Carmichael, no less. Had his father still been alive he'd have whipped him for the stupidity of it.

Never lose your cool.
Always keep a level head.
Don't resort to violence unless you yourself are attacked.

He'd ignored those words of wisdom completely this evening. All because Lundquist had dared to smile – because Adrian had needed a target for all his anger and pain.

It wasn't fair and it sure as hell wasn't wise.

He had to do better.

With his jacket rumpled and his shirt still slightly askew from the altercation, Adrian entered his home where he handed his hat and gloves to Elks.

"Please see to it that a bath is prepared and that Murry is ready to attend me," he told the butler before heading into the parlor. There he poured himself a large glass of brandy from which he proceeded to sip while staring into the fire that burned in the grate.

He needed additional clues – something more substantial – but finding them was proving a chore. All he had was a button, a man who might or might not have been eating sugar-glass, and Miss Fairchild's connection to Lundquist.

None of it amounted to much. It wasn't enough to prove a damn thing.

Frustrated, he downed the remaining contents of his glass and re-filled it. A visit to Lady Camille's family might be in order next. Hell, he'd not even discerned if she'd been involved with Lundquist somehow. Or if Miss Irvine had been acquainted with him as well.

If not, then it was unlikely he'd somehow managed to lure them to their deaths. Unless he'd accomplished the feat by applying his rank and some sort of threat or promise or…

Adrian scrubbed his palm over his brow and pinched the bridge of his nose. "Bloody mess."

Instead of making headway, the paltry bits of information he'd managed to gather left him more confused and uncertain than he'd been last week.

"Sir?" Murry interrupted from the doorway. When

Adrian glanced at him he jutted his head toward the stairs. "Your bath is ready."

Adrian nodded against the sudden weight of exhaustion that clung to his shoulders. He set his glass aside and made his way toward his bedchamber with Murry following close behind.

"Rough evening?" Murry inquired while untying Adrian's cravat. The slackening of the piece of linen eased the constriction around his neck.

"I went after Lundquist," Adrian said, his voice strained with self-deprecation.

"Did he deserve it?"

"Possibly, but it was too soon to know for certain. I ought to have waited."

"You snapped." Murry didn't fuss over the word. He stated it matter-of-factly while helping Adrian off with his jacket and waistcoat.

"I did," Adrian admitted. He shucked his shirt and handed it to Murry.

"Can't say I'm surprised." Murry tossed Adrian's shirt and cravat into a basket for the maid to collect. "Tragedy can take a terrible toll on even the most self-controlled individual. It would be strange if the nature of Miss Croft's death didn't add to the strain."

Adrian scoffed. "My father would have been appalled."

"Perhaps. Perhaps not. Let's not forget that Miss Croft was his daughter."

Of course she was, and had his father still lived, Adrian knew he'd have embarked on his own path of vengeance. The difference was, he would have been more subtle. He would not have allowed emotion to rule him.

Instead of having an outburst in front of the London elite, he'd have done substantial research, checked that research, and then made the guilty blighter disappear off the face of the earth.

It would have been slow, carefully planned, thoughtful.

"Miss Carmichael came to my defense," he said, eager to shift the subject of their conversation away from himself.

"How so?"

Adrian stripped off the rest of his clothes and tossed them aside while thinking back on the whole ordeal. In the midst of the chaos, he'd not had time to reflect on the part Miss Carmichael played in smoothing things over.

"Lundquist called for my arrest," Adrian said as he settled into his bath. "Miss Carmichael appealed to his conscience and managed to convince him against it. In the end, I was simply asked to leave and to stay away until I'd finished mourning."

"Not terrible advice, I should think." Murry padded about the room to collect clean clothes. "You should know that all your employees are as eager to find your sister's killer as you are. We cared for her, but we care about you as well, and if I may speak as your friend instead of your valet, I would tell you that it will take time for you to come to terms with what happened."

"Figuring out who killed her would help," Adrian muttered, allowing himself to sink lower into the soothing warm water.

"She cares for you by the way," Murry said, a pensive note to his voice. "Miss Carmichael, that is. Having found nothing dubious about her, I see no other motive for her to defend you. Especially not given all that we know. Considering her recent entrance into Society, which has been made at a rather advanced age for a woman, her lack of pedigree, and her personality which you've described as politely reserved, it must have taken courage for her to speak up."

Knowing she'd chosen to do so for him made his heart beat slightly faster. Warmth spread through his veins, fanning out through his body until he felt wrapped in a comforting blanket.

It pleased him immensely to know Miss Carmichael liked him enough to stick up for him even when he'd gone too far. Where most other people would turn away, sever all ties, and save their own hides, she'd chosen to stay by his side and speak up. Had it not been for Murry assuring him she wasn't a threat, he would have been certain she must have ulterior motives.

The fact that she didn't was an immense relief.

∼

Lady Lavinia knew she ought to be climbing into her bed instead of out of it. But the note she'd received that afternoon encouraged her to be just as reckless as she'd been last night when she'd finally learned what it meant to be kissed.

Not chastely, but in a wild way that brought her alive. It was the oddest thing ever. She'd always been active and ready for a bit of fun. Yet that one kiss – electrifying and sensual – had jolted her out of a slumber she'd not even known she'd been in.

So she dressed and slipped from her room, heart racing with the eagerness of exploring more kisses. She knew it was highly improper, but her body craved Julian's touch – craved it in a way that risked seeing her ruined.

Not that she cared. What did it matter when she hoped to spend the rest of her life with him? He had to feel the same way or he'd not have sent her the note.

This certainty amplified her excitement as she left the house, exiting through the kitchen door and climbing the steps to the pavement. The cloak she'd put on helped ward off the nighttime chill while the hood she'd pulled over her head provided the anonymity she required.

Walking with purpose, she made her way to the Hyde Park end of Green Street where Julian said he would meet her. They would have privacy there, he'd assured her. This promise alone made her speed up her pace, quickening her breaths.

There, just up ahead, was the entrance to the alleyway where they could find some time alone. For her safety, he'd told her not to enter it unless she found a red rose tied to the drainpipe of the first building she reached.

She grinned the moment she saw it, both from relief and exhilaration. Pleasure seized her as she untied the ribbon and raised the bloom to her nose, allowing its sweet scent to brighten her senses.

This was more than an illicit meeting. This was romantic and thoughtful. It proved that Julian cared for her and that he'd embarked on their courtship in earnest.

Eager to prove her own affection, she entered the alleyway, her anticipation rising with each careful tread.

"Julian?" she whispered when she failed to spot him.

"I'm here," he murmured, his voice directly behind her as he wound his arm around her middle and pulled her back firmly against his chest.

The tie at the front of her cloak was swiftly undone, the bulky garment removed immediately and promptly discarded. His mouth found the side of her neck and she leaned into the caress – leaned into him as the same need she'd felt the last time they'd kissed began to consume her once more.

"Miss me?" he asked, his voice a notch lower than what she was used to.

"Yes."

He caught her earlobe between his teeth, the gentle tug producing a cascade of shivers that only made her crave more. She tried to turn in his arms, to seek his mouth with her own, but he held her in place and something about that possessiveness increased her physical need.

So she didn't complain when he tugged at her bodice. This was what she'd dreamt of since their last encounter – his hands on her body, soothing each ache he created while driving her want to new heights.

"Please," she whimpered when he moved his other hand over her thigh.

"I wonder if you would return the favor."

Again, his voice sounded off, but Lavinia dismissed it, deciding their scandalous meeting and where it could lead affected him as much as it did her.

"Would you?" he pressed, his touch fogging her mind with endless pleasure. "If I satisfy your desire, will you do the same for me?"

"Yes. Of course."

His answering chuckle was low and hollow. It shrouded her in sudden unease. More so when his grip on her tightened, the fingers he'd used to caress her now digging into her flesh.

Lavinia gasped. "Julian. Please stop. You're hurting me."

"Am I?" He pulled his other hand free and gentled his hold while kissing the side of her neck.

The effect was wondrously calming, encouraging her to tilt her head back and relax while praying he'd soon return his attention to where she wanted it most.

Her breath hitched in response to him nipping her skin. The cool night air drifted across her face. From a few streets over, came the clatter of carriage wheels rolling over uneven cobblestones.

Julian lifted his head. An icy shiver brushed Lavinia's neck where his lips had just been. One second later, a cat's screech from somewhere nearby gave sound to her muted scream.

∼

Seated at the breakfast table, Adrian smiled at the invitation Elks had delivered to him a few moments ago. Miss Carmichael wanted to see him again. At her home, no less. For luncheon. The day after tomorrow.

His chest expanded with pure pleasure. A sigh of relief followed. Last night's incident didn't deter her from spending additional time in his company. She'd not been put off by his beastly outburst. On the contrary, her missive stated that she dearly hoped he'd be able to join her.

Adrian tucked the invitation into his jacket pocket and stood. He reminded himself not to get too excited. Perhaps all she wanted from him was friendship. Thus far, she'd given no other indication.

It was too soon for that anyway he decided as he went to fetch his horse from the mews. Best take things slow while laying the groundwork for a potential romance. Rushing headlong into something like that would be unwise.

For although Murry had assured him there was no cause for concern when it came to Miss Carmichael,

Adrian had to be sure she would accept him the way he was, that she would stand by him when his darker side chose to rise from its slumber. That she would still care for him even if the blood of his sister's killer stained his hands.

A life at his side was not for the weak. It required strength. Whether or not Miss Carmichael had enough remained to be seen.

And yet, despite all of this he chose to have hope as he swung himself into his saddle and trotted toward Hyde Park. In all the years he'd spent navigating one social season after the next, she was the first woman who'd made him stop to think of his future. Surely that had to mean something.

He gripped the reins and steered his mount onto Park Street. The morning light was slightly hazy today, the temperature already pleasant despite the early hour. It wasn't yet nine, which suggested Miss Carmichael must be an early riser. Her home was a good half hour away without any significant traffic, yet her invitation had reached his home before eight.

Choosing to take the quieter route, Adrian rode onto Green Street and was nearing Park Lane when a group of people milling about up ahead caught his notice. He slowed his horse when he spotted Kendrick.

The chief constable chatted with one of his Runners, the grave look in his eyes putting Adrian on alert. He dismounted and walked his horse through the small crowd of people who'd gathered near the entrance to an alley. Another Runner kept them back, but he couldn't silence their comments about the woman someone had found.

Throat dry, he walked straight up to the Runner while equal parts dread and hope raked his skin. He had no wish to look at another victim – feared he might not be able to do so without seeing Evie – but knew that the chance of finding the killer increased every time a new victim was found.

Eventually, he'd leave behind more useful clues than the ones Adrian had discovered thus far.

"What's going on?" he asked the first Runner he reached.

"That's not for me to say."

Impatient, Adrian started to push his way past him, but the Runner was quicker than he'd expected and blocked him with his arm. "You've got to stay back, sir. We can't have all of London interfering in our crime scene."

Adrian glared at the fellow even though he was only doing his job. "Get out of my way."

"Can't do that, I'm afraid. Now take a step back or—"

"Kendrick!" Adrian didn't even bother with looking toward the chief constable while he shouted his name. Instead, his cool gaze remained on the man who blocked him.

"It's all right, Jackson. Let him through."

Adrian offered Jackson his reins. "Hold these, will you?"

"That's not my job," Jackson protested.

"Shall we see about that?" Adrian challenged.

Jackson scowled at him but took the reins, allowing Adrian to cross to where Kendrick stood. The chief constable jerked his head at the Runner with whom he'd been chatting, sending him away.

Crossing his arms, he gave his attention to Adrian. "I suppose you want to know what's happened."

Adrian held his gaze with steely resolve. "One of the onlookers said that a woman was found. Murdered, I'm guessing?"

"Same as the previous victims," Kendrick confirmed. He glanced toward the alleyway. A frown puckered his brow. "It's slightly different this time though."

"How so?"

"The woman's bodice was pulled down, leaving her more exposed than the others."

Adrian swallowed past the increasing aridness in his throat as he too glanced toward the alley. "Do you know who she is?"

"I've never seen her before, but her clothes are quality and her hands without calluses. She has to be upper class."

"Mind if I take a look? See if I can identify her?"

"It's not an easy sight, Mr. Croft." Kendrick looked genuinely reluctant to push him. "Considering your sister, I imagine you'd rather avoid the scene."

"Not if it helps us track down the villain." Adrian turned, his long and even strides taking him into the alley before he could second guess his decision.

It didn't take long for him to spot the body, bile

filling his throat the moment he did so. She lay on her side, a rumpled discarded mess pressed into the wall of the building that stood to Adrian's left. Her blank eyes stared straight through him, and the blood...

However awful it had been for him to see Evie after, this was somehow worse. The coroner hadn't yet had the chance to clean this woman up. Dark red, nearly black, splotches stained the gash at her throat. Stained her breasts and lilac gown too.

As with his sister, a note had been pinned to her crumbled bodice, accusing her of being a whore. Kendrick was right. This wasn't an easy sight in the least. It made his eyes sting, knowing what Evie must have looked like when she had been found. Before the blood had been washed away.

Even then, it had been a hellish experience.

"Well?" Kendrick asked, his voice apprehensive as he came to stand beside Adrian.

"I was wrong to suspect Lundquist." Adrian stared at the woman who'd made her debut last year together with Evie. The rosy tinge to her cheeks was now gone, hidden beneath a pale mask of death. "It seems unlikely to me that he'd kill his own sister in such a way."

A sharp hiss alerted Adrian to Kendrick's surprise. "Are you telling me this is—"

"Lady Lavinia." Adrian took a step closer to her, his gaze now searching her body, noting her posture, looking for anything that might be useful. A question began taking shape, the sort he'd no wish to ask, much less know the answer to. But given the state she was in, it seemed important. "Was she…"

God, he couldn't get the word out, so he gestured with his hand instead.

"Raped?" When Adrian nodded Kendrick told him, "We won't know for certain until the coroner takes a look, but I don't believe so. Such an act would have required force. The perpetrator would have had to get her onto her back, lift up her skirts, and do the deed while holding her still. This would have left at least one of her hands free at some point or other, allowing her the chance to fight. Yet her gown isn't torn and her nails appear clean."

"So he came at her from behind and seduced her?" Adrian tried to imagine how it could have happened but found it a challenge. "How the hell does a murderer lure a young woman out of her house late at night?"

"Judging from what we know of the previous victims, I expect he's taking advantage of their desires."

It took extreme restraint for Adrian not to round on Kendrick and slam him into the nearest wall. He took a few breaths to slow his pulse, then told him, "I trust that statement doesn't apply to my sister."

"Of course not. I know she was killed by mistake."

And yet, Evie's death had been very deliberate. He could only hope that solving this case would help him figure out who was behind it.

"When will you tell the marquess?"

Kendrick clasped his hands behind his back. Another couple of Runners brought a stretcher for the body and a sheet to drape over it. "As soon as we're done here."

"I think I'll resume my ride then." Adrian didn't bother extending his hand, but he did thank Kendrick for sharing the crime scene with him.

Staring straight ahead, he suppressed the shiver stealing across his shoulders as he walked away. Lundquist's world was about to change in the same tragic way his own had a few weeks ago. Adrian owed the man an apology and planned to stop by his house tomorrow to pay his respects.

Had their positions been reversed, he'd have welcomed the distraction. Not to mention the chance to speak with someone who understood his pain.

What he wouldn't share was what he himself had witnessed at the Ottersburg ball when he'd gone for a bit of fresh air. Seeking privacy, he'd exited one of the parlors and stepped onto a secluded balcony so he could be alone with his thoughts.

The private moment he'd glimpsed had been none of his business, although he had filed away a few details in case he required leverage later.

He'd deliberately kept that piece of information from Kendrick. After all, he'd had his go at Mr. Walker already, and had chosen to set him free. It was Adrian's turn now. And if Walker turned out to be the killer – if he'd somehow managed to double back and murder Miss Irvine on that September evening in Vauxhall – then *he* would be the one to end him.

CHAPTER TWENTY-SIX

Lundquist House was teeming with people when Samantha stopped by to pay her respects. Servants hurried about, attending to guests and family members while Kendrick spoke with Lundquist in the hallway. A steady stream of Runners moved up and down the stairs, the overall look about them suggesting they were terribly busy and important.

Samantha stepped aside to let one past her as she entered the house. News of Lady Lavinia's death had reached her the previous evening when Harlowe brought it up over dinner. She'd thought of it at great length since and knew she had to learn more.

Another death meant another chance at catching the killer.

The bouquet of lilies she'd purchased on her way over weighed heavily in her hands. Despite the resolve with which she'd come, melancholia crawled through her veins like a sickness attempting to find a foothold.

This had to end, but a year had now passed since the first murder, and it didn't look as though Bow Street was closer to catching the killer than they had been then. As for Mr. Croft's own attempts, they'd clearly led him astray. He'd been so certain the man he hunted was Lundquist, but that seemed highly unlikely now.

Hopefully, by coming here, Samantha would discover something more useful – a piece of information to aid the investigation and bring these pointless deaths to an end.

"The parlor is fully occupied at present," said the butler, his lifeless eyes a perfect match for the somber mood. "Please wait here a moment. I'm sure a seat will be made available shortly."

The butler vanished, leaving Samantha alone, save for an elderly man who also waited. She nodded a greeting at him, then glanced along the length of the hallway to where Lundquist stood with Kendrick. Neither man had noticed her yet, and since they spoke in muted tones, it was impossible for her to hear what either one said.

A nearby clock chimed the hour. Four in the afternoon.

Another Runner descended the stairs and went to join his colleagues outside. The man who waited with her proceeded to study a painting, his disinterest in chatting with her made all the clearer when he turned his back.

Just as well.

Intent on finding her own answers, Samantha took a deep breath, placed her bouquet on a nearby table, and climbed to the first-floor landing with confident steps.

A swift sweep of the hallway assured her she was alone. Conscious of her limited time, she moved with purpose, striding directly toward the only door that stood open. Taking a quick look inside, she confirmed it must have belonged to Lady Lavinia. The Runners had not been considerate in their search, which appeared to have been quite thorough.

There wasn't a mess as such, just an overall sense of things having been moved.

Samantha walked to the center of the room and turned around slowly, assessing every surface, each drawer, cupboard, and corner until...

She approached the windowsill. The slight misalignment would have escaped her notice had she not been searching for something unusual. Her hand slid over the wood, adding pressure until it rocked ever so slightly beneath her touch.

Sliding her fingertips under the windowsill's lip, she gave it an upward nudge and was unsurprised when it opened toward a hollow space beneath.

A collection of letters were hidden within.

Samantha grabbed them, stashed them in her skirt pocket, and closed the windowsill so it looked just as undisturbed as when she'd found it.

The sound of approaching footsteps reached her. A woman's voice followed.

Samantha crossed to the door and peeked out into the hallway just in time to see a maid disappearing into another room.

Although she did have an explanation at the ready if anyone found her up here, she'd rather avoid the altercation and chose therefore to slip from Lady Lavinia's room with a silent tread.

She descended the stairs to the foyer where the man no longer waited, sent the lilies she'd brought a quick glance in passing, exited the house, and climbed into her awaiting carriage.

The conveyance took off at once, allowing her to relax against the squabs without the fear of discovery.

~

Adrian had begun reviewing what little he knew from the very beginning, this time with the idea of Mr. Walker being the killer. Considering Walker's alibi on the eve of Miss Irvine's murder, he would have had to have found a way to return to Vauxhall and kill her without those vouching for him being any the wiser.

If such a thing were possible, Adrian meant to find out.

To do this, he'd need to visit Vauxhall. The pleasure park was walled in, but maybe a tree could be climbed to allow easy access. He'd have to check, so he told his driver to take him straight to the front entrance. There, he paid the small admittance fee, then a slightly larger fee for the information he needed.

The park attendant who welcomed the coin he offered showed him to the spot where Miss Irvine was found. The area was perfect for all manner of mischief. Cut off from the main pathways and filled with vegetation, it felt like a woodland scene instead of a place in the City.

Adrian stepped between the trees and bushes, moving deeper into the brush until he arrived at the boundary wall. A few nearby trees could have been climbed to escape unnoticed. But what about getting in?

He'd have to check the opposite side, and since it was too high up for him to mark the location, there was no other choice but to measure the distance to the next corner. Not a straightforward feat when bushes interrupted his path in numerous places. The result was an estimation. Give or take a few yards either way, he should get a sense of where the culprit had entered the park *if* he'd climbed over the wall.

Once he knew this, he'd have a much better sense of whether or not Walker could have parted ways with his friends, doubled back, and killed Miss Irvine without anyone knowing.

It seemed like a stretch, but it was the best lead he had at the moment.

Turning, he prepared to head back to the main entrance when he spotted Miss Carmichael out for a stroll. She was accompanied by Miss Violet Greene and

Lady Octavia Burley, Lady Heathbrooke's companion, Miss Roberts, and the same woman he'd seen her with at Reed's Boxing club. Her name escaped him at the moment.

Unable to resist, he called out Miss Carmichael's name to draw her attention. A smile lit up her face when she saw him. "Mr. Croft. What a lovely surprise."

"I couldn't agree with you more," he said as he walked toward her and her friends.

"You remember Miss Stevens?"

"Of course." He bowed toward the red-head.

"And are you acquainted with Miss Roberts, Miss Greene, and Lady Octavia?"

"We've seen each other in passing," Miss Roberts answered, "though we've never been formally introduced."

"It's a pleasure," Adrian told her. He greeted Miss Greene and Lady Octavia next, then directed his attention back to Miss Carmichael. Her smile had faded a little, but that didn't make her any less radiant. He cleared his throat, straightened his spine, and gestured in the direction the ladies were heading. "Shall we?"

A bit impertinent of him to force himself into her company, but he'd always been driven – the sort of man who went after what he wanted as soon as he figured out what that was. Right now, he wanted to learn if he and Miss Carmichael had a chance at more than friendship.

He offered his arm and felt the space behind his ribs expand the moment her hand touched it.

They proceeded at a casual pace, allowing her friends to take the lead while they followed behind. It was odd seeing the pleasure garden during the light of day. The place lacked the vibrance found after dark when lackluster objects were cast in shadow and lanterns spread a magical glow across every path.

"Do you come here regularly?" Miss Carmichael asked while they strolled. Wisps of her blonde hair curled from beneath her bonnet, falling against the curve of her neck. It was rather distracting.

Adrian tore his gaze away when she sent him a questioning look. "I tend to frequent Hyde Park since I prefer riding when time allows. However, I did feel the need to stretch my legs today, and this seemed as good a place as any in which to do so."

Not a lie, exactly. Moving helped ease the tension that gripped his nerves these days, when he stayed home too long with his own thoughts.

A soft smile captured Miss Carmichael's lips. "I visited Lundquist House earlier. It seems you made a mistake regarding the marquess."

Adrian nodded. "I apologized to him this morning when I went to pay my respects."

The marquess had accepted his apology with grace. Truth be told, he'd looked too exhausted for feelings of anger or resentment.

"That was very good of you."

"It was the right thing to do." Even if Adrian still believed the marquess had deserved to be punished for striking a woman, he'd not killed anyone and would now have to bury his sister.

They continued in silence for a while before Miss Carmichael asked, "Are you looking into anyone else?"

Adrian paused. There was Mr. Walker of course, but nothing had come of that yet. Besides, he was wary of making another mistake. If he was to mention someone's name in connection with the murders, he had to be sure of the man's involvement this time.

"Not really. But the nature of Lady Lavinia's death compels me to warn you. You must be extra careful when venturing out. Promise me you won't go anywhere alone. Especially not at night."

"Of course."

Relief poured through him, but it wasn't enough. He had to make sure she'd stay safe. So he gritted his teeth and told her bluntly, "Whoever the murderer is, it would seem he's evolving."

Her beautiful eyes filled with endless concern. "How do you mean?"

"Lady Lavinia's murder was different. I saw her body and…" He paused to consider his next words. However important the subject he wanted to broach, he could not forget with whom he was speaking. Miss Carmichael was still a young lady whose sensibilities had to be taken into account. And yet, there was no delicate way around it. "He's no longer killing for the sole purpose of ridding the world of unworthy women. It would seem he's…begun enjoying the act."

"In other words, it's not just a mission for him anymore but also something he craves?"

"In a manner of speaking." It was as close as she'd come to comprehending the horror with which Lundquist's sister had met her end.

"Then I shall be sure to heed your warning, Mr. Croft, and will warn other women to do the same."

"Maybe encourage them to join you at Reed's." It couldn't hurt for them to learn a few tips on how to defend themselves.

"I'll be sure to do so."

Neither said anything more after that. Sensing he ought to leave so she could enjoy the rest of her walk with her friends, Adrian drew to a halt after a few additional paces. "I believe I ought to get going."

"Very well." Was that a hint of regret in her voice? "It was lovely to see you again, Mr. Croft."

He tipped his hat. "Likewise, Miss Carmichael. I look forward to lunching with you tomorrow."

He wished both her and her friends a good afternoon and then strode for the exit, arriving on Kennington Lane five minutes later. Heading east, he paced the length of the wall until he'd taken ninety-two steps.

Here he stopped to inspect the masonry and quickly decided that finding a foothold on the brick wall would not have been easy. Scaling it would have been impossible without a ladder.

Not exactly the most inconspicuous item.

Adrian shook his head. It didn't look like Walker could have committed the crime either.

Unless...

He turned to stare back along the length of the street. All this time, he'd dismissed the killer's use of the entrances. He himself had concluded that the one leading through the Proprietor's House would have been an unlikely choice for anyone needing a quick in and out. Not only was it farther from the crime scene but accessing it required the use of a boat.

The Kennington Lane entrance, however, was easily accessible by carriage or on foot. He just hadn't considered it after Kendrick claimed Walker hadn't been in the park at the time of Miss Irvine's death.

But the admission clerk didn't take names and wouldn't have known if or when Walker arrived or left. So how could Kendrick be certain of his absence from the park during this timeframe?

Returning the way he'd come, Adrian spotted a tavern directly across from Vauxhall's main entrance. He proceeded toward it as soon as a break arose in the traffic. The dimly lit venue was only half full at this hour, its patrons clustered into small groups around a few tables.

As afternoon turned to evening, the place would likely begin to fill. Men would engage in card games and dice, laughter and conversation would make for a noisier atmosphere than what was presently found.

Retrieving his calling card from his jacket pocket, Adrian crossed to the counter and slid it toward the barkeep who busied himself with drying a glass. "I'd like to test your memory if you've a moment to spare."

The barkeep glanced at the card and nodded. He set the glass aside and braced both hands on the counter. "I'll do my best, Mr. Croft."

"A murder took place in Vauxhall last September."

"Aye. Bow Street sent a constable here around that time. Wanted to know who was here that night."

"Did they inquire about anyone in particular?" Adrian collected a couple of coins from his pocket and placed them on the counter. He waited until the barkeep grabbed them before leaning closer. "A Mr. Walker, perhaps?"

Recognition flashed in the barkeep's eyes. A slow nod followed. "A man who fit his description was present that evening between the hours of eight and midnight. He came with friends – a raucous bunch who were all deep in their cups by the time they left."

Four hours. From before Miss Irvine was reported missing and a good while thereafter. Kendrick must have interviewed Walker's friends, then stopped by here to double check their statements in order to determine the veracity of his alibi.

It seemed fairly solid. Walker had been here during the time of the murder. Enough people had seen him to ascertain his presence. Which made it impossible for him to be the culprit.

Adrian surveyed the space. According to the barkeep, Walker's group had enjoyed their fair share of drinks. They'd been foxed by the time they departed.

Perhaps a bit sooner. Would such men even have noticed if one of them disappeared for a spell?

Frowning, Adrian made a quick calculation. The scene of the crime could likely be reached in about five minutes, provided one ran. But that would have drawn attention. As would a hurried stride.

A moderate pace should cover the distance in roughly ten. That made twenty for a round trip, plus whatever time was needed to commit the murder.

Half an hour, Adrian decided. That was the minimum Walker would have required. And since it had been a masquerade, he could have returned to the park unnoticed. Especially since the direction he would have been headed was off to one side, away from the popular paths.

But he'd still have had to sneak away without detection.

Adrian glanced at the barkeep. "I don't suppose you recall if Walker was gone for a lengthy duration that night?"

"Afraid not. This place gets pretty busy late in the evening. There's enough to see to without paying close attention to where all the customers are at a given moment."

"Of course." Adrian gave the barkeep a few additional coins. "Thank you for taking the time. Do you mind if I use your privy before I go?"

"Not at all." The barkeep gestured toward the left back corner. "It's straight through there."

The door he indicated led into a courtyard where

two narrow structures with green wooden doors offered privacy to anyone needing to heed nature's call.

Adrian pulled one door open and scrunched his nose in response to the stench of piss that assailed him. At least the privy was clean besides that. The wooden seat above the cesspit even appeared to be newly lacquered.

After completing his errand, he found the pump in the courtyard and used it to rinse his hands. Which allowed him the time to stop and notice the gate in the fence sealing off one side of the courtyard.

He wiped his hands on the back of his trousers and went to undo the latch. Beyond was a narrow alleyway where the tavern kept its rubbish. It was no more than a couple of arms lengths wide, but it did provide a walkway between the tavern and the next building. One that led straight to Kennington Lane.

Adrian blinked. Walker could theoretically have left his friends inside, come through here, returned to Vauxhall wearing a mask, then rejoined his friends after killing Miss Irvine.

Could he have accomplished the feat without his friends questioning what would have been a lengthy absence?

Possibly, if they'd been as foxed as the barkeep suggested.

But what about bloodstains? The murder had been messy. If Walker had done it he would most likely have needed to clean up afterward, perhaps change his clothes, before returning to the tavern.

Unless he'd been calculating enough to remove his jacket and shirt first so he'd only had to wash the blood off his hands. That could have been done with the very same pump Adrian just used.

He pondered all of this for a moment, then shut the gate and returned the way he'd come. His theory, while a stretch, did mean that Walker's alibi didn't hold up as well as Kendrick might think. The opportunity, however cumbersome, was there and as such, it could not be fully dismissed.

CHAPTER TWENTY-SEVEN

Samantha chose a light blue day dress for Croft's visit. According to her lady's maid, it complimented her fair features and accentuated the color of her eyes. A useful thing when she meant not only to gain the man's interest but keep it.

If only it would serve as a form of armor and shield her against the effect he'd begun to have upon her. She had to stay strong in his presence, focused and on target. Allowing herself to lose sight of the mission would be a disaster. Failure would follow and that was not an option she would allow.

She reminded herself of this as she stood by the drawing room window, watching the gardeners cut the grass next to the driveway while she waited for Croft's arrival. The three men swung their sickles with practiced skill, leaving a neat and uniform blanket of green in their wake.

Harlowe and Hazel, who sat behind her, occupied the armchair and the sofa, respectively. Harlowe with that day's newspaper and Hazel with some knitting. Tara and Holly had not come to join them, though they were expected to put in appearances during luncheon.

A movement out of the corner of Samantha's eye made her shift her gaze sideways. It looked like one of the Clearview House cats had disrupted a group of pigeons. By the time Samantha spotted the birds they'd already taken flight, their wings wildly flapping while the cat stared after them from below.

She shook her head and returned her attention to the front of the drive just as Croft came into view. Seated upon a gleaming black horse, he sent the gardeners a nod in greeting as he trotted past them on his way to the front door.

The gesture left Samantha slightly dismayed. Not only because most members of the upper class strove to ignore servants, but also because of the visceral effect it had upon her. Once again, she found a reason to like something about him. Which complicated matters since it made her job so much harder to do.

Unhappy with the soft spot she seemed to be developing for him, she stiffened her spine and clenched her jaw to steel her resolve, then announced to Harlowe and Hazel, "He's here."

"We'd best go greet him then," Harlowe said, folding away the paper and rising while Hazel returned her knitting supplies to a nearby basket.

Together, the trio entered the hallway, arriving

there at the same time as their butler opened the door, allowing them to watch Croft dismount and hand the reins to a stable boy.

Harlowe stepped forward onto the front step. "Welcome to Clearview, Mr. Croft. I'm glad you were able to come."

"Thank you for inviting me," Croft said, extending his hand so he could shake the one Harlowe offered. "Having never been here before I really must say that you have an admirable property. It's close to the City while offering all the benefits of a country estate. I can't deny I'm a little bit envious of you."

Harlowe grinned in response to Croft's wry smile and ushered him into the house. "You could have a place just like it. There's plenty of land for sale in these parts though it's likely a great deal pricier now than when I purchased mine some twenty to thirty years ago."

"Nevertheless, it could be worth it." Croft, who'd removed his hat and gloves while Harlowe spoke, handed the items to Branton, the butler, and directed his gaze toward Samantha and Hazel. "It's lovely to see you again, Miss Carmichael. And you, Miss Stevens. I trust you are both well?"

"Indeed," Samantha said, a funny sensation gripping her heart when she noted the pleasure with which he watched her. "And you?"

He dipped his head, the corner of his mouth dimpling slightly due to the smile he gave her. "Much improved, now that I'm here."

"I hope you brought your appetite with you," Harlowe said. He turned to Branton and asked him to have someone fetch Tara and Holly before saying, "From what I gather, Cook has prepared quite a feast. But perhaps you'd like a drink to start?"

They removed themselves to the parlor where Croft requested a glass of port instead of the brandy Samantha would have expected. Sitting on the sofa next to Hazel, she held her tongue while the men discussed the upcoming elections. Although she had strong opinions on the subject and favored Lord Grey, she knew it wasn't a young lady's place to comment on such matters. Best say nothing at all then, lest she raise Croft's suspicions.

But when they were finally seated at the dining room table and the first dish – a seafood terrine – was served, providing a lull in the conversation, she decided to ask, "Have you settled on what to read next, Mr. Croft? After finishing *Herakles*?"

The sound of cutlery clinking against everyone's plates was incredibly loud in the brief pause that followed. Until he said, "Perhaps something lighter. One of Shakespeare's comedies could be refreshing."

"Another play," Tara remarked, voicing Samantha's thought. "Do you generally favor them?"

"Not especially." A soft crease appeared on Croft's brow as he seemed to consider the bite-sized piece of terrine suspended on the end of his fork. His eyebrows rose as if to suggest he'd just had a moment of realization. "I've little preference in the type of material I read.

My only requirement is that it be thought-provoking. It ought to leave me with a feeling of personal growth upon completion."

Samantha gazed at him. How curious he was – how different from what she'd expected. It was difficult for her to think of him in a negative light – to imagine him aiding foreign enemies, coercing women into prostitution, selling counterfeit goods, and whatever else he supposedly did – when there was no hint of illicit dealing about him.

She sipped her wine while Harlowe voiced his agreement with Croft's point. Of course, she too wore a mask. The woman Croft currently saw when he looked at her bore no resemblance to the one who'd taken on four thugs and won.

"Did you acquire your schooling from Oxford or Cambridge?" Harlowe asked.

Samantha blinked, not having realized the conversation had moved on without her. Noting that her terrine remained mostly untouched, she ate an additional bite while Croft spoke.

"Neither, to be honest. My father didn't see the merit for someone in my position."

"Why not?" Holly asked with an owlish sort of curiosity.

"Because he expected me to join the family business, not enter into law or become a physician. As such, he believed the expense would be a waste. The time too, I imagine."

"And what exactly is your family business?"

Harlowe managed to make the question sound casual by taking a sip of his wine. "If you don't mind my asking."

Croft smiled with the ease of a man who had nothing to apologize for. "Anything profitable really, from farming, to fishing, some shipping, factory construction, and mining."

"Hmm…"

That was Harlowe's only response before he mentioned his fondness for music and how pleased he was to have four accomplished pianists in the house. A comparison of various composers followed, during which Samantha's gaze happened to meet Croft's, the mischievous look he gave her reminding her that she'd told him of her dislike of playing.

Pressing her lips together to keep all hints of humor at bay, she spent the next half hour concentrating upon her food.

"You could invite him to see the aviary with you," Hazel whispered when luncheon was over. She and Samantha followed the men to the terrace where tea would be served. "It would give you the chance to spend more time together. As you must if you are to bond with each other properly."

"An excellent idea," Samantha agreed, "although the suggestion ought to be made by Harlowe. If I make it, Mr. Croft will surely wonder at my forwardness."

"But it's so lovely this time of year," Hazel said, raising her voice as she and Samantha arrived on the terrace where the tea things awaited. The comment interrupted Croft, who'd been remarking on the staggered pillars. "Do you not agree, Harlowe?"

"What's that?" Harlowe asked while Samantha prayed Croft would not find Hazel's remark too transparent. Or wonder overly much at the folly's unusual appearance.

"The aviary. Your budgerigars are especially fun." Hazel lowered herself to one of the bamboo chairs and turned to Croft once the rest of the party was seated. "He's taught them to speak."

"Really?" Croft chuckled. "What an interesting hobby."

"A rewarding one," Harlowe murmured, the pensive look in his eyes informing Samantha that he knew precisely why Hazel had raised the subject. "You're welcome to take a look if you like. Miss Carmichael will be happy to show you the way, I'm sure."

"After we've had our tea," Samantha said. She picked up the pot and proceeded to pour, all the while conscious of Croft's gaze tracking her every movement.

It left her feeling a bit like a specimen in a glass case. More concerning was the added warmth she experienced in her cheeks because of his increased attention. She did her best to ignore it while she drank her tea, allowing herself to relax as she listened to Croft argue with Harlowe over the best way to gauge a good horse.

She sent Hazel a wry look and watched her suppress a grin in response.

"If it's no imposition," Croft said when he finished

his tea a few moments later, "I'd love to see the aviary now."

"Of course." They descended the terrace steps and proceeded to stroll toward an iron-framed structure, their pace slow and unhurried. Samantha eyed her companion. "Will you remain in Town for the summer or do you plan on visiting your estate?"

"That depends." His voice had a harder edge than before. "I intend to stay in London until my sister's killer is caught."

"Speaking of your sister, I have something for you." Samantha produced the small parcel she'd tucked inside her skirt pocket and handed it to him. "I believe it might help."

He turned the parcel over between his hands, his fingers stroking the pink silk ribbon with which it was tied. "What is this?"

"Letters belonging to Lady Lavinia." He looked at her sharply. "I didn't want anyone else to know I took them, so I couldn't give them to you until now."

They reached the aviary then and positioned themselves so they could admire the birds, though Samantha doubted either of them paid the creatures much attention. "How did you come by them?"

"I, um...may have pilfered them from her room. When I went to pay my respects." She sent him a wary glance but failed to discern his thoughts. "I realize it was badly done, but I know you're in need of clues and I wanted to help. Hopefully you won't think too poorly of my actions."

"Not at all. If anything, I thank you." He dropped a look in her direction. "These may prove valuable in my search for the truth."

"Having read them, I have to agree. Which is why I must ask you to use them with care. Especially after the warning you gave me yesterday. This individual you're hunting is dangerous, Mr. Croft. I fear what he'll do if he learns how determined you are to discover the truth."

His lips quirked. "Your concern for my wellbeing means a great deal, Miss Carmichael. I promise to be cautious."

∾

Standing there, surrounded by bird chatter, Adrian tried to figure out what to make of Miss Carmichael. Honestly, he wasn't entirely sure.

Outwardly, she appeared like any young lady, yet he knew from her own admission that she contained a rebellious streak. At least if her penchant for wearing breeches while riding astride was any indication. She'd also stood up for him at the musicale, which had both surprised and impressed him.

Furthermore, she now revealed herself to be a bit of a thief, albeit one driven by a desire for justice. In this regard she was already proving to be a strong ally.

"Thank you for trusting me with the letters." He noted the softness in her eyes and her hesitant smile. "I'm honored, but also surprised. In all honesty, I would have thought you too proper to steal something from someone else's home."

Her smile faltered just enough to convey a hint of concern. "I simply want the killer caught. No woman is safe until he is and we obviously can't rely on Bow Street to get the job done. The fact that they missed the letters proves their incompetence. Which means it's up to us. As far as I'm concerned, I'll do whatever it takes to keep myself and my friends safe."

He nodded. "I understand and I appreciate the faith you're placing in me. But remember, I've made mistakes too. As it turns out, I was wrong about Lundquist."

"True. But that doesn't mean you won't get it right in the end. The letters…they suggest Lavinia fit the killer's profile. She was supposed to be an innocent debutante, but it would appear she was headed for ruin. There was a man in her life, one who wrote to her anonymously and with an escalating degree of… um…suggestiveness."

"Interesting." Adrian mulled over this detail while watching a lovebird fluff its colorful plumage. He turned to face Miss Carmichael more directly. "I saw her with Mr. Walker once. Perhaps he's the lover who wrote her those letters."

Miss Carmichael nodded. "It could be worth looking into. If only to discover who else might have seen them together."

Adrian agreed. He tucked the letters into his jacket pocket and offered his arm, suggesting they should start heading back to the house.

"How are you finding your boxing lessons?" he asked as they approached the terrace.

"Productive. I already feel more confident in my ability to protect myself."

He slowed his pace slightly to give them more time alone. "When will you be returning to Reed's?"

"In three days." The length of her arm brushed his as she leaned in closer. "That's when I have my next lesson."

"In that case I'll see you then."

"Looking forward to it, Mr. Croft." Pleasure softened her voice.

Dropping a look in her direction he felt his heart squeeze in response to the warmth he found in her eyes. "Me too."

Despite wanting to spend more time in her company, he didn't linger when they arrived on the terrace. Eager to return home so he could study Lady Lavinia's letters, he thanked Harlowe for his hospitality and took his leave.

Catching the killer wasn't just about avenging Evie's death. Not anymore. It was also about ensuring Samantha Carmichael's safety.

CHAPTER TWENTY-EIGHT

Muscles straining, Samantha pulled herself onto the roof and broke into an immediate run, racing along the flat ridge until she reached the opposite end. Her foot met the edge, allowing her to push off and jump toward the next building.

Knees bent, she landed with a soft thud and vaulted over a pair of chimney stacks before continuing onward to her destination – a spot directly across from Number 5 Portman Square.

Perched there, she pulled a spyglass from her jacket's inside pocket and settled onto her belly. The rooms visible from this angle were few in number. A parlor, a study, two bedchambers upstairs, and the staff quarters on the top floor.

She focused on the study first. Judging from what little she was able to see, it wasn't much different from Harlowe's, though in her opinion the space was too bold to suit Mr. Croft. The gilded lion statue she glimpsed didn't quite suit the man she believed him to be.

Someone entered the room and she stilled, her breath caught, until she saw it was merely a maid. The woman moved about as though clearing a few things before leaving once more. Samantha frowned, her focus on the bookcase that stood beyond the desk.

Was that where Mr. Croft kept the blackmail information he was supposed to possess?

He'd not be so careless, surely.

She slid the spyglass higher, over the bedchamber to the right and then across the white brick façade to the left. Her pulse leapt and she nearly sprang from her spot when Mr. Croft's magnified face came into view.

Recalling the distance between him and the vantage point from which she watched, she blew out a slow breath and gave him her full attention. He was already turning away, his hands yanking his shirt and...

Aware that he was undressing, she started to lower the spy-glass, only to still when a welt traversing his back caught her gaze. It wasn't the only one. More came into view as he pulled the shirt over his head. Her heart froze in response to the awful sight. Hundreds of lines were embedded upon his flesh, some more pronounced than others.

She dropped the spyglass and swallowed against the sick feeling that gripped her.

Who had done this?

What kind of monster had tortured him so?

If she ever found out, she'd drag the bastard into the darkest hole she could find and whip him as soundly as he had whipped Croft. Good God, she was so spitting mad on his behalf, she wished she had someone to fight as an outlet for some of the rage.

Closing her eyes briefly, she reminded herself that whatever had happened to him in the past was not her concern. She should not care. Couldn't afford to.

So she shoved the spyglass back into her pocket and headed back to the room she'd rented. It took her less than half an hour to arrive on the sloped roof. Without pausing, she slid to the eve, grabbed the drainpipe, and dropped down to the open window below.

In one fluid motion she swung herself into the space where she came to collect her thoughts, poured herself a large glass of water, and drank. She couldn't afford to lose focus because of some ugly scars.

She shook her head, forced herself to reflect on yesterday's conversation with Croft. His expression had been guarded when she'd confided stealing the letters.

Maybe giving them to him had been a mistake.

Sneaking into a dead woman's bedroom and riffling through her belongings wasn't exactly the sort of behavior one would expect from a respectable young lady, but rather from a trained operative on a mission.

Stupid.

She drank some more water, then set the glass aside. If he took the time to think about it, he'd surely suspect her of being up to something.

A telltale knock at the door alerted her to Isak's

arrival. She let the boy in and offered him part of the minced meat pie she'd purchased for herself earlier.

He took it and handed her the letter he'd brought before shoving the pie in his mouth.

Samantha tore the seal Kendrick used and unfolded the paper, frowning as she read the message.

Meet me at St. Mary's Church tonight. Your progress is unsatisfactory. We need to talk.

She crumpled the paper and shoved it into her pocket. The chief constable's impatience was beyond frustrating. Sighing, she trudged to a rickety wooden table and pulled out a chair. She was aware of the strain the man was under. According to Harlowe, Lundquist was pressuring Bow Street, insisting they meet with results soon. And he wasn't alone, having enlisted Moorland's and Eldridge's support. Not easy, facing the criticism of a marquess and two dukes.

She also realized she ought to have been much closer to Mr. Croft by now. Her assignment was dragging on, taking longer than expected. Although to be fair, she could have warned Kendrick it would be like this if she'd met Croft before she received her assignment.

"Is everything all right?" Isak asked, chewing his food.

"Yes." Samantha retrieved her writing supplies and proceeded to pen her response, the tip of her quill scratching against the paper with each stroke she made.

I'll be there. Make sure you're not followed.

Meeting in person was dangerous, so it was with

serious unease that she sealed her message and handed it back to Isak for delivery.

"There's something else," he said, a cagy look about his eyes.

A cool sliver of foreboding lodged itself at the base of Samantha's spine. "What is it?"

He raised his chin, eyes too old for a boy his age meeting hers. "Wycliffe wants to collect the debt you owe. You're to meet him tomorrow evening, ten o'clock at Seven Dials. A disguise is recommended."

She dared not wonder why. "And if I don't show?"

"He'll let Mr. Croft know you're spying on him."

Breathing became a sudden chore. Teeth clamped together so hard it felt like her jaw might snap, she stared at the boy before her. "How the hell did Wycliffe discover this information?"

Isak swallowed hard and retreated a step. "It wasn't from me. He never even asked me about it. I swear."

"So then?"

"I'm guessing one of his other boys tracked our movements."

She stood immobile for a second, allowed that detail to settle. Bloody hell, she'd been careless, and now she'd pay the price.

"Very well." There was no way around it. "Tell him I'll be there."

∼

With the brim of his hat pulled low so it shielded his face, Adrian kept an eye on Walker's movements across the street. He'd been trailing him for the past half hour in an effort to gain some insight – some hint of the type of man he might be.

Walker didn't strike him as a murderer so far, his stopping to help an old lady climb the steps to a shop not exactly on par with a cold-blooded killer. But looks could be deceiving.

A bakery drew Walker's attention a few seconds later. He stopped to admire the goods in the window, then entered the shop. Despite the distance and the slightly impaired view caused by passing carriages and pedestrians, Adrian could tell his exchange with the woman behind the counter was amicable.

When he re-emerged with a parcel tucked under his arm, the smile on his face was warm and genuine. By all appearances, he lacked the demeanor one would expect from a monster.

Adrian mulled that over while matching Walker's steps. Could it be he was once again chasing the wrong man?

Unsure, he continued to track his movements, interest rising inside him when he spotted Lundquist. The marquess was exiting The Gentlemen's Emporium and didn't seem to have noticed Walker until the other man called out to him. Another clue Walker wasn't the killer? Or simply that he was incredibly skilled at deception?

Lundquist turned, the pain of loss evident in the

bleakness of his gaze. Walker approached and Adrian moved a bit farther along the pavement to better gauge Walker's expression as he and Lundquist spoke. Sympathy showed in the dip of his eyebrows and etchings upon his brow, which seemed like further proof that he wasn't the killer.

Adrian frowned as concern slipped through him. For if it wasn't Walker, then who the hell was it?

CHAPTER TWENTY-NINE

Confident Kendrick hadn't been followed, Samantha emerged from the added darkness she'd found against the church wall and stepped into his path. Ignoring his jolt of surprise, she told him directly, "We shouldn't be meeting like this. It isn't safe."

"Perhaps not," he agreed, the flatness of his tone conveying annoyance, "but it seems to be necessary if I'm to get the answers I need. Your notes don't exactly provide detailed updates. If anything, they suggest a lack of progress."

His dissatisfaction with her only caused her own irritation to flare. "Your impatience could jeopardize everything. Especially since I suspect Mr. Croft of keeping his guard up. I've not yet earned his absolute trust."

"And whose fault is that?" Kendrick hissed, the words too loud in the silence of night even though he kept his voice muffled. "You're not the only one whose job depends on following orders. In case you're unaware, you work for the Crown. As does Harlowe."

"You need not remind me."

"Don't I?" Shadows spilled across his face as he took a step closer. "The project you've been a part of these past seventeen years was funded by taxpayer money. In other words, your residence at Clearview House and whatever comfort it entails is entirely dependent upon your ability to prove your worth."

True apprehension formed in her stomach. She swallowed and quickly steeled herself against it, ever grateful for the darkness which helped her conceal her brief moment of weakness.

"Are you suggesting I'll be cast out if I don't live up to your expectations?" she scoffed, feigning defiance. "Harlowe will never allow that to happen."

"He may fight the decision, but ultimately it won't be up to him."

Samantha stiffened her posture, refusing to let his words shake her. She didn't believe Harlowe would willingly turn his back on her, but he might not have a choice if the order came from the Home Office or from the Prince Regent.

"I need more time," she said, her voice tight.

"You have one week. Not a day more."

"And if I fail you?" Given what she'd just learned, she had to ask. And remind Kendrick of the value she offered. "You won't be any closer to getting the answers you seek or of bringing Mr. Croft down."

His next words, however, surprised her while sending a chill down her spine. "There are other means, Miss Carmichael. Accidents happen." He collected a box from his pocket, pulled a cheroot from it, and placed it between his lips before lighting it with a flint. A quick inhale preceded a puff of smoke. "Let's not make more of the situation than necessary. You're no different than I. We're both government employees with jobs to accomplish. Do yours and you'll be rewarded. Don't, and you will be sacked."

Samantha gritted her teeth. Blood pounded in her ears, encouraging her to lash out against the man who had her cornered. Knowing it would most likely be a mistake, she took a deep breath in an effort to calm herself.

"Fine, but I have to warn you. Mr. Croft is a cautious man. He doesn't trust easily, so if what little trust I've earned from him thus far is to be preserved, our friendship must continue to develop naturally. It cannot be forced to suit your agenda."

"I understand your concerns, but this has already taken longer than what was expected. A week is all you get, so I recommend you don't waste it." He turned, tossed the cheroot, and started walking away. "I trust you'll keep me informed."

Samantha watched him mount his horse, the squeak of leather sharp in the still night air. A soft whinny followed, and then the thud of hooves as Kendrick rode off, his shadowy figure blending with the darkness.

She knew of only one way in which to achieve her

goal before time ran out. Her heart raced at the idea. It would require more from her than all her years of training combined. But given the stakes, she might not have a choice.

Her hands, she realized, were trembling. Not because of what she might lose if she failed in her mission, but because of the threat Kendrick issued against Mr. Croft. He'd have him killed if need be. And she would do whatever it took to prevent such an outcome.

∼

Mr. Reed greeted Adrian when he arrived at the boxing club. "It's good to see you again, Mr. Croft. Would you like to train alone or do you prefer to engage in a match?"

"A match would be welcome if one of your trainers can spare the time."

"Certainly. Jones should be free for the next two hours." Mr. Reed called for the stocky Welshman to prepare himself, then leaned closer to Adrian. "Before you begin, you might want to see how the ladies are doing. Barrow is training them in the next room, and I've got to say, they've made exceptional progress so far. It's quite impressive."

Adrian glanced in the direction Reed indicated. He'd known of Miss Carmichael's plan to be here today. It was the reason he'd come – so he could see her again and enjoy her delightful company.

"I'll just be a moment," he told Jones, waving him off as he started toward the closed door to the left.

He pushed it open and stared, a little taken aback by what he saw. For there she was, together with her friend, Miss Stevens, and a few other women. All of them dressed in loose fitting shirts and snug breeches and doing their best to murder the wooden dummies they'd been provided.

"What do you think?" Barrow asked when he came to greet Adrian. "I myself was skeptical when Mr. Reed told me to teach them how to defend themselves. But it turns out they're remarkably capable and quick learners."

"It would seem so," Adrian agreed, his attention on Miss Carmichael's perfect technique as she threw a series of punches. It was hard to believe this was only her third lesson.

He caught her gaze when she turned, his chest expanding with pleasure in response to her smile. She crossed to where he stood, her damp skin glistening slightly from the exercise. The effect, Adrian realized, was not the least bit off putting but rather…exhilarating.

"As you can see, I've been practicing." She rocked back on her heels, her gaze drifting to the other women before returning to him. "I took your advice, adjusting my posture in front of my mirror until it was perfect. Hazel helped."

"It would seem the effort paid off. You've made remarkable progress in very short time."

Her answering grin nearly robbed him of breath. "I'm determined to learn."

"Will you excuse me a moment," Barrow asked. "I need to have a quick word with Reed. Won't take long. Maybe you can give the ladies some pointers in the meantime?"

Adrian nodded, the thrill of engaging Miss Carmichael in another mock fight spiking his pulse. "I'd be happy to."

He shucked his jacket, rolled up his sleeves, and strode to the center of the room before calling for everyone's attention. "Allow me to introduce myself to those of you who don't know me. I'm Adrian Croft. Barrow had to step out for a bit, so he asked me to manage the class until he gets back.

"First of all, I've got to say I'm impressed by your efforts. Did Barrow tell you what to try first if a man attacks you?"

"Kick him where it hurts," someone said. The comment was followed by snorts of laughter and furious blushes.

Adrian nodded. "That's right. Of course that'll only work under certain conditions. If an assailant attacks from behind, you'll have to apply different tactics."

He gestured for a woman he did not know to step forward and then proceeded to show a series of moves that might help in the situation he'd just described.

"Excellent work," he told her once they were done. "Now everyone find a partner and take turns trying to make that work."

Knowing the numbers weren't even, he told Miss Carmichael, "You're with me."

She stepped toward him, a look of determination burning bright in her eyes, and turned so he could attack her. A breath to keep his heartbeats even, before he placed his hand at her throat, his other hand grabbing her arm.

A pause followed, just long enough for him to smell the fragrance of jasmine in her hair. They were close, so close he could feel her breaths in the slow movements of her back as he pressed up against it with his chest.

Focus.

No sooner had the thought formed than she bucked her hips backward, attempting no doubt to strike him straight in the groin. A move that would have been quite effective, had he been positioned a little bit more to the left.

"Nice try," Adrian muttered as he caught her wrist, only to grunt with surprise when her elbow jabbed him hard in the ribs.

He brought his arm around her, attempting to trap her against him, but she twisted away, putting him slightly off balance and...

Releasing her, he did what he could not to crush her as they hit the floor with a thud.

Her breath rushed over his chin as the air was forced from her lungs.

Swallowing, he pressed his palms into the floor and pushed himself upward, catching the look of surprise in her eyes. "Are you all right?"

"I...Yes. I believe so."

Adrian stilled. There was something incredibly tempting in her expression – something that drowned out all else and made him forget that they weren't alone. He leaned in. Only to freeze in response to a shout.

It was followed by a gunshot.

He was on his feet and racing for the door before he took his next breath. Halting, he peered out into the front room where Barrow, Jones, and Reed stood with a few of the club's other members. Their hands were raised while two familiar scoundrels threatened them with pistols.

"We know you're 'ere, Croft," Chubbycheeks shouted. "Show yourself and we'll let these men go."

Adrian muttered a curse. It was the same blasted pair who'd attacked him before. If only he'd been wise enough to kill them then, he'd not be in this situation now.

He glanced at the women. "Stay here. I'll handle this."

"Come now, Croft," Scarface hollered. "Don't be a coward."

"What do you want?" Adrian asked the scoundrels as he entered the front room. He'd bloody well murder the pair for showing up here.

"Same as before."

"A beating then?"

"Don't try to be clever or..." Chubbycheeks glanced past Adrian's shoulder and grinned. "Looks like we won't be needin' you gents any longer. Not when there's ladies about. Go on. Get out."

"Leave the women be," Adrian growled. "This is between the three of us."

"Agreed. So just go get the files and we promise they won't be 'armed. Provided you don't do anything stupid, that is."

Adrian's mind raced. He didn't trust the men to keep their word and feared what would happen if he left the women alone with them. These men were violent. Anything could happen before he returned.

He had to stay and fight. With one pistol already fired, only one proved a threat. The question was which.

"Fine." He stepped forward slowly and made his approach, moving toward the exit until he was level with Scarface. "I've a question though."

Scarface aimed his pistol directly at Adrian's face and pulled back the hammer. "Go on."

"Have you forgotten what I told you when we last met?" He didn't wait for an answer before he lunged, spinning sideways while using the back of his hand to knock the pistol from Scarface's grasp.

The shot exploded from the barrel, the noise ringing in Adrian's head as he sent his fist flying. Knuckles connected with bone and Scarface crumpled. But even as he fell, Chubbycheeks slammed himself into Adrian's body and sent him reeling.

CHAPTER THIRTY

Samantha watched in horror as Croft scrambled to fight off the man who'd knocked him over. Light bounced off the edge of a blade the villain had managed to draw from a sheath. A short distance away the other man started to push himself upward. Soon it would be two against one and then what?

The pair on the floor rolled, grunting as they exchanged several blows.

She had to help.

Reaching into her hair, she felt for one of her lethal pins, only to feel a firm hand halting her movement.

"You can't use that," Hazel hissed. "Remember who you're pretending to be."

Right. Samantha lowered her hand and glanced around, seeking some sort of makeshift weapon.

An unlit oil lamp on a table nearby caught her attention. She grabbed it without overthinking the matter, ran for the man Croft was fighting, and smashed it over his head.

Glass shattered, splattering oil. The villain cried out in pain and released his hold on Croft, his blade clattering to the floor. Blood oozed from countless cuts as he tried to brush shards from his face.

Catching the back of his collar, she started to drag him off Croft, but the second assailant, having regained his footing, lunged at her. His size and weight pushed her off balance and stopped her from bracing for impact.

Her head hit the ground with a sickening crack, causing her vision to blur. Rough hands squeezed her throat.

"I'm gonna enjoy this," the brute spat as his thumbs dug into her flesh.

Samantha choked, her arms arcing straight up and outward in an attempt to dislodge his grasp. When that didn't work, she went for his eyes.

He reared back, but didn't release her. "Damn bitch."

His effort to kill her increased. Samantha tried to suck in some air but her windpipe had been restricted. She stared up at the ugly face hovering over her as it grew fuzzy. Her limbs felt increasingly numb, the need to pull air into her lungs forcing tears to her eyes.

"Miss Carmichael." Croft's voice was filled with alarm.

Hazel called out, the sound cutting the space between them. Additional shouts followed. The weight pressing Samantha into the ground disappeared. She managed a breath.

"Search them for additional weapons," an unfamiliar man's voice ordered while gentle hands brushed her face, pushing stray locks of hair from her brow. It felt like time was missing. Could it be she'd blacked out?

"Are you all right?" Croft asked with what sounded like genuine worry. She managed a nod. "What the hell were you thinking?"

"That you needed help." She coughed and swallowed past the ache in her throat, then turned to one side and began easing herself into a sitting position, despite Croft's protestations. "Who's that?"

Croft followed her gaze toward the tall, broad-shouldered man who kept the two thugs restrained. "Murry. He's my valet. Reed went to fetch him."

"Smart man."

Croft searched her face as though looking for something specific. He eventually sighed. "The lamp was a good idea. Thank you."

She nodded and rubbed the back of her head. "It sounded like they knew you. Any idea what they wanted?"

They'd mentioned files. Considering the lengths the thugs had gone to in order to acquire them, their contents had to be extremely desirable. Perhaps they were filled with information pertaining to illicit business dealings? Or maybe this was where Croft kept all the damning details used to force people's hands.

Either way, her interest was piqued.

"Something I'm not prepared to hand over." He knit his brow. "Are you sure you're all right?"

"Not entirely, but I will be once I put something cold on this bump that's forming."

"We'd best get you home then. Do you think you can stand?"

She almost laughed. She'd taken a rather serious hit to the head, but she wasn't some delicate flower.

Still, Croft didn't know that. So she pretended to think on the matter before deciding to tell him, "With your help, I should manage."

He got her upright with the utmost of care and urged her to use his arm for support. Glancing around, she saw that the rest of the women who'd been there, save Hazel, were gone.

"What will you do with those men?" Samantha asked a few minutes later when Croft escorted her and Hazel to their carriage.

"Make sure they pay." His manner, so warm when he'd asked about her wellbeing, was now cold and steely. He helped her into the carriage. "I regret what happened today. My only hope is that the next time we meet, it will be under more pleasant circumstances."

"Likewise."

Stepping back, he shut the door, then ordered the driver to take her home.

∼

There was no escaping the heavy regret weighing on Adrian's shoulders. Those men might have come after him, but they'd done so publicly this time, disrupting other people's lives in the process. Their thoughtless use of those pistols could have resulted in tragedy.

And then there was Miss Carmichael, whom Scarface would have deliberately murdered had Murry not shown up at the right time and neutralized him. Adrian himself had been too busy fighting Chubbycheeks, whose weight had continued to pin him down.

It was a damn miracle no one had died.

"I'm sorry this happened," he told Mr. Reed who was sweeping glass off the floor when Adrian returned. "I'll naturally pay for the damage."

"Thank you, but there isn't much besides the broken lamp."

"I'll have it replaced." When Mr. Reed nodded and went back to sweeping, Adrian glanced at the scoundrels who'd ruined everyone's day. Their wrists had been tied behind their backs, their mouths gagged with lengths of fabric. Disgusted by their behavior, Adrian turned to Murry. "Let's get them into the carriage."

The journey out of town seemed never ending. Jaw tight, Adrian kept his eyes on the captives who sat on the opposite bench, his loaded pistol on Scarface while Murry directed his at Chubbycheeks.

Anger curled in his gut, spreading through every limb until the rigidity pained him. It wasn't just caused by the attack or by thoughts of what it could have led to, but by what he was now forced to do.

He had no choice even though it stood in direct opposition to what he'd hoped to achieve. But the truth was he'd already made a mistake by letting them go the first time they'd attacked him. A decision that nearly cost Miss Carmichael's life today.

For her and any other innocents these men might harm, he had to act with unforgiving force.

Of course, there was also the issue of his reputation. If he showed additional mercy now and word got out, it would be destroyed.

Not an option. It was time for him to send a message to anyone foolish enough to cross him – to those who thought him weak and incapable of living up to his father's notoriety.

CHAPTER THIRTY-ONE

Samantha marched into Harlowe's office as soon as she got back to Clearview. She planted her palms on his desk and leaned forward, her gaze meeting that of the man who'd provided her with a home.

"Did you send those cutthroats?"

"What cutthroats?"

"The men who attacked Mr. Croft at Reed's. I need to know if you were involved."

"Of course not. Why would you think such a thing?"

"Because they wanted *his files*." She sank into one of the two leather armchairs that stood across from the desk. "My guess is they're after the same thing as us."

"I swear, I had nothing to do with any cutthroats." He regarded her seriously. "Looks like they might have attacked you too."

"On the contrary, it was the other way around. I tried to help Croft fend them off."

"Not by revealing too much, I hope."

"You needn't worry. It looked like he truly feared for my safety." What she would not confess was that one of the thugs had managed to get the best of her. It shouldn't have happened. And it wouldn't have if she'd been able to use all her skill.

Harlowe chuckled. "Go clean yourself up and have one of the maids bring you a slab of meat for your bruises."

She'd do so as soon as she'd dispatched a message to Kendrick, asking if he was involved.

It was past nine o'clock by the time his answer arrived.

I know nothing about the men you mentioned.

Samantha tossed the note into the fire that burned in her room. She was no closer to figuring out who had ordered those men to attack. But one thing was clear: Mr. Croft was in danger. Not just from her, but from an unknown enemy.

It bothered her deeply and made her feel out of control. So she did what she always did when frustration tugged at her nerves. She stormed to the training room and snatched up a sword, slashing it through the air until her anxiety started abating.

He's just a mission, she reminded herself while moving through a series of attacks. *I mustn't care about him.*

But she did. In her heart, she knew he wasn't merely a target. He'd become so much more, though she dared not acknowledge how much.

The afternoon light grew increasingly dim as Adrian's carriage rumbled onward. Leaving the cobbled streets of the City behind, it made its way along uneven country roads, heading west before turning down a bumpy lane. Another half hour passed before they drew to a halt, by which time the sinking sun was casting long shadows along the ground.

"Time to get out," Murry said once he'd opened the door and alit.

Chubbycheeks scooted forward and pushed his head through the doorway, only to jerk back against the squabs, his eyes wide as he shook his head, muttering something against the gag wound tightly around his head. The reaction agitated Scarface, who started to wrestle against his own bindings.

Impatient to have the entire ordeal over and done with quickly, Adrian found the dagger he wore in his right boot and pressed the tip against Chubbycheeks's neck. "Do as he says. Now."

When Chubbycheeks just continued to whimper, his eyes welling with tears, Adrian grabbed him by his arm and shoved him toward the door. He landed knees first on the carriage floor.

Adrian glared at him briefly, then placed the sole of his boot against the man's arse and shoved him forward. "Bloody coward. Grab him in whatever way you're able, Murry. Get Phelps to help if need be."

Together, they managed to get the unwieldy man

from the carriage. His friend, who showed the same resistance, received a similar treatment. Adrian sent them both a disgruntled look while sheathing his dagger and thrusting his pistol into his pocket.

"Are you sure you want to do this?" Murry asked once they'd dragged both men a fair distance from the carriage.

Adrian turned to him with surprise. "You ask me this now?"

"I simply mean that you don't have to be the one pulling the triggers."

The comment resulted in further distress from the captives, their garbled pleas for help disturbing the peace in this desolate spot. In Adrian's opinion, it was a senseless waste of their final moments since none of those able to hear them actually cared.

"Thank you." He took a deep breath, inhaling the smell of wild grass before extending his upturned palm – a silent request for Murry to hand him his pistol. "It's nothing I've not done before."

"Of course not." The valet handed the weapon over, the weight of it a familiar thing that helped settle Adrian's nerves. Calmed by it, he retrieved the second pistol from his pocket and jutted his chin at the men. "Let's get those gags off so they can speak."

No sooner had Murry done so than both men launched into a series of pleas, each drowning out the other with a degree of eagerness Adrian found disgusting. There was no doubt in his mind he could have made both of them do as he pleased in exchange for their lives.

But nothing was worth the worry of knowing they'd probably hunt him down yet again if he let them go. So far, luck had been on his side. The same might not be true next time.

He raised the pistols.

"Please," Chubbycheeks cried. "We meant ye no harm."

"Didn't you?" No hint of sympathy. "You'd have happily stabbed me if you hadn't been stopped."

"I only meant to threaten ye with the blade, not actually use it."

"Have mercy," Scarface begged.

"For trying to strangle a lady to death?" Adrian scoffed. "Sorry. You'll have to ask that of God, for I am not as forgiving."

The gunshots that followed were quick and precise. They were drowned out by squawking birds who'd been frightened from nearby trees. The deed was done. Adrian glanced at Murry. "Let's go."

Together, they trudged back to the carriage where Phelps waited. Neither spoke a word as they rode back to London, and Adrian was glad of it since he'd nothing to say. What he'd done kept him tied to a past he'd longed to escape, anchoring him to the darkness corrupting his soul.

The opera was a lively place to visit – a venue where spectators watched each other with equal, if not more interest, than what they showed the performers. Theatre glasses were pressed to everyone's eyes as they sought to discover a new affair, a ghastly choice of attire, or some other detail to gossip about at the next social gathering.

One man, however, sought something different as he took stock of those present, his focus on finding a debutante guilty of wicked behavior. Smiling at those who glanced his way, he kept the dark thoughts that swirled through his mind carefully hidden.

They stood in sinister contrast to the shimmering light provided by hundreds of gilded wall sconces, but they also reminded him of his purpose. A purpose that was becoming increasingly easy for him to fulfill. Hell, his most recent murder had quenched a thirst he'd not even realized he had. The power he'd found in seducing Lady Lavinia right before slitting her throat had been wonderfully thrilling.

He needed to experience that again.

So he kept on scanning the youthful faces of women who prided themselves on being untouched. Somewhere among them were those who were anything but. And sooner or later he would find them. If only to appease his own hunger.

CHAPTER THIRTY-TWO

It took a good couple of hours for Adrian to return from his unpleasant journey. Elks greeted him and Murry in the foyer before conveying a message.

"Marsdale stopped by an hour ago. He said to tell you he'd be at the Hog Tail Tavern until eleven, if you'd like to join him there for a drink."

"My bath will have to wait until later then," Adrian said, walking to the stairs and proceeding to climb them two steps at a time.

He'd been looking forward to washing the filth from his conscience, but Edward was family, so if he wanted company, Adrian would deliver. It had been a while since they'd last spoken. A lot had happened during that time. "Help me freshen up, Murry. I want to be on my way within fifteen minutes."

It was nearing ten by the time he strode into the noisy alehouse. He surveyed the space, but it was so packed with patrons near the front where the ale was served, he'd have needed to stand on a stool in order to find anyone.

Pushing forward, he squeezed his way past a series of tables until he reached a more open spot. He turned, his gaze catching the bounce of two dice being used in a game of hazard. A roar of laughter erupted behind his left shoulder before someone shouted for one of the barmaids to fetch additional tankards of ale.

He could use a drink of his own to silence the censorious thoughts flooding his brain. The blank-eyed stares of the men he'd killed remained in his mind's eye, taunting him – reminding him how he had failed in his promise to Evie.

No. He shook off the voice that taunted him. Those men had deserved what they got. He'd not minced words when he'd threatened them in the alley. They'd chosen to ignore him and now they'd paid the price.

Besides, they were no different from the other men he'd killed while enforcing his father's will.

Perhaps not, but this time, you made the call entirely by yourself.

Clenching his jaw, he rounded a wooden post and was happy to spot his friend's familiar profile. He stood with a few other people – Lords Glendale, Ottersburg and Midhurst, as well as Mr. Nigel Lawrence.

Adrian stepped forward, swept his hat from his head, and greeted them each in turn – ever conscious of their gazes assessing the bruises on his face. No one commented on it, however. In fact, the only one who showed any interest in his arrival was Edward. Understandable, since they were friends. The rest were, as his father had put it, a potential means to an end.

None of them argued when Adrian proposed he and Edward excuse themselves from the group. Moving away from the others, they found a table in a far corner, and grabbed an extra chair.

"Will you tell me what happened?" Edward asked once they'd settled into their seats. He gestured with his hand to gain a barmaid's attention. "Looks like your face may have met with a fist."

The barmaid arrived and Adrian ordered them both a couple of drinks.

"Remember my accident with the low hanging beam?" When Edward nodded, Adrian confessed, "I was actually attacked by a couple of thugs."

"What?" The question was spoken in anger – anger on Adrian's behalf. "Why didn't you tell me?"

Adrian shrugged. "The same men attacked me again today. They were after the files I inherited from my father."

"And they came after you twice." Edward stared at him in dismay. "You realize this means they'll be likely to try again, right?"

"They won't."

The barmaid returned. She placed two mugs on the table and took the one Edward was done with before walking off.

"How do you know?" Edward asked, his hard gaze boring straight through Adrian.

"Because I made sure of it."

Edward blew out a breath and sank against his seat. "Don't tell me anything more. I don't want to know but...damn it, you should have told Bow Street to handle this."

"That wasn't an option." Good lord, the very idea of involving the authorities in his private affairs was enough to make his skin itch. He drank a measure of ale.

"Look, our friendship is based on me not knowing what you're involved with, so all I'll say is this: Knowing who your father was, I'm fairly sure you didn't send those men who attacked you off to Bath on holiday. Which worries me, because if you get caught doing something...questionable...I'm not sure I'll have the power to save you."

"I understand, and I appreciate your concern." He genuinely meant it. "Please don't worry."

"How can I not?" Incredulity filled Edward's eyes. "With your sister gone you're..." He shook his head. "Just promise me you'll be careful."

"Always."

Edward didn't look fully convinced. Concern was still etched on his brow, but when he spoke next his thoughts had clearly shifted. "They say time heals all wounds, but I miss Evie more with each passing day."

Edward's use of Evelyn's pet name came as a jarring surprise. It shouldn't have, Adrian reflected, and yet the intimacy and loss it conveyed was poignant.

A sad smile tugged at Edward's lips. "If only I'd told her how I felt."

If only.

Maybe he would have married her and she would still be alive today. Adrian swallowed that thought when he took his next sip and opted for offering comfort instead. "I'm sure she knew."

"Maybe," Edward conceded. His gaze suddenly darkened. "I want her killer to hang."

"He'll do more than that," Adrian vowed.

The comment brought Edward's head up with a snap. He stared across the table between them, his knuckles bright as he gripped his mug. "You promised me less than ten minutes ago that you'd stay out of danger. Let Bow Street handle this matter so they don't find cause to go after you as well."

"As much as I appreciate your concern, Evie was my sister. Bow Street is doing bugger all to catch the man who, may I remind you, butchered her throat. So I will do whatever I can to sniff him out. And once I do, the bastard will rue the day he was born."

Noting how pale Edward looked, Adrian realized he'd probably said too much. A notion he thought on at greater length later when he returned home. Edward was like the brother he'd never had. They'd always gotten along. But only because he'd kept the ugly part of himself and all his dark family secrets carefully tucked away so his friend wouldn't see.

It occurred to him now how exhausting that was, constantly having to tiptoe around the edges for fear of what Edward might think. Or worse, what his moral compass might prompt him to do.

By contrast, Miss Carmichael seemed more inclined to safeguard his secrets. Maybe. He took a moment to explore that thought. Unlike Edward, she'd encouraged him to seek vengeance on Evie's behalf. Hell, she was trying to help him track down the killer.

He sipped the tea he'd ordered before retiring, his heart finding a steadier rhythm the more he thought on the woman who'd come to his aid in the midst of a fight. Unique was one way to describe her. Brave was another. As were resilient, remarkable, surprising, attractive, compelling, and…

He could not wait to see her again tomorrow.

~

Having opted for a snug pair of breeches, a comfortable shirt and jacket, Samantha accompanied Wycliffe into a narrow street. The hooded mask she wore concealed all but her eyes, the daggers tucked into her sleeves a welcome reminder that she could protect herself from whatever danger she might be about to face.

Wycliffe had not been specific. He'd merely informed her that he was about to meet with a disgruntled business associate. Things might get rough. It was her job to keep him safe.

They crossed to a shadowy doorway and Wycliffe gave the door a few solid knocks. It opened a smidgen and someone peered out through the gap, took quick stock of them, then pulled the door wide to grant them entry.

Samantha followed Wycliffe inside, her attention on the man who'd let them in. His thick arms stretched the sleeves of his jacket taut, his broad torso forcing the garment to gape at the front. Built from pure muscle, he'd prove a dangerous foe if she had to fight him.

"This way," he said, his voice gruff.

He led them through a hallway toward another door and out into a courtyard lit only by the occasional touch of moonlight. Two other men stood here, both of solid build, though one appeared slightly shorter.

"Who's your friend, Wycliffe?"

Samantha tilted her head, her eyes on the shorter man as he stepped closer. She knew that voice but couldn't quite place it.

"One of the older lads," Wycliffe said. "The right side of his face melted a few years ago in a fire, so he keeps it hidden from view."

A moment of silence to gauge this response, and then, "Where's my delivery?"

"Still on the ship. The boy I sent to collect it was caught trying to find it." The last was spoken with bitterness, the only indication Wycliffe regretted the loss.

"Then I've really no use for you, have I?" The shorter man gestured toward his protectors, the slight movement allowing a sliver of moonlight to touch his face.

Samantha sucked in a breath as she recognized Wrengate, his hard eyes glinting with merciless calm. A thousand questions filled her head all at once, all of them just as quickly forgotten when Wrengate's men charged. She sensed rather than saw Wycliffe move, her own attention on shifting away from the fist that was flying toward her.

She ducked, spun, and grabbed her attacker's ankles, then pushed herself upright so her momentum could send him headfirst into a sprawl. A curse followed before he leapt back into action. His speed was impressive for a man his size.

Another fist flew and she darted sideways, careful not to get struck since one blow would probably kill her. Something crashed and a grunt followed. Ignoring the sound, she kept her gaze trained on the beast she'd been paired with.

He lunged and attempted to grab her while she swung her leg, kicking her foot toward his groin with as much force as she could muster. A roar of pain shook the surrounding buildings and yet he remained upright.

Rage twisted his features, the cruelty in his eyes warning her she wouldn't leave here alive. Metal glinted in the next instant, the dagger he'd unsheathed arcing toward her with menacing swiftness.

Instinct ripped through her veins. Her hands moved, curling around smooth wood and pulling twin blades free from her sleeves as she dropped to one knee. Her attacker's blade met with nothing but air while she thrust hers upward, straight into his belly.

A swift stab, just as she'd practiced again and again with those burlap sacks Harlowe had filled with hay. It felt no different – soft and yielding. She pulled them free and dodged the body now falling toward the ground with a choked-out groan.

Still he moved, shifting onto one forearm and turning while cursing her to perdition. Footsteps hitting the ground behind her was all the warning she got before his companion was there with death in his eyes, his arm rising to showcase the dagger he wielded.

Samantha lowered her stance, one hand preparing to block him as the other shot forward, straight into his throat. His eyes bulged, a spray of blood wetting her face before he buckled.

She wiped it away with the back of her hand and shifted her gaze to the other man. His chest rose and fell with strained breaths before he went limp.

There was no telling how long she stood there, hands trembling while coming to terms with what had transpired. All she knew was that Wycliffe was gone. A cat's screech eventually snapped her out of her stupor.

Crouching, she wiped her blades clean on the dead men's clothes, sheathed them, and started making her way back to her lodgings. Her debt had been paid ten times over. If Wycliffe ever asked anything of her again, she'd carve him into little pieces.

∽

The hallway clock at Stanton House chimed the eleventh hour as Clive Newton donned his hat. He was on his way out to meet with some friends, but turned back when his father's voice, coming from the study, drew his attention because of the door being left ajar.

"Is there anything to suggest Croft might know we're involved?" Papa asked.

"No." The answer was clearly spoken by Owen and was followed by a more muffled comment.

Curious to know what they might be discussing, Clive moved a bit closer.

"Damn him and those files," Papa cursed. A thud followed, suggesting he'd slammed his fist into his desk. "I'd hoped he'd be different from his father, but the threat he issued Mr. Abernathy is added proof that he's chosen to take up where the old bastard left off."

A brief hesitation before Owen asked, "What else has he done?"

"Nothing. Forget it."

"Perhaps," Owen began, only to lock eyes with Clive through the gap in the door. He quickly shut it, preventing Clive from discerning anything more.

CHAPTER THIRTY-THREE

Although she was perfectly able to hold her balance, Samantha made a show of gripping the curricle's bench whenever Mr. Croft steered the horses around a sharp bend in the road. He claimed to have brought the vehicle due to the excellent weather, but also, he'd later confided, so they could enjoy an excursion without the need for a chaperone.

It was the first indication he'd made of an increased interest in her, and while it pleased her for the sake of her goal, she'd be lying if she claimed it did not thrill her on a more personal level. However dangerous that might prove for her later.

For now, she would simply enjoy her excursion with him. She would not, *could* not, think of last night. Only anger and fierce self-loathing would come of that, for while common sense told her she'd done what she had to, the fact still remained: she'd taken two lives.

"Everything all right?" Croft sent her a curious glance. "You're unusually quiet all of a sudden."

She forced a smile. "I'm just admiring your excellent driving skills."

He sent her a wicked grin and she laughed. This was where her focus should lie. Not on Wycliffe or Wrengate or the men who would have killed her had she not killed them.

There was no point in mourning their loss or in letting the incident shake her nerves. For the sake of her mission, she'd do well to steel herself against it.

So she took a deep breath and considered her handsome companion, a principled man who'd stop at nothing to see justice served, who made sure women received the training required to fend off assailants, despite it going against social standards, who saw to a lady's comfort and punished those who preyed on the weak. The fresh bruise marring the edge of his jaw reminded her of the latter.

Did she suspect him of killing the men who'd attacked him at Reed's yesterday? Without doubt. She'd seen the murderous look in his eyes when he'd helped her into her carriage.

Could she fault him for it?

No. She would have done the same had she been in his position.

But what of everything else Kendrick claimed Mr. Croft was a part of? The forced prostitution, the aid he provided criminals and foreign agents, the information he supposedly used for blackmail?

She wasn't entirely sure, so she glanced at him and was instantly struck by the softness currently framing his eyes and mouth. He'd always looked tense during each of their previous encounters. Driving the curricle seemed to offer a welcome escape. It seemed like it helped him relax.

A pity she'd have to ruin that, but since she'd no idea when she'd see him again and time was of the essence, she had to make the most of it. "I've been thinking…"

He shifted slightly beside her, his upper arm brushing hers. "About what?"

She took a deep breath.

"How to discover the killer's identity." Hard lines instantly gathered upon his brow. His mouth firmed and his grip on the reins seemed to tighten. As much as Samantha regretted the shift, she had to press on. "It might be useful to bait him."

The horses cantered onward, their hooves pounding into the firmly packed dirt. Air swept past Samantha's face, cooling her skin. The curricle bounced, perhaps because of a stone, and Mr. Croft pulled the horses into a gentler trot.

He glanced at her with interest. "The idea has merit, but how do you propose to do so?"

"There's a meadow up ahead," she informed him, avoiding the question for a brief moment. "If you turn between those trees right there, we can stop to talk while we stretch our legs."

The spot was lovely – a welcome retreat she'd visited often over the years. Surrounded by trees and blackberry bushes, it also offered a lovely display of wildflowers with the added benefit of a small lake.

It was also secluded and wonderfully private.

She'd never shared it with anyone else. Until now.

Having reached the trees she'd indicated, Mr. Croft steered the horses off the road and toward the meadow as she suggested.

"It's the perfect subject for a landscape painting," he remarked as soon as he'd pulled the horses to a standstill and allowed himself a moment to take in the view. When he glanced at her next, his eyes were filled with equal amounts of interest and curiosity. "A bit hidden away though, wouldn't you say?"

"That's the benefit of it," Samantha explained while hoping her purpose was not too transparent. If Mr. Croft suspected her of encouraging him to take their relationship to the next level, he'd probably suspect her of a great deal more. She shoved the concern aside and gave him a serious look. "Chances are you won't like what I am about to suggest. In fact, I believe you may wish to shake some sense into me once you hear it. In which case I thought it best if you were to do so without the risk of encountering anyone else. Or while attempting to drive."

He stared at her, then firmed his mouth and gave her a hesitant look. "What do you have in mind?"

"Just remember that you yourself agreed my idea to bait the killer has merit."

His eyes narrowed. "Miss Carmichael."

"Well, my plan involves me playing the part of the—"

"Absolutely not." A thunderous expression darkened his gaze. "Are you out of your bloody mind?"

"No. I—"

"Do you honestly think I would ever place you in that sort of danger?" He grabbed her upper arms and held her firmly in place, his fingers digging into soft flesh while searching her gaze. "What sort of man do you take me for?"

"The sort who would walk through hell to do what is right." Inspired by the fierceness with which he'd spoken, the raw emotion that burned in his gaze, and their close proximity in this moment, she set her palm against his cheek and whispered, "The sort who would come to my aid as soon as the murderer shows his face."

He stared at her, his posture rigid, each breath a ragged reminder of how close he was to losing control. She licked her lips and his mouth collided with hers in a feverish kiss for which she was utterly unprepared.

After all, no man had kissed her before and…

Honestly, she'd been a fool to imagine Mr. Croft's kisses would ever be gentle and sweet when everything else about him conveyed some degree of danger. Men feared him for good reason if he was as unforgiving as she believed.

He wasn't the sort to mince words, to pretend he was something he wasn't. And the lack of restraint in this moment was like a reflection of that. It was like getting caught in a storm from which one had no wish to ever escape.

So she curled her fingers around his neck, her other hand clutching his shoulder. Teeth grazed her lips. A warm hand flattened against the base of her spine, scattering heat as he pulled her against the hard, muscular plane of his chest. A new sensation wove its way through her.

She tried to examine it closer, to understand her body's response, only to groan with frustration when he drew back. Pressing his forehead to hers, he panted for breath.

"Good lord. You must think me feral." He withdrew even farther, his brows dipping as he met her gaze. "My apologies. I hope you can forgive me."

The underlying hint of uncertainty lacing his words made her smile. "Doing so would suggest you did something wrong. Or that I was opposed to what happened between us just now. But I'm not, so there's nothing for me to forgive."

"You're certain?"

His question made her begin to have doubts, so she forced herself to say, "Unless you regret it, Mr. Croft."

"Adrian. After what we just shared, I must insist you use my given name."

"Only if you will agree to use mine."

"It would be my absolutely pleasure." Raising his hand, he brushed a stray strand of hair from her cheek and tucked it behind her ear. "And to answer your question, I could never regret kissing you. As it is, I'm doing my damndest to stop from taking things further."

"You mean…" She had to hear him say it – to have him confirm that her plan was working and that she had some sort of chance in hell of meeting her deadline.

"I want you." The words were delivered with raw emotion, his eyes filling with fresh desire as soon as he spoke them.

"As your lover?" He gave a quick nod and she made a show of pretending to give his answer some thought before saying, "My questionable birthright makes marriage unlikely for me in the future. However, I cannot deny being drawn to you or that I'm tempted to know what it might be like to share your bed."

He gave her a roguish look filled with promise and mischief. "I'd make it worth your while."

She cleared her throat and glanced to one side, affecting an air of uncertainty. "I should probably give this some serious thought before committing."

"A wise decision." He snatched up the reins as if preparing to nudge the horses back into motion.

Samantha stopped him with the press of her hand against his arm. He stilled and turned to her slowly, a question burning in his dark eyes. "I meant what I said. If we make a plan to draw out the killer by using me as bait, I'm confident I'll be perfectly safe as long as you're somewhere nearby."

He shook his head. "What you're suggesting goes against my every instinct. I've already lost my sister. I'll not risk losing you too."

"What's the alternative? To hope he'll slip up and reveal himself?" She grabbed his hand, lacing their fingers together. "Other women may die before then."

The look he gave her was pained. "Samantha…"

Her name was a heartfelt plea filled with dread. It proved more than anything how much he cared for her safety.

"I won't forgive myself if that man claims additional victims, knowing I could have done my part to stop him. Will you?"

"Of course not. I want him caught as soon as possible, but I will do so without you getting involved." He squeezed her hand. "You're too important to risk."

"No more so than anyone else." Leaning in, she pressed her mouth to his in a gentle caress. "Please. Let me do this."

"Your resolve and courage surprise me." He placed his fingers against her chin, cradling her there while studying her with incredulity. "You don't seem the least bit afraid."

Samantha's mind raced. She was supposed to be a gently bred lady, not a woman trained to do battle.

Aware he waited for some explanation, she picked the argument she believed in the most – the truth she'd have found in this moment had she lacked the skill to fight for survival. "Will you come to my aid the instant I need you?"

"Of course."

The smile she gave him was purposefully sweet. "Then I have nothing to fear, do I?"

Dark eyes stared into hers. "Your faith in me is a bit overwhelming."

"I watched you fight off two men yesterday. One of them larger than you."

"Only because you helped."

"Which proves we make an excellent team." She held her breath and waited for his response, her stomach clenching due to the wary look he gave her.

"I pray I'll never regret this." Sighing, he tied the reins to the seat rail and gave her his full attention. "How do you wish to proceed?"

CHAPTER THIRTY-FOUR

Adrian's heart refused to slow. It continued thumping wildly against his chest as he helped Samantha from his carriage and led her across the field. She'd suggested they stroll while they crafted their plan and he'd been in full agreement. He'd felt like a wolf trapped in a cage for the past half hour.

The tension gripping his body was like an insatiable hunger. It had to be satisfied somehow and since a violent fight and a shag were both off the table, he had to settle for walking.

Dog's bollocks, the woman had him vexed, anxious and overheated, all at the same time. Hands clasped behind his back, he glanced at her, matching her paces while she began stitching a plan together. Had she been offended when he'd invited her to become his mistress? It hadn't seemed that way, but he could be wrong.

At least she'd said she'd think about it, but would

she accept? He desperately hoped so. Now that he'd had a small taste, he wouldn't be satisfied until she came to his bed. Not just to sate his desire, but to mend his damaged soul.

"It will involve the two of us showing an increased interest in one another," she said, her suggestive comment sending a thrill down his spine.

The edge of his mouth quirked. "That shouldn't be hard."

She rolled her eyes but the twitch of her lips was evidence of her amusement. "We have to be very public about it to make sure word spreads."

"Although I'm not supposed to attend social functions at present, a ball would probably serve as the best location. With hundreds of people in attendance, the killer is bound to hear what happened even if he's not there himself."

"Agreed. The one Harlowe's hosting will make for the perfect setting. I'll make sure you're not turned away at the door." Halting, she faced him. "We'll need help though. From someone we can rely on to be discreet."

"Why?"

"So we can be absolutely sure the killer will know I'm the sort of woman he's after." When he failed to respond she reminded him boldly, "There tend to be two men in the victim's life – the one who believes she'll make him the perfect wife, and the one with whom she's finding her pleasure."

"In other words," Adrian murmured while tamping

down the sick feeling that roiled in his stomach, "you need to be courted and compromised at the same time."

"Yes."

A series of deep breaths helped fight the red haze before it descended over his eyes. He'd never believed himself capable of jealousy, but the idea of anyone other than him so much as touching Samantha put murderous thoughts in his head.

She was his. No one else's.

"Adrian?"

"What?" His muscles were straining so hard he was practically shaking.

"You look…furious."

He glared at her while trying to come to grips with his increasing feelings for her. They were bloody inconvenient, made worse by the terror of knowing their plan, however good it might be, could fail. That *he* could fail. And that going ahead with it put him at risk of losing her forever.

He slammed the door shut on that thought and leaned toward her, shoulders tense. "Which one will I be? The lovesick fool or the scoundrel who gets to push up your skirts?"

"Naturally the first," she said with a bite to her voice. "We've spent enough time together at various social functions for a courtship between us to look like a natural progression. I can't sell that with somebody else."

Her comment appeased him a little, though not

nearly enough. He flexed his fingers. "And your seducer?"

She crossed her arms. "What about Marsdale?"

He opened his mouth, prepared to argue, only to close it once more as the idea sank in. There was no denying the wisdom in it. Edward could certainly be trusted, but could they convince him to help? "He's a stickler for law and order. When I met him last night he urged me to leave the killer to Bow Street. I'm not sure we can get him to help."

"Will you let me try?"

"Certainly, but we'll need an alternative if he refuses." Honestly, he could not believe he was saying this. It sounded ludicrous to his own ears. And yet, he still told her, "I'll give it some thought."

She nodded. "The Clearview ball is on Friday. It would be good if we could be ready by then."

"If you're free tomorrow afternoon, I'll make arrangements for you and Marsdale to meet."

"Thank you." Happy the conversation had come to an end, Adrian turned with every intention of heading back to the carriage, but her hand caught his arm and kept him rooted. "Whatever happens between him and me, it won't be real. Not like it is with you."

No sooner had she spoken than he hauled her against him and pressed his mouth to hers. She gasped, lips parting, allowing him to deepen the kiss – to claim that part of her for himself.

Whatever they'd shared in the carriage, this was

rougher, more elemental, a dark reminder of what he wanted and what he would give in return. It ought to have scared an innocent woman like her, and perhaps it did, though only for a brief second.

After that…

She matched him every step of the way, pressing her body to his, hands roaming and gripping, exploring every spot she could reach. And the taste of her – the soft little sighs of pleasure that spilled from her lips when he touched her in just the right way – drove him wild.

It pushed him straight to the brink of madness. For even though his most burning desire right now was to lay her down amidst the flowers, his heart, that part of him that had felt like a charred piece of coal for most of his life, resisted.

The resulting effort caused him to growl in frustration. He grabbed her wrists and stilled her movements, then pushed her back gently. "We should stop, before I forget myself completely."

"I…" She brought her fingertips to her lips and suddenly blinked. "Good lord. Whatever must you think of me?"

"That you've the same inclination as I to get carried away." He offered his arm. "Come. Let's return to the carriage and get you home. We've much to do if we're to be ready for Friday's ball."

A smoldering heat still singed Samantha's skin when Adrian dropped her off. The pleasure she'd found in the kisses they'd shared was something else entirely. Unexpected was one way of putting it. Life-altering, enlightening, and altogether astounding also worked.

Standing on the front steps of Clearview House, she watched him drive away while doing her best to convince herself it was merely a means to an end. And yet, there was no denying he'd made her insensible. Even now, she longed for additional kisses and in that field...

Heaven's, she'd have let him do whatever he wished– would likely have begged him for more – had he not ended things.

Unacceptable.

Cursing herself, she spun on her heels and continued inside, only to find Harlowe leaning against the stairs, his elbow on the newel post. "How did it go?"

Schooling her features as best as she could, she forced herself to meet his gaze directly. "I managed to make some progress."

"Oh?" Harlowe pushed himself upright and gave her a studious look. "How so?"

She wouldn't lie. He'd see straight through that. "Croft kissed me."

Harlowe's expression remained unchanged. It was impossible to tell what he might be thinking. "Did you welcome it?"

Yes.

"In light of what we hope to achieve, I thought it unwise to push him away."

"Naturally." His sharp gaze lingered on hers. "Anything else?"

"He made his interest in taking me to his bed abundantly clear."

A slow smile materialized. "And did you accept?"

"I told him I'd think it through."

"Good. You made the right decision." He swept his hand toward his study. "Join me for a drink. We've much to discuss."

Harlowe poured them each a glass of port and handed one to Samantha. Eying her with that inscrutable expression of his, he asked, "Are you prepared for what comes next?"

"How do you mean?" Just to be sure she understood him.

"Croft's proposition. It's not exactly what you trained for." He leaned against the edge of his desk and stretched out his legs, crossing them at the ankles. "Might be useful to bring in an expert to walk you through the details. So you know what to expect."

No question as to whether or not she wanted to do it.

Her interest in discovering what it would be like to have a man like Adrian Croft as her lover was beside the point. Harlowe didn't know her mind. In his eyes she was an agent, raised to serve the country, and apparently to sacrifice her innocence in the process, if need be.

She was expendable.

Not loved or cared for, as she'd believed, but a weapon. To be used without thought for the impact it would have upon her.

She sipped her drink slowly. Allowed herself time to process what he was saying. All the while eyeing the silver letter opener on his desk. It would be so easy to stab him in the throat and watch him bleed out.

But what would that lead to? A quick hanging or a life on the run?

She'd no desire for either. And besides, pretending nothing had changed might prove useful. In case she needed Harlowe later.

So she did what she had been trained to do and buried her anger as deep as it could possibly go. "That's not a bad idea. Thank you for looking out for me."

"It's what I'm here for." He swirled the contents of his glass while considering her. "I'll have Blush's owner drop by in the morning. Mrs. Butler's her name. She'll give you the information you need and answer whatever questions you have. Any idea of when you'll be sealing the deal?"

Deep breaths kept Samantha grounded. She'd not considered it yet, but the intensity of Harlowe's gaze pressed her to answer. "Perhaps after the ball, if I'm able to tempt him with the suggestion."

The edge of his lips curled with approval. "I'm sure you'll manage. Just be sure you're prepared when you go to him. I recommend that you take a vial of laudanum with you. Put a few drops in his drink so he doesn't disturb you while you search through his things."

No suggestion as to how she would make sure Adrian drank the concoction she served him. That would be up to her. Provided she did as Harlowe instructed. Assuming Croft brought her into his home instead of using an inn.

She drank the last of her port and returned her glass to the sideboard. "If that's all, I'll go write a message to Kendrick. Make sure he's kept up to date."

Not until she'd reached her room and locked the door behind her did she permit her mask of agreeability to slip and her rage to show. She'd never felt so used or betrayed in her life.

Snatching her pillow from her bed, she pressed it firmly against her face and screamed, allowing the down-filled item to block out the sound. She punched at her mattress next, forcing the anger and hurt through her fists until exhaustion took over.

Sinking to the floor, she sat with her back to the bed and her knees curled up under her arms. Hard breaths followed. She tilted her head back, stared at the ceiling, and contemplated her next move. For now, she'd feed the illusion of following orders without asking questions.

But if she went to Adrian's bed, she'd damn well do so for herself.

Not for Harlowe.

Not for Kendrick.

And not for some bloody Prince Regent she'd not even met.

CHAPTER THIRTY-FIVE

"This just arrived." Peter Kendrick handed the note he'd received from Miss Carmichael to the chief magistrate. "Looks like the ultimatum I gave her worked."

Sir Nigel scanned the paper and nodded before returning it to Peter. "While this may suggest our odds of arresting Croft are greater than catching that blasted murderer, it's no guarantee. Our agent may have formed a closer attachment with our target, but her ability to use it against him remains to be seen."

"I understand." Peter shoved the note in his pocket.

"We need results, Kendrick." Sir Nigel's voice was as grave as their failure to solve the murders. "Eldridge has already been to see me twice more. He's questioned our worth and has threatened to advocate for our replacement."

Kendrick shivered. As a duke, any suggestion

Eldridge made would be considered with the utmost seriousness. "I'll let you know as soon as I have something more."

"Please do, or you may find yourself on a clerk's salary come next week."

~

Relief flooded Samantha's veins the next day when she stepped back into the room she'd rented. The message she'd received from Adrian shortly after breakfast invited her to meet him and Marsdale in front of the Hyde Park entrance at two.

This wasn't for another couple of hours, but she'd rather wait them out here than at Clearview. She clenched her jaw and fisted her hands. God's teeth, she'd not been able to get away fast enough. Not after speaking with Mrs. Butler.

The woman, a buxom blonde with a coy smile slapped onto her painted face, had been shockingly frank. So much so, Samantha wondered if the woman had thought her a whore in training instead of an innocent woman who merely required some guidance.

Sitting, she unpacked the fried piece of chicken she'd bought on her way here and took a large bite. The savory flesh dissolved in her mouth and filled her stomach while street noise two floors below kept her company.

Not that she needed it. Her own thoughts on all that had happened since Harlowe gave her the mission was enough to hold her attention for decades to come. Like a well-trained dog, she'd done as he'd asked without stopping to think for herself.

But now that she stood on the precipice of a momentous decision, with Harlowe eagerly pushing her forward, questions flooded her brain.

What was his motivation in all of this? Was he just following orders? Or had Kendrick threatened him too?

And why was Kendrick so hell-bent on Adrian's arrest? She pondered that for a while until something finally clicked. The blackmail information in Adrian's possession.

Was it possible it could be used to keep other disreputable people in check? Could one such person want Adrian gone?

Of course. It made perfect sense. In order to be open to extortion, one had to have acted immorally – done something ruinous. And if the person were powerful enough, they might have managed to put some pressure on Bow Street.

If that was the truth, the legal system had been corrupted and she might have been sent to destroy an innocent man.

Yes, she'd read the information Kendrick had gathered on Adrian, but what did it really prove? The newspaper articles, while topped by impressive headlines, were all based on conjecture.

There were no named witnesses with whom to double check facts.

She took another bite of her chicken, chewing the

meat while mulling all of this over. One carefully filed Bow Street report did mention a smuggler who'd tried confessing to murder because he'd rather hang than have Croft think he'd betrayed him. Kendrick had let the man go, only for him to turn up dead.

And then there was the report of two men who'd begged for protection. They'd claimed Adrian's father threatened to kill them. These same men were found two days later, hanging from Blackfriars bridge.

But who was to say they didn't deserve what happened to them? Or that Adrian had been involved in either of these incidents? Nothing about him suggested he was a cold-hearted killer. If anything, his every word and action gave her reason to believe he never did anything without good cause.

A belief that was further compounded later when Adrian left her alone on a bench with Marsdale while he went to purchase some treats from a vendor. The setting was public, right on Rotten Row, ensuring she and Marsdale were seen engaging in private conversation. And this, in turn, would make it more plausible for them to carry on with each other during a ball. Should the earl agree to participate.

She sent him a smile and shifted closer to where he sat, angling herself and dipping her head to convey an intimacy they did not share.

He stiffened, the tips of his fingers digging into his thighs, puckering the fabric of his trousers.

"I apologize for making you uncomfortable," she whispered. "That's not my intention, but given the nature of what I'm about to say, it would be best if no one else hears us."

The pressure in his hands eased. "Go on."

Deciding she might as well get to the point, she took a deep breath and dived in. "Croft and I need your help catching his sister's killer."

"What?" His outrage was only marginally outdone by his shock. "I can't believe he's dragged you into this. If you'll excuse me a moment, I'll just go and see what's wrong with his head."

She placed her hand on Marsdale's arm and pushed down firmly. "Please lower your voice and let me explain."

"There's no need. Whatever he's gotten you into, it's not worth the risk."

"I have to disagree with you there." Raising her chin, she met his gaze squarely. "Every innocent life is worth it. One lost is one too many."

He scoffed. "I'm beginning to see why he holds you in such high regard. You're two of a kind – a pair of crusaders."

She tilted her head and smiled. It hadn't occurred to her how similar she and Croft were. No wonder she struggled to view him as the villain. "How many murders have there been thus far?"

"I… Four?"

"There's been five. Any idea when the first one took place?"

"It was last autumn I believe."

"No. It's been more than a year. Miss Fairchild was

killed in the first week of June. Yet Bow Street is no closer now to catching the man responsible for it than they were back then. Even more disturbing, the murders are increasing at an exponential rate."

His eyes widened just enough to suggest he'd missed this important detail. "Are you certain?"

She listed the dates. "If this pattern continues we run the risk of having a murder each week. Perhaps more often."

"Making it more likely for the killer to reveal himself in error."

"True. But how many women will have died by then?"

"Too many," he murmured.

Good. He was finally in agreement. "Whoever this individual is, he's clever, but the increased frequency of his attacks suggests he may have developed a taste for it – that he's eager for victims. And once the ones fitting a certain profile have all been killed, he'll surely move on to others."

Horror drew Marsdale's features tight. He stared at Samantha. "What's your plan?"

"Promise you'll hear me out before judging?" He gave a quick nod, upon which she told him what she and Adrian had in mind.

"And where would all of this take place?" Marsdale asked once she'd finished.

"At Clearview House. During the ball."

He scrubbed his jaw. "This is insane. Beyond that, it goes against my firmly held belief that private citizens shouldn't be hunting down dangerous men. It's perilous and stupid. However, I understand your reasoning in this instance. You've made an excellent argument, for which I commend you. So I'll help. Provided Croft approves every part of this scheme. I'll not have him challenging me to a duel for daring to kiss his woman."

"What?" The comment was so unexpected he might as well have told her he knew of his friend's proposition and hoped she'd accept.

Heat rushed to her cheeks and her gaze instinctively shifted to Adrian's tall frame. He was approaching the bench, his dark eyes fixed upon her while he carried three paper cones.

"He's taken a liking to you," Marsdale murmured. "An understandable one, I might add. The manner in which he speaks of you leaves no question about his intentions."

Despite the pleasure this comment instilled somewhere deep in her heart, she still had to ask, "What if I'm not of like mind?"

"That would be between the two of you." Marsdale straightened as Adrian neared, his final words before he reached them so softly spoken Samantha barely heard him. "He may be rough around the edges, but he's a reasonable man - the most dependable of my acquaintance."

"What's the conclusion?" Adrian asked, offering them each a cone filled with a mixture of nuts and sweetmeats.

"Miss Carmichael can be very persuasive," Marsdale

informed him. "I daresay she would work wonders in Parliament."

"So you'll help?" No hint of humor or willingness to make light of the situation.

Marsdale's expression sobered. "Yes."

Adrian couldn't have looked more somber if he'd been carved from granite. It made Samantha wonder if he'd secretly hoped the earl would refuse. His jaw was firmly set, his mouth a tight line of precision. Fierceness sharpened his gaze.

Extending his hand to Samantha, he told Marsdale boldly, "I need to speak with her for a moment."

No words of gratitude.

"Of course."

Adrian's gaze shifted, finding hers and locking with it, creating a pull that forced her hand to clasp his and her body to rise. They strolled for a number of paces, arms linked, before he spoke. "I worry our plan will go wrong and I won't be able to protect you."

No request for her to give him an answer regarding his proposition. She wasn't sure if she found that disappointing or if it gave her relief.

"You're thinking of what happens after the ball." An observation, not a question.

"We'll only have so much control. The rest will be up to…" He stopped, turned to face her, his posture stiff. "Were you serious when you said you never go anywhere without a pistol?"

Among other things. "Yes."

His expression remained the same: hard and inscrutable. "Show me."

"Hold this." She handed him her cone, then opened her reticule so he could look inside. A grunt conveyed his opinion. "I realize it's small but—"

"Are you an accurate shot?"

"Certainly." Better than anyone else she'd seen, though it wasn't her weapon of choice. She much preferred the blades hidden in her sleeves and tucked firmly against her thighs, or the long razor-sharp pins concealed in her hair. But she didn't mention any of that.

He handed the cone back to her and reached inside his jacket pocket. "I want you to have this as well."

She stared at the silver dagger he offered, her fingers reaching and curling until they gripped the smooth mother-of-pearl handle. The blade had been etched with a swirling design and polished to a high sheen, reflecting the leaves from the tree behind her. It sparkled as she turned it against the light.

Stunning and lethal. Easily the most wonderful gift she'd ever received.

She swallowed against a sudden surge of emotion, shutting it down and locking it back into place before meeting his gaze. "Thank you."

"Stop by Reed's tomorrow and I'll instruct you on how to use it."

His enigmatic expression couldn't quite hide the unease in his eyes. So she nodded, even though she was sure her skill was superior to his.

And tried not to think overly much about just how important his concern for her was.

~

"Have you considered courting her?"

Adrian watched Samantha's retreating figure, the confidence in her stride as she walked toward the park entrance after parting ways with him and Edward.

"No." He glanced at his friend. "I propositioned her instead."

Edward's mouth fell open. "Tell me you're not serious."

"She's not the sort of woman one might consider—"

"Are you blind or just plain stupid?"

Adrian stiffened. He clamped his teeth together. "Insult me again and I'll break your nose."

"Don't be an arse." Edward matched his scowl. "Miss Carmichael may not have respectable parentage, but she is prepared to risk her reputation and her life to help you catch your sister's killer."

"There's no need to make it sound like she's doing me a personal favor when she has her own reasons for wanting the killer caught."

"Fine. Let's suppose she does. It still doesn't change the fact that she's got more courage than most men I know. Add to that her determination, intellect, and need for justice, all of which set her apart, and I think you'll struggle to find a woman more suited to be your wife. But that's just my opinion. For whatever it's worth."

This was one of the reasons Adrian valued his friendship. Because Edward always found a way to cut through the clutter and get to the heart of the matter. He told him what he needed to hear, offered up a different perspective, and opened his eyes to the truth.

His heart gave an unsteady thud. Taking Samantha as his lover was something he could adjust to. Marrying her, however…

"Aside from the fact that I'd likely make a horrific husband, I'm not prepared for that sort of commitment with anyone."

"No one is." Edward snorted. "Take it from someone who's forced to live with regret. Don't squander your chance when you've found the right woman."

The comment produced a tremor deep in Adrian's gut. Edward's point was solid, delivered with the effect of an ice-bucket dumped right over his head. He stared straight ahead, his focus exclusively on his own thoughts as he turned his gaze inward.

His father had recommended he set his mind on finding a wife. Lord knew he needed an heir. If anything were to happen to him, as it very well might, everything built by generations before him would be lost – turned over to the Crown.

Air clawed its way down his throat and into his lungs with the effort it suddenly took to breathe. He couldn't allow that. A wife would be needed – a capable woman strong enough to stand by his side, not some gently bred creature who flinched at the sound of thunder.

He wanted a partner, a friend he could turn to but also a lover he longed to come home to. He wanted a wife who'd accept him because she'd have the good sense to let him explain who he was and why he did what he did. And the only person who came even close to fulfilling these standards, was Samantha.

Edward had seen what he'd been too blind to. She was perfect. Provided she'd have him.

He blinked on that thought and told his friend. "Let's see how this plan of ours goes before we start making wedding arrangements."

CHAPTER THIRTY-SIX

Lit by a thousand candles, the Clearview House ballroom beckoned its guests like a lighthouse guiding sailors to shore. Beads sewn into lace-trimmed gowns shimmered alongside dazzling jewels. Champagne served by a fleet of footmen bubbled in glasses while music wove its way in between laughter and chatter. A country dance was presently underway, a lively start to what promised to be a fun-filled evening.

Standing near one of the French doors leading to the terrace, Samantha enjoyed the cool air wafting over her shoulders while taking quick stock of her surroundings. Her dress, cut from ivory silk, concealed the weapons she wore underneath, including her gift from Adrian. Held in place by a leather strap, the sleek dagger lay flush against her right thigh, reminding her of the man who'd made her question and doubt her superiors.

A footman approached with a tray full of glasses. She took one and sipped the chilled drink. Yesterday's training session at Reed's had been a farce. She'd hated every second of it – the act that kept her from fighting Adrian on equal terms, the strain of pretending she'd no idea what she was doing, her gradual attempts at showing improvement until he was satisfied with her progress.

The lies.

What she wished for most of all was honesty with him.

Harlowe would say she'd been compromised if he learned how conflicted she had become. He'd pull her from the case, tell Kendrick they'd failed, and set a series of unacceptable measures in motion.

She couldn't allow that. Could not let Kendrick send an assassin after Adrian any more than she could permit herself to be responsible for what happened to Hazel, Melody, Tara, and Holly if the program got shut down.

They were the ones who kept her on track. Not Harlowe.

She glanced across the room at where he stood, conversing with some of the guests. He'd saved her from the jaws of hell when she was a child, had offered warmth and comfort instead. She'd never wanted for anything while in his care. In exchange, all she'd had to do was train.

Not once had she wondered where it might lead or how far he'd push her in order to win.

Anger pulled her spine into a rigid line. She tightened her hold on her glass, drank a bit more, and forced her resentment into a box before slamming it shut. She could not afford to reveal what she thought of the man who'd raised her, or let her feelings get in the way of tonight's plan. It was too important to botch for any reason.

Spotting Melody near the refreshment table, she made her way toward her. "Is Lady Heathbrooke not insisting you stay by her side?"

Melody glanced away from the plate she was filling. "She's found a seat for herself in the gaming room and has asked me to bring her some food."

"I can see to that if you'd like. Might give you a chance to dance for a change."

"Thank you, but I'd rather play cards if possible."

"Hmm…" Samantha made a deliberate show of looking toward the entrance while craning her neck.

"Waiting for someone?"

"In a way." She finished her drink and set her glass aside. "Croft said he would be here."

Surprise flickered in Melody's eyes. "I thought he was meant to stay away from social events for a while. Because of his outburst at the musicale."

"Yes, but I also need to be able to form a closer attachment with him. Balls allow for that more easily than anything else, especially when there's a waltz."

"And I suppose there shall be since you and Harlowe have made the arrangements?" She gave Samantha a wicked look. "Perhaps you've a private spot in mind too – somewhere for you and Croft to sneak off to?"

If only that were true. "Maybe."

Melody shook her head, a soft chuckle escaping her lips. "I hope you know what you're doing."

So did she. "Of course."

"Anything I can do to help?"

"Just make sure Lady Heathbrooke suspects me and Croft of being involved." One seed was all it would take for the rumor to spread, lending fuel to the fire once everyone saw them together.

"I can do that, but are you sure?"

Samantha's attention shifted toward the front of the room, to the new guests arriving and to the man flicking his dark gaze in her direction. "Trust me. Public opinion will make a world of difference."

She gave her friend a firm look before making her way to Adrian, whose strong presence dominated the ballroom. Tall and smartly attired in evening black, he stood beside Marsdale, surrounded by whispers and scowls from those who'd noticed his entrance. If it bothered him, it didn't show in the slightest since his attention was placed on her as she made her approach.

Try as she might, she couldn't ignore the effect it was having. Being Adrian Croft's sole focus proved more intense than balancing along the edge of a building. Her cheeks burned by the time she reached him. More so when he looked directly into her eyes, his smoldering gaze reminding her of the heated kisses they'd shared.

She swallowed, extended her hand for him to catch, and dipped into a low curtsey – a sign of allegiance and surrender to everyone present. If Melody did her part, no one would doubt Adrian's claim to her.

"Miss Carmichael." The velvety softness with which he whispered her name fanned out across her skin. Raising his voice, he added, "You're absolutely stunning."

"I completely agree," said Marsdale, his compliment carrying with enough strength to be heard by those who lingered nearby.

Clever.

Allowing a timid smile, she affected a look intended to show that he too had the power to flatter her ego. "You're much too kind, my lord."

Adrian sent him a stern look and drew Samantha close to his side, away from Marsdale. A part of the act, or something more real? She wasn't quite sure.

His palm settled firmly against the base of her spine in a scandalous show of possessiveness few men would dare exhibit in public. He seemed not to care. "Let's take a turn of the room, shall we?"

Guided by his touch, she allowed him to steer her past the inquisitive looks from the guests standing closest. Pretending indifference wasn't an option. No amount of training could have prepared her for the spark of awareness his touch instilled or the hot little shivers that shot through her limbs.

It was like an assault on her nerves and she hadn't the skill or the will to fight it.

Linking his arm with hers, he dipped his head. "I have a confession to make, Samantha."

"And what's that?" She'd never sounded so raspy before.

"You're making me go slightly mad."

A powerful revelation from someone who always appeared in control. Provided it was the truth.

Not that it had any bearing on how she would answer. "Perhaps I should make a confession too."

"Please do."

She took a deep breath, made sure to lock her gaze with his when she spoke her next words. "I've missed you."

A world of meaning in those few words. They'd seen each other frequently during the last few days, but one shared moment stood out above all the rest.

His eyes sharpened, revealing the instant he understood. The walls seemed to tilt in toward them, making the ballroom too small to contain the fire that burned between them. An almost desperate expression strained his features.

He leaned in, his breath hard and heavy against her face. "I want to kiss you."

She glanced toward the end of the room, her gaze catching Mr. Nigel Lawrence's for a brief second. His eyebrows dipped even as he sent her a nod. She dismissed him, her attention back on Adrian. "As much as I'd like that, you can't. Not if I am to fit the killer's profile."

The look he gave her was fierce. Pained, even. He

steered her sideways, circumventing a group of women who blocked their path, not stopping until they'd reached the wall. Releasing her arm, he faced her. "You're right." His palm found her cheek – improper but proof of the intimacy they wished to evoke – before falling away. A disingenuous smile followed. "We'll dance the waltz and I'll take my leave so the rest of this blasted charade can play out as planned."

She hesitated, not liking the cool aloofness with which he addressed her. "Adrian."

"It's fine." Not a warmly spoken assurance but rather the bite of steel.

Uncertainty crept through her veins. If he failed to play his part to perfection then what was the point? Her hand caught his wrist, pulling him farther away from the rest of the guests. "You know it will just be an act. I have no interest in Marsdale."

"Doesn't make it any easier to accept."

"Listen to me," she insisted. "I am yours. I have been since the moment you kissed me. But this, what we're doing here tonight, must take priority."

He paused in mid-stride, his gaze searching hers until she feared he might see every action she'd taken against him. A satisfied nod suggested he'd only found the truth in her most recent statement. "I'll try to remember that after the fact, so I don't end up killing my friend for something I asked him to do."

Despite the annoyance rippling off him, it took but a second for him to leash and conceal it behind a façade of charm that gave nothing away.

For the next two hours, he proved himself the doting suitor – a gentleman who exuded pride at gaining her notice, who praised her to anyone willing to listen, and who hung on her every word.

It was unsettling, this ability of his to play the lovesick pup with a level of skill that nearly convinced her of something she knew wasn't true. So much so she was almost relieved by the time he bid her goodnight and departed, the dreamy look in his eyes making more than a few other ladies sigh with envy.

Incredible.

No sooner was he gone from view than Marsdale stepped up beside her. Leaning in, he spoke so softly only she could hear. "Pretend I've just said something vastly amusing."

Her lips twitched at the unexpected request and she laughed with genuine humor. She turned to him, allowed her gaze to catch his. "Lord Marsdale. How positively delightful to find you still here."

A smirk added a hint of mischief, easing the grave expression he so often wore. "I've been wanting to dance with you for the better part of the evening."

"You should have said."

"I'm doing so now." He winked, his playfulness affording him with a boyish appearance that made him look five years younger. A reminder that this man had once known what it was like to have fun – to be happy – before his ability to do so was cruelly snatched away.

She pursed her lips and glanced at the dance floor. "We'll have to wait for the next set."

"Or the one after that." He extended his arm. "In the meantime, I'd love nothing more than to chat with you in a quiet corner."

They took the long route to the adjacent room where settees and armchairs stood scattered about, whispering and chuckling, making every guest they passed privy to their flirtation. Shocked expressions suggested severe disapproval from most. Mr. Lawrence looked especially critical. As did Birchwood. The viscount even went so far as to warn them of Croft's disapproval.

Samantha's response was clear. "He doesn't own me." She promptly waved Birchwood off with a laugh and clung harder to Marsdale's arm.

What followed was made to appear like an intimate conversation between two people who longed to be alone behind closed doors. Although they mostly spoke of Adrian, they made sure to add the occasional touch, to lean in a bit too close, and to send each other needy looks.

"Shall we take this show back to the ballroom?" Marsdale asked when their conversation eventually started to drag.

Samantha sent him a sly look. "By all means, my lord. Please lead the way."

They reached the edge of the dance floor soon after and paused to wait for the current dance to end. Dipping his head, Marsdale whispered, "Pretend I've told you something shocking. Maybe gasp a little and fan yourself with your hand."

She did exactly as he suggested, even going so far as to add a chuckle and making a pretense of telling him off. Several guests shook their heads. Another censorious look came from Wrengate, who watched her as though he'd enjoy biting her head off.

For one fleeting second she worried he might know that she'd been Wycliffe's masked companion, but then she recalled their clash at Reed's and allowed herself to relax. Of course the duke would resent her for that.

Someone tapped her shoulder, prompting Samantha to turn and find Harlowe there, his brow furrowed and his eyes full of censure. "A word?"

"I'm afraid it will have to wait," Samantha informed him. "The Earl of Marsdale and I are about to dance."

Harlowe glowered. She'd made a deliberate use of Marsdale's title so it would be more difficult for him to interfere. He narrowed his gaze on the earl before shifting it back to her. "Afterward then."

"Of course."

"What will you tell him?" Marsdale asked as soon as they'd positioned themselves in preparation for a quadrille.

It was a question she'd pondered at great length as soon as she, Adrian, and Marsdale had all agreed to move ahead with the plan. Harlowe was certain to wonder at her behavior. Explaining it wouldn't be easy unless she told him what she was up to.

A conversation she'd rather not have for a number of reasons, the most important one being discretion.

The fewer people who knew what they meant to accomplish, the lower the risk of mucking things up.

Beyond that, there was the issue of trust. If Harlowe wanted Adrian gone so badly he'd whore her out just to get the deed done, then what might he do if he figured out Adrian's ultimate goal? Lurk in the shadows and wait for him to unleash his wrath? Tell Kendrick so he could attempt to set up a trap?

No. She'd not risk it.

"I'll think of something," she promised Marsdale, despite having already done so.

The dance started and he caught her hand, his gaze holding hers as they spun in a circle. If looks could undress, he'd certainly mastered the skill. A ploy, she realized, to draw the kind of attention they sought.

Beyond the dance floor, a few older matrons started to whisper behind their fans. Evidence that their attempt at creating a stir seemed to be working, though she would have to do better. For while the earl might be dashing and rather good looking, he didn't affect her in the slightest.

So she let her thoughts wander to someone who did, to the burning desire in Adrian's eyes and the basic possessiveness binding her to him with increased force whenever they met.

The earl caught her hand and her pulse fluttered. His fingers curved round her waist and illusion took over, her breath quickening as she pretended his touch belonged to another.

"I could whisk you away right now," Marsdale

murmured, his voice so raw she wondered if he thought of someone else too. "Help you avoid the chat with Harlowe."

Tempting. But would it work? Or would Harlowe just track her down and prevent her from seeing this through?

She shook her head. "Make your way to our agreed upon spot in about half an hour. I'll meet you there as soon as I can."

The music faded. He brought her hand to his lips and pressed a much-too-long kiss to her knuckles. Samantha withdrew slowly, allowing everyone standing nearby to get a good look at the scene playing out.

She turned, and was met by Harlowe's thunderous glare. He caught her upper arm with punishing strength and forced her into a hasty step that brought her straight to his study. The door clicked shut behind them.

CHAPTER THIRTY-SEVEN

"I want to know what you're playing at." Arms crossed, Harlowe stood before her as he'd done so often before – an authoritarian figure demanding effort, results, and compliance.

She planted one hand on her hip and sent him a glare of her own, not caring how annoyed she might look when the truth was she wanted to gut him. "You've always taught me to use every weapon at my disposal. And you told me when I began this mission to use my best judgement. That's what I'm doing."

He stared at her. "Explain."

She ought to insist on the same. He'd lied to her from the very beginning, crafting a pretty illusion of fatherly love, pretending she was more than a discarded mongrel whose only value had been her potential.

"Marsdale may be Croft's longtime friend, but he's also a staunch supporter of law and order. He could prove a valuable asset if I can convince him Croft is in danger. There's a chance he might offer up valuable information in order to help."

"In other words, you want to play the pair against each other."

"There's no telling what I'll be able to find once I gain access to Croft's home. Making Marsdale my ally will help."

"He certainly seemed quite smitten by you." Harlowe tapped his nails against the edge of his glass. The ringing sound jarred her nerves. "I'm surprised he'd risk Croft's wrath by daring to look your way, never mind engage in an open flirtation. Word will likely reach Croft's ears. Are you sure this isn't a test?"

"It's not."

"How do you know?"

There was no easy answer to this, none she could think of at that very moment. So she held herself completely still and spoke with as much conviction as she could muster. "I just do."

He held her gaze for what seemed an eternity before giving a slow shake of his head. "Not good enough. You'll not risk what you've already gained. Forget Marsdale and focus on Croft."

"Bu—"

"That's an order, Samantha."

It took every ounce of her training to fight her instinctual defiance, to stop from cursing him to damnation or flinging her blasted glass at his head. She nodded without even blinking and turned for the door.

"And since Croft has already taken his leave," Harlowe added before she could slip from his grasp, "there's no need for you to return to the ballroom. Get some rest. Lord knows you'll need it for what lies ahead."

The assignation she was supposed to have with Croft tomorrow. She'd not even mentioned it to him, had made no commitment regarding his offer, and would surely pay for it dearly if Harlowe found out she had other priorities.

She took a sharp breath, ignored the tension boiling within, and slipped from the room. Her only advantage right now was Harlowe's misplaced belief in her total compliance.

Moving swiftly, she walked to the stairs at the front of the house. It didn't take long to reach them or to make her way to the first-floor landing. Once there, she strode to the end of the hallway, past her bedchamber door, and straight to the service stairs.

A second to pause and listen, followed by a hasty decent. She opened the door at the end of the stairs, and exited into the hallway where Marsdale waited, directly behind the ballroom. A wooden screen had been placed there to block the view of the service entrance.

"We don't have much time," she whispered, closing the distance between them and sending a swift glance over her shoulder. "Harlowe doesn't believe you'd pursue me and risk falling out with Croft. He suspects I'm up to something."

Marsdale arched a brow. "He's not wrong. His reasoning is also cause for concern. If he doubts I'd seduce you, chances are the killer will too."

"I know." It was an angle she'd stupidly failed to consider, but not an impossible one to deal with. Provided she was willing to stake everything, including her freedom, on catching the bastard who slit women's throats for the pleasure of watching them bleed. "It's a risk we'll have to take."

She couldn't tell him what she had in mind. He'd walk away this second if he had an inkling.

Marsdale glanced at the screen. Doubt creased his brow. He was starting to question his resolve. It was evident in his posture, which was slacker now than when she'd arrived.

They didn't have time for this. Not with the chance of Harlowe insisting the servants notify him if they saw her. She had to act fast.

Her hand caught Marsdale's. "Croft is depending on you to see this through. If it goes wrong, then so be it. But if it goes right, his sister will be avenged. As will the rest of the victims."

Marsdale's jaw hardened. His gaze found hers with unforgiving resolve. Less than a second to breathe was all he gave her before he'd pinned her against the wall. He leaned in, anger and pain colliding in an expression filled with unspeakable loss.

"Damn Croft and damn you." The fury with which he spoke stilled the beats of her heart. It slashed at her with commanding force as his mouth found hers, his hands gripping her waist to hold her steady.

It was a kiss that would mark her forever, much in the way her first encounter with death had done. Nothing about it compared with what she and Adrian had recently shared. That had been a passionate declaration intended to cut through the clutter, expose their longings, and forge a stronger connection.

While leaving them both wanting more.

By contrast, this was a deep dive into an unexplored well of emotion, a purging of the soul and a desperate search for peace.

There was little doubt in Samantha's mind she'd be glad when it ended.

And yet, she could not forget her own part in it.

So she set her mind to unbuttoning Marsdale's jacket.

He pulled back, his breaths coming hard as he dropped his gaze to her fingers. "What are you doing?"

"Ensuring my absolute ruination." She tugged his shirt free, then pulled up the left side of her skirt, exposing the thigh where no blade would be found.

Marsdale stared at her. The swift shake of his head warned he was having a crisis of conscience. She grabbed his hand and forced it against her pliable flesh, holding it there even as he attempted to pull it away.

"Think of the woman you wish you were with in this moment." Curling her fingers into his lapel, she caught the fabric and drew him closer. "Kiss *her*."

His mouth was on her again, trailing down the

length of her neck, the words he murmured begging forgiveness.

Samantha threw her head back, made sure her hold on him was secure, then shifted position and leaned against the screen. The wood creaked and groaned beneath her weight. Somebody gasped and Samantha slid her gaze sideways to where a maid stood, her hand at her throat and her eyes impossibly wide.

"Now," Samantha hissed, hoping Marsdale would hear and prepare for the impact that followed as she used her strength to pull him with her. The force of the movement threw the wood screen completely off balance. She heard it snap as she slammed down onto the floor, crashing into the brightly lit ballroom and sending it into a frenzy.

A woman shrieked. Other guests gasped. The music came to an instant halt. Samantha blinked and focused on Marsdale. The earl, who'd landed beside her, his legs tangled with hers, had never looked more stunned.

A silent pause followed and then…

Heels clicking on marble approached. A pair of men's shoes came into view.

"Get up." Harlowe seethed.

Marsdale managed to push himself upright. He offered Samantha his hand and she took it, allowed him to help her stand. Ignoring Harlowe for a brief moment, she made a show of putting herself back in order – smoothing her skirts and tucking stray strands of hair back in place.

"My apologies," Marsdale said, his voice carrying

loudly in the still room. "My intention was not to disrupt the festivities."

A male guest snorted. "No worries, Marsdale. Your intentions could not be much clearer."

Someone snickered.

"Too bad the screen was not made of sturdier stuff," another man shouted, his comment resulting in wild hoots of laughter.

Samantha finally looked at Harlowe, unsurprised to find his expression tight with rage. "It appears we got slightly carried away."

"You were supposed to have gone to bed." Every word Harlowe spoke was sharp enough to cut steel.

"As you can see," Samantha murmured, "I had more important matters to deal with."

"Isn't she being courted by Croft?" an elderly woman asked. It sounded like Lady Heathbrooke. "Where is he, by the way?"

"His whereabouts are inconsequential." The masculine voice that spoke carried vast amounts of authority. Even Harlowe turned to see who'd made the remark. The Duke of Eldridge stepped forward, his lean figure conveying both power and confidence. "The only question of interest is what happens next?"

"I…" Marsdale cleared his throat. He turned to Samantha, his green eyes holding an unspoken promise to follow her lead.

She raised her chin. "Nothing. The earl and I had a brief lapse in judgement. That is all."

The resulting murmurs were in disagreement.

Harlowe stepped right up to her. His hand caught her arm in a hold so tight she knew it would bruise.

"I don't know what you're playing at," he hissed, "but rest assured I will find out."

"Two angles. One goal. I told you that already."

"And I told you to abandon that plan."

"While I understand your anger, Harlowe," said Eldridge, "rough handling your charge doesn't paint you in a positive light."

"Release her," Marsdale told him with an added touch of firmness.

Harlowe loosened his hold and let his hand drop. He gave Marsdale a hard look. "You're a scoundrel. Had she been a gentleman's daughter, you'd never have done this. Not without making an offer of marriage."

Marsdale flinched but swiftly recovered. He straightened his spine and seemed to grow a few inches taller. Hands clenched with such force his knuckles turned white, he leaned toward Harlowe, a deadly gleam in his emerald-green eyes. "You forget yourself, sir."

Samantha clasped her hands together and prayed her next words wouldn't be a colossal mistake. "Has it not occurred to anyone yet that I might have a prior attachment?"

The room went entirely still, like a memory frozen in time.

She shrugged one shoulder, a careless gesture she hoped would incite the right person. "Croft proposed to me earlier this evening and I accepted. We're to be married."

∼

The Mayfair Murderer, as he'd most recently been dubbed by the papers, considered the scene playing out before him. It was hard to believe Miss Carmichael could be so careless with Mr. Croft's feelings. Not that the man seemed the least bit sensitive, but he had looked fairly enamored with her this evening. He'd looked like he cared.

Which he probably did if he'd asked her to be his wife.

Yet here she was, throwing herself at his friend.

Outrage on Croft's behalf – that long-detested taste of betrayal – gripped him once more. It burned through his veins, sank its claws deep, and awakened his hunger.

She'd humiliated Croft this evening, had left a stain on his reputation. Whatever happened from this point onward, whether he cast her aside or not, that stain would remain. And yet, she seemed not to give it much thought, her blasé manner showing no sign of remorse.

There was no regret there, no sense of wrongdoing, just an almost callous degree of entitlement that was destined to touch Marsdale too. The poor fop would likely wind up at the wrong end of Croft's dueling pistols for this.

Shoving his hand in his pocket, the murderer stroked his thumb over the watch he kept there – a soothing exercise keeping his lethal compulsions in check. For the moment.

He studied the look of defiance on Miss Carmichael's face as she spoke with Harlowe, disgust turning his stomach to ice.

Women like her had no place in the world. They had to be snuffed from existence.

Although…

He paused to consider, his head tilting slightly while thinking through all the events leading up to this moment. Something wasn't quite right. It felt like a perfectly laid out mosaic with one single tile out of place.

Croft and Marsdale were friends. Croft had spent the better part of the evening showering Miss Carmichael with attention. No sooner had he departed than she'd begun flirting with Marsdale. Marsdale had always come across as the honorable sort – beyond reproach. It seemed unlikely of him to seduce the woman his friend was keen on.

And then of course there was the fact that Croft was intent on catching his sister's killer. He'd made no secret of it.

So maybe…just maybe…all of this was a trick intended to lure him out.

A far more plausible notion than anything else he'd witnessed these past ten minutes.

With a smirk, he proceeded to ponder his next move. If Croft was indeed attempting to trap him, caution would be required. To better assess the situation, he'd have to come up with a trap of his own.

By the time he arrived home later that evening, an idea was already taking shape. He took a seat at his desk and retrieved two pieces of foolscap, then proceeded to pen the first of two notes.

CHAPTER THIRTY-EIGHT

Having concluded his unexpected meeting with Harlowe, Adrian had to make a conscious effort to keep from bursting into the Clearview House parlor and giving Samantha a good shake. Instead, he entered the room as though all was as it should be.

At least she'd had the sense to warn him of what was to come.

Be aware. Harlowe thinks we're engaged. I'm sorry.

He would have liked some additional details - some hint as to what had occurred. Not quite ready to take a seat on the sofa beside her, he stayed near the window overlooking the driveway. "Tell me everything."

She sent the door a pointed look, and he instantly shut it, not caring if anyone thought it a lapse in social conduct. He arched an eyebrow, a silent command for her to proceed.

"Very well." Back straight, she clasped her hands in

her lap, ignoring the tea tray for now as she laid out the details of what had transpired. "Harlowe got in the way. I had to explain myself to him which forced me to improvise on the spot."

"So you concocted the fake engagement."

"That was later. But the idea did arise from something Harlowe said during that conversation. He questioned the effect my flirtation would have upon you."

"It must have been quite the show for him to take issue and pull you aside." He feigned a casual stance, but every muscle was strained to the point of snapping.

"We did as agreed."

A nerve began ticking at the edge of his eye. He ignored it. "Why would Harlowe care about my reaction to you and Marsdale?"

"Most likely because he, like most others, has no wish to earn your disfavor."

"I still don't see why you chose to announce our engagement."

"Because without it, you'd just be another man looking to get beneath a loose woman's skirts. But as my fiancé, you'd be thrown over, embarrassed, with no easy way out. Making you exactly the sort of man the killer would sympathize with and me the sort of woman he'd want to murder."

He dug his nails into the palms of his hands until pain distracted him from the image of her lifeless body covered in blood. It would not come to that. He'd make damn sure to take whatever precautions were needed to keep her safe.

"And the kiss?" There was no avoiding the bitterness in his voice. "Tell me about it."

She dropped her gaze, refused to look at him, choosing instead to reach for the teapot and fill their cups.

Her silence was worse than any words she might have spoken. Breathing became a chore. Something dark and ugly caught him in its thorny grasp.

One second he was by the window, the next, he was leaning in, spine curving as he clasped her jaw and forced her gaze to meet his.

"Did you enjoy it?"

Her expression hardened. "It was a means to an end."

"That doesn't answer the question." He drew a harsh breath, set his other hand on the armrest to block her escape. "What I want to know is how far you took it and whether or not you forgot yourself in the moment."

Annoyance simmered in her blue eyes. It looked like she wanted to slap him. He almost smirked. So the genteel woman he'd gotten to know had a temper. This was something he understood and something he'd like to explore.

"We took it as far as we had to," she gritted. "I undid his jacket, pulled his shirt free, and made sure my skirt was pushed up past my knees by the time we fell into the ballroom. But no, I did not forget myself in the moment. My focus was on the details and on making sure Marsdale didn't back out."

The thorny vines gripping him tightened. "Did it leave an impression?"

"Yes." He pulled back as if struck. "To say it didn't would be dishonest. Your friend needs help. He behaved like a wounded creature in need of comfort. I think there's a weight bearing down on his chest. It might be good for him to share it with someone."

Not at all what he'd been expecting. The tension within started to ease. "Anything else?"

Her crystal-clear eyes snared him. "He didn't affect me. Only you have the power to do so."

Adrian's mouth was on hers in an instant, the kiss he gave her as hard and punishing as his desire to claim her.

He sank to the sofa and pulled her into his lap, her sighs and gasps sending him straight to the edge. His hand pushed under her skirts and curved over her knee before slipping higher.

"Adrian." A breathless word - his name - so perfect when she spoke it.

His palm settled firmly against the curve of her hip. Breaking the kiss so he could observe her response, he splayed his fingers across her soft flesh.

Desire made her breath hitch, but she still sent the door a look of concern.

"I'll go no further than this," he promised. "I just had to make sure my touch left a mark more intimate than his."

"I've told you before," she murmured, "but I'll say it

again, just to be clear. I am yours. No other man will be able to claim me."

He growled with immense satisfaction and brought his mouth back to hers. She'd made no mention of his proposition, and he'd not asked if she'd given it any more thought. Nor would he. Not when the world thought she'd soon be his wife.

Edward had been correct. The idea of her with his ring on her finger, bound to him in a way she never would be as his mistress, was unbelievably thrilling.

Not that he was in any rush to reveal his intentions. There would be time for that later, once the mess they were currently dealing with had been concluded. And if he'd had any second thoughts on the matter, they were quickly dashed by a knock at the door.

Adrian lifted Samantha and placed her on the sofa beside him before quickly moving to a nearby armchair. He gave her a nod and she told whoever was at the door to come in.

Her butler entered. "A letter for you, Miss Carmichael."

She picked it from the silver tray he held toward her. The butler gave a stiff bow and departed, leaving the door wide open.

Samantha turned the letter between her hands. "The seal is generic. No crest or initial."

Adrian picked up his cup and sipped his tea. "Open it."

Part of the paper stuck to the wax and was peeled away in the process. Samantha unfolded the sheet of foolscap and scanned its contents. Her eyebrows rose. A satisfied smile captured her lips.

"My dearest Samantha," she read. "The events of last night compel me to reassure you, not only of the impact our kiss has had upon me, but of my steadfast devotion to you. I long to explore it further and to offer whatever support you need, should Croft decide to break your engagement.

"Please meet me tonight at The Toothless Cat Inn, ten o'clock. Provide the innkeeper with your last name, and he'll show you to a private room where we can discuss the details of our affair. Whatever your wishes, I'll seek to accommodate them in full.

"Your servant…Marsdale"

An uncomfortable mixture of dread and excitement settled in Adrian's stomach. He took the letter and re-read the words. The script was neat and precise, similar to both his and Edward's, but with slight variations. "It appears our plan worked."

All they had to do now was go to the rendezvous point and see who showed up.

CHAPTER THIRTY-NINE

Adrian arrived at The Toothless Cat Inn well in advance of the scheduled time, just to be sure the killer wouldn't be there to see him. The late afternoon light was beginning to dim. A group of dockyard workers passed him on their way in. He took a moment to survey the building's exterior and its location before he followed, just in case an escape route would be required later.

"Has a room been rented under the name of Carmichael?" Adrian slipped a few coins to the innkeeper when the man crossed his arms and held his tongue. The faintest nod confirmed it. "Which one?"

Additional coins got him the answer he wanted and made sure the occupant in the adjoining room was moved elsewhere so Adrian could have it instead. A maid showed him to the small space which was crowded by a simple bed, table, and chair.

Adrian crossed to the window and peered out into the murky side street that ran between the tavern and the building next door. The ground wasn't far – he could easily make the jump if needed, but he couldn't expect Samantha to do the same. The only exit available to her would be through the tavern.

Raising his gaze, he spotted a woman through one of the opposite windows. She pulled a small boy into her lap and proceeded to feed him, the oil lamp on the table they sat at making the pair stand out against the dark shadows behind them.

The room to the left of them showed an old man reading a book by candlelight while the room to the right remained dark, either because the occupants weren't yet home or had already gone to bed.

Satisfied nothing looked out of place, he turned to the maid. "What's on the menu this evening?"

"There's a mutton stew, roast chicken, or pork on the spit. All with boiled potatoes and stewed mushrooms."

"I'll have the pork and a mug of ale," Adrian told her.

It didn't take long for the food to arrive, the fragrant aroma filling the room and increasing his hunger. He paid the maid and waited for her to leave before taking a seat at the table and digging into his meal.

∼

Like a hunter tracking its prey, the Mayfair Murderer stood in the darkness, patiently waiting to see if his bait would have the desired effect. He leaned against a tree – one of many that stood in the center of Wilton Crescent – his gaze firmly trained on Avernail House, where Nigel Lawrence resided.

The letter he'd paid a young scamp to deliver had been filled with passion and longing. It spoke of a desperate need for comfort, the uncertainty of what was to come, and a plea for help in the face of potential rejection. Signed with Miss Carmichael's name, it offered Nigel exactly what he'd been dreaming of since the first time he'd seen her.

He'd not have the strength to resist.

Sure enough, the front door opened at nine thirty. Casually attired, Nigel stepped down onto the pavement and headed east. The murderer followed at a distance, all the way to Oxford Street where Nigel hailed a hackney.

The next one stopped in response to his own raised hand.

"Where to?" asked the driver.

"Just follow that carriage." If his suspicions were correct, Croft would believe Nigel to be the killer. He'd attack him, creating the perfect excuse to banish Croft from existence.

If he was wrong, Miss Carmichael's immoral nature would be confirmed, in which case he'd take great pleasure in spilling her blood.

His stomach tightened in anticipation. He hoped she'd be the one whose life he claimed. It had already been too long since he'd last known the rousing control of turning bliss into terror.

∼

Adrian paced the constrictive space of his rented room with impatience. Restlessness kept him from sitting still. He'd finished his meal an hour ago and had since been waiting for something to happen.

During which he'd turned over every decision he'd made this past week a thousand times. He should have done this without Samantha. Involving her had been selfish and stupid. But she'd convinced him and he'd agreed because her plan had seemed so easy. Until it came to the moment of truth and every conceivable thing that could go wrong began playing out in his head.

Gritting his teeth, he checked the time on his pocket watch. Still five minutes until the designated hour. He ought to meet her when she arrived, inform her he'd changed his mind, send her home.

If any harm came to her, he'd never forgive himself.

He shoved his watch into his pocket and started toward the door, only to pause at the sound of footsteps in the hallway. Then came the muffled sound of Samantha's voice as she thanked whoever had shown her upstairs.

It was too late. Adrian's gut clenched. The plan was already underway.

∽

The room Samantha entered was dimly lit by her oil lamp's low-burning flame. A dry and musty smell tempted her to open the window, but the air she'd inhaled in the street outside made her reconsider. Smoky, with a lingering stench of refuse, it would be worse than the dust and mildew she presently breathed.

Her heart pulsed in anticipation of what was to come.

With lethal blades strapped to each thigh, an additional one concealed in the sleeve of her spencer, a pistol tucked into her skirt pocket, and razor-sharp hairpins, she was prepared for whatever came next. Her only weakness lay in her pretense. She wouldn't be able to use the skill carved into her bones, but having the weapons on hand gave her comfort.

They were her safety net, an assurance that all would be well. Even if she had to knock Adrian out and chase down the killer herself.

She flexed her fingers, rotated her shoulders, took a deep breath. The noise from the tap-room downstairs increased as more people arrived. A good thing, since it would prevent anyone from hearing a scuffle upstairs.

Additional minutes passed. She lowered herself to the edge of the bed and stared at the door. Either the killer was purposefully late, or he'd changed his mind about showing up.

Her limbs were stiff with anticipation. The need for

action, built on the hope of finally reaching some sort of conclusion, coiled firmly around her. Slowing her breaths, she forced herself into a state of calm, a quiet before the storm. Her fingers slid over the blade pressing snugly against her left forearm. It would take less than a second for her to retrieve it.

A knock finally came – three solid taps against the wood.

Pulse leaping, she stood, and crossed to the door. "Yes?"

"It's me," a hushed voice spoke. "Nigel Lawrence."

She took a sharp breath and turned the key, the lock producing a scraping sound before it clicked into place. The door swung open and Samantha stepped back, inviting the man who stood before her to make his approach.

His eyes, a rich shade of toffee, danced with a hint of amusement and keen expectation. Dark brown locks of mussed hair swept his brow as he took off his hat and entered the room. His elegant jawline complimented the straight line of his nose and the mischievous slant of his mouth.

Undoubtedly, Nigel Lawrence was beautifully built.

Of greater note was his debonair manner, which lacked the cold calculation she would have expected. A clever trick to lure his prey closer.

His gaze swept the length of her body with interest. "I must say, your invitation to meet surprised me."

She smiled sweetly. "I made no such invitation. It was you who invited me."

He gave her a funny look. A chuckle followed. "If that is how you wish to perceive it, I'll make no dispute. All that matters is that we are here. Christ, you've no idea how many times I've dreamt about this."

"About what, exactly?" She knew the answer, but was curious to know if he'd actually say it.

"Come now, Miss Carmichael. *Samantha*. There's no need for you to play coy. I know the sort of woman you are and what you're after."

"Really?" She began sliding her hidden blade into her right hand.

"Rest assured, I'll see to your needs with complete discretion." He nudged the door shut, locked it, and licked his lips. His eyes gleamed with ready desire. "I'll take no issue with the number of men I share you with. Just as long as—"

One swift motion was all it took for the tip of her blade to find Mr. Lawrence's throat. He stiffened, eyes wide and whatever he'd planned on saying forgotten. Samantha watched as he swallowed, the action shifting the elegant knot of his white cravat.

She'd stain it with blood if he made any sudden movements.

"Like I said, I didn't invite you here, Mr. Lawrence." Her grip on the dagger's mother-of-pearl handle tightened. This was the man who'd slit women's throats without second thought. He'd delighted in their deaths. Every cell in her body ignited until liquid steel poured through her veins. She'd gut him where he stood if given the slightest excuse to do so. "You invited me."

"No. I didn't." The words shook and his body trembled even as somebody tested the door from the opposite side. Adrian. "If it's proof you require, I'll show you the letter."

No such chance occurred before the door shook in response to a powerful force. Wood splintered as Adrian came crashing into the room with all the ferocity of a demonic beast. In one swift movement he'd regained his footing and launched himself squarely at Mr. Lawrence.

One second he was standing before Samantha, looking as though he might piss himself out of fear. The next, he was being pressed into the ground by Adrian's weight and feeling the pain of each blow delivered.

An ugly crunch sounded, grunts of exertion mingled with anguished gasps. Bone connected with bone and blood started flowing. Samantha stared at the blind rage gripping the man who ought to mean nothing to her, and recognized it as though it were her own.

And yet, something felt off. Mr. Lawrence's mention of her invitation to him and what he'd said since. His being here had compelled her to make an assumption. But what if she'd made a mistake? What if her confidence in the plan she'd devised prevented her from seeing how it could be used against her?

She didn't want to believe it, but Mr. Lawrence had mentioned a letter and—

"Adrian." Deaf to her plea, he closed his hand around Mr. Lawrence's throat. The man clawed at him, legs kicking as he fought to break himself free. Adrian's fingers just tightened. A murderous smile of pure satisfaction curled his lips, baring his teeth. Samantha grabbed his shoulder and shook him as hard as she could. "Stop and listen for just one second. Adrian. I think there's a chance we've got the wrong man."

CHAPTER FORTY

Words of warning, barely perceptible, whispered somewhere beneath Adrian's quest for vengeance. A shift in his body as somebody shook him broke through the haze. He blinked, absorbed the demand to cease his actions.

Confusion descended upon him like murky fog. He shook his head, attempted to focus on his own breathing – a series of strained sounds wheezing through him with every tense muscle and tendon.

"Release him."

Again, that solid voice ordering him to comply.

He had no wish to, but something in the sound – a spellbinding sweetness – halted his movements.

"Adrian." A firm press of a hand against his shoulder. "Let him give you the letter."

He shook his head. "What letter?"

"The one I supposedly wrote, inviting him here."

It could be a ruse, an attempt at gaining the upper hand. Adrian forced air into his lungs while staring at Lawrence's battered face. Multiple bruises were starting to form, his left eye was swollen shut and blood dribbled from a cut on his lip.

The wrecked individual sprawled beneath him could easily be overpowered again if need be.

With this in mind, Adrian braced his knee against the floor and prepared to let up, but doing so was no simple feat.

Fingers locked in position, it took a near insurmountable effort to pry them free from the neck he was squeezing. Extreme force of will and determination were required, a relentless struggle against every instinct driving him to end the man who'd murdered his sister.

But what if it wasn't the right one?

Adrian's fingers unlocked, his hand opened, and he drew back. Lawrence gulped down a series of breaths, then proceeded to cough and sputter while desperately fumbling for something inside his jacket pocket.

Adrian prepared to knock him back onto the floor in case he produced a weapon. Instead, a crumpled piece of paper was thrust in his direction. It bore a broken seal and was indeed signed with Samantha's name.

He read the rest of it – the impassioned longing for Mr. Lawrence to meet her at this location. Words intended to lure him with the promise of bedsport.

Now that I'm ruined, the letter said, *I no longer need to pretend. I'll seek the pleasure I crave, indulge in whatever desires I please, and welcome whomever I choose to my bed.*

It went on, suggesting Mr. Lawrence would be but one of her lovers.

Crafty, since this would have stopped him from questioning why she had written to him alone. According to this, she had not. She was merely accepting auditions.

∽

The Mayfair Murderer cursed beneath his breath as he watched the scene unfold from across the alley. He'd paid the occupants handsomely for the use of their lodgings under the pretext of needing them for a very important home office assignment.

Croft should have killed Nigel by now. Instead, he'd stopped his attack to examine a piece of paper. The Mayfair Murderer gnashed his teeth. It looked like it might be the blasted letter he'd used to lure Nigel here – the one that proved Nigel wasn't the killer.

Additional hesitation followed. Tension worked its way through the Mayfair Murderer's body. The plan to get rid of Croft and Miss Carmichael wasn't working. If they didn't kill Nigel, then there would be no grounds to step in as witness and have them arrested for murder.

Instead they would leave the inn and continue their hunt. Croft's obstinance would not let him stop. He'd review every detail and expand the list of possible suspects until he eventually identified his sister's killer. Now, with the additional clue of Nigel being used as scapegoat, Croft's attention would soon find its mark.

The only way to prevent it would be to remove Croft and Miss Carmichael from the playing field.

He reached into his pocket and withdrew the pistol he'd brought along for this eventuality. He'd kill Croft first, then wait for Miss Carmichael, the weaker opponent of the two, to leave the inn. She'd be distraught, he'd happen upon her as if by chance and offer her comfort, then slash her throat.

His pulse leapt in response to the pleasure he knew he'd soon find in spilling her blood. Lips curving in anticipation, he opened the window and aimed his pistol.

∼

Furious with the additional stain Mr. Lawrence's letter caused to Samantha's reputation, Adrian crumpled the page in his fist. "It's a trap."

He started to rise, extended his hand to help Lawrence up, was almost fully upright, when Samantha glanced at the window. She didn't utter the slightest sound before flinging herself in front of his body. Glass exploded in the next instant, shards flying in every direction, like sharp pieces of frozen rain in a storm.

Lawrence cried out and Adrian dropped, catching Samantha as she fell. His knee struck the floor, the jarring impact no more than a minor nuisance compared with the dread sliding through him.

"Samantha." A plea trapped in emotional torment, the knowledge of what had occurred sending chills down his spine. A series of feverish shivers rushed through him. Hands trembling, he felt for her wound, a patch of wetness soaking her gown at the shoulder. "No. No, no, no."

"Adrian." Her voice was surprisingly calm. Steady. Insistent.

Raising his gaze, he looked at her, and caught the flint in her eyes. Fury burned in her veins – a savage need to punish whoever had done this – a merciless thing born from so much hate he almost recognized it as his own.

Taken aback, he stared at her, at the woman who'd captured his heart and mind with her sweetness. He shouldn't have involved her in any of this. He should have done it alone. He—

"I'm shot," she said, "but I'm not mortally wounded. I'll be fine as long as you don't let that murdering scoundrel escape."

"How do you know?" His attention returned to her wound, experience gauging the severity of it.

A small grin. "I've no essential organs there as far as I know."

True, but there were important veins nearby. She'd been lucky. Damn lucky. He blew out a breath. "You're right."

"Which means you can leave me. Go after him. Catch him."

He gripped her hand. "You're sure?"

"Yes." She gave him a shove. "Hurry."

Despite his reluctance, Adrian stood. It was true that she would survive a shot to that part of the shoulder as long as she got proper treatment later. He just didn't feel right about leaving her when she was wounded. Then again, with the killer so close, it made sense to give chase.

He spoke to Lawrence. "Keep her safe until I return."

Not waiting to gain the man's agreement, Adrian ran from the room and clattered down the narrow staircase leading toward the tavern's front entrance. He shoved his way past some men blocking his path, ignoring the protests that followed him into the dimly lit street.

Turning toward the building from which the pistol was fired, he spotted the swiftly retreating silhouette of a figure no more than fifty yards farther along the pavement. Adrian broke into a run, his booted feet heavy against the ground. Intent on catching the bastard who'd sliced Evie's throat, he pushed himself faster.

A street light cast a hazy glow, allowing a clearer glimpse of the man he chased as he darted around a corner, but the distance was still too great and with his back turned, it was hard to note significant details besides a hint of golden hair.

Conscious of the fact that failure to catch him now

might mean he never got caught, Adrian dashed after him, weaving and winding his way through increasingly narrow streets.

Until he erupted onto Weymouth Street and nearly crashed into Clive Newton as he came the opposite way.

The younger man leapt from Adrian's path, pulling what looked like a snuffbox close to his chest, shielding the contents with his hand while trying to calm his breaths. Shock showed on his face. "What the hell, Croft? You're the second person to nearly collide with me in under a minute."

"Might the other person have been the man I'm chasing?"

"I'd say it's likely. He looked like he was fleeing a fate worse than death." Newton gulped down a breath and jutted his chin toward Thayer Street. "He went that way."

Adrian nodded and turned, was about to take off once more when a crunching sound drew his attention. Stiffening, he glanced at Newton who was already strolling away. A lingering scent of orange blossoms hung in the air. "Is that by any chance sugar glass you're eating?"

Newton stopped. The gaslight overhead brightened his teeth as he grinned. "Indeed. The man you're after almost caused me to spill the box."

Guided by an instinct he'd garnered from nearly a lifetime of dealing with rotten scum, Adrian stepped toward him.

He considered their empty surroundings, the length of the street, and the fact that he should have spotted the man he was chasing as he ran off into the distance. Though Newton's hair was a dark shade of blonde instead of the much fairer color belonging to the man whom Adrian had been chasing, the gaslight made it glow in much the same way.

Add to that the treat Newton chewed – the very same kind enjoyed by the man Mr. Adams had mentioned – and it all started coming together.

It was an easy ploy, pretending to be out and about for a walk, heading toward the person chasing instead of away, stopping to talk and then misdirecting. Feigning shock to account for the unsteady breaths.

A bold move.

Adrian met Newton's gaze. The edgy look in his eyes betrayed the calm he tried to convey.

He took a step closer.

Newton extended his hand, offering him the box filled with sugar glass treats. "You want one?"

A predatory stillness descended on Adrian's body. He tilted his head and studied his prey. "Why did you do it?"

"Do what?" It genuinely sounded like he didn't know, but Adrian would not be so easily fooled.

"Don't pretend ignorance, Newton. I know you murdered those women."

"A harsh accusation, Croft." Anger began to pull at Newton's expression. "I should call you out for the insult."

"Come now." Adrian stalked toward him and snatched the box from his hand before tossing the thing aside. It clattered against the pavement, the contests flying in every direction. Teeth bared in a smile he hoped would strike terror, he leaned in. "We both know you'd take more pleasure in killing an innocent woman than you would me."

A slight pull at the edge of Newton's mouth proved the remark struck a nerve. "Everyone knows why the killer targeted them. They weren't innocent, Croft."

"I beg to differ," Adrian snarled. "My sister was virtuous and pure, the very embodiment of goodness."

Newton's jaw tightened. His breaths deepened. Irritation flickered within his cool gaze. "A tragic loss that had nothing to do with me."

"Stop. Lying." God help him, he'd rip the man's tongue out if he didn't start confessing.

"I'm not. You're casting blame on someone who doesn't deserve it. Just like you did with Lundquist."

Adrian didn't believe it. He wanted to smash Newton's skull against the ground, beat him until he begged for his life, and then slit him open so slowly he'd have time to feel death creeping in.

A fantasy he knew he couldn't afford if he wished to avoid getting messy. He'd have to resort to other means. But not before Newton admitted his guilt.

"You're wrong." A slow whisper, so confident it forced a brief look of unease to fill Newton's gaze. Adrian smirked. "I know you're the man I was chasing. There is no one else. The street is empty, besides which

I managed to glimpse you in detail when you passed beneath the streetlight earlier. It took a moment for it to register, but there's no denying it now. You're dressed exactly the same."

A laugh of disbelief. "Brown jacket with trousers to match? I'm sure I'm dressed the same as half the men in London."

"Your clothes and hair are also messier than usual. As would be the case if you've been running."

"Or leaping out of the way of two men."

Fair point, but not enough to dissuade Adrian from his increasing certainty.

Additional steps brought them closer. Newton moved as though to retreat but Adrian caught him by the arm. He leaned in, drew a deep breath, and acknowledged the lingering hint of smoked wood combined with the acrid smell of rotten eggs. It was faint, so much so he'd initially missed it due to the sweet scent from the sugar glass.

Straightening, Adrian dropped his hand and prepared to attack if need be. "You're right. Everything I've mentioned so far is hardly enough to stand as proof. Combined with the stench on your person, however, it's fairly solid. You've recently fired a pistol, Mr. Newton, or will you deny that as well?"

Newton dipped his chin, shoved his hands in his pockets and shrugged. A snort followed. When he looked back up, a malicious grin was pasted upon his face. "Bravo. You finally figured it out."

Adrian held himself perfectly still. If he moved, he'd

tear Newton to pieces right here. "You realize I plan to avenge my sister."

Not a hint of remorse showed in Newton's expression, even as he said, "I'll admit I may have made a slight error where she was concerned."

It took every ounce of control Adrian possessed not to murder Newton where he stood. But no, he had to resist. If only for a while longer.

"But the rest of those women," Newton continued, "were nothing more than manipulative liars taking advantage of unsuspecting men. Someone had to put an end to their wicked deceptions. I merely did what was necessary."

"By murdering them?" Adrian curled his fingers into a fist.

"By making sure no other man would fall prey to the sort of woman Miss Fairchild turned out to be. Like so many others, she played the innocent debutante, but she was a whore in disguise – a despicable creature and a disgrace to her–"

Adrian's fist landed squarely against Newton's jaw, replacing his words with the cracking of bone. His head snapped back, knees buckling as he crumpled into a messy sprawl.

Adrian flexed his fingers, then bent to check Newton's pulse. It still beat where his neck met his jaw, thank God.

Shifting into a crouch, Adrian hauled Newton's body up over his shoulder and stood. It was a good ten-minute walk from here to his house, longer when he had to carry what felt like eleven stone.

He shifted the weight and kept an eye out for a hackney. None appeared until he turned onto Bulstrode Street, the horses' hot breaths misting in the cool air as they approached. Adrian raised his hand to signal the driver, and the carriage drew to a halt, wheels grating against the axels.

"What's with him?" asked the driver, a hunched over man with heavy jowls and thick bushy brows dipping low over shadowy eyes. He gripped the reins and jutted his chin toward Newton.

"Too much drink led to a brawl. I'm trying to get him home so he doesn't wake up in a gutter."

"Right then. Whereto?"

"Number 5 Portman Square." Adrian pulled the door open and shoved Newton's body inside, leaving him on the floor of the cabin while he himself took a seat on the bench. He yanked the door shut and knocked on the roof. The vehicle lurched into motion, rocking Newton's head from side to side as they travelled west.

Adrian glared at the limp body. Never before had he hated someone as much as he hated this man. He'd taken Adrian's sister from him and forced him to further darken his soul with the punishment he would now have to enact.

There was no choice but to harden himself against the inevitable. If he was to satisfy his need for vengeance, he'd have to embrace the demons he'd hoped to banish. Forgiveness wasn't an option.

It didn't take long before the carriage arrived at its destination. Five minutes at most. Adrian alit, told the driver to wait, then yanked Newton out of the cabin and left him on the pavement while he went to fetch Murry.

"Get him inside and dismiss the servants for the night," he told his valet. "I don't want any of them involved in what happens next."

"Of course." Murry accompanied Adrian to Newton's body.

"There's something I've got to do before dealing with him," Adrian added. "Shouldn't take more than an hour."

"I'll see to our guest in the meantime," Murry promised, already squatting to pick Newton up.

"One other thing." Adrian stared at Newton's limp face. "See if there's a file on Clive Newton. If not, find the one on Viscount Stanton. I'd like to review it when I return."

"Of course."

Satisfied with his valet's assurance, Adrian instructed the driver to take him to The Toothless Cat. It was imperative he check on Samantha before anything else. He needed to make sure she was all right and that she got the care she required.

CHAPTER FORTY-ONE

Nearly an hour passed between Adrian's departure from The Toothless Cat and his return. Panic reached beneath his sternum when he found Samantha gone from the room where he'd left her. The floor, he noted, was swept, not a shard of glass remaining, the curtains billowing in the breeze wafting in through the broken window.

Turning his back on the scene, he raced back downstairs.

"Miss Carmichael," Adrian snapped, his hand grabbing a maid's wrist and halting her progress. It was the same one who'd shown him upstairs earlier. When she shook her head with incomprehension he said, "The woman who was shot. Where is she?"

"The innkeeper put her in one of the supper rooms over there. The one farthest to the right. A physician's attending her."

Adrian muttered a quick, "Thank you," and strode toward the spot she'd pointed toward. Without pausing to knock, he opened the door he believed was correct and froze when he spotted Samantha.

She was alive, yes, but lying on a table, her face turned away from the door. An elderly man of slim build, his thinning grey hair neatly combed to one side, bowed over her. The needle he wielded pierced Samantha's skin and slipped through, catching the opposite edge of raw flesh and pulling it neatly shut.

Adrian drew a ragged breath and shifted his gaze. He spotted Lawrence, his overall appearance that of a man who'd been trampled by a runaway carriage. Slouched in a chair in the corner, he pressed a slab of meat to his puffy eye.

"How is she?" Adrian asked, of no one in particular.

The physician glanced up, peering over a pair of spectacles. "She'll be fine. We're almost done."

Relief flooded Adrian's body, washing away much of his apprehension, though it didn't quite slow his pulse. It would likely keep racing until she'd fully recovered.

"I thought it best to get help," Lawrence said, his voice hoarse.

Adrian nodded. "You did well. Thank you. And um...I hope you can forgive my attack. It shouldn't have happened."

"No, I don't suppose it should have," Lawrence agreed. "But I understand and I do forgive your mistake."

"Did you at least catch the right man in the end?"

Samantha asked. Her voice was steady, though it did sound as though she was gritting her teeth.

"I did. Turns out it was Clive Newton."

"Really?" Samantha would have sat up, had the physician not used a firm hand to hold her against the table.

"He's...in a safe place," Adrian added, already regretting how much he'd said in front of Lawrence and the physician. "I'll speak with him later, after I help you get home."

"Thank you, but you don't have to do that," Samantha told him. The physician tied off the thread he'd used and placed a compress on top, which he secured with a bandage. "I can easily take a hackney on my own."

"Absolutely not." If there was one thing he needed to do for his own peace of mind, it was see her safely back to Clearview. "I'll escort you as soon as you're ready."

"But what ab—"

"We're not discussing this." Hoping to avoid additional protests from the stubborn woman, Adrian told the physician, "I'll pay you whatever you're owed."

He made the innkeeper a similar offer before taking his leave, assuring him he'd cover all the repairs if he sent him the bill. Once in the street, Adrian hailed two hackneys, one for himself and Samantha, the other for Lawrence.

He handed Samantha up into the first one and turned to Lawrence. "I'd also like to express my sympathy for your brother. Losing the use of one's legs cannot be easy."

"He's in a terrible state, truth be told. It's a daily struggle."

Adrian could only imagine. He nodded. "Once again, my apologies for what happened. If there's any way in which I can make it up to you, don't hesitate to ask."

"Thank you. I'll keep that in mind."

Adrian nodded and gave directions to his driver before climbing into the carriage. It took off as soon as the door had been shut.

"What the hell were you thinking?" he asked. The dread he'd experienced, briefly buried while he dealt with Newton, pushed its way back to the surface. "You could have been killed, Samantha. Did that thought enter your head even once?"

"No." She leaned against the opposite side of the carriage, her gaze on the dark view beyond the window. "I caught a movement out of the corner of my eye. When I turned, I spotted a figure leaning through the window across the way. Despite the dark, there was no question about his intentions, and in that moment, my only thought was of saving you."

Adrian's heart shivered with some sort of deep ineffable feeling. His arm came around her, drawing her close to his side. He pressed his lips to the top of her head – a gentle kiss to comfort and reassure her.

"Promise me you won't ever do something so foolish again."

A soft laugh rippled through her. "You ask the impossible. I cannot curb my instinct. Nor would I forgive myself if I stood by and watched you get hurt when I was in a position to stop it."

"Samantha…"

"Don't tell me to do what you yourself would not be able to, Adrian."

He sighed. Perhaps a different subject of conversation would serve them better. "Harlowe won't be pleased when he sees you like this."

"He's furious with me after last night. Ordered me to stay in my room until further notice. I'm not supposed to be out of the house."

"Another reason for me to see you home." He caught her hand and gave it a squeeze. "As your fiancé, I've every right to your company, Samantha. I'll remind him of that."

She sighed. Her head settled heavily against his shoulder. "He'll see I was shot and will want to know what happened. And besides, our engagement isn't real. With Newton caught, there's no reason to keep up the ruse."

"Isn't there?" That deep indefinable feeling filled him once more, only this time it twisted and turned as though trying to free itself from something awful.

He took a deep breath, focused on what it was like to have her back in his arms safe from harm, on the warmth of her hand, the soft exhale flowing over her lips, that sweet scent of jasmine caught in her hair.

"I'd be a liar and a fool if I didn't admit my fondness

for you. You've proven a constant friend, beyond supportive at every turn. To be honest, no woman has ever impressed me more." He drew her a little nearer. "Add to that the fact that we get along, enjoy similar interests, and share an attraction. I believe I'd be making the biggest mistake of my life if I didn't propose to you in earnest. So I ask you now, Samantha Carmichael, if you will do me the honor of taking me as your husband."

A brief hesitation followed. It was enough to make his stomach contract. But then she lifted her head, allowing their gazes to meet while she gave him her answer. "I will."

Her words calmed him, eased away tension and doubt, replaced them with deep contentment and a strong faith in the future. An unsteady breath revealed how much her agreement meant to him.

Cupping her chin, he stroked the delicate edge of her jaw with his thumb before leaning in.

A kiss to seal the new bond they'd forged. The first of many to come. A flickering hope of light vanquishing darkness. As long as his world didn't destroy her.

She'd no idea what she was getting into, and if he were noble and good, he'd warn her, accept the risk of losing her forever. But he wasn't either of those things. If what he intended to do when he returned home proved anything at all, it was that he was utterly ruthless.

∽

A dull ache permeated Samantha's entire left side. It would take days for it to subside and more than a week for the wound to heal. The brandy Harlowe had given her when she returned to Clearview was a soothing balm.

She took another sip and considered Harlowe's somber expression. He'd met her and Adrian in the foyer, his attention going straight to the torn fabric of her spencer before he'd ushered both of them into his study.

"I don't believe an explanation is too much to ask for," he said, his cool blue gaze on Adrian. "Within the course of two days, Samantha's reputation has been ruined beyond compare, yet you still declared a desire to wed her. Surprising, though not as much as her getting shot immediately after. While in your company."

"We were—"

"Not you," Harlowe snapped, cutting Samantha off. "I want to know what Mr. Croft has to say about this."

Adrian's entire bearing changed in response to Harlowe's sharp tone. He drew back his shoulders and pushed his chest forward. His dark eyes reflected the light from the oil lamp on Harlowe's desk, the overall appearance that of a dangerous cat ready to pounce.

"I'll explain," Adrian said, his voice terrifyingly smooth. "But if you ever raise your voice to Samantha again or disrespect her in any way, you'll make a permanent enemy of me. Is that clear?"

A stubborn gleam entered Harlowe's eyes, but he eventually nodded.

"As my fiancée," Adrian went on, "she's under my protection. Apologize to her so we can move on with our discussion."

Samantha froze. She'd never heard anyone pressure Harlowe before. Adrian, it seemed, had zero qualms about doing so, which made one thing blatantly clear. He was confident enough in his power to know he could force other men to yield. It was that threat of what he might do, the suspicions of what he was capable of, that could bend other men to his will.

Concrete proof of his involvement in criminal conduct could strip him of that control.

As his wife, she'd be in the perfect position to find any evidence that might be used against him. If she desired to do so. Harlowe and Kendrick would both expect her to stay on mission, but neither of them truly cared about her, whereas Adrian did.

A deciding factor that shifted the balance.

Going forward, her loyalty would be to her husband.

Harlowe slid his gaze over to her. His jaw worked, clenching against the words he'd have to utter. "Forgive me for interrupting you in such a curt manner. It was inconsiderate of me and shan't happen again."

"Good enough," Adrian said. He leaned back, the movements he made with his glass causing his brandy to swirl. "Samantha was shot while helping me track down the Mayfair Murderer. She and I devised a plan, part of which included last night's scene with Marsdale. I'm sorry about the disruption that caused to your evening."

"You were attempting to bait the killer," Harlowe said, his voice hardening as he spoke. "In doing so, you deliberately put her in harm's way."

"A regrettable outcome." Adrian's comment contained no hint of the open distress he'd shown in the moment. Had she not experienced it first hand, she'd have thought him indifferent. "Unfortunately the killer proved more cunning than we expected. I…wish our efforts had led to his capture, but…"

Samantha's mind raced in the wake of the lie, even as she made every effort to hide her surprise. Was Adrian testing her to see if she would stand by him no matter what? Or were his plans for Newton such that he didn't want anyone tracing what might happen next back to him? Perhaps a bit of both?

"You mean to say he got away?" Harlowe asked. "After everything you put her through, he slipped through your fingers?"

"I wasn't about to leave Samantha wounded and alone while I chased down the villain." Raising his glass, Adrian took a moment to let the remainder of his brandy slide down his throat. "No need to worry, though. Her wound will heal soon enough and her reputation will be restored once she and I wed."

"Might I suggest a special license and an imminent union in order to speed that along?"

"Of course. I'll see to the special license in the morning. If all goes well, we should be able to speak our vows as soon as tomorrow evening." He glanced at Samantha. "Unless you desire more time to plan, in which case we might be able to wait a few days."

"No." It felt like the walls were caving in on her. Everything was happening so fast, her head was spinning. But with Kendrick's deadline nearly up, it was imperative that she place herself in a position to keep Adrian safe. A hasty wedding would do precisely that, so she forced herself to look excited. "The sooner the better."

The edge of his lips dimpled – a swift hint of approval before he told Harlowe, "As for the Mayfair Murderer, one can only hope what happened this evening will force the scoundrel to go into hiding."

"Has it not occurred to you that you may have hindered Bow Street's investigation by getting involved?" It sounded like Harlowe believed what Adrian told him. Samantha found no hint of suspicion in any part of his manner.

"I don't believe they would ever have caught him." Adrian stood, the conversation as far as he was concerned apparently at an end. He took Samantha's hand and, bowing, raised it to his lips. "I'll call on you tomorrow afternoon to see how you're doing and to confirm the time and location of our nuptials."

"I look forward to it already."

He smiled, the warmth in his eyes snaring her for a few seconds until he turned away, his long strides taking him from the room as he made his departure.

"You should have told me what you were up to," Harlowe informed her as soon as they were alone. "Instead, you deceived me."

"A necessity for the sake of authenticity. Your response to my indiscretion with Marsdale was real. It lent credence to the act."

"For all the good it did." Harlowe stood and crossed to the fireplace. He stared at the flames. A log snapped. "At least he's serious about getting married. As his wife, you'll have full access. More than you would have as his mistress."

The only thing of importance to Samantha was her ability to thwart potential attacks against the man who'd become her future. To Harlowe she said, "If there's proof of Croft's criminal dealings, I'll find it. You have my word."

CHAPTER FORTY-TWO

Satisfaction was draped across Adrian's shoulders like a cloak woven from pure pleasure as he climbed the front steps of Croft House later. Samantha would soon be his. She'd agreed to become his wife.

But first...

He entered his home and shut the door on the outside world. The foyer was cast in shadow, the longcase clock next to the stairs filling the stillness with sharp ticks. A broad-shouldered figure appeared in the parlor doorway, his tall frame silhouetted against the dim light behind him.

"I've locked him in the basement room," Murry said while Adrian pulled off his gloves and removed his hat. Nothing more needed saying. There was no questioning which room Murry referred to since it had been used for similar purposes in the past, including his own punishments growing up.

"And the files?"

"I located Stanton's. It's on top of your desk in the study."

Adrian flipped it open as soon as he found it, scanning the pages until the notes started to mention the viscount's children. Four sons in total. Owen, Randolph, Philip, and Clive. The heir, the barrister, the physician, and…the disappointment.

According to the information compiled on Stanton and his family, Clive had been encouraged to join the clergy, only to fail his examination with the bishop due to his lacking knowledge of Latin and scripture. He'd had a brief stint in the army after, but had found the training too difficult, the discipline too demanding.

After that, he'd appealed to the foreign secretary, the Marquess of Londonderry, who'd managed to acquire a position for him as an aide to Henry Goulburn, the undersecretary at the War and Colonial Office.

Adrian flipped the page and read what followed. Remarks made by Clive during last year's Season suggested low self-esteem on his part, along with the need for his father's approval.

"Would you like a glass of brandy before we head down there?" Murry asked when Adrian finished reading.

"No." He straightened. "Just grab the oil lamp."

The valet lit the way and Adrian followed into the hallway, past the library, then down the servants' stairs. The soles of his boots scraped the tiled floor as he stepped off the bottom step.

They turned left, away from the store rooms, the butler's pantry, and the kitchen, and toward the room that still made his heart lurch in ways nothing else could.

This was where nightmares were made. The scars crisscrossing his back had been dealt here by his own father.

Dank and miserable, the space had introduced him to pain and to death. It had molded him into the man he'd become, enabled him to mete out punishments under his father's rule.

Now, with his father gone and Evie's killer confined to this place, the responsibility of ensuring justice was served fell squarely on him. He would determine what happened to Newton. There would be no one else for him to pass the blame onto. He was in charge and the weight of that knowledge made every cell in his body pulse with alertness.

They reached the arched door leading in. Crafted from a knotted dark wood, it was held in place by thick iron hinges. The large key protruding from the keyhole kept it securely locked.

Murry turned it and pushed the door open so Adrian could enter.

He stepped across the threshold and a chill crept through his bones. How long had it been since he'd last set foot here? He couldn't recall, but he'd be damn glad if tonight was the last time he did so.

Murry followed him in, the light from the oil lamp filling the space and bringing their prisoner into view.

He sat in a wooden chair, his forearms bound to the armrests, ankles tied to the chair legs, hatred burning in his eyes. A length of white fabric, an old cravat perhaps, had been used to gag him, though it failed to stifle his grunts of protest.

Ignoring him for a moment, Adrian glanced at the table that stood near the wall as Murry set down the lamp. A glimpse of the past stiffened his spine – his father's hand closing around the whip he'd selected, the anguish that followed.

He blinked, focused on all the tools Murry had gathered, made a mental note of each one, and went to undo Newton's gag.

"You'll be arrested for this," Newton seethed. "My father will make sure you hang."

"You're assuming your father will take your side in all this," Adrian murmured. "I've got my doubts. When he learns of what you've done, there's a good chance he'll cast you off. Not just because your actions repel him, but because you'll have shamed your family once you make the newspaper headlines."

Teeth bared, Newton jerked his arms against his restraints. "You're a bloody bastard, Croft."

Adrian tilted his head in quiet reflection. "You're not wrong. I can be harsh and unforgiving, but I also have a clear understanding of right and wrong. You, on the other hand, are a monster."

"Because I tried to prevent trusting men from being deceived?" A snort of disgust followed. "I'm not the monster in all of this, Croft. The whores are."

"Those young women's actions may have been selfish, immoral even, but that didn't give you the right to kill them. Their sins did not warrant death. In Miss Fairchild's case, the only victim who affected you directly, social ruin would have sufficed. No other man would have touched her had her behavior been revealed. But that wasn't enough for you, was it? Because deep down, this is who you are, a madman looking for any excuse to spill the blood of others." Adrian crossed to the table and slid his hand over a length of rope before picking it up and testing its strength. "Be honest, Newton. You enjoyed it."

"You're wrong." Newton's gaze tracked Adrian's every movement with pure contempt. "It was unpleasant, but necessary. I merely did what had to be done."

"So you found no thrill in knowing they came to you with the expectation of finding pleasure?" Adrian circled the room slowly, until he stood at Newton's shoulder. "Tell me, did they mistake you for their secret lovers?"

A rough bit of laughter escaped Newton's throat. "Always."

Adrian's grip on the rope tightened. He sent Murry a quick glance and saw his own fury reflected in every tight line of the valet's face. "But not my sister."

"No. She met with me for a different reason."

"What was it?"

"As if I'd tell you."

Fueled by the rage that had taken root at The Toothless Cat Inn, Adrian wound the rope around Newton's neck and pulled it tight. A gasp and a strangled sound followed along with a series of spasmic movements.

This was just the beginning.

Adrian loosened the rope and Newton wheezed as he drew in some air, upon which he started to cough as though he were choking.

"I'll ask you again," Adrian told him, his hand pressing down against Newton's right shoulder. "How did you lure my sister?"

"Go to hell, Croft."

The rope was tightened once more, then again, and a fourth time, until Newton sputtered and swore when Adrian let it go slack.

Red-faced and watery eyed, with each breath scraping his throat, he surrendered. "I…I told her I'd… give her the name of the person…who'd spread the rumor about her."

The comment was like a stab to Adrian's chest. He'd promised Evie he'd find that information for her, but rather than wait, she'd accepted help from another source.

How could she have been so careless with her own safety when he'd warned her against going out on her own? It was hard to comprehend as he stood there, a mixture of loss and failure spearing his soul.

"Whose name did you sign to the letter you sent her?"

One corner of Newton's mouth rose. "My own."

Of course. Evie had known him well. They'd moved in the same circles, danced at various balls. He was a viscount's son, for crying out loud. If he'd told her he had information to give her, what reason would she have had not to trust him?

Despite his every intention to leave Newton's body unmarked, Adrian's gaze slid over the tools that lay on the table. The temptation to use them was irresistibly strong. "You despicable son of a bitch."

"Your sister didn't think so." Newton managed a hoarse laugh. "She was more than happy to pay for what I'd promised. Hell, I can still taste her sweetness upon my tongue."

Adrian lunged.

Fingers curled around Newton's jaw in a rigid hold, every muscle locked with the effort it took not to bury his fist in the bastard's face. But that wouldn't do. He had to hold back if he was to make sure none of what happened here got linked to him. "Liar."

"Or maybe you didn't know her as well as you thought."

A red haze was swiftly descending on Adrian's vision. The instinct to lash out pulsed with urgent need at the base of his skull. Intent on regaining control, he closed his eyes, drew his attention inward, focused on slowing his breaths and bringing his heartbeats back to an even rhythm.

A predatory sense of calm wrapped itself around him, shielding him from the impulse to strike without thinking. He shoved Newton's face from his hand and took a step back.

Tossing the rope aside, he turned to Murry. "I need some writing supplies."

Murry nodded and went to collect the items. Adrian crossed his arms to prevent himself from grabbing a dagger and shoving it through Newton's throat. "I'm going to give you two choices. You can either confess your sins to your father in writing and face his wrath, or I can slit your throat right now and let you bleed out. It's your choice."

Newton narrowed his gaze and leaned forward as much as he could. "You would honestly let me go?"

"Make no mistake," Adrian told him darkly. "Your father will know what you've done. There will be no escaping that if you pick the first option."

"But I'll live." Not a question but a deduction.

Adrian picked up the dagger and studied it briefly before glancing at Newton once more. "What will it be?"

The door opened and Murry returned. He swept the tools on the table to one side and set down the writing supplies. Adrian thanked him then shifted his attention back to Newton. "Well?"

Body hunched as he stared at the floor, Newton curled his fingers around the ends of the armrests. His breaths were ragged and loud, filling the space with a saw-like sound. When he finally raised his chin, an involuntary need to comply was imbedded in his murderous gaze. "I'll write the confession."

"Make sure to mention all of your victims," Adrian

said once Newton began. "And don't forget to describe how you lured them or why you did what you did."

The tip of the quill scratched over the paper, the words flowing with notable swiftness. Adrian glanced over Newton's shoulder and read a few lines. No hint of remorse could be found in the matter-of-fact account he gave.

"Showing regret and begging forgiveness might soften your father's response, don't you think?"

Newton paused, finished the sentence he was working on, and followed Adrian's advice before signing his name to the bottom.

"Blot this please," Adrian told Murry while he himself went to collect the rope he'd been using earlier.

Roughly ten yards long, it would serve his purpose nicely. He proceeded to casually loop and twist one end, enjoying the soothing effect of the process and where it would lead.

"Wha…what are you doing?" Newton asked. His attention had been on Murry before, but was now directed at Adrian.

"What does it look like?"

Newton shook his head, dread showing in his stricken expression. "You said you'd let me go if I wrote a confession."

Finished with the noose he'd been making, Adrian climbed onto a stool and slipped the rope over a hook in the ceiling. He jumped down and secured the end of the rope to an iron ring embedded in the wall.

"I don't negotiate with curs who murder women."

Arms crossed, he considered the noose that would hang the bastard. "Let's get him over here, Murry."

Screaming for help, Newton struck them with fisted hands, landing blows that were sure to bruise as they dragged his chair backward. When they reached the right spot, Murry untied the rope from the iron ring, lowering the noose.

Adrian dropped it over Newton's head and pulled it tight, all the while fighting Newton's every attempt to free himself from his fate.

A sideways swipe put Adrian briefly off balance, but when Murry drew the rope taut, Newton's attention shifted toward his own neck.

He grabbed the noose with desperate hands, tried to create a gap between it and his neck – some room in which to breathe.

Lowering to a crouch, Adrian untied Newton's ankles then gestured for Murry to pull a bit harder. "Let's get him up."

Sputtering, Newton continued to grip the noose while his feet began scrambling for purchase. Lifting him slightly, Adrian helped him gain his footing before yanking his hands away from the noose.

Grim faced, Murry pulled the rope until Newton stood on his tiptoes then retied it to the iron ring.

"You'll burn in hell for this," Newton croaked.

Adrian didn't doubt him for a second. He'd compromised his soul a long time ago, but it had never felt more worth it than now. "In that case, we'll see each other again."

With nothing more left to be said, Adrian kicked the chair away with violent force.

Newton's body dropped, his eyes bulged and his lips parted. He clawed at the rope with desperate fingers while small gasps of air were squeezed from his lungs. His body jerked, like a fish dangling at the end of a fisherman's line. A choking sound followed. His legs twitched and then his body went limp.

Adrian took a deep breath and expelled it. Had he been free to do as he pleased, he'd have carved Newton into a thousand pieces, starting with his fingers. Instead, this would have to do. The vile creature who'd brutally murdered Evie was finally gone.

Satisfied, he turned to Murry. "Let's get him into the carriage."

CHAPTER FORTY-THREE

A thin morning fog crept over the damp London ground. Hunched in an effort to ward off the chill, Kendrick entered St. Bartholomew's churchyard and cast his gaze upward, toward the top of the church tower.

It was exactly as the curate had described. Kendrick had brought the shaken man back to the church with him, along with a couple of Runners. He'd need them to help get the hanged man down.

Bloody nuisance.

Whatever his thoughts might have been when he'd tied one end of the rope around a parapet and the other around his neck before jumping over the side, they had not been on the people tasked with having to fetch him.

"Any idea who it is?" one of the Runners asked.

Kendrick shook his head. "Not from this angle. I'll need a closer look. Maybe search his pockets for clues."

Half an hour later, thanks to a series of calling cards and one hell of a damning letter, he had his answer. It was Clive Newton, one of Viscount Stanton's boys.

Blast it. This news would not go over well, but at least it helped put an end to the most puzzling investigation of Kendrick's career. The Mayfair Murderer was, according to Newton's own admission, found.

Already dead, he'd saved his family the embarrassment of a trial and the pain of enduring his execution. His self-murder was neatly accomplished.

Kendrick regarded Newton's face, a twisted expression of anguish still straining his features, and felt a brief pang of regret. Hanging, in his opinion, was far too easy a way for a man such as him to go.

∽

It was nearing eleven by the time the special license Adrian had requested, or rather purchased, from the Archbishop was ready. Having tucked the document into his jacket's inside pocket, he returned to his carriage and ordered the driver to take him to Clearview House.

When he arrived there some forty minutes later, he spotted Kendrick, who appeared to be on his way out. Adrian, who'd alit from his carriage, kept his expression neutral while greeting the man with a nod. "Didn't expect to find you here. I trust all is well?"

"Indeed. The Mayfair Murderer was identified earlier." Kendrick cleared his throat. "I'm doing the rounds, informing those who put in requests for immediate updates."

"You finally tracked him down? I suppose apologies are in order then. I underestimated your abilities."

A high color rose to Kendrick's cheeks, turning them slightly ruddy. "I'm afraid I can't take credit. He killed himself, you see. A confession was found on his person."

"Lucky you," Adrian murmured. He followed the comment with a wry smile. "Will you tell me who it was?"

"Of course. I was actually planning to call on you next since your sister was one of the women killed, but now that you're here..." Kendrick gave him a sober look. "It was Viscount Stanton's son, Clive Newton."

Adrian held the constable's gaze for a long, drawn-out moment, then nodded. "Thank you for letting me know."

Concern creased Kendrick's brow. "I've done so as a courtesy, Croft. You're not to go anywhere near Lord Stanton or his family. Is that understood."

"Yes."

"Do I have your word on that?"

"Without question," Adrian promised, dismissing the constable as he turned his attention to Clearview's imposing façade and approached the front steps.

Kendrick went straight to Sir Nigel's office after returning from Clearview. "Harlowe doesn't think Newton hung himself from the top of that church tower."

"Oh?"

"At the very least, he believes he was encouraged to take his own life." Kendrick dropped into the vacant chair that stood across from Sir Nigel's. "Croft had him within his grasp last night, but something went wrong and Newton escaped. Or so Croft claims."

"But Harlowe doesn't believe that?"

"No, and neither do I. Croft would never have let that happen."

Sir Nigel steepled his fingers, his expression pensive. "So he got Newton to write that letter somehow, then killed him and made it look like self-murder?"

"There's no way to prove it."

"Of course not." Sir Nigel grunted. "One has to admit it's rather clever."

"Providing he got the right man." If Croft had indeed been involved, he'd played both judge and executioner. Viscount Stanton had lost a son. It was no small matter.

"Time will tell, I suppose. For now, we'll consider the case closed and pray no other murders occur."

"And Croft?" The deadline he'd given Samantha was in two days. If she didn't deliver, he'd need Sir Nigel's approval to follow through on the threats he'd made her.

"You're to leave him be until further notice."

Kendrick stared at his superior in disbelief. He couldn't be serious. "Our agent is finally in the perfect position to take him down. She's going to marry him for that exact purpose."

"And she'll be informed if she is to move ahead later. For now, a request has been made for her to desist."

This couldn't be happening. Not when they were so close. "By whom?"

Stern-faced, Sir Nigel told him crisply, "The highest authority."

Kendrick sank against his seat in a state of deflated stupor. The Prince Regent would not have given this order without someone else advising him to. The question was who.

It had to be someone who stood to gain from Croft's freedom.

The problem was no such person within the Prince Regent's circle came to mind. But Kendrick vowed in that moment that he would figure it out. He'd worked too damn hard on backing Croft into a corner. There was no way in hell he'd give up when victory was so close at hand he could practically taste it.

To Sir Nigel however, he simply said, "Duly noted."

∽

"How are you feeling?" Adrian asked Samantha as the two of them strolled along one of the paths behind Clearview.

"The wound still aches. From what I gather that will be true for several more days. Besides that, I am well."

"I'm pleased to hear it."

She sent him a smile. It finally felt as though the events of the last two days were beginning to settle. His coming here as promised reassured her of his intentions. He'd not changed his mind as she'd continuously feared he might. The special license had been obtained. At six o'clock this evening, she would become his wife.

Before then, she had one pressing question.

"Last night, you told Harlowe the killer had gotten away. Why?"

His expression was grave, his words more so when he answered. "Because anything else would complicate matters tremendously. Why didn't you correct me?"

"Because that would have been disloyal." An honest response.

He stopped walking and faced her, his gaze assessing. "I never would have asked you to be my wife if I didn't believe I could trust you. That said, I should be completely forthright. My past is filled with dark corners. If you look hard enough, you'll find things you'd rather not see, things that will make you think the worst of me."

"Adrian, I could never."

"Listen to me, and listen well. I've done things – terrible things – some on my father's orders, others of my own volition. Newton was…" He shook his head as though struggling with a decision. His jaw hardened and when he met her gaze next, it cut straight through her like shards of glass. "I couldn't leave his punishment to others. Not after what he did to Evie. Do you understand what I'm saying?"

"I do." He'd taken matters into his own hands, just as she'd known he would. Newton's death had not been self-inflicted. She reached for Adrian's fingers and wove them between her own. "It doesn't change the way I feel about you. Nothing else you've done will either, for if there is one thing I've learned these past weeks, it is that you are a just man, not a cruel one."

If she were to place a bet, she'd stake her life on the fact that Adrian Croft would only harm those who deserved it. He was like an avenging angel in human form, punishing wrongdoers for their sins. For that reason alone, she could not be the one who destroyed him – not when she didn't believe he was guilty of half the things Kendrick insisted upon.

His father might have forced women to whore themselves, just as Harlowe had tried to force her, but Adrian could never be so unfeeling.

"You still want to marry me then?" An unexpectedly uncertain plea from a man as harsh as he.

"Yes."

No words of love had been spoken between them, not that she minded. In her heart, she knew she felt something deeper than friendship and sensed he might too, but it would be foolish of either of them to make declarations unless they were spoken without any shadow of doubt.

For now, the bond they'd managed to build would

suffice. Beyond that, their marriage would be practical for them both. He would give her a way out from under Harlowe's control while she would guard him against any further attempts made against him.

So she did not hesitate later when asked if she would take Adrian as her husband. Nor did she feel any guilt over choosing to keep her directive a secret. All that mattered was what she did moving forward. No sense in giving Adrian cause to doubt her when marrying him was essential to his own safety.

Already, Harlowe had issued a stark reminder, that she was expected to locate the files and discover the names of the people they mentioned. He'd given her three days. Kendrick's orders.

Samantha sipped her celebratory champagne, her thoughts already on all the lies she'd deliver to keep Kendrick busy. The wedding was a small affair. Marsdale was there along with Harlowe and Hazel. A delicious dinner had followed and then the cake, hastily prepared and yet an incredible marvel of chocolate and cream.

She took another bite and chased it down with more champagne. So good.

"It's strange to have no urgent tasks to attend to," Adrian said once the others had taken their leave and it was just the two of them in the parlor. He sent her a mischievous smile before taking a seat beside her on the sofa. "With the murders resolved, I almost wonder what I will do with myself."

"I think it will be nice to have some peace and quiet

for a change. It should give us a chance to get to know each other better. For instance, I've still no idea of what time you rise, what your daily schedule looks like, or what might irritate you."

He stretched his arm out behind her and stroked the back of her neck with his thumb, making it hard for her to think. "I'm up before eight. Whatever my daily routine was until now, it's likely to change to accommodate you. We'll figure it out together. And finally, I hate being interrupted while reading. Unless it's urgent of course."

"I'm of a like mind."

The warmth in his smile darkened his eyes. His thumb stilled at the edge of her neckline. "You've not yet received a tour of the house."

"There's hardly been any time."

"There is now." He tilted his head, his boyish grin making it nearly impossible for her to equate this man with the brutal one who'd hunted Newton down and forced him to pay with his life. "Shall we?"

She placed her hand in his, happy to follow, not the least bit afraid. They were so similar he and she. In due course, she hoped she'd be able to show him how much, but for the present, she had to take care. However jovial he might be right now, he wasn't a man to be trifled with, and she'd be wise not to forget that.

They started with the music room – a colorful place with difficult memories since it had been his sister's favorite spot in the house. They entered his study next. The large wood-paneled room she'd seen through her spyglass had a view of the street to one side while overlooking the garden to the other, though it was too dark beyond the beveled windows for her to get a good look at what lay beyond.

She considered the golden lion that sat by the fireplace before taking in the rest of the room's decor.

"It's masculine and yet I don't feel as though it suits your personality." The space was too austere, suffocating in a way with a large wall to wall carpet and various rugs placed on top.

"It was my father's. I've not had a chance to redecorate since he died."

No mention of not wanting to. Seeing the fierce look in his eyes, as though he were seeing unpleasant ghosts from the past, she chose not to comment.

They moved on to the dining room, then the ballroom, before taking a look below stairs where she received a quick tour of the kitchen, the butler's pantry, and the housekeeper's room. The servants, she noted, followed her every movement with sharp alertness. It would take time to win their loyalty.

"What's through there?" she asked, gesturing toward what looked like a dungeon door. It appeared ancient.

"Storage," Adrian told her, his hand at her elbow guiding her back to the stairs. They returned to the foyer and started climbing the stairs to the first-floor landing where Adrian paused.

He gestured toward the door to the right but made no attempt to open it. "Please don't go in there. That room belonged to Evie, and I…I've not yet mustered the courage to enter it since she died."

Unsure of how to respond without saying something inane, Samantha rose up onto her tiptoes and pressed a kiss to Adrian's cheek. "I won't overstep. I promise."

The sadness that welled in his eyes was enough to shatter her heart. A silent nod was his only response as he led her away from the haunting memories, past a private drawing room, and toward the door on the opposite side of the hallway.

He opened it and ushered her into a space warmly lit by three strategically placed oil lamps. It was familiar yet different from when she'd studied it from a distance, the intimate atmosphere filled with promise.

Adrian was also fully clothed this time, the terrible scars on his back concealed beneath layers of fabric. Bile rose in her throat at the memory of it, at the horror he had endured. Anger started to work its way through her body, straining her muscles until she feared it would soon reach her face.

It took more effort than usual to bank the emotions. She managed to do so with pure force of will while watching the fire that burned in the grate.

A four-poster bed dressed in rich damask silks dominated the room. At the foot of the bed was a space, separating it from the two velvet-clad armchairs located before the fire. A dresser stood to the right of the doorway but there was no wardrobe. Instead,

Adrian pointed out an adjoining door that led to another room where their clothes could be stored.

"I'll make more space for you tomorrow. And we can have a vanity table brought in if you like."

Samantha turned. "You're sure you want me in here, interfering with your private space?"

He gave her a hesitant look. "Would you rather have separate rooms?"

"No. This is marvelous. I just don't want to impose."

"You couldn't possibly." He dipped his head and kissed her, the tenderness in the sweet caress so achingly perfect she wanted to hold onto it forever. But then it ended and he led her forward.

Samantha glanced at the bed once more and drew a shuddering breath. As if sensing her unease, Adrian turned her toward him and told her gently, "Whatever you think might happen between us tonight, please set it from your mind. You are still wounded and I'm not a beast. We have time – a lifetime worth. Our wedding night can happen later. For now, we'll simply enjoy each other's company. As you pointed out, it's a good opportunity for us to get to know each other better. Tell me, are you also an early riser or do you like to sleep in?"

It was the first question of many. One that led to countless others.

For the next three hours they talked, sharing information about themselves, their interests, and life experiences. Sitting in front of the fire, an open bottle of port on the table between them, Samantha savored the comfort she found in Adrian's company.

Their conversation flowed with a natural ease. It was filled with moments of humor as well as more serious reflection. What counted most was the growing kinship she felt with him, like an unbreakable thread forming between them. It extended beyond the close friendship she'd known with him until now, laying open a series of wonderful possibilities, including what promised to be an incredibly strong marriage.

CHAPTER FORTY-FOUR

The afternoon sunlight spilled through the windows of Adrian's study, warming his face as he looked out at the garden where Samantha strolled. A smile pulled at his lips when she glanced toward him with happiness in her eyes and waved. He raised his hand to return the gesture.

Two days had passed since their wedding, and they had been the best damn days of his life. For the first time since he could recall, he was content. It was as though Samantha had filled a gap he hadn't realized was there.

And to think they'd not even consummated their marriage yet. He'd have thought that would make him go slightly mad. To his astonishment, he didn't experience any need to rush ahead in that area though. Instead, he enjoyed speaking with her, learning her thoughts about various issues, figuring out who she was as a person.

The result was a deep satisfaction that seeped through is body and left him with a wonderful feeling of rightness. For the first time since Evie's death, he looked forward to what tomorrow would bring, to moving ahead with his future. He no longer had to do it alone. Samantha would be there with him, every step of the way.

He took a deep breath and allowed himself to accept the joy that settled within the deepest recess of his heart. Tonight they would go to the theatre, and tomorrow they'd head off to Deerhaven Manor.

He looked forward to showing her where he'd spent the earliest years of his childhood.

A knock at the door preceded Murry's arrival. Adrian abandoned his view for a moment and glanced at him, a sliver of apprehension forming between his shoulder blades when he saw how grave his servant looked. "Yes?"

Murry stepped forward, as solemn as a pallbearer at a funeral. "Forgive the intrusion, but there's been a development that I'm forced to address with you at once."

Adrian turned to him more fully. "What's happened?"

"The matter pertains to your wife. It turns out she's not what she appears to be." The pained look in his eyes was nothing compared to the ice that was forming in Adrian's stomach. "She has secrets I failed to uncover until this morning, when I was out running an errand and happened to see her step into an alley."

"So?"

"She glanced over her shoulder first, as though to make sure she was not being watched or pursued. Standing across the street and some distance away, with a parked carriage between us, she failed to spot me. A scruffy looking errand-boy emerged from the alley less than a minute later, followed by your wife, who checked her surroundings once more before stepping back onto the pavement and walking away."

"It's probably nothing," Adrian said even as his heart trembled. He refused to believe what Murry suggested. Samantha was loveliness incarnate. The idea of her posing a threat was absurd.

"I chose to chase down the errand boy and finally caught up with the lad. Took me until now to get the truth out of him. He's loyal to her, but my threats eventually managed to sway him." Murry looked directly at Adrian, just as Kendrick had done when he'd come to deliver the news of Evie's death. "Your wife passed him a note in that alley – a note intended for Chief Constable Kendrick. I let the boy deliver it but not before I read it."

"And?" Adrian gripped the back of the chair standing before him, his fingers digging into the wood until it felt like his knuckles might snap.

"It merely said, 'Please confirm that my orders remain the same.'"

This couldn't be happening.

It felt like the ground had opened up beneath his feet.

She was his bloody wife now.

His lungs grew unbearably tight. He couldn't breathe, yet he somehow managed to ask, "Anything else?"

"Apparently, she's been in constant contact with the chief constable since the two of you met. More than that, she used the boy to track your movements. I...I have no words, sir. No excuse will suffice, so I understand if you want to punish me for failing you."

Adrian stared at him while the happiness he had experienced these past few days unraveled. "If I didn't see what was right in front of my bloody eyes, how can I expect you to have done so?"

"Sir, I—"

Teeth clenching as steel pushed through every limb, banishing all traces of softness, he turned his back on Murry. "Leave me."

The valet was wise enough to know not to linger or to say anything more before slipping out of the room. The door closed with a soft click that stood in complete contrast to what Adrian felt. He wanted to smash his fist through the window – shatter the glass as surely as the illusion his wife had crafted had just been shattered.

Whatever dreams he'd had of sharing the details of his life with her had been torn from his grasp. She'd deceived him, wormed her way into his heart, convinced him she was on his side—while actually working against him.

Incredulous, he stared out onto the garden where she still strolled. Rage didn't come close to describing the ravenous beast now sinking its teeth deep into his flesh. Betrayal. The woman upon whom he'd thought he could fully depend, the person closest to him, was his greatest foe.

He couldn't trust her.

Worst of all, he was stuck with her until death did them part.

She sent him another smile. A wave followed – an eager request for him to join her.

He'd rather eat poison, but managed to smile past the anger instead. A painful knot in his chest reminded him of the place where his heart had once been as he stepped out into the garden. Strolling through beams of sunshine, he went to greet her. She met him with fondness in her blue eyes, and he placed a soft kiss to her cheek, murmured something sweet in her ear, all while allowing one truth to cement itself in his mind.

There was no coming back from this. He would never forgive her.

E ager for the next book? Grab *A Tainted Heart Bleeds* to find out what the future holds for Adrian and Samantha.

And sign up for my newsletter at www.sophiebarnes.com so you don't miss out on my freebies, special deals, and giveaways. You'll receive a complimentary copy of **No Ordinary Duke** with your subscription!

Did you enjoy **A Vengeful King Rises**? If so, please take a moment to leave a review since this can help other readers discover books they'll love.

Keep turning for a sneak peek of *A Tainted Heart Bleeds.*

Get a sneak peek of the sequel!
Keep reading for an excerpt from
A Tainted Heart Bleeds

CHAPTER ONE

August, 1818

Lady Eleanor dropped onto the stool in front of her vanity table. Exhausted from entertaining dinner guests with her parents, she looked forward to climbing into the soothing comfort of her bed.

Something pushing against her leg made her lower her gaze to Milly, the miniature poodle her parents had gifted her with for her sixteenth birthday. Rising onto her hind legs, Milly shifted her paws to better press her damp nose against Eleanor's thigh, her stubby tail wagging with eager affection.

Eleanor chuckled and scooped the pup into her lap. She raked her fingers through Milly's fur, scratched her a few times behind one ear, and allowed her to settle comfortably in her lap.

"Are you ready, my lady?" The question was posed by Audrey, Eleanor's lady's maid. A short woman with dark brown hair and eyes to match, the servant was five years Eleanor's senior and possessed a positive outlook to match her own.

Eleanor glanced at her and smiled in response to the warmth she found in Audrey's eyes. "Yes. Please begin."

Audrey raised the comb she'd collected earlier and drew it through Eleanor's hair. Molly snuggled farther into the circle of her arms, nails scratching a little at Eleanor's lap as she repositioned her legs.

Eleanor sighed and sent her bed a longing glance. The coverlet had been folded back to display the crisp white sheets that beckoned. It would be good to climb between them and let the weariness seep from her body.

Molly's curls compressed beneath the weight of her hand as Eleanor stroked the fluffy fur. Glancing up, she caught Audrey's gaze in the mirror, her thoughts returning to the charity visit she'd planned for tomorrow. "Maybe you're right about the brown woolen spencer. I never wear it, so I might as well include it in the donation."

"Are you sure?" Audrey set the comb aside and collected a glass bottle containing Warren & Rosser's Milk of Roses lotion.

The question was a legitimate one since Eleanor had argued against the suggestion yesterday when she and Audrey had prepared the box that would go to St. Augustine's Church. The spencer had been a gift from her aunt three Christmases ago. It was undoubtedly lovely, but every time she'd put it on she felt it didn't quite suit her.

"Yes," she said, her mind made up. "There's no sense

in it taking up space in the wardrobe when it can keep someone less fortunate warm."

Audrey dabbed a bit of lotion on Eleanor's face and began rubbing it in with wonderfully soothing circular motions. "I'm always impressed by your kindness, my lady."

But was she always kind? Guilt gathered in Eleanor's stomach, becoming so heavy it felt like a block of lead. The choice she'd made for herself – for her future – had not been easy. She hated how selfish it made her feel.

Yet she managed to smile and pretend Audrey's comment was welcome. "Thank you."

Audrey responded with a smile of her own and proceeded to plait Eleanor's hair. The peaceful activity calmed her mind. She allowed herself to focus on what was to come, instead of worrying over the past.

She'd had her say, and in so doing, she'd paved the way to a new adventure.

A surge of excitement filled her breast at this thought. Everything would be fine. All she needed was rest. The maid finished her ministrations and tidied up. Eleanor set Molly down and climbed into bed. The mattress sagged beneath her weight, the cool sheets inviting her to sink deeper.

"Would you like me to close the window before I go?" Audrey asked.

"No. Leave it open." The afternoon sun pouring into the room several hours before had made it unbearably warm and stuffy. She couldn't sleep like that.

"I'll bid you good night then, my lady." Audrey called for Molly to join her and the dog complied without question, knowing full well that a walk and a treat awaited.

"Good night," Eleanor replied, "and thank you for your help."

The maid left and Eleanor reached for her book. This was her favorite time to read, when all was silent and there was no risk of being disturbed. She opened *Pamela* and flipped to the spot where she'd left off the previous evening.

A gentle breeze streamed through the window, toying with the curtains. Distant laughter reached her ears. It was followed by a horse's faint whinny. Eleanor's eyes grew heavy. The book began sagging between her hands.

She yawned and it felt like only a moment had passed before she was startled by a loud noise. Her eyes snapped open, adjusting and observing. The light by which she'd been reading had burned itself out. Her book had slipped from her grasp. She must have fallen asleep.

Light flashed beyond the window. A resounding boom followed. The curtains flapped with wild abandon while rain poured down from the heavens. She blew out a breath and went to close the window. It was just a storm. No need for alarm.

Barefooted, she padded across the Aubusson rug and noted that parts of it were now damp from the rain. She leaned forward through the window's opening, her abdomen pressing into the sill, wetting her nightgown as she reached for the handle.

Her hand caught the slick wood and she pulled the window shut. A welcome silence followed, cocooning her from the elements. Pausing briefly, she watched water streak down the smooth window pane, saw lightning flash across the sky.

Intent on returning to bed, she took a step back, prepared to close the curtains, and froze when her toes connected with something unpleasant. Not just water, but a thick and squishy substance of sorts. But how could that be? Confused, she dropped her gaze, but the darkness was blinding. She'd need a candle or an oil lamp in order to see.

She straightened and started to turn, her aim to locate the tinderbox she kept on her nightstand, when a pair of large hands captured her throat. She opened her mouth, attempted to scream, but couldn't even manage a gasp as the fingers dug deeper and cut off her breath.

Terrified, she stared at the window, at her own blurry figure reflected in the wet glass, and the larger man standing behind her. Tears welled in her eyes. She clawed at the hands that gripped her, kicked her attacker's shins, and did what she could to wriggle free.

None of it worked.

He was much stronger than she, and her strength waned with each breath she was denied. Her heart fluttered desperately. It begged her to keep on fighting. But it was no use.

She had already lost

∽

Chief Constable Peter Kendrick removed his hat as he entered Orendel House. Given the circumstances, a somber atmosphere wasn't surprising. But the gloom he encountered in the elegant foyer was unparalleled.

Servants stood near the walls, slumped like wilting plants. Maids wept while the male servants stared into nothing, their stricken expressions underscoring the horror they'd woken up to. Even the butler struggled to speak when he offered to take Peter's hat, his voice cracking before he averted his gaze.

"Where are the earl and countess?" Peter asked.

The butler gave his eyes a quick swipe and straightened his posture. "In the parlor with their…remaining children." Someone sobbed and the old man's expression twisted with grief. "As you can no doubt imagine, this is terribly difficult for them. They asked me to show you upstairs."

"Very well."

He followed the butler, one step at a time, a couple of Runners at his back. They arrived on the landing, their footfalls muted by the plush carpet lining the hardwood floor. A few more paces and then…

The butler paused and gestured toward a door. "Through there. I realize I ought to come with you, but… Do you mind if I remain here?"

"Not at all." Peter reached Lady Eleanor's bedchamber doorway and froze. A sick feeling caught hold of his stomach. Ghastly didn't come close to describing the scene he beheld. This was the sort of thing that could make men lose all hope in humanity. It was…barbaric.

"Good lord," murmured Anderson, the Runner standing at Peter's right shoulder.

Anderson's colleague, Lewis, only managed a faint, "Excu…" before he bolted for the stairs, no doubt hoping to make it outside before he vomited.

Peter swallowed and took a deep breath, then entered the room. It hadn't been so long ago since another young woman's body was found – the last in a series of brutal murders that left him baffled for more than a year. But that killer was dead, so it couldn't be the same man who'd acted here.

Besides, this was different and shockingly worse.

He clenched his jaw, reminded himself that he had a job to accomplish. There was just…so much blood. It felt like the room was bathed in it. And the victim…

Forcing himself to employ an analytical mindset, he considered her position on the bed and the clean blanket draped over her torso and legs.

"I'll need the usual sketches," he said.

"Already working on it," Anderson told him, his voice gruff.

"You may want to wait a moment." Peter studied Lady Eleanor's face and the empty eye sockets that seemed to mock him. "Until I've removed the blanket."

"Sir?"

"It doesn't belong. Someone placed it here after the fact, no doubt to protect her modesty." He shot a look over his shoulder. "If you'll please shut the door."

A firm click followed and then, "Why would the bastard take her eyes?"

"I don't know. Could be a trophy of sorts. There's no telling what goes on in such vile creatures' heads."

Slowly, with respect and consideration directed toward the poor young woman whose body lay on the bed before him, Peter folded back the blanket and shuddered. Whatever nightgown she'd worn to bed was gone, her naked body left on display.

Air rushed into Peter's lungs on a sharp inhalation. She'd been stabbed too many times to count, as though her attacker hadn't been able to stop. And her neck – the skin there was a bright red shade.

Swallowing, he surveyed the rest of the room while Anderson kept on drawing.

A vase lay on the floor near one of the windows, smashed to pieces. The flowers were strewn across the Aubusson rug. They'd probably ended up there during a struggle. Peter lowered himself to a crouch, his fingertips testing a dark brown stain and feeling the wetness. Mud.

"Take notes too, will you?" Peter retreated until he'd reached the bedchamber door. He grabbed the handle. "And cover her with the blanket once you're done. I'll question the servants in the meantime."

∽

The parlor was made available for interviews, each servant introduced to Peter by the butler as he showed them into the room. Peter considered the latest arrival. Audrey was her name. Short in stature, with mousish features and lackluster hair, she'd been Lady Eleanor's lady's maid.

"I...I don't..." Audrey gulped.

She dabbed at her watery eyes again. Her handkerchief looked heavy and wet. Peter handed her a fresh one and gave her a moment to try and collect herself. Not easy, he realized, since she'd been the one who'd discovered her mistress's body when she'd gone to rouse her.

"Did you always wake her in the mornings?" Peter gently asked.

A nod accompanied trembling lips. "She was always so...active. Liked making the...the most of each day. Today... Oh dear. Please forgive me."

"It's quite all right," Peter told her and waited once more for the woman's tears to abate. "Take your time."

She swallowed, licked her lips, and seemed to straighten a bit. "We planned to visit St. Augustine with a few donations. My mistress...she was so very kind I... I don't understand why anyone might have wanted to hurt her."

"So you can think of no enemies?"

"None."

"No hopeful suitors she might have spurned?"

Audrey shook her head. "She's engaged to Mr.

Benjamin Lawrence. They were supposed to marry three months ago, toward the end of April, but his horse-riding accident forced a postponement."

Peter recalled news of the tragedy. The event had turned the young man into a cripple. He'd lost the use of his legs. "She still meant to go through with it, despite what happened?"

"Of course." Additional tears slid down Audrey's cheeks. "My mistress loved Mr. Lawrence and intended to stand by him. That's the sort of person she was."

And yet, the nature of her death suggested someone had loathed her beyond all reason. Peter made a few notes in his notebook, his pencil scratching the paper with quick and efficient strokes.

"Thank you, Audrey. That will be all for now." He accompanied her to the door and called for the next servant.

Again, his thoughts wandered back to the murders that took place earlier in the year. Those women had all seemed like proper young ladies. Friends and family had vouched for them. Yet they'd each had a secret that had gotten them killed.

In all likelihood, Lady Eleanor had secrets too. If he was to figure out who killed her, he'd have to discover which of hers had led to her death.

∽

There was no greater nuisance than murder.

It was hard to predict how one would play out. Killing Lady Eleanor had been messier than he'd intended. Perhaps because he'd allowed himself to get carried away.

His lips curled. At least he'd had the foresight to stash a change of clothes for himself at St. George's burial ground. Returning home covered in blood would not have helped him get away with the crime. As he intended to do.

Hands shoved into the pockets of a clean pair of trousers, he stood by his bedchamber window and watched the London traffic go by.

He had no regrets. She'd deserved every part of what he'd done.

His attention focused on the carriages filling the street and on the people hurrying by. It was the busiest hour of the day, when men of consequence made their way to Parliament while those who belonged to the working class went off to start their jobs.

Bow Street would have its hands full this morning. He casually wondered if they were examining Lady Eleanor's body right now and where the clues they discovered might lead them.

Spotting a young girl who carried a crate of eggs on her head, he tracked her as she walked along the opposite side of the street. A man coming the other way nudged her shoulder as he pushed past her, but failed to disrupt her stride.

She threw a quick glance toward him then stepped

off the pavement and hurried between two carriages, making her way to this side of the street.

A couple of street urchins came from the left at a run, most likely fleeing someone whose pocket they'd picked. Leaping into the street at the same exact time as the girl with the eggs attempted to exit, they crashed into her, tripping before regaining their balance and sprinting onward while she was sent reeling.

Down went the crate and all of her eggs, straight into the gutter.

Not one person stopped to inquire about her well-being. She was invisible to the crowd – just another lowly individual doing her best to scrape by. Too much trouble for the middle or upper class to get involved with. Too time consuming for the rest.

And yet, as he watched the poor wretch try to salvage the few eggs that somehow remained intact, there was no doubt she'd prefer her situation to Lady Eleanor's at the moment.

He watched the girl until she'd gathered whatever she could and continued along the street, vanishing from his view before he turned from the window. His gaze went to his bedside table and he crossed to it, retrieved a small key from his jacket pocket, then dropped into a crouch.

With adroitness, he set the key in the lock of the door beneath the drawer and turned it. The door opened and he reached inside, retrieving a jar that he held up against the bright morning light.

A pair of eyes contained in a clear solution stared

back at him while his lips twitched with amusement. The last time they'd talked, Lady Eleanor had insisted she'd no desire to see him again.

It was a wish he'd been more than happy to fulfill.

Order your copy today!

AUTHOR'S NOTE

Dear Reader,

If you've made it this far, then it must be because you enjoyed this story enough to read all the way to the end, for which you have my sincerest gratitude. Embarking on a new series and waiting to find out if it will catch on, is always a little nerve-wrecking.

So much work goes into completing one novel. Starting one that's completely different from anything else I've written before, was a risk. But it was one I was willing to take, not only because the idea for this story (and series as a whole) wouldn't let go, but because I trust my readers to trust me.

It is therefore with the utmost appreciation that I thank you for daring to go on this journey with me. I hope you've enjoyed it so far and that you look forward to finding out what happens next. Because this is just the beginning. There's a lot more intrigue and romance to come, and I can't wait to share it with you!

Sophie

xoxo

ACKNOWLEDGMENTS

I would like to thank the Killion Group for their help with the editing of this book.

Thanks also go to Liz G, Kelly Kuntz, Jennifer Wagonner, Becky Mayr, Angela Killion, and Marlene Harris for offering valuable insight on the opening chapter.

And to my friends and family, thank you for your constant support and for believing in me. I would be lost without you!

ABOUT THE AUTHOR

USA TODAY bestselling author Sophie Barnes is best known for her historical romance novels in which the characters break away from social expectations in their quest for happiness and love. Having written for Avon, an imprint of Harper Collins, her books have been published internationally in eight languages.

With a fondness for travel, Sophie has lived in six countries, on three continents, and speaks English, Danish, French, Spanish, and Romanian with varying degrees of fluency. Ever the romantic, she married the same man three times—in three different countries and in three different dresses.

When she's not busy dreaming up her next swoon worthy romance novel, Sophie enjoys spending time with her family, practicing yoga, baking, gardening, watching romantic comedies and, of course, reading.

You can contact her through her website at www.sophiebarnes.com

For all the latest releases, promotions, and exclusive story updates, subscribe to Sophie Barnes' newsletter today!

And please consider leaving a review for this book. Every review is greatly appreciated!

Printed in Great Britain
by Amazon